# FUGUE
# STATES

# FUGUE STATES

# PASHA MALLA

ALFRED A. KNOPF CANADA

PUBLISHED BY ALFRED A. KNOPF CANADA

Copyright © 2017 Pasha Malla

www.penguinrandomhouse.ca

Alfred A. Knopf Canada and colophon are registered trademarks.

The quotations at the start of each section in this novel come from *Fugue* by Ebenezer Prout (London: Augener & Co., 1891).

Library and Archives Canada Cataloguing in Publication

Malla, Pasha, 1978–, author
Fugue states / Pasha Malla.
Issued in print and electronic formats.
ISBN 978-0-345-81133-2
eBook ISBN 978-0-345-81135-6

I. Title.

PS8626.A449F84 2017          C813'.6          C2016-906015-2

Book design by Lisa Jager

Cover image: (topographic map) © DmitriyRazinkov,
(silhouettes) © grynold, both Shutterstock.com

Interior image: (topographic map) © DmitriyRazinkov / Shutterstock.com

Printed and bound in the United States of America

2 4 6 8 9 7 5 3 1

Penguin
Random House
KNOPF CANADA

*People who remember court madness through pain, the pain of the perpetually recurring death of their innocence; people who forget court another kind of madness, the madness of the denial of pain and the hatred of innocence; and the world is mostly divided between madmen who remember and madmen who forget. Heroes are rare.*

–JAMES BALDWIN, *Giovanni's Room*

*Among the tortures and devastations of life is this then—our friends are not able to finish their stories.*

—VIRGINIA WOOLF, *The Waves*

*And I've only lived a couple of my dad's lives. A couple of my dad's lives.*

—SWIRLIES

*A fugue is a composition founded upon one subject, announced at first in one part alone, and subsequently imitated by all the other parts in turn . . . The name is derived from the Latin word* fuga, *a flight, from the idea that one part starts on its course alone, and that those which enter later are pursuing it.*

## 1

SOMETIMES THIS WOULD HAPPEN.

In the middle of an interview, Ash would stray off-script to pursue some tangential idea and along the way discover he was lost. Whether his thoughts snagged on a word or phrase, or his own dull voice began to fill his ears, or the author across the table assumed an irked or patient or pitying look, in an instant whatever he might have meant went galloping away. Rarely then did he have the sense to stop. Instead he'd resume the chase with renewed desperation and even more words, each sentence annihilating the last until he'd talked himself into a void: he was a fool, and a fraud, and he still had no clue what he'd been trying to say.

It was Sherene, of course, who'd come to his rescue. Her voice would enter his headphones like a float tossed to a drowning man. Or a suggestion to put his feet down and touch bottom.

'Whoa there, Ash,' she'd say. They'd lock eyes through the glass. Winking, she'd suggest, 'Why don't we take another crack at that?' and reset him at a pre-written question. They called these episodes 'losing the plot.' In the studio they were easy enough to fix; time could be erased and the interview edited so that no one might ever guess the depths of Ash's panic.

Not so when you lost the plot in real life, Ash thought. At his sudden silence he sensed all those people—strangers, mostly—tilting toward him. There was a touch of rapture upon their faces, stunned and wary. What a mistake, this speech. His sister's eulogy had been brief and heartfelt. With her husband clutching her elbow, Mona had spoken without notes, choking back tears. And here Ash was, alone, reading in a voice like a polished stone—what? An essay, a story. Parts of it weren't even true.

Ash scanned the crowd again but couldn't pick out Sherene. Thought he felt his phone humming in his back pocket. Reached for it, resisted.

Someone coughed. His hand fell back to the lectern. The pages spread upon it were titled 'Brij' and numbered 1 and 2. Still to come was the ending, which struck him now as false. Though he didn't trust himself to improvise.

'I hope he's home,' Ash read, not looking up. A sob from the back of the hall nudged him to his final excruciating line: 'Wherever my dad is, I hope he's finally home.'

And then he waited, as though for applause, before he fled the podium, banging the microphone stand and sending a warp of feedback honking up through the rafters.

IN THE FUNERAL HOME'S carpeted parlour their father's friends and colleagues queued to greet Ash and Mona, proceeded to a photo display propped between two lurid eruptions of flowers, and dispersed into whispering clusters. Some roamers caromed from one group to the next, caressing the backs of the especially bereft: three circles with the palm of the hand, as if wiping clean a window. No family had made it from India.

Ash was furious with Mona's husband, Harj, some make of doctor without boundaries whose gaping nostrils betrayed the exploits of a serial nose-picker, and who now loitered behind his wife like a bad henchman in a baggy suit and moccasins. (Mona was so *clean*; couldn't she do better?) Having handled the funeral arrangements Harj had insisted on local catering. But this was rural Quebec, not the Napa Valley. The results were three cling-wrapped platters of sandwiches, cubed cheese, cold cuts coiled into tubes and an assortment of pale, dreary fruit. Ash watched the guests—was that the right word?—fill their plates. A man had died and they were serving baloney!

Since the phone call from his sister, the news lurking amid that terrible emptiness on the end of the line, over the week Ash's grief had putrefied into rage. On the train from Toronto every overheard conversation became a target for his bile, quoted and viciously annotated via text to Sherene. (*I feel your pain*, she'd replied. *Hugs!*) It wasn't until arriving in Montreal, wheeling his luggage through a wet snowfall, shoes soaked through to his socks, that Ash stopped short: his dad was dead. The hard-edged fact of it caging him there, unmoving and bewildered, in the slush.

Here was the next mourner, a tall brown man bowing like a geisha. 'Doctor Echebbi,' he whispered. 'I was a Fellow with your father at the Sleep Centre.' The subdued tenor of his voice seemed to convey sincerity. 'Brij was a great friend.'

'Thanks for coming,' said Ash.

As this Echebbi slid along to his sister, Ash considered his own friends: who would consider their friendship great? The thought vanished as the woman next in line stepped up. As this person, whoever she was, extolled his father's virtues Ash realized that a soundtrack—panpipes, Peruvian or Casio, likely another selection of Mona's globally minded husband—was playing. Why the music? To make things easier? Sadder? More fun?

On and on they came, dressed as if for job interviews. Sometimes Ash recognized a face: a law school classmate of Mona's, some ancient neighbour, a coterie of his dad's students, a pair of 'aunties' waddling up in their least flagrant saris. These two were old family friends and of that same obstinately maternal mode as Ash's own relatives: busts like shelves, affectionate to the point of molestation.

Ash was seized and smothered with kisses.

'We've not seen you in years,' said one, awestruck. 'You're a man!'

'I am,' Ash confessed.

'Anything you or your sister need,' said the other, 'please ask.'

What Ash needed was for his father to be alive. Could they help with that?

The aunties fell upon Mona. Following them was a guy in jeans and a bowtie, scuttling past with such haste that Ash wondered if he were at the wrong funeral.

Then a beaming couple who presented their two children as though posing for a portrait. 'They're eight and ten now,' Ash was needlessly informed.

Then a high school friend of his sister's whom Ash had once tried to kiss. 'Thanks for coming,' he said, and she hugged him with one arm.

Then that woman's husband, shaking Ash's hand with clueless vigour.

Then Ash's old pal Chip, pushing his palsied son in a wheelchair with the heft and carriage of an SUV. It was a long, tedious drive from Southern Ontario, through Montreal and over the Champlain Bridge into farmland, and Chip seemed accordingly annoyed. He wielded the kid like a battering ram, plowing through the crowd with a grimace of daring: *just try and get in our way.*

But when he reached Ash, Chip's ferocity crumbled. 'Man, I'm so sorry,' he murmured. 'Losing your dad, I can't imagine.'

'It's okay,' said Ash. 'We're getting together at his place after this, if you . . .' He trailed off, eyeing the kid gurgling away in his chair, head lolling.

'Thanks, but Ty's never been to Montreal. Going to head back shortly, see the sights. Got a hotel right downtown. Here till Tuesday. Any chance you can make it in?'

'Sure,' said Ash. 'I'll call you.' And then—he'd almost forgotten— 'Thanks for coming.'

Chip and Ty rolled down the line. On came the next mourner. And the next. Faces blurred as Ash's role turned mechanical, a factory worker in an assembly line of grief: shake hands, agree death was sad, 'Thanks for coming,' pass to Mona, repeat. Repeat, repeat, repeat.

Eventually, back on the sidewalk in Montreal, Ash had returned to the flow of pedestrians. Swept along, he thought about time: its passing, its irrevocability. And longed not for his father to be alive— impossible—but simply to revisit that moment before remember-ing he was gone. The old chestnut: one second a person was here and the next, not. An absence both swift and massive. 'Passed away' or 'deceased' felt too delicate. More conclusive, more honest, was the abrupt, fatal thud of *dead*.

A bald head appeared at the door, lofting above the others like a zeppelin. As Ash watched, Matt's eyebrows arched into the stupefied expression he believed to convey sympathy, the same look he'd presented that morning when he'd shown up on the family doorstep, hat literally in hand, like some long-lost uncle returned to assume his portion of the family grief. 'I'm here as long as you need me,' Matt had announced, plopped his backpack in the hall, and embraced Mona with such melodrama that there had seemed something scripted in how she'd wept into his jacket.

Now the big man skipped the line like a VIP and ducked to haul Ash into the same rib-cinching hug. He'd always enjoyed touching people, craved it even. So after failed careers as a pro skier and actor, his latest scheme, massage therapy, almost made sense.

'Great speech,' he murmured into Ash's neck. 'Your dad would have been proud.'

Ash squirmed free. 'There's food, if you've got the munchies.'

'You know me too well,' said Matt, though he lingered. And intercepted the next mourner, Mona's father-in-law: 'Good to see you, such a loss for us all.'

Two years prior, in Winnipeg to record his show live at Thin Air, Ash had missed Matt's mom's funeral. ('We were never that close,' Matt had said by way of absolution; it had taken Ash a moment to realize this *we* was supposed to mean Matt and his mother.) So there was something consequential, even punitive, in how readily Matt assumed his role of best friend. Whatever his game, he stood at Ash's side as stalwart and proud as a grooms-man, beaming at some woman who swooped in upon a gush of silks and scent.

'Here he is,' she crooned, engulfing Ash's hand with both of hers. 'I listen to you every week.'

'Thanks for coming,' said Ash.

The woman stroked his fingers as she might a wounded bird. 'I loved your interview with that Spanish writer . . . What was his name?'

'Spanish?'

'Don Quixote,' offered Matt, in the accent of Zorro.

'I'm Barbara,' she said, eyeing Matt—first dubiously, and then, when he winked, with a coy smile. 'The Dean of Medicine?'

'Hi,' said Ash. As Barbara lingered, the queue bloated.

'How long are you in town?'

'I'm—'

'The reason I ask is that we have a book club—the Secret Literary Auxiliary of Westmount—and we'd love for you to come in and speak to us.'

'SLAW,' said Ash; Barbara nodded. 'And what would I be speaking about?'

'Books!'

'Guy sure does know his books,' confirmed Matt.

In the pile-up behind Barbara, Ash spotted Sherene. His heart lifted a bit, although no other co-workers had shown: no top brass, no talent, not even one of the interns to whom Ash generously imparted wisdom, every day. Sherene was it. A delegation.

'And I so admired what you said at the funeral,' said Barbara. 'So different from your interviews—or your book. I'd love to sit down and pick your brain about writing.'

Ash caught Sherene's eye. She clasped her hands at her chin in a gesture of prayer or solidarity—or triumph? No: an apology. She held up her phone, lip-synched, '*Sorry*,' and veered out of line with it to one ear and a finger plugging the other.

In the meantime Matt had insinuated himself between Ash and Barbara, laying a paw on her shoulder. 'If you're interested, I've known Ash his whole life. Ask me anything you want about him.' He slid his hand to her waist. '*Anything.*'

BY MID-AFTERNOON the Dhars and their companions—Matt, that is, and Harj—were back at Brij's house in a nearby anglophone enclave of the Eastern Townships. Since its purchase their father had referred to this place, a cedar A-frame with sightlines to a nearby ski resort, as 'the chalet.' Pretentious, yes. But the place was cozy, with an open kitchen and adjoining den anchored by a big fireplace, one bedroom and a study upstairs and a cinderblock basement that Brij had long threatened to finish. After a series of prefab townhouses, it was the closest to an actual home that their dad had ever lived in.

They sat around the dining table snacking on leftover catering and sharing a six-pack of skunky Heineken. Mona, four months pregnant, cracked one and Matt raised an eyebrow—which she caught.

'One beer's not going to kill me,' she said. 'Or the kid.'

'It's her choice,' said Harj, and drank from his own beer in solidarity.

Matt shrugged and took an egg salad sandwich over to the window to ogle the ski trails across the highway. Ash's phone, sitting expectantly on the tabletop, flashed. At last, an apology from Sherene: *So sorry I had to run, sweetie. Just getting everything ready for Tuesday, see you then?* Ash wrote back to invite her to join them. Waited. No reply.

'Okay,' said Mona. 'Might as well get on with this.'

From a suitcase at her feet she produced Brij's will and placed it on the tabletop. Next came a grey cardboard container, six inches square. This she set beside the will. For a moment, no one moved or said a word.

Matt returned for another sandwich, noticed the box. 'Is that—' he began.

'It's what's left when you're gone,' said Ash. 'Your powdered bones in a shoebox and instructions for divvying up your stuff.'

'Ash,' warned Mona. 'Don't.'

But he wasn't just being difficult. Ash wanted no part in any inheritance—to profit in some way—nor in that vain project of sublimating the dead man's memory into his things. Besides, 'estate' seemed such a grandiose term for a two-bedroom cottage, some savings bonds, a modest rug collection and a Volvo. And then there were the ashes: garbage disposal duties as a last living rite.

'There are no instructions for the . . . remains,' said Mona, turning officious. 'But I thought it could be something for us to talk about.'

'What about joint custody?' said Ash. 'Just like when we were kids: Monday to Wednesday with you, I'll take him Thursdays and Fridays, and we'll alternate weekends.'

Mona laughed a little, despite herself. It was Harj who swept in with the required gravitas, murmuring in the voice of a hypnotist, nostrils flaring: 'Ash, you don't have to hide behind jokes.'

'Hide?'

Harj closed his eyes, nodded. When a few seconds went by and he still hadn't opened them, Ash winked at his sister. But she only frowned and took her husband's hand.

How could Mona allow, even cultivate, space for this interloper at the family table? At least Matt, back at the window, had the sense to butt out. Within hours of Brij passing, Harj had been on a flight home from some refugee camp, an act of sanctimony all the more vile for how he downplayed it, and made worse when he actually *forgave* Ash for not making it to Montreal until after the cremation.

'If you don't want to talk about the ashes, what about the house,' said Mona.

'Whether we sell? Be a shame.'

'Says the kid who lives a province away.'

'What does that have to do with it?'

'You think I can just swing out here every weekend to clean the eavestroughs?'

'Not once the baby's here,' said Harj. And quickly corrected himself: 'Though of course I'll be taking a pat leave too.'

'That's not a bad-sized hill over there,' called Matt from the far side of the room.

Ash checked his phone. Sherene had written back: *If you need to skip the interview that's fine, I can get someone else.* No acknowledgement of his invitation. Nor in his next message, which he tried not to read as an afterthought: *Hope you're doing okay! XO*

'Who are you texting?' said Mona. 'There's so much that needs doing!'

'Listen,' said Ash, turning the phone facedown on the table, 'I don't want to say the body's still warm—'

'Ew,' said his sister. 'Then don't.'

Ash chuckled, but her wounded expression chastened him. He softened his voice: 'Just, maybe we shouldn't rush into all this stuff while we're still . . . sad.'

Too late: she was crying. Harj draped over her like a shawl, clucking softly. Ash swept up his phone and tapped out a reply: *I'm fine.*

Matt appeared with a fistful of Kleenexes. 'Don't worry,' he said, indicating a box on the mantle, 'they're not mine.'

Mona accepted one, wiped her eyes. Asked Matt how long he was planning to stay.

'Told you guys, as long as you need me.'

'But aren't you in school?'

'Yeah. About that.' Matt held out his right hand, scrunched his fingers: each one but the pinkie tucked at the knuckle. 'Dropped digit.'

Ash pictured him blundering into some candlelit spa, solemnly kneading some poor geriatric's bones to glue—and wounding himself in the process. 'Jesus, what did you do?'

'Check this out: in my head I think I'm moving it but the tendon's just flapping around loose inside!'

'It will heal,' said Harj with beleaguered expertise.

Mona leaned in to get a better look. 'Does it hurt?'

'When I did it, yeah. Now it's just numb.'

'I'm waiting for the story,' said Ash. 'Because there has to be one, right?'

Matt grinned. 'So this bartender I met out west, he's an Ironman. With the swimming and biking and running and everything. Casper. Guy is forty-eight and *jacked.* Does the race every year. And, get this, he used to be a junkie, woke up in a gutter in Vancouver and was just like, *Gotta get my life together*. So he started training. Total carpe diem mentality. And just super happy in his own skin, you know?'

Ash had seen this before: between failed auditions, non-speaking parts on unwatchable TV shows and the occasional commercial gig, Matt would meet a stranger to whom some hobby had brought purpose and fling himself at it wholesale—Ultimate Frisbee, improv comedy, a disastrous turn as a drum and bass DJ for which he went shirtless in faux-fur pants.

'So you skipped Regular Person and went straight to Ironman.'

'Part of making myself happen, bro.'

Mona tipped back her beer. She'd never had much time for people who floundered through life. Yet what had once been about asserting her own resolve had a tinge of elitism to it now—the stain, Ash thought, of Harj.

'Except,' Matt continued, on the verge of losing his audience, 'my first long bike ride we're going through the Kootenays, seventy clicks in freezing rain. Brakes are *locked*, no stopping. I go around one corner and everything just slips out from under me—bike goes one way, I go the other and slide right up to the edge of the mountain. Literally gravel avalanching down two hundred feet, and it's lucky I was baked out of my tree because instead of tensing up and going over? All I did was smush my hand and burn up my backside something fierce. But'—he looked around the table to confirm he had everyone's attention—'not only was that it for training, I had to take the semester off school too. Which sucks, because we were just starting to work with actual bodies.'

'So, wait,' said Mona. 'That means you don't have anything to go back to?'

'I told you: I'm yours however long you need me.'

'How long before it heals?' Mona asked her husband.

Harj's shrug suggested that he reserved diagnoses for significant ailments only: malaria, typhoid, landmines.

'Could be weeks,' said Matt forlornly. 'Maybe even months. Could miss this year's ski season entirely.' He displayed the busted finger again, like a sad Mafioso wielding a ring to be kissed.

So it was with Matt's injuries, always turned into spectacle. A sprained ankle, a stubbed toe—even a sneeze!—became an occasion for theatrics, from grunts and groans to writhing on the floor screaming for a surgeon. Performances aside, he'd suffered his share of trauma: broken bones (eight), surgeries (two scopes on his left knee, a jaw hinged with plates and screws), concussions ('Four officially,' he claimed, 'though probably more'). Vainly he'd turn in profile like a Roman emperor and sigh, 'Busted my nose three times. Never breathe the same again.'

Though it wasn't quite masochistic, Matt wanted to be hurt. Not to revel in the pain, but to have something to showcase for sympathy. Even as a kid, long before his mom took her own life, he'd been this way too.

'Well, if we're not going to go through the legal stuff,' said Mona, returning the will and box to her bag, 'what's the story with dinner?'

'Whatever you'd like, my darling,' said Harj, stroking her hand.

But Mona's eyes were on Ash, the family cook. Ash checked his phone. No new messages. So he scrolled through his conversation with Sherene, thinking that if Harj were taking requests, he could go ahead and make his own fucking supper.

'Tons of chow right here,' said Matt, nibbling grapes from the bunch.

'I guess we could go out,' said Mona.

'Eat in public, are you insane?' said Ash, looking up. 'What if someone starts crying?'

'What if we do? Aren't we meant to cry? Our *dad* just died.'

'Exactly!'

'I, for one, will not support some chain restaurant,' said Harj.

'Well, there's Chez Whatever,' said Mona. 'Remember that, Ash? That BYO joint down the highway where Brij said the wine was off?'

Ash pushed his beer away and snarled, 'It's corked,' through gritted teeth.

Mona laughed her wild, chirruping laugh, covering her mouth with her hand. Just as she'd laughed as a kid.

At the time, it hadn't been so funny. The waiter retreated two steps while Brij scowled at the bottle. With no explanation he stood, went to the car and drove off, leaving his adult children to fondle their menus for forty minutes before he returned with a replacement.

Mona shook her head, still smiling. Something had opened up.

'That same weekend,' began Ash carefully, with the warm look on his sister's face urging him along, 'you told us about *jizz*, remember?'

Matt leaned in. 'Go on.'

'Not like that! Mona was just back from Istanbul and she said that in Turkish the word *jizz* means *sizzle*, so when I served this sizzling reduction, we called it "jizz"—'

Mona smacked Ash's knee under the table. 'Oh my god! I totally forgot! Too funny. And then Brij—'

'Right?' Ash voice lifted. 'We were cracking up, and Brij was laughing that big booming laugh of his—'

'The fake-sounding one,' said Mona. 'The one you can spell.'

'*Ha ha ha! Ho ho ho!* And I asked him if he knew what was so hilarious. And he got mad. "Of course I do, idiot."'

'Too much!' shrieked Mona. 'You sound exactly like him!'

'So I asked him what, then, he thought *jizz* meant.'

Mona placed her hands on her belly. 'What did he say? I can't remember.'

'He got quiet, replaying the story, trying to piece it together. And then he stares us down, totally sure of himself, and with this gloating look goes, "It means . . . pubic hair."'

The laughter felt symphonic: Ash and Mona and Matt (even Harj, a little) howling in chorus, almost desperately, cresting out of grief and threatening, when it began to wane, to maroon them in sorrow. So when Matt reprised, *'Pubic hair!'* the hysterics reignited with something like gratitude.

The second wave subsided. A round of final chuckles. A round of sighs.

'Oh, man,' said Mona. 'Too funny.'

'My stomach hurts,' said Matt.

'My everything hurts,' said Ash.

'Jizz,' said Matt. 'Pubes . . . Priceless!'

A pause, from which a flatter silence surfaced and settled over everything like a lid.

'Brij,' said Mona, smiling distantly. 'What a guy.'

The words, her wistful tone—it was the saddest thing Ash had ever heard.

She yelped, her hand flew to her throat, her face collapsed, her body lurched. Ash reached for his sister across the table. But Harj, bursting into tears himself, swept Mona into his arms. From across the table Ash watched them hold each other, foreheads pressed and bodies heaving, their sobs coming in gasps.

He felt a hand on his shoulder, a squeeze.

'We're out of beer,' Matt whispered, shaking his empty. 'You think your old man would mind if we got into his wine?'

STANDING BEFORE A WALL of bottles in the basement, Ash tried to imagine which one Brij would pick to go with cold meat and cucumber spears. Yet for his dad wine was less of an accompaniment to food than an occasion for ceremony: the opening, the swilling, the sniffing, the nod. Having long ago forsaken

Hinduism, like most apostates he'd adopted new sacraments. It felt right to honour his rituals, now. It was, maybe, all they could do.

Except Ash knew nothing about wine. He got his phone out to text Sherene but no signal reached the basement. She'd told him once, maybe sarcastically, to bet on rural origins (villages, mountains, farms, etc.), so he grabbed some dusty French number—2005, was that a good year? He looked over the bottle for some memo of complementary foods: none, not even a schedule of how it would taste.

Whimpers trickled downstairs. Ash hoped his quick exit had seemed less an escape than allowing his sister her space. The way he grieved was just different. He wasn't a crier. Nor had his dad been, either. At ten, when his parents announced their divorce, while Mona and their mom wept Ash had absconded to shoot hoops in the driveway; he'd looked up at one point to discover Brij observing from the window. It wasn't until high school that sadness arrived—the brutal, adolescent monsoon of it, manifest as vandalism, negligent hygiene and shoplifted CDs.

Matt's voice rumbled down the stairs: 'You stomping grapes down there or what?'

'Coming,' Ash called.

Yet he couldn't bring himself to head back up. His failure to cry suggested some more profound deficiency. (Though Harj, who could bawl on command, surely had defects of his own.) Even before Brij's stroke Ash had been feeling a little lost to himself, waking each morning in a disoriented panic. Back in October he'd got in a cab and been struck by the voice on the radio, discomfiting and oddly familiar. It wasn't until the speaker laughed—a hiss, like air escaping a slashed tire—that Ash recognized himself.

IN THE END, Matt's suggestion of takeout won the day. But first, Mona announced, there was still time to 'climb the mountain,' which meant the 45-minute trudge up a nearby hill that had provided Brij his daily exercise. Another ritual, another way to pay homage. Yet to Ash it offered a chance, with the house emptied, for solitude.

'Should be nice,' said Ash. 'Great views if you can get to the top before dark.'

Mona looked dismayed. 'You're not coming?'

'I really want to'—Ash winced in a pained, regretful way—'but I've got this interview on Tuesday that I need to prep for. Also the house needs cleaning . . .'

'I'll go get the food in the meantime,' Matt volunteered. He seemed twitchy; his edges were showing. 'Can't do hills anyway with my knee.'

Watching his foot thrum under the table, Ash realized that Matt likely hadn't smoked up since before the funeral. So this was less helpful errand than self-care. Even after twenty years he could still get secretive, almost embarrassed, about his weed habit. Not always, and sometimes he'd coerce Ash into joining him. The shame was of dependence, of weakness.

Once Ash was alone, the house settled into an eerie stillness. Heading upstairs, he even imagined a spectral presence at his heels and, upon reaching his dad's office, slammed the door and pressed his back to it. Once his pulse had steadied he sat in Brij's reading chair with the book he would be discussing in two days, but had yet to start.

The best part of Ash's job was when he and Sherene picked their guests and sketched out the interviews together. She was the most confident and insightful reader he knew, tempering Ash's need to impress the author with a steady critical eye. With their co-written scripts in hand Ash approached these episodes with vigour, and when the on-air light extinguished and the headphones came off, nothing pleased him more than being told how good it had been to be read so closely, so accurately—to be *understood*. He felt sanctioned, a peer and not just a patron.

However. Occasionally interviews were handed down from on high. For their Christmas Eve programme, Ash and Sherene had been appointed, as they called him, 'The Behemoth.' The Behemoth's novels (manually typed, of course, in some log cabin on some lake in some deep dark woods) tended to launch directly from the printers to the bestseller list. His sixth book, the portentously titled *Into the Night*, had already received the expected, weirdly combative notices (*an absolute triumph* over what?) and could now be found stacked like sandbag barricades by the cash registers of the nation's biggest, boxiest bookstores. In his jacket photo, The Behemoth glared headlong into the camera while caressing the cinderblock of his jawline, presumably to communicate a hostile intellect—or intellectual hostility.

In Ash's opinion *Into the Night* was, probably, a 320-page epitaph for literature. Though he'd yet to read a word, he could predict what was in store: its touchstones would be Hemingway, manual labour and the films of Clint Eastwood. Its main character would be a Broken Man of few words fuelled by booze and penance. Its politics would be 'common sense,' viz. intolerant of anything beyond their own chauvinistic purview. The prose, like The Behemoth himself, like his fictional proxy, would be *muscular*. The plot would be one of vengeance, illuminating the innately violent nature of Man. The movie version would make a trillion dollars; a sequel was likely already in the works.

Here was the novel's opening line: *Man is pain.*

Ash pulled out his phone, took a photo, and sent it to Sherene with a sad face. Set book and phone down. Scrubbed his eye sockets with the heels of his hands (a gesture inherited from Brij, performed in moments of weariness or disbelief).

Sherene's reply: *Tell me please you're further in than that!*

Ash put aside *Into the Night* to look through Brij's stuff. Among folders dedicated to TAXES and HOUSE he found one labeled WRITING. Inside was a story, 'Lines of Control,' Ash's own last real foray into fiction, a decade old now and never published. Its prominence among his dad's papers, printed on the corny marbled stationery Brij favoured for documents of import, struck Ash as both comical and depressing.

Begun a year or two after the publication of Ash's first and only book, the story had seen many drafts but never gone anywhere. Sharing it with Brij had been a capitulation to his requests to see Ash's fiction in its infant and most mortifying stages. ('When's your new novel coming out?' he would ask; 'I'm working on it,' Ash would lie; 'Well then send me what you've got.') Brij seemed to believe that fatherhood entitled jurisdiction over his son's creations, whatever state they were in. Ash's book, after all, was the closest he'd come to continuing the family name.

Reading the story was like encountering some past version of himself, one yet to see his dreams wither and perish. 'Lines of Control' wasn't good, but there was a lightness to it that, as he read, made Ash embarrassed, then amused, then nostalgic. Life had been simpler then. His only goal had been to make up things that were both funny and sad, as if striking that balance were some grand artistic feat.

Still, it *was* kind of funny, and maybe even a little sad. Though not really a story, more a quirky vignette about a young man and his dog bumbling through a warzone looking to buy, of all things, a peach. After twelve pages it attempted a metaphysical ending: while gunfire crackles around him, our hero bites into his peach, finds it rotten, and hurls it straight up in the air, as high as he can—*and it never comes down.* If he'd intended some symbolic resonance Ash couldn't think of one now.

On the back of the printout was a letter in his dad's handwriting, that jagged scrawl Ash had described in his eulogy as *a polygraph readout spiked with lies.* 'My thoughts,' it began. Why had Brij bothered to write out comments on the story, only to never share them with his son? Whatever his reasons, Ash stopped short at the first line: 'If one is to write about Kashmir . . .' Confusing! The story was not about Kashmir at all. He'd intended the setting, a war-ravaged village amid mountains, to be generic.

Certainly Ash's second book, if he'd ever got round to writing it, was supposed to have been 'about Kashmir.' Yet for various reasons (an inability to invent characters, resistance to research, misgivings about treating tenuous cultural heritage as *material*) he'd been too paralyzed to begin. Besides, who was he to speak about a place whose name he couldn't pronounce? Ash had tried imitating his dad's *Kuss-meeher* once, to Sherene, and her cock-eyed response had flooded him with shame.

What would a novel 'about Kashmir' even be? Surely there were stories 'about Kashmir' that never touched on Partition, or the Troubles, or the military occupation, or the exile of Pandits like the Dhars. A book truly 'about Kashmir' would be the size of a sofa, a tale from all sides that included the subjective, the objective, the factual, the impressionistic—even the clueless and misguided, even the ideologically deranged. Anything less would be akin to summarizing a film with a single frame snipped from the reel. But such a project was impossible. So—for virtuous reasons, Ash preferred to tell himself—the novel was never begun, and now he only read other people's books, and talked about them on the radio, and was considered successful in a small, Canadian way.

So what was 'Lines of Control' actually about? The story shared the gently ironic, amiable tone of his novel, and the character was once again just a hapless and naïve version of himself—Ash, but inured to darkness. He did no wrong and every wrong he suffered was a ploy to elicit sympathy, to be likeable so in turn the author might be liked. When his novel had been published, readers had spoken to Ash as though he were his character; a stranger telling him, 'I felt so bad for you!' had been a type of victory. But Ash was not that sweet and sunny man, and 'Lines of Control' slouched one sentence to the next as if in acknowledgement of its own deceit.

But this was not his father's critique.

My thoughts—

If one is to write about Kashmir one must understand a few basic things about the place. You have been to India if not Srinagar in recent memory. It is a shame you have not paid attention. Firstly if this story is meant to take place during the height of the Troubles the notion of dogs as pets is preposterous. Perhaps you have been confused by this new middle class which has been Americanized sadly. Now one sees dogs in homes and not simply in the streets. But it is a recent phenomenon. Secondly one wonders what message you are attempting with this pathetic ending. Such nihilism is disingenuous to the passion many people still have for the Valley's autonomy. Also there are few if any cobblestone streets in Srinagar. Peaches do not grow there. Apples yes. Kashmir produces the best apples in the world. Walnuts also and saffron. You have made the city vague. You have missed its particulars. Where is Dal Lake? One must either go to Kashmir so one might write something accurate or one must write about some place one has been and knows. One has a debt to the people of any forgotten and ignored place. There are responsibilities. What you have done instead, is foolish.

-Brij.

Such vitriol! Brij's penmanship furrowed the page. This from someone who so enjoyed *Amerika*, written despite its author never having set foot in the United States. Brij had especially delighted in the lampoon of Kafka's Statue of Liberty lofting a sword. 'Serves those stupid Americans right,' he would chuckle.

Ash went over to the bookshelves to find the novel. Aside from a shrine-like section dedicated to his homeland (the Gervis and Molyneux histories, *Midnight's Children*, some coffee-table mountain photography), Brij's books were, as ever, a mess: medical journals stacked three and four deep, first editions tucked behind cookbooks, Gandhi's *Experiments with Truth* crammed alongside two copies of Ash's own novel, one each in paperback and hardcover to stir double jolts of humility. There were still, as far as Ash could see, no books by women in his father's entire library.

One title had its spine facing in, a Neruda collection; a poem in Brij's handwriting graced the inside cover. As he had as a teenager, discovering this inscription during the height of his dad's Hispanophilia (Spanish classes, a week in Tulum, teabagged maté), Ash read only the first two lines—*Entre las hojas/Dos amantes se encuentran*—before hastily reshelving the book.

Oh, Brij's phases: born from envy, enacted as parody (ultimately of himself). Upon moving to Montreal, he had taken to wearing cravats and serving cheese after supper, whether the meal were rogan josh or fondue. Later, inspired by Moroccan friends, there had been some misguided forays into the cultures of North Africa, which included the purchase of a fez (never worn) and a disappointing trip to Tangiers. 'Idiot sightseers,' Brij claimed, had ruined the package tour.

Midway through his graduate degree, Ash had visited Brij in the Townships and discovered a crop of basil plants thriving in the kitchen window and the *Godfather* trilogy stacked by the TV. Brij's phases were always prompted by some man-crush, consummated in cultural appropriation and borrowed vocabulary. This time his muse was a Calabrian research fellow named Nico.

Ash was in the den pretending to understand Lacan when a voice full of portent growled down the stairs: 'Join me in my study.'

Brij was stationed behind his desk with the jade-shaded lamp twisted away, a misty cone of light fanning up the wall.

'Sit,' said Brij.

Ash sat.

Brij pushed his car keys across the desk. 'Take the Volvo to Nico's.' He wrote an address on his notepad and placed it face-down beside the keys. 'He is in LaSalle.'

'That's like an hour's drive!'

'In the trunk of my car . . . is a lamb.'

'A lamb.'

'A lamb.'

'Not living, I hope.'

'A frozen lamb.'

'Phew.'

'Take this lamb—'

'To your new boyfriend's house.'

'To Nico.'

'Gotcha.'

'He will know what to do with it.'

'Can I ask how you got your hands on a lamb?'

Brij settled back in his chair with a furtive smirk. 'I know . . . people. Now go.'

'Should I kiss your ring first?'

'*Go.*'

The delivery was clandestine. Ash arrived at Nico's, a town-house by the canal, at dusk. The lights were off. A shadowy figure lurked inside the open garage.

Ash idled in the driveway.

Nico approached, leaned in the window. 'Did you bring it?'

'The lamb?'

'*Sì.*'

'It's in the trunk.'

'*Buono.* Let's have a look.'

This scene was a bit too much like the confirmation of a mob hit: the hatch wheezing open, the shudder of light over a carcass in tarpaulin. Nico pulled back the plastic and revealed the lamb's face—it had a face!

'*Buono*,' he said. 'Follow me.'

Ash held the lamb at arm's length and moved at a trot into the garage, its frozen musculature a little too articulated beneath the thin plastic. From atop the lid of a deep-freeze Nico removed a GT Sno-racer and a rolled-up Slip-and-Slide.

'Here.'

The lid opened; a pale and icy light flooded out. Ash dumped the lamb atop some turkey burgers.

Nico closed the lid, casting the garage in darkness, produced a billfold and tucked a stack of twenties into Ash's shirt pocket. 'Tell your father—*grazie*.'

During this time his father had taken to reading Italo Calvino. A shelf down from Neruda, Ash found *Invisible Cities* wedged between *Oh Canada! Oh Quebec!* and *An Area of Darkness*. An expired Metrocard marked page 69; a section of text had been underlined in pencil. This was strange; often Brij ranted about respecting books. 'Vandalism!' he would cry. 'A book is for reading. You want to write, write your own damn story.' So Ash only folded down corners, though failing to locate the intended passage on a dog-eared page always seemed a betrayal of some prior version of himself.

The bit his father had highlighted was this, spoken by Marco Polo: '*Perhaps I am afraid of losing Venice all at once, if I speak of it. Or perhaps, speaking of other cities, I have already lost it, little by little.*'

Ash read this again, centering his mind upon what it might have meant to his dad, and lowered the book. His eulogy had focused on Brij's nostalgia. *My dad moved backward through life, eyes fixed on the receding horizon of the past*, Ash had read aloud at the funeral, *until it vanished. By the end he was left with an ideal of where he'd come from, which might have been the only real home he ever knew.* Was this bad writing? Worrisome that he could no longer tell.

Out the window the evening light was settling over a yard strewn with leaves, pocked here and there with the granular scraps of the first failed snow, sooty and hushed. Framed in the window the scene looked like the sort of naturalist painting plied at craft fairs upon the aesthetically naive. Yet the stillness also felt expectant. Ash thought about ghosts: an absence so palpable it becomes present.

The house seemed suddenly stuffy, musty, oppressive. Ash, sensing that he ought to do something other than read, decided that the leaves needed raking. For once, he thought, bounding downstairs, his sister would come home to find him being useful.

Except the leaves, left too long, had splintered to confetti. The rake clawed but the little shards danced through its teeth. Ash scraped and tilled; he was only making dust. He propped himself on the rake. The smoky odour of autumn whisked down from the woods on a chilly breeze. A few loose leafy bits swirled and went scattering. Everything was quiet. From a striation of purple above the treeline the sky ascended into blackness.

Of course, Ash's eulogy hadn't been a eulogy, really. He'd written it years before, when Brij was still alive, and even tried to get it published. In their rejection the editors at the magazine had commented, *There's a great piece in here about the son.* Obediently Ash had excised his dad and angled things selfward. The revision was accepted; it won an award. At an agent's encouragement Ash expanded those fifteen pages into a book: a book about a softer proxy who breezed through life's foibles with naïve and hilarious folly. One who learned, and grew, and changed.

All these years later, writing about Brij had seemed impossible. How to sum up a life once it was gone? Ash's attempts at a eulogy had felt like trying to sculpt fog in high winds. At one point he'd even emailed Sherene for help; she'd responded with the Beckett line she trotted out whenever he panicked. *Easier said than done*, Ash replied, *when I've got so little to 'go on' to begin with.* And then he remembered that old story, 'My Dad, Nostalgic.' In a box of memorabilia he found the original draft, the paper gone yellow and brittle, the paperclip bleeding rust. The writing was maudlin and seemed to be reaching for insights never quite attained. But at least it was something.

So that was what he'd read. And people had wept. Though his show, which attracted a modest but committed audience, occasionally taped live (a funny term—anything recorded surely died a little), Ash preferred the disembodiment of a darkened studio and reciting scripts into the ether. Getting up before the crowd, speech in hand, reminded him of piano recitals as a kid, that same looming threat of familial disgrace. Each expectant face mirrored Ash's presence in the room. His hands had been shaking. He'd felt vulnerable and fraudulent. He'd been a bit too aware of his own face. And then everything had collapsed.

How had his sister spoken so naturally? She didn't care about sounding familiar, for one thing. As a lawyer Mona trafficked in language with the practicality of a statistician pecking out num- bers on a calculator. If a rote phrase expressed what she needed, in it went. And maybe tapping into some common experience was the whole point of a funeral—or a wedding, or any type of ritual. Clichés were the currency of such things. Whose dust might be so unique, anyway, to warrant some special send-off?

Part of Ash's struggle to get at some elusive essence of his dad was that he lacked a firm footing from which to begin. Growing up, Mona had been the target of Brij's instincts toward paternity (curfews, mistrust, fear), and even though they'd warred through her teens, it had at least made for a parental dynamic. Brij and Ash had been more like two joggers running in tandem: intermittently he might check over his shoulder, satisfied if his son were still there.

Forgoing the rake, Ash got down on the ground and with his hands tried to corral the powdery leaves into a mound. They crumbled; he was only spreading them about. The earth felt damp beneath his knees. And still he knelt there, as the night's first stars or satellites blinked feebly into existence and the temperature began to plummet. Remarkable in the Townships how distinctly day ceded to night, and autumn to winter.

His sister and her man were coming down the mountain. Mona's voice preceded them like a little stream murmuring down the hill through the dark. From the other direction tires crunched up the gravel road. Matt arrived first, his truck swinging wildly into the drive. Carrying bags of grease-roasted chicken, he was almost in the house before noticing Ash on his knees in the garden. 'Doing some yardwork?'

Ash's reply was froggy, strangled: 'Hey.'

'You okay?'

As Matt approached through the twilight, the skin behind Ash's ears drew taut and his throat swelled. All week, what had begun as gathering himself had tightened into constriction. Now he felt choked by it, his heart knotted in his chest.

His old friend was upon him, setting down the takeout and hauling Ash to his feet. 'Okay now,' said Matt. 'You're okay.'

Ash was cradled. The smells were body spray and deep-fry and weed.

The voices of his sister and her husband approached. Ash couldn't let them see him like this, clutched by this mawkish ox. He wriggled. But Matt held him fast.

'Easy, bro,' said Matt. 'I got you.'

Ash swallowed the hard sharp disc lodged in his throat. Tensed as it scraped down through him. Closed his eyes. Clenched his body into stillness.

Matt seemed ready to let go, and then Mona and Harj were coming off the road onto the driveway.

'He's a brute,' Harj was saying. 'An alpha male monster.'

'I just don't know what he thinks he's doing here,' said Mona, 'acting like he's family.'

And Matt wrapped Ash even tighter.

His sister and her husband went in the front door, neither noticing the two men clasping each other in the shadows. Ash felt smothered. Lights came on inside the house. The only sounds were the faint huff of Matt's breath and a distant drone from the highway. Still he didn't let go. So Ash let his friend hold him, there on the lawn in the dusklight, and waited to be released.

**2**

SINCE MONA AND HARJ HAD CLAIMED the master bedroom, the remaining sleeping spots were in the den: Ash on the pull-out and Matt on a foam mattress on the floor, face hidden beneath the mask Brij had diagnosed to regulate his sleep apnea. Between stabs of rotisserie-induced heartburn and the machine's percolations and Matt's Darth Vader rasping, Ash couldn't sleep. Not that he was an expert sleeper anyway, but now at least he had someone to blame. What *was* the guy doing here?

As kids their friendship had begun easily, instantly. They were sports fanatics with divorced parents who lived a block apart in London's north end; were ten-year-olds still monarchs, such harmonies would be enough to end wars and merge kingdoms. And while Matt acknowledged, with mild astonishment, what different paths their adult lives had taken, he seemed to believe that the childhood unity of their friendship remained.

After high school, when Ash moved to Toronto, he became something like the island nation upon which Matt had long ago staked his flag. With each reunion he grew a little more sovereign, a little harder to claim. So Matt preferred to reminisce: 'I don't care what you're up to,' he'd say. 'With us none of that matters.' And while anything new, any change or development, only strained the tether of history between them, occasionally he'd offer a surprising show of support: showing up at Ash's MA defence like it was an Olympic trial, for example, where he'd torn around the room slapping high-fives when the committee announced a 'pass with changes.' This from a guy who'd dropped out after two semesters of an undergraduate degree, buried by debt and, possibly, dyslexia.

Shortly after Ash landed his show Matt had coaxed him back to London 'to celebrate,' which meant watching ski videos and smoking weed in his basement apartment. Ash arrived to discover that Matt's girlfriend-of-the-moment had been missing for three days, stranding him with her pug, Gertie. 'I figure if she's dead I'd have heard something,' he reasoned between bong-hits. 'She's probably just somewhere getting nailed by some Japanese guy.' (Matt's imagined sexual rivals were, inexplicably, always Japanese.)

Midway through *Extreme Moguls 6*, the dog began whimpering, and before Ash could suggest a walk, a turd appeared gleaming on the living room floor. Matt tented a magazine overtop, and then they were out on the streets with Gertie snarling at the end of her leash and Ash blinking like an unearthed mole in the daylight and Matt beaming at passersby, demanding, 'How's your day going?' with an edge to his voice, a challenge. He often pursued excuses to feel slighted, to cast adversaries. 'You see that?' he spat when someone snubbed him. 'Dumb homophobe thought we were gay.'

Out at the bar a similar offence would have been enough for Matt to flip a table and start swinging, though this 'homophobe' was a middle-aged woman in business casual who disappeared into a taxi. Matt turned the corner in a black mood, yanking Gertie along. But everything was forgotten minutes later at the jingle of an ice cream truck. 'Ice cream!' he cried and bounded off, stranding Ash with Gertie on the curb.

Lying a few feet away and masked like a spaceman, Matt's sleep-face contorted between peaceful and scowling, like a puppy externalizing its dreams. Slave to his own id, a mind possessed by itself. 'My mind's got a mind of its own,' he liked to say, by way of apology, whether for a momentary lapse of reason or a lifetime of mistakes. 'Ash, honestly?' he'd continue, suggesting confession, though what followed was usually some equivocation: 'I'm no teddy bear's picnic, but . . .'

Honesty. This too was big for Matt. Albeit a curated and capricious version, one that served grander narratives of integrity and self-worth. Even so, through every career change and relocation and marital engagement and STI, Ash had done his best to support his friend—skeptically, sure, but also with genuine hope that *this* might be the thing to finally work out.

'Dhar?' The mask was off; Matt cupped it in his hand while the machine puffed away on the floor. 'You awake?'

'Yeah,' said Ash, feeling ambushed. 'Can't sleep. Gut's a little jumpy.'

'Right, the muscles. From trying so hard not to cry.'

'No, that's not why, you lunatic. From dinner. Too much grease.'

The meal had been depressing: brown chicken and brown fries with brown gravy heaped onto Brij's best dinnerware. Ash regretted not cooking. What they'd needed was nourishment, sustenance. Something green and lively. Something he could offer.

'Anyhow,' said Matt. 'I was thinking.'

'Go on.'

'Remembering. Our sleepovers. When we were kids.'

'Okay.'

'Like the one we had in your dad's yard, that last weekend before grade nine?'

Ash sat up.

'Probably the best night of my life.'

'Last night of my childhood, I've often thought.'

'Honestly?'

'Honestly.'

'Remember how we built a tent out of ski poles and tarp? Your dad got all excited, started drawing up blueprints and everything.'

'And then it rained.'

'But before that, remember how we snuck out into the neighbourhood?'

'Right!' Ash chuckled. 'And the barramundi.'

'The what?'

'You don't remember? My dad called us into the TV room and was like, "Boys, look at these things. They're born men and turn into women. Remarkable!" For the rest of the night we kept doing fish faces and in this bad Indian accent saying, "I'm a man . . . I'm a woman . . . Remarkable!" and laughing till we pissed ourselves.'

'Was that jizz story for real?'

'Why wouldn't it be?'

'Was just trying to think of the last time I laughed that hard.'

'Without drugs, you mean.'

'Yeah.' Matt got distant. 'Wanna blaze one?'

'Now?'

'Might help you sleep.'

Ash was doubtful. Weed made his mind and mouth race, often into realms of the obnoxious. But he followed Matt outside all the same. And when the joint came his way he accepted it greedily.

'That's it, take your medicine,' said Matt, leaning back and gazing up at the heavens. 'Wow, it really cleared up. Lot of stars out here, huh?'

'Cold, though. No cloud cover.'

'Pass that?' Matt smoked expertly, smoothly, making Ash aware of how self-conscious he looked sucking on one end of the joint while eyeing its blazing tip in faint terror. Matt cradled it backwards in his palm to shelter the cherry from the breeze, released the smoke as naturally as he would his own breath. An elegant performance.

Ash declined a second round, gazing past Matt out into the yard. The chalet was surrounded by pine and poplar, and the trunks seemed to jostle in the night like a crowd of onlookers. *My dad is dead*, thought Ash, and shivered, and hugged himself.

'Crud,' said Matt. 'I nearly forgot: that lady, that old vixen who wants you to come to her book club? I told her we'll be staying in Montreal tomorrow night. She said she could get her gang together to meet with you Tuesday morning.'

'What are you, my agent?'

'Does that mean I get a cut?'

'A cut of what?'

'Well, actually,' Matt giggled, 'I might've already took one.'

'Oh god, what did you do now?'

'What didn't I do, is the question.'

'At my dad's funeral?'

'I can't help it! I'm only one man! And don't get me wrong, I feel bad. I mean, considering. And we didn't go all the way or anything—'

'That's Brij's boss!' *Was*, Ash amended, but didn't say.

Matt blew smoke over his shoulder. 'Hush now. You'll wake up your sister.'

'How the hell did you manage this?'

'She asked me to show her the bathroom, but then she found out I was in school for massage therapy and she told me her shoulders were tight so I gave them a little squeeze and she pulled me inside and closed the door and was like, "I need to see your cock."'

'This did not happen. How does this stuff happen to you?'

Matt finished the joint with two big sips, stubbed out the roach on a licked thumb, and pocketed it. 'Nothing happens *to* me, bro. I make it happen.'

'You sound like a serial killer. Or a despot.'

'So anyhow, all's I told her was, "You gotta show me yours first."'

Ash shook his head. Partly at Matt, but also at the jealousy flitting on the periphery of his disgust.

'We didn't blast, just a little . . . *you know.*' A demonstration followed. But then his voice shifted registers. 'I didn't nut, or mean any disrespect.'

'As long as you're making memories, right?'

'Barbara.'

'What?'

'I don't want to forget. That was her name: Barbara.'

THOUGH HE'D DABBLED IN pretty much everything else, Matt's drug of choice was weed. For nearly two decades he'd committed to a strict routine: bong hit on waking at noon, a few toots on a one-hitter over the course of the day, a joint in the early evening, and a nightcap with the bong at bedtime. Wake at noon and repeat, repeat, repeat.

Matt liked to say, with pride, that he didn't drink. 'I'm not supposed to,' he'd explain, as if on medical advice—x-rays on the wall, cirrhotic guts revealed—rather than best practices after wayward boozy escapades had left him shamed or gonorrhoeal or jailed. (Though he did claim to have heart problems, too, something arrhythmic, some valve flapping the wrong way or jamming like a stuck door.) But of course he did drink, regularly, announcing each time, 'Honestly, I shouldn't be doing this!' By last call, wallet emptied, he was either looking for a fight or a fuck or he had his arm around Ash, slurring into his face, 'You're my best friend, you little maggot.'

Sometimes he'd even consummate things with a kiss. Not really sexual, more as a misguided father might smooch his estranged, reluctant son. Though he kissed everyone, from lovers to co-workers. His mom had been the same way, insisting when she dropped him off at school on a goodbye kiss on the lips. This seemed beyond ridicule, into the territory of the incestuous, the unhinged, the possibly illegal. And yet there was something showy about it too, so once, at a pool party in front of a girl they both liked, Ash had teased him about it. 'So my mom loves me!' screamed Matt, and in a blind rage thrown all the patio furniture into the pool—and then chucked Ash in too.

Matt's adolescence had been like an attack from within: he sprouted to six feet and began shaving in grade seven, lost his virginity at thirteen, the same year of his first arrest (for crapping into his math teacher's sunroof). But his tempers had their maudlin extremes too. In grade eleven gym class, volleyball unit, he'd pounded a third consecutive bump into the ceiling and couldn't take the razzing of his classmates. 'I'm a frigging nationally ranked junior mogul champ!' he'd screamed, tears running down his face, and gunned the ball as hard as he could into the crowd, breaking a girl's nose. (He'd sent her flowers, they'd ended up dating, and then Matt had slept with her older sister.)

Another crying episode had occurred in English class, during debates. Matt did not care to be made to look stupid, and Ash knew this, and Ash liked getting laughs, and so during their discussion of Hamlet's existential crisis he'd taken full advantage of the heckling option, parroting everything Matt said in the voice— half an octave up, interrogative—his friend affected for phone calls and friends' moms. Matt lost it, punching him so hard in the shoulder that Ash couldn't use the arm for a week. (Seeking redemption, Matt took him to Wendy's: 'Anything you want, bro. It's on me.')

These were Ash's thoughts as he lay awake again, high, now,

as well as heart-burned. Matt's sleep machine wheezed and gasped. The hour ticked toward two, passed it, approached three. He'd always been ashamed of his insomnia, considering his dad's medical speciality. Like the petty criminal son of a cop. Both Brij and Mona were sound and instantaneous sleepers: their heads hit the pillow and out they went. But not Ash. As a kid he'd spent too many nights staring wretchedly into the dark, dreading the morning with everyone burbling around the kitchen, bright-eyed and rested, while he blearily poured orange juice into his Cheerios.

Such a basic thing, sleep, into which lucky souls *fell*, as if each bedtime afforded some glorious accident. Yet for Ash the night offered nothing so passive as a dreamy tumble. It wasn't sleep that echoed death: no, death was that purgatory of lying awake, forsaken, as the hours slunk toward the fresh hell of dawn. And now, with his sister sleeping, and her husband sleeping, and Matt sleeping, Ash felt like a ghost, abandoned and alone. He struggled to coax his mind into silence. But thoughts swirled and clanged, the pillow was too hot, the sheets twined into snakes that crept neckward to choke him.

At a quarter past three Ash got up to read. *Into the Night* seemed the perfect analgesic for a twitchy brain. He turned on the light over the dining table, reread the novel's first sentence, hung his head, checked his phone—far too late to text Sherene, who slept the sleep of a dead and buried log—and, with a sigh like a desert wind rasping across the sands, continued.

The story unfolded more or less as expected, beginning with a prologue that detailed, in italicized and bludgeoningly lyrical language, a man building a cabin in the woods. Tearing out stumps, hammering, framing, sawing, whatever. The writing was manly. The man was manly. He cussed and roared and roasted shirtless under a blazing sun, hydrating with whiskey while his blood and sweat (no tears, never tears) pollocked the ground. The work was pure masochism; the suffering deserved. *The past lives in the body,* summarized the narrator, *so it must be wounded free.*

Then the novel proper began. Or rather backtracked to life before the fall—a wife, a child, a dog: the man had it all. But tragedy loomed. He'd been a soldier, he'd beheld horrors and maybe committed some too. And it haunted him. As time passed the man's behaviour turned erratic, his thoughts became paranoid. Convinced that spectres from his troubled past were planning to kidnap his wife and son, the man locked his family in the cellar and headed off to hunt down his demons. Except there were no demons to be found, only whiskey, and when he returned, the house with his family trapped inside was engulfed in flames. The man sank to his knees there on the lawn in the shuddering glow of his own ruination and watched the last embers of his dying world scatter off *into the night* and no, no, no, what had he done?

And here Ash cried.

Just a little. A tear or two, easily wiped away.

Down on the floor, Matt rolled over, grunted and groaned.

Ash froze, waited. Smeared another stray tear from his cheek to his ear.

And Matt began rasping away again.

Ash dog-eared the page and flipped the book. The Behemoth stared unflappably from his author photo, a man who'd waded into an abyss of hard truths and emerged to tell the tale. A man with such clout and power, and in such high demand, that there was no rescheduling his interview, tragedies be damned. Ash felt bullied. What might Sherene have planned for Tuesday? What might he ask the author of this dreck? There were no revelations here, just manipulations and make-believe. The abyss was the guy's own creation, its battle-won wisdoms self-serving and contrived: it was no great trick to build up a hard man only for the tear-jerking purpose of making him fall. This wasn't a novel, Ash thought, blowing his nose softly into a napkin. It was a con.

THE NEXT MORNING MONA, upon waves of morning sickness, walked in on Matt shaving his crotch with what seemed—though she didn't look long or close enough to confirm it—to be her razor. She slammed the bathroom door moaning, 'Ew, ew,' fled downstairs with her hand over her mouth and unleashed a torrent of vomit into the kitchen sink.

After bleaching the drains clean, Ash joined her and Harj on the couch.

'He was all hunched over and gross,' she explained, 'washing his pubes down the drain. Why, Ash? Why would someone do that?' She lowered her voice, pressed her face into Harj's chest. 'How long is he going to be here?'

Ash resisted mentioning that, having known them all for twenty-five years, Matt was more family than Harj, now cooing like a mother bird into the top of Mona's head.

Brij had always claimed to like Mona's husband, called him 'thoughtful and kind,' though Ash felt that he mostly appreciated having another doctor around to talk shop. Sometimes they'd even switch to Hindi, which, after decades away from India, Brij spoke haltingly, deferring to his son-in-law for pronunciation and vocabulary.

'What about a bath?' Harj asked Mona, nuzzling her neck. 'Shall I bathe you?'

Ash fled to the kitchen to scramble some eggs.

But then Harj appeared in the doorway. 'Are those farm fresh? Free range? We're trying not to feed the baby any GMOs.'

Ash knocked the eggs around the pan as if searching for incrimination in their midst. 'No idea.'

'I'll make Mona some toast then.'

'No, that's fine. I'll do it.' Ash brandished the spatula like a cutlass.

'We brought our own bread—'

'The gluten-free stuff. In the freezer. I know.'

Still Harj lingered. Ash busied himself with breakfast preparation. Finally he turned and met his eyes.

'Oh, Ash,' said Harj. Was this pity? Ash felt an urge to hurl something at him, a steak knife or a fridge. 'Your friend—don't let him bully you.'

'Sorry, what? Bully me?'

'Ash, please.' Harj stepped toward him. He wasn't speaking so much as purring. 'For too long white men have been emasculating us, feminizing us.'

Ash laughed. 'They have, have they?'

Harj nodded. His hand was on Ash's shoulder now. It felt like a blessing. 'The history of colonialism is exactly this: they ridicule our manhood with their version of what it means to be a man. They say we're not man enough, they make us feel small.'

'And this, you're saying, is playing out in my dad's living room.'

'The legacy of colonialism runs long and deep.' Now Harj had Ash by both shoulders, nostrils flaring with each breath. Distantly Ash was aware of his eggs scorching. 'But the secret is to embrace what they deem feminine. That's how we beat them.'

'Go team,' said Ash.

Harj, oblivious to his sarcasm, added something in Hindi or Bengali that Ash had no way of understanding. Before a translation could be requested, Matt came thumping down the stairs and interrupted Harj's and Ash's strained embrace. 'You guys slow-dancing?'

'Give us a minute,' said Harj.

Matt pushed between them. 'Is there coffee?'

'I thought you weren't supposed to have caffeine,' said Ash.

'True.' Matt turned to Harj, tapped his chest. 'On account of my heart.'

'We were talking,' said Harj, looking to Ash for solidarity.

'Honestly?' said Matt. 'I doubt Ash wants to talk to you. He doesn't even like you.'

Ash grabbed Matt by the back of his shirt, pulled him away. 'Seriously?'

'Well, you don't.'

Harj stared hard at Ash and, with a shake of his head, slipped out of the kitchen.

'Come on,' Ash called after him. 'We're family.' But his words sounded weak.

Before Harj was out of range Matt lifted a leg and farted. 'That'd be all those sandwiches yesterday,' he said, wafting. 'What do you think, Doc? Can you smell the egg salad?' He let go another one, a greasy squeak. 'And there's the ham and cheese, too.'

'THAT GUY HAS GOT TO GO.'

'Harj?' said Ash. Having dispatched her husband for groceries Mona had brought Ash up to the master bedroom to go through Brij's clothes. Matt was out back chopping wood and every thirty seconds the whack of the axe echoed across the yard. 'If you say so. Shame he has to leave so soon.'

Mona kept balling loose socks, dropping matched pairs into a garbage bag at her feet. So dutiful, such resolve. But there was fragility about it too, a slight tremble in her hands.

From outside sounded a great crack of split lumber.

'Matt means well,' said Ash. 'You know that, right?'

Mona looked up. 'Does he? Aside from the fact he's disgusting and takes up half the space in the house? That he threatened my husband? I don't trust him. Never have.'

'Threatened? By gas attack?'

'And, really, Ash—*means well*? This is the person, remember, who used to steal wallets from the change rooms at Thompson Arena during family skate.'

'He's here for us.'

*Thock*, sounded Matt and his axe from outside.

'Wrong.' Mona moved to the dresser. 'He's here for himself.'

Dimly Ash watched her manoeuvre an armload of sweaters to the bed. The previous night's lack of sleep was catching up. He felt sludgy and detached, and his sister's purposeful sorting and stacking made him feel especially peripheral to the whole affair. All he'd contributed so far was dumping a drawer of his dad's briefs onto the floor. But then what? Kicking them into the donation bag was surely wrong.

'It's just like when he was a kid,' said Mona. 'Always hanging around our house. No family of his own so he adopts us. Or pretends we've adopted him.'

'His mother killed herself!'

Mona looked up sharply. 'Don't use that. Don't let him use that as an excuse.'

Ash escaped into the walk-in closet. Surrounded by a dangling army of empty suits, he was overwhelmed by the smell of his father: coffee, mothball, a vaguely fecal musk. Brij had boasted about not needing deodorant (true), though his breath had borne the reek of death. Once, returning home from vacation, Ash had discovered a sludge of rotten kale and furred yogurt in the trash that recalled his dad's mouth-smell exactly.

Ash emerged from the closet with six hangers of pants. 'Well, you'll be rid of us soon enough. We're going to Montreal tonight. Matt and Chip planned drinks.'

There was a splintering sound from outside, and a shout— 'Frigging cripes!'—and then silence.

'Did he cut off his hand or something?' Ash moved toward the window but Mona straight-armed him back. He'd forgotten how strong she was, still very much the older sister who'd dragged Ash's sixth-grade bully around by the ear before dumping the kid face-first in a puddle.

'You're leaving.'

'Don't poke me, that hurts.'

'Couldn't stand it here any longer?' Her tone was fierce, her expression wounded.

'Shit, Mona, you either want us here or you don't. Which is it?'

'Ash, I want *you* here. Just not him.'

'That's what I want too! Just us.'

She sat on the bed. 'Yet you're leaving.'

'It's not like that. Chip came all the way from London! He doesn't get much chance to go out, what with his kid and all. And plus I have this interview . . .'

Mona shook her head: no excuses, no bluster. She gestured at the clothes piled around her on the duvet. 'Some of this stuff would fit you,' she said. 'You should try it on. Before you go, I mean.'

'I'm good for Y-fronts, thanks.'

'Well, what about this?' She held up a Kashmiri housecoat with a tasselled sash and intricate embroidery up the lapels. It had been their dad's home-wear before giving way to a pair of grey joggers and an Expos T-shirt.

'Hmm . . . I *was* looking for an outfit for my next puja.'

'Just try it on, smart guy.'

A chance for absolution, maybe. So Ash slid his arms into the sleeves. With his hands at his forehead he bowed, rose with a head-wobble and a sly grin. 'Memsahib.'

'Come,' said his sister, and tied the tassel. Her eyes glistened. 'There.'

'Could I pass for full Brahmin now or what?'

Mona wiped away a stray tear. Sniffled. But then laughed a little. 'You look nice.'

'Wouldn't it be better on Harj?' said Ash. 'A real Hindu, I mean.'

'No.' Mona's expression was wistful. It made Ash feel like a lens: not looked at, but through. 'Keep it,' she said. 'It suits you.'

—

AFTER HE'D SPLIT WITH THEIR MOM, Brij had taken a few, faintly tragic cracks at homemaking: the dutiful replication of Ikea showrooms, a 'play tent' in the basement (commandeered by Mona; off limits to Ash) and some calamitous attempts at microwave cookery before discovering premade curry sauces: dump over meat, heat, 'enjoy.'

He'd also stocked a games cupboard to rival any toy store, minus the awkward domestic values of Life. On the alternate weekends Mona and Ash spent at their father's, this cupboard helped salvage Brij's required Saturday morning of family time. Eyes on the clock, Ash and Mona trudged plastic avatars around the boards of Sorry! or Snakes and Ladders while their father cheered them on, delirious with caffeine, until his competitive streak took over and he crushed them both.

But as the years wore on the tradition turned nostalgic, and games before lunch became something they almost enjoyed on visits to the Townships. So just before noon Ash called everyone into the den to enact another old rite. The assembly happened grudgingly, like rival nations gathering for a forced truce. While Harj crafted a teepee of kindling and newsprint in the fireplace, Ash, still wearing his father's robe, knelt by the games cupboard and proposed options. 'Jenga?'

'You're too anxious,' said Mona. 'You knock it down every turn.'

From the window, watching snow machines paint the distant slopes, Matt called, 'He can't play Operation either. Shakes like a leaf.'

'How about Monopoly?'

'Capitalist propaganda,' said Harj. He struck matches and flicked them into the fireplace. The kindling began to crackle.

'Trouble's more socialist,' said Ash, 'but I think the popper is broken . . . Scrabble?'

'With you, Mister Word-Nerd?' said Mona. 'No thanks.'

'Hey,' said Matt. 'I'm no Tolstoyevksy but I'll lay tiles with frigging anyone.'

'No, Mona's right. Scrabble's boring.' Ash scanned the remaining games with urgency: Risk, chess, Chinese Checkers. Each more dreary than the last.

'There we go,' said Harj, stepping away from the fireplace, where a mighty conflagration snapped and snarled. 'Now, that's a fire.'

'Clue's a no for me,' said Ash. 'Mona always used to make me be Mrs. Peacock.'

She laughed. 'Well, you're certainly dressed the part now in that robe.'

'What about charades?' said Matt.

Ash turned from the cupboard. 'What is this, drama camp?'

'Don't be a turd,' said Matt. 'It'll get us off our butts and that.'

'I haven't played charades in years,' said Mona. 'Could be fun. Us versus you two?'

Matt moved away from the window, cracking his neck, limbering up. 'Remember I'm a professional actor. You guys don't stand a chance.'

Harj, who seemed to consider this a challenge to his marriage, swept onto the couch beside Mona like a general into battle.

'Charades it is,' said Ash with, he hoped, conviction.

With the fire roaring away, clues were written on Post-its and dumped in a bowl. Mona selected herself, the eldest, to go first. She opened with the movie camera motion.

Harj nodded, chin in hand. 'Film.'

From there she operated with the bodily semaphore of a third-base coach: syllables tapped out on her forearm, an earlobe tugged, vigorous affirmations when her husband guessed a word. How in synch they were. How familial. And with the firelight shuddering over her, Mona looked radiant. What a good mum she was going to be, thought Ash.

'A *Passage to India*,' yelled Harj—and he and Mona high-fived.

This had been Ash's contribution, though he'd meant the book, not the movie.

Mona returned to her spot. 'You guys are up!'

'Let's save me for the home stretch,' Matt advised. 'Ash, why don't you give it a shot.'

Harj passed Ash the bowl and excused himself to the bathroom.

'Okay, little buddy,' said Matt. 'Let's do this.'

The clue was *cold-snap*. Easy enough. Ash loosed an arm from the sleeve of his dad's robe and held up two fingers.

'Peace,' said Matt.

Ash shook his head.

'War?'

One finger, then a second.

'Counting . . . Counting to two . . . One, two. Uh, duh . . . twah?'

Ash tried a different tack: he held himself at the elbows and shivered.

'Parkinson's disease! Muhammad Ali, Michael J. Fox—'

Ash shook his head. His smile had faded.

'Wait, are those guys dead?' Matt sounded panicked.

Ash shivered again, then snapped.

'Snappy? Sounds like: snappy. Snoopy? Snoop Dogg? I know—Charlie Brown!'

The room was cast in a spell of bafflement and wonder.

Ash shivered, then snapped.

'Shiver-snap.'

He shook his head again. Repeated the simple, clear actions.

'Snap . . . cold?'

With relief, Ash nodded and pointed at Matt.

'Me?'

Ash shivered, snapped.

'Me, snap? I'm cold? Sorry, bro, you lost me.'

Ash crossed his hands in a gesture of reversal: other way round.

'Spell it backwards?' Matt closed one eye; his lips moved. 'Is it *pans?*'

Ash shivered. He snapped.

'Snap, cold . . . Snappity-snap, chilly willy . . . Oh snap, that was *cold!*' Matt guffawed. Mona looked stunned. Ash sighed.

And shivered. And snapped.

'You're cool, but you're also snappy . . . Ice-T? West Side Story?'

Ash tried again, with urgency.

'Snap, cold; snap, cold.'

And again—though the actions had become weary.

'Tylenol Cold and Flu and Snapping . . . Frozen Fonzie . . . *Cool Runnings* . . . Snap! Cold!' Matt reclined on the couch, looking like a beached walrus prospecting for a mate. 'This is hard. Do another clue!'

Ash slumped against the hearth. He watched Harj's fire shudder. From upstairs came a flush, the woof and roar of it, and the door opening. Surely sufficient time hadn't elapsed for hand-washing?

'Jack Frost!'

Here was Harj, back and bemused: 'You two still at it?'

Now Matt was snapping and shivering. 'Snap!' *Snap.* 'Cold!' *Shiver.*

'Keep it up,' said Ash, loosening the tassel on the robe; the lapels flapped freely. 'I'll be over here self-immolating. Just let my scorched carcass know when you figure it out.'

'Hey,' said Matt. 'You're not allowed to talk.'

'Pay attention.' Ash demonstrated. 'Cold, snap . . . cold snap. *Cold snap!*'

'Cold what?'

Ash closed his eyes. Opened them in a slow, pained way. 'Seriously?'

'Oh, *cold*-snap. Right. Duh, when you say it like that it seems so obvious.'

'When I fucking did it, it was obvious too.' There were echoes of his father in this petulance: how fragile the man who cares to win. When he looked up the room felt clenched. Everyone stared at him.

'Don't act like you two'd be any different, stuck with this idiot on your team.'

'Hey. I'm right here.'

'I know. You always are.' Ash looked out the window. The day was overcast, the trees mostly bare save a few dead and orphaned leaves. He stood. 'I need the bathroom. For once in your life, can you not follow me?'

As Ash stomped upstairs, Matt's voice broke the silence: 'Got him.'

'What?' said Mona. 'That was a *joke*?'

'Cold—*brr*—snap.' And Matt snapped. 'I told you guys I was an actor!'

Locked in the bathroom, Ash pretended he hadn't heard this. He was struck by a distinctly Indian smell, that sickly, putrid stench of shit-pasted latrines. And floating in the toilet was a single wisp of toilet paper bearing a brown tinge. This was too much: Harj had wiped once, then left the evidence like some sick calling card!

Ash pissed upon it hard.

Once the flush had quieted he noticed that the voices downstairs had gone hushed. Sensing that he was being spoken about, Ash cracked the door slightly. Yes, there it was: whispering, a conspiracy. He thought to stride out onto the landing and interrupt: *What are you all gossiping about?* And then crush them each, one by one.

Matt—all it took to ruin him was to claim that he was just like his father, heedless, self-obsessed and doomed, an abandoner of people and an absconder from life.

Then there was Harj, whose smug self-righteousness was the

flimsy armour of an inadequate soul. Never mind his hygiene: twice Ash had caught him knuckle-deep in his nose. And with him dripping from her like dank lichen, Mona's fiery spirit had dampened. What sort of kid would they have? A self-righteous, deluded snob whom the real world would summarily crush. Better if the pregnancy—

Too vile, too much. Ash retreated instead into his dad's office, where what had risen as loathing collapsed in despair. He felt hollow, gutted by his own malice. His presence in the house had soured from inept to toxic. Brij's robe was suddenly oppressive. Ash shrugged it off and closed the door.

Better, he thought, to leave Mona alone.

And maybe better still that he was leaving altogether.

THE LAST DOCUMENT in the WRITING folder was double-sided and single-spaced, with no paragraph breaks, like a readout from the subconscious or a missive written in a fever dream. There was no title. It simply began:

On the day in question our hero ceased to be a hero, perhaps he had never been, perhaps none of them had, he was only the first.

What was this? Ash leafed through. Such strange, halting diction, as if translated poorly from some lost language. On the final page, things cut off mid-sentence:

And when he reappeared

That was it. The ending was missing, or unwritten.

He returned to the opening line and began to read. It was a story. Maybe even the beginning of a book. The author, Ash assumed, was his father. Or, more so, a version of his father he'd never known: one who wrote fiction. The voice was alien. It did not suggest the man he thought he knew. Yet the setting—snow-capped mountains and pale glacial lakes—was certainly Kashmir. These forty-odd pages were Brij's attempt to novelize his homeland. His vitriolic response to 'Lines of Control' now made sense. Ash's story had seemed like competition.

The novel continued:

The hero woke and the mountain loomed above and atop its slopes he knew was the answer. He gathered his things and crossed the meadow gone golden in the sun and along the path once trod by so many thousand pilgrims he went, yet alone, down first and then up over a little bridge over a brook chortling along, the icy blue tumbling water haunted with silver, and saw no one save a few sheep, strays perhaps from a nearby flock. So a shepherd was nearby. But he could not be seen. Swirling mist gathered. The hero walked alone.

And on it went, and on he read, turning pages in a sort of reverie until the spell was broken by a knock. Ash looked up: the room was unfamiliar; the walls seemed to reel. He felt roused from sleep, and at the edges of waking life lingered the shimmer of a dream. It took a moment to place himself: Brij's office in the Townships. Reading a book his father had written. About a man climbing a mountain. A *hero*, at that. And something high above, it seemed, that might save or heal his broken soul.

Another knock.

'What?' Ash called sharply.

Matt peeked in through a crack in the door. 'You've been up here over an hour, everything okay? It's gone one o'clock . . .'

'Yeah, just a little tired. Didn't really sleep last night.'

Matt's eyes were glazed and pink. And Ash understood the

real reason he'd come up. Not to apologize. To satisfy his munchies. To order a meal.

Ash tucked his dad's novel back inside the folder. 'So I guess you're hungry.'

Matt grinned. 'I'm glad to make lunch, long as you don't mind Doritos sandwiches and pickle juice straight from the jar.'

'No, let's not do that.'

'Find anything juicy up here?'

'What do you mean?'

'Oh, you know. A secret family, a map to buried treasure.' Matt closed the door behind him. His face turned grave. 'Sorry. I know I'm too much about me sometimes. Just, my mind's got a mind of its own.'

'Right.'

'Honestly, I know what you're going through. This stuff's hard. But you have your best friend here to crap on if you want. So go ahead. Crap away. Crap on my face if it'll help. Or in my mouth. Drop a hot two right in here.' Matt tilted his head back and yawned.

'Is this meant to be helping?'

'I just did it again, didn't I?' Matt pounded his forehead with a closed fist. 'I'm trying, Dhar. I'm trying. Do you wish I hadn't come?'

'No,' Ash said obediently. 'Of course not. It's great you're here.'

'I'm glad you think so! There's nowhere else I'd want to be. Though it'll be good to go out tonight in the city with Chip, really tie one on like old times.' He paused. 'And no problem, is all I meant. As far as you losing it on me.'

'Okay.'

'I just want to be the right amount of here for you.'

Ash laughed. 'You sound like a Neil Diamond song.'

'Honestly?'

'Did you just take that as a compliment?'

Matt struck a baritone: '*I'll be what I am . . . A solitary man . . . Solitary . . . man.*' Then there was some humming.

'Very nice,' said Ash.

'My mom's favourite tune.' Matt ran a hand over his head. Seemed on the verge of something else. Instead nodded briskly and slipped back out into the hall. And, like a summons, failed to close the door.

WHAT A BIG, BIZARRE HEART thumped in that huge body, thought Ash, spinning lettuce for a salad for lunch. In high school, when his chemistry lab partner had died in a car accident, Matt had claimed her suddenly as 'one of my best friends' and required a week off school to recuperate. Or, years after graduation, when a vice-principal whom Matt had never liked—who, in fact, had suspended him twice—passed from cancer, Matt had sat front row at her funeral, holding her sister's hand.

And then there were his 'memories': the time he and an associate piloted a hot air balloon over the cornfields outside London in search of weed, logged some grow-op's coordinates into their GPS, and returned under cover of night only to have their asses spackled with buckshot. Or the boss's daughter he pleasured orally in the company van—while *he* was driving ('Just hold the wheel and enjoy,' he quoted himself in the retelling). Or the time he'd eaten poison ivy for cash. Matt didn't make memories for himself; these stories were a way to exist in the thoughts of others. So he blundered from one set-piece to the next, always with the goal of recounting it all to someone—anyone!—later.

Brij, too, had existed through stories, though whenever he'd summoned one, usually from his youth in Kashmir, he'd gazed past his audience to tell it. Never a performance, more of a retreat. But then what, thought Ash, tearing leaves onto plates, about this unfinished novel or whatever it was? What did it *mean*, this interminable climb? If fiction offered keys to the author's soul, then Brij's manuscript ought to have unlocked some secrets. Yet with no ending it only obscured him further.

From outside came a crack and hollering. Ash moved to the window. Although he'd already split enough kindling to warm the house through spring, Matt had returned to finish off the wood-pile. But now this: the axe had lodged in the block and he had a foot up to jimmy it loose. 'Come on, you frigging jerk!' Matt roared, and toppled backwards, and lay there in the dirt like a clown pandering for laughs. When none came he stood, dusted himself off and, after glancing around, pulled the thing free with one hand—the hand, Ash noticed, allegedly stricken with a dropped finger.

'SO,' SAID MONA, BETWEEN MOUTHFULS OF SALAD, 'anything interesting up there?'

'I asked him the same thing,' said Matt. 'Treasure maps, dick pics, whatever.'

'Classy,' said Mona.

'Well?'

Ash drank wine. 'Not really. Standard stuff, most of it for the shredder.'

'When I went up he looked like I'd caught him watching porn,' said Matt.

'If there's porn up there,' said Mona, 'I don't want to know about it.'

'There's no porn.'

'What'd you find then, Dhar?' said Matt. 'I know you too well, can totally tell when you're hiding something. And he's hiding something.' This was directed at Mona, who smiled tersely.

'Nice idea to add the grilled chicken, Harj,' said Ash.

'Simple enough,' said Harj from the head of the table. 'Organic meat and fire.'

'Nah, I hate it when my meat's on fire,' said Matt. 'Like, say, when you pee.'

Mona ignored him. 'Ash, what did you find?'

'Some writing.'

'Of Brij's? What kind of writing?'

'A novel, maybe?'

'Really? Brij wrote a *book*? Let's see it!'

'Like father, like son,' said Matt, nodding sagely. 'Mee pah-dray, soo pah-dray.'

Harj, poking at his salad, had lost interest: how frivolous to make up stories when there were war orphans to be saved!

'Will you do anything with it?' said Mona.

'Do? What would I do?'

'Try to get it published or something?'

'Just like that? "Get it published?" As one might "get groceries" or "get fat?"'

'Or get an STD!' added Matt.

'How am I to know how it works,' said Mona. 'You're the one who wrote a book.'

'Here's an idea, Dhar,' said Matt. He'd taken command of the conversation and his captaincy was deranged: Ahab without a whale, madly harpooning the waves. 'Just put it out under your name. None of us would say anything.'

'Plagiarize my dead dad's book, you mean,' said Ash.

'Can you not say that?' said Mona. '"My dead dad"—you sound almost gleeful.'

Harj went outside to take a call. Matt, now in comic mode, glanced around for fresh material. Ash headed him off: 'Do you want to hear what it's about?'

'Please,' said Mona.

'Far as I can tell it's just about a guy climbing a mountain, in Kashmir, I think, to some cave. And there's something up there that's going to, I don't know, save him?'

'Sounds like Amarnath,' said Mona.

'What's that?'

'Shiva's dink,' said Mona.

Matt perked up again. 'Tell me more!'

'It's this pilgrimage that Hindus do,' said Mona. 'They walk up into the Himalayas to this cave, which they insist on calling a temple, where there's an ice stalagmite they claim is Shiva's dink. And they ogle it and come back down, protected by the army, while meanwhile the Muslims who live in the villages they go parading through are digging up mass graves of their family members murdered by those same soldiers, probably.'

'Well, no. What Brij was writing is a story. It could be based on anything—'

'It's totally Amarnath,' said Mona.

'So, wait,' said Matt. 'Dinks are holy in India?'

'A lingam,' said Ash, 'is a *symbol* of Shiva that has a phallic shape. Not a dink.'

'And dudes hike up to this . . . symbol?'

'Women too, Matthew,' said Mona, and gazed out the screen door to the deck, where Harj, with his phone to his ear, nodded and laughed and furiously picked his nose.

'Anyway,' said Ash, 'Brij's book seems less about dink worship than the quest itself.'

'Can you hold off on interpretations until we've heard the actual story?' said Mona.

'Yeah,' said Matt. 'What *happens*?'

'That's the thing. That's it. Just climbing.'

'Just climbing,' said Mona. 'The guy—'

'The *hero*, Brij calls him.'

'Right. The *hero*, then, never gets to the top?'

'Yeah.'

'Sounds riveting.'

'I want to read it when you're done,' said Matt. 'Frozen dink quest, I love it!'

'Except there's no ending,' said Ash. 'Like, it just cuts off. So maybe he did have something else planned.'

Matt slapped the table. 'You've got to write one!'

'I can't believe Brij wrote a book,' said Mona. 'When did he do this?'

'I don't know. There's no date on it or anything. I was thinking that when Matt and I head into Montreal—'

'So you're really leaving?'

'I told you this. Sherene's scheduled studio time tomorrow morning for this big interview for our holiday show. Plus a book club visit. And since they've got me staying out by the airport, after that I'll likely just fly home to Toronto. And I can help with everything here from home. Right? Sorry, Mona. Not my fault. I just really have to go.'

'*We've* got to go,' said Matt. He turned to Mona. 'I'm leaving too.'

'What book club, Ash? Tell me you didn't take Doctor Bloch up on that invite.'

'What was I going to say?'

'I don't know, maybe, "Sorry, my dad just passed away, can't make it?" Or, "Not sure this is the time or place to be soliciting celebrity guests for your literary luncheons?"' His sister stood to clear the dishes.

'Oh, come on, I'm not much of a celebrity.'

She swept past him with an armload of plates.

'Hey, wait!' Ash called after her. 'What I was saying was that we're going by Brij's office to see if there's a finished version of this thing on his computer. The Amarnath story, I mean. And obviously if I find anything I'll email it to you and we can read it together!'

No reply, just a great thunder of silverware clattering into the sink.

'Could be cool? Mona?'

The taps came on. But his sister said nothing.

Matt, though, was keen. 'Don't worry, Dhar,' he said, with a bounce of his eyebrows. 'I love a good mystery. Just like Jekyll and Hyde, chasing down the clues.'

'Do you mean Watson and Holmes?'

'Whatever.' Matt leaned back, laced his fingers behind his head. 'All that matters is you and me, bro, finishing your dad's quest to see the ice dong.'

# 3

SO THEY ESCAPED: down through the hills in Matt's pickup. As the roundabout wheeled them to the highway Matt wistfully watched the ski resort fade from view, the mountain like a pound cake drizzled with some pale and creamy sauce.

'Next time,' Ash said.

And off they went to Montreal.

In the duffel at Ash's feet was his dad's manuscript. For now, he took out *Into the Night*. Two hundred pages remained unread. On the back cover was its author, gloating in full colour.

'That's who you're interviewing?' said Matt. 'He looks cool, not like a writer at all.'

'Why don't you read it for me then?'

'Nah, I'm no reader. Last book I read was ... Yours, probably.'

Ash returned *Into the Night* to his bag.

They were quiet for a while. The world rolled by: half-frozen fields and black barren trees. Matt turned on the radio, discovered only French stations and flipped it off. Wet snow began slashing down and melting on the windscreen. Ash watched the wipers swish back and forth, the glass spangled and wiped clean.

'Get my one-hitter from the glove box,' said Matt. 'Should be loaded. Help yourself.'

The pipe was modeled to look like a cigarette and came in a sleek wooden case. Ash smoked, exhaled, enjoyed the heat in his chest spiralling outward, passed it to Matt as his head went loopy and strange. Yet for Matt, a couple puffs turned him focused. Normal.

'So that hike? The one into the mountains?'

'The one in my dad's book?'

'Yeah. The one Mona was talking about. Why do people do it?'

'I don't know. Religion, I guess. You should have asked Mona, she's the India expert. She was actually in Kashmir a few years ago doing her Mother Teresa thing.'

'I searched it online. Looks like Banff. With way more brown folks.'

'When my dad really missed home he used to go to Lake Louise. There was one spot he said that looked just like this place where his family went on holiday when he was a kid, the Golden Meadow or something like that . . .'

'Did I tell you about the German girl I dated the summer I spent out there?'

'Yes. You told everybody. Please don't—'

'Dhar, honestly? Getting peed on can be a beautiful thing.'

'Stop. Just—stop.'

Matt giggled. 'Load that thing up again.'

Ash did, took a toot, passed it over. He felt giddy and loose. His mouth was woolly.

'So can anyone go on that hike?'

'Pilgrimage. For Hindus. It's not a tourist thing.'

'Frigging French drivers!' Matt hammered the horn. 'Tabernacle!'

'Why, are you thinking of going to India?'

'For a fistful of god-cock, bro. I'm going to ride that thing to freedom.'

'Don't. Ever. Okay? This is thousands of years of history and tradition.'

'Come on,' Matt said. 'Could be fun, me and you. When was the last time we took a vacation together?'

'We're going to Montreal right now.'

'That's not what I mean. Remember our trips to Tremblant and Blue Mountain? I'd always have to tighten your boots because you couldn't do it yourself.' Matt snorted. 'Imagine us riding moguls down the Himalayas?'

'Are you out of your mind? Kashmir is a *war zone*. You've seen those kidnappings and decapitations on CNN? That'd be you, with your big dumb bald head sawn off and dangled before some jihadist's camcorder.'

'So is that a maybe?'

'The Champlain Bridge should be coming up in a bit. Just drive us off it. Full speed.'

'Know what your problem is?'

'I've got one idea.'

'You need to get laid.'

'Right. Your solution to everything.'

'Honestly, when was the last time?'

'Once we hit the bridge, take a hard right, okay? Do us both a favour.'

'When, Ash? Honestly. When?'

'Leave me alone.'

'That's what I thought.'

They drove for a while in silence, Matt with a cheeky smile and Ash watching the snow gust across the highway in phantasmal wisps. The fields on either side were a washed-out murk. Something about them reminded Ash of his dad's book. All those looping, ethereal sentences leading to that final, unfinished line, like a pathway to the mouth of a cave, with whatever followed lost in gloom.

Here was the river, the city, the mountain hefting out of the misty snowfall like some dormant beast. Though *mountain* was such a funny word for that hump of gravel and scrub. 'Some mountain,' Brij had scoffed. 'Hardly royal, either.' Having been born among actual mountains, the subject of an actual king, in his more exasperated moments Brij had liked to cast the whole province as a mockery of his homeland. 'Separatism?' he'd cry. 'These stupid Quebecois don't know how good they have it.'

And he'd been so resistant to French, too. Despite years of private tutoring, as if in protest his *bonjour* still rhymed with ganja, his *noir* came out 'nwah'—like a burlesque kiss—and his consonants gurgled and hacked. There was something Arabic about Brij's French: a little too glottal, a little too phlegmy.

The bridge was gridlocked.

'Rush hour, looks like,' said Matt. 'La ur da rush.'

They inched forward. Matt laid on the horn.

'Why?' said Ash.

Matt shrugged, eyeing the city, its downtown a cluster of tombstones in the dim light. 'Hey,' he said, with sudden brightness. 'Let's make a stop.'

'Oh dear god. Where?'

'Dhar, trust me. I'm thirsty. And you need to loosen up.'

ASH HAD NOT BEEN to a strip club in a decade. Following Matt inside with his eyes on his shoes, he felt the need to text Sherene. To confess, but also to justify his unease in terms of sexism—the objectification, the abjection—rather than a lack of expertise. But an ominous *No pictures, no video* sign banished his phone to his pocket. He already felt like a kid sneaking in somewhere dubious and forbidden. No sense getting in trouble too.

Matt, of course, was a pro, nodding collegially to the doorman and leading Ash toward the stage. 'Not pervert's row,' Matt instructed. 'One table back. So the girls can see you but don't figure you for a total creep.'

Flirting brazenly with the waitress Matt ordered 'duh sankaunts, see-voo-play' while Ash eyed the woman twisting around the pole a few feet away. The place smelled of stale beer and tobacco guttering amid the floral malaise of a funeral parlour; the lighting recalled a submarine. The clientele at this hour—mid-afternoon—was scant: one guy alone at the bar thumbing his phone and a couple of American college boys (backward caps, goatees) a few tables over, gawking like toddlers plopped down before a TV.

The song faded. The dancer readjusted. Everything went still for a moment.

*My dad is dead*, thought Ash.

A second number began. Their beers arrived. Ash swallowed half.

'That's the spirit,' said Matt, clapping his back. 'You like her, eh?'

The woman was dark-complexioned, possibly Middle Eastern. As she knelt and tilted back, humping the air with her pelvis, Ash struggled not to think of Sherene. 'Mare-see bow-coupe, sherry.' Matt lifted his beer, turned to Ash. 'Man, if we go to India I'm going to have to do some serious Karma Sutra training.'

'You and I are never, ever going to India,' said Ash. 'And it's *Kama*. Karma is the infections you'll bring home.'

'But what if you can't find the end to your dad's book? We'll need to head over there to figure it out. Jack off the ice dick and that. See what comes out.'

'Why do you care?'

'Meh, I guess it doesn't really matter,' said Matt with a shrug.

So dismissive! Who was he—this interloper, this fool—to decide what mattered and didn't? Angrily Ash downed his beer and signalled the bartender for another.

The announcer came on and told them to give it up for Cyprus. Matt hooted. Waving, she dismounted the stage, collected three beers from the bar, and brought them, shockingly, to their table.

'No French,' apologized Matt. 'Nuh-pah parlay frawn-say.'

'Good,' said the girl, sitting between them. 'I can practice my English.'

'Cyprus, meet my best buddy Ash.'

'Hi,' said Ash.

'Enchantée,' said Cyprus.

'His dad just died.'

'Smooth,' said Ash.

Cyprus reached across the table, took Ash's hand. The contact was not unwelcome. 'That's terrible,' she said, caressing his thumb. 'I'm sorry.'

'Thanks.'

'I was to say to buy me a drink,' she said. 'But maybe I'm going to buy you?'

'That's okay,' said Ash. 'We're just here for this last one, and then . . .'

A new dancer was introduced: 'Please welcome Sylvie!' Cyprus clapped and whistled. The woman strutting out from backstage gave her a wink. Ash, his hand orphaned on the tabletop, felt forsaken.

Sylvie began her first number from a handstand.

'Gosh-*dang* I love black women,' said Matt.

Ash sighed. 'Can you not say stuff like that, please?'

'It's true! White women too. Not to mention'—he nodded at their guest—'brown.'

'Sorry,' Ash told Cyprus.

But she was watching the stage with a grin. 'This girl, she is my . . . *coloc?*'

'Roommate,' said Ash.

'Room, mate.'

'Look at you two getting along like a Taj Mahal on fire,' said Matt, punching Ash in the shoulder, spilling his beer. 'How about a little private session?'

'No,' said Ash.

'VIP, bro. Dons-con-tack. It's on me.'

'Only if you want?' said Cyprus. Once again, she took Ash's hand, squeezed his fingers. Ash squeezed back.

'One thing though,' said Matt, handing his car keys to Ash. 'If you're getting a dons, I'm going to pound a few bee-airs, so you're driving. Now go allay-zee a bun time.'

Cyprus stood, lifting him by the hand. And Ash went, feeling bullied, limp and led.


ASH HAD BEEN THE RECIPIENT of one previous lap-dance in his life, when he was seventeen, courtesy of—who else?—Matt, already among the lunchtime regulars at London's Fabulous Forum. Out of curiosity and a dim instinct toward rebellion Ash had joined him one noonhour. They'd barely sat down before one of the dancers straddled his knees.

'I can't pay you,' he whispered.

'It's okay,' she told him, draping her arms around his neck. Braces glittered on her teeth; her breath smelled of peanut butter. 'Your friend's got a tab.'

That Ash had ejaculated less than a minute later had been a secret until a moment of drunken candor months later, when he confessed stashing his soggy boxers in the toilet tank. He expected ridicule. Instead Matt tousled his hair—as a father might, imparting some life-lesson—and said, 'Ah, whatevs, Dhar. Happens to the best of us.'

This time, nearly twenty years later, was different. In a space reminiscent of a police interrogation room (complete with two-way mirror), Cyprus deposited him on a lumpy couch, pressed play on a boom box in the corner and came at him, swaying at the hips.

'Tell me what I'm going to do,' she said, slipping out of her top until it hung loosely around her waist.

'You don't have to do anything,' Ash said.

'Viens,' she said. 'Touch me if you wish.'

She turned her back to him, bent over, took his hands and placed them on her hips.

Ash felt like the passenger on a motorcycle.

'Touch my breast,' she said.

Ash groped upwards. She placed her hands over his, squeezed. The pocks of her nipples pressed into his palms. Cyprus turned to face him, wedged a knee between his legs and, moving between them, began massaging his thighs.

He moved his hands to her buttocks, one cheek cupped in each.

She leaned in so close her nipples brushed his lips.

He closed his eyes.

She popped two buttons, reached inside his shirt, caressed his chest.

Everything was so gentle, almost tender.

Ash stroked Cyprus's back up to her shoulders.

She eased onto his lap.

He held her to him.

She ground her hips. 'Like that?' she said.

Ash said, 'Okay.'

She took his face in her hands. 'Do you want to tell me about your father?'

He opened his eyes.

Cyprus was staring into them.

'My father.'

'You don't have to.' She stopped moving; her face flashed with panic. 'Sorry.'

'It's okay.'

'But if you want?'

What did he want? Ash stared.

'My father, he is also dead,' she said—plainly, simply, in a way Ash almost envied.

'I'm sorry,' he said.

'Long ago, when I was just a child. In Lebanon. In Beirut.'

'In the civil war?'

'Yes.'

'My dad was from Kashmir,' Ash told the half-naked woman on his lap. And felt immediately preposterous. Yet blundered on: 'He left there a long time ago, but if he'd stayed . . .' He let the pause suggest the same fate as Cyprus's father: solidarity!

'The world, it's hard,' she said.

'It is,' Ash agreed, sealing their compact of suffering.

'Was your father in pain?'

'At the end? No, it was all very quick.' But before that, thought Ash: yes. Brij had been in pain—the discreet pain of longing, of loss—most of his life.

Cyprus nodded. 'C'est tout qu'on peut demander.'

'Oui,' said Ash stupidly. 'Exactement.'

She reached out and touched his face, drawing her fingers down his cheek where a tear ought to fall.

Ash moved his hands to the small of her back.

Cyprus wiggled a little closer. Her breasts pressed against his chest. Their faces were inches apart. Her breath fell warmly upon his lips.

The moment opened up, expanded. Cyprus's eyes were wide and kind—and quizzical. They seemed to search his own for a way in.

———

'YOU *WHAT*?'

'Shut up, let's just get out of here.'

'Oh man. You didn't.'

Ash dropped two twenties on the table. 'Leave your beer. Let's go.'

On the way to the truck Matt had to race to keep up. 'Who tries to kiss a stripper?'

Ash ducked between two businessmen in suits, around an elderly woman pushing a cart of groceries through the slush.

Matt followed, his laughter booming up St. Catherine. 'The one thing you're not allowed to do and you just go for it.'

Turning down a side street, Ash clawed in his pocket for the car keys. 'How am I in the wrong here? You act like an asshole and yell shit at these women and it's fine?'

'It's just out of the rules, bro.'

'Insane. The whole thing makes no sense.'

'Yeah, right. It's the rules that are insane, not you.'

In the truck Ash sat for a moment behind the wheel, watching traffic putter by. 'I swear to god she wanted me to do it. There was something between us.'

'Nope.'

'What do you mean, "nope"? You weren't there!'

'Dhar, listen to me. I've spent enough time at the peelers to know that no stripper, ever, wants you to kiss them.'

'Specifically me?'

'You're lucky she didn't sic a bouncer on your ass. It's a bad idea to mess around in Montreal clubs. Hell's Angels run half these places.'

'So now a biker gang is going to hunt me down for trying to kiss this woman.'

'Cyprus.'

'There's no way that's her real name!'

'As if you know her.' Matt shook his head; the code had again been breached. 'There's your number one problem in the first place.'

AS HE QUITE LITERALLY opened a new room of Brij's life, Ash had to resist the Hollywood anthropology of it: chamber by chamber, the mystery unlocked . . .

'I feel like a super-lame Indiana Jones,' he said, entering his father's office, tucked away in a corner of campus with Mount Royal looming up behind.

'*India* Jones though,' said Matt. 'India Jumanji.'

'That's Africa.'

'Same diff. They both have elephants and hungry people.'

On Brij's desk was a framed photograph of Ash and his sister, dressed up for Ash's grade eight graduation. His head was shaved ('You've got plenty of time to go bald,' his dad used to carp. 'Why not enjoy your hair while you have it?') and he wore a billowing silk shirt and tie, its clumsy double-Windsor as big as a fist. Mona was fifteen, standing with her arms crossed and the distant look of someone with better places to be.

'Nice duds, Arsenio,' said Matt, plopping into the swivel chair behind the desk and picking up the photo. 'God, your sister is beautiful, you know that?'

'Stop it.'

'No, honestly.' Matt put the picture down. 'I'm not trying to be a creep. You guys are lucky to have each other. Me, I've got nobody. No brothers or sisters, no mom or dad.'

Ash looked away.

'And hey? I know sometimes I act dumb and say the wrong thing and embarrass you and whatever, and your sister probably hates me—'

'Hate might be a strong word.' Matt lifted a hand as if pledging an oath. 'What I'm saying is I'm here for you guys. You're like my second family. I'm here for you, bro. Your oldest, best bud.

Which is actually better than a husband or wife or whatever because we can't break up. And way better than that nose-picking commie Mona's married to. Right?'

Ash nodded.

'But if I'm in the way, just tell me.' Matt cringed as if preparing himself for a slap.

'It's probably good we came to the city,' said Ash. 'Just to give Mona some space.'

'And to get wasters with Chip tonight,' said Matt, recovering. 'And for you to kiss a stripper.'

'Okay, get out of the way. Let's see if I can find this stupid thing.'

While Ash fired up the old PC, Matt sprawled on the floor with his phone. After a minute he sat up and announced, 'In 2000 thirty people were murdered on that pilgrimage.'

'Amarnath?'

'Yeah. Would that be terrorists?'

'Or freedom fighters, depending what side you're on. You're looking this up?'

Matt shrugged, sunk back into the cushions, returned to reading his phone.

The login screen appeared and Ash keyed in what he hoped was still his dad's password: *Srinagar*. It worked. As the old Dell began to chirp and gurgle Ash felt invasive, on the cusp of trespass. Computers were such strange repositories of the subconscious; among Matt's bookmarks he'd once unearthed a folder marked *Sweet Pussy Vids* of—astonishingly—kittens doing adorable things. What might Ash discover about his dad? Secrets, revelations, a hidden life. Maybe even some other family back in India, one he'd left behind and sent monthly payoffs and never ceased to love.

Though as the home-screen loaded a breakthrough seemed impossible. His dad's desktop resembled his bookshelves. Atop a background image of Dal Lake, dozens of icons and files floated like leaflets strewn by the wind.

'So why would anyone go see this thing?' Matt's voice was the honk of a trombone through the small room.

'What thing?'

'Ice cock. Like, what's the goal?'

'It's a shrine. It's one—'

'—*of the most important sites in Hinduism.* I know. It says that right here. But, like, why walk up into the mountains just to look at it? Does it work like Viagra or something?'

'God, no. I don't think?'

But Matt had gone quiet again, frowning, tapping away at his phone.

Ash returned to the wild mosaic of files. Stupidly he'd left his dad's manuscript in the truck, and lacking a title he struggled to think of an exact phrase to narrow the terms of a search. He typed 'lingam.' No results. 'Amarnath' also revealed nothing. 'Kashmir,' conversely, returned more than a thousand hits; Ash clicked on one—a conference paper, 'J-K Sleep Deprivation and Psychosis,' co-authored with some researchers in the Lolab Valley.

Perhaps Brij had written that story years ago on some other, older machine. Ash leaned back in his chair, knocking his fist against his chin, another gesture he'd inherited from his father. Now it felt mimetic. His hands fled to the keyboard. But what to type?

'It doesn't look like a dick at all,' said Matt. 'No nuts, no glans. False advertising!'

Ash looked briefly away from the screen. 'I really don't know much about this. My dad kind of gave up on the Hindu thing when he moved to Canada.'

'Is seventeen-fifty expensive for a direct flight to India?'

Ash tried 'pilgrimage'—no results. 'You're not really thinking about going, are you?'

'I told you, bro. Me and you. Road trip. Or air trip, I guess. Like old times.'

'I've got a job. I can't just leave. Besides: brown boy's dad dies, brown boy flees to the fatherland to discover who he really is? No thanks. I've seen that movie and it sucks.'

'Yeah, exactly. Isn't India where people go to find themselves?'

Ash laughed.

But Matt didn't seem to be joking. 'This one's cheaper but it goes through Frankfurt. That's in West Germany, right?'

'Right. On the happy side of the old Iron Curtain.'

'Jesus H. Vishnu, eighteen hours in an airplane! Do you think my one-hitter would set off the fire alarm in the can?'

'I think if you went to India you would be dead in an hour,' said Ash, punching 'novel' into the search bar. All this revealed were papers that used the word adjectivally and a few old emails goading Brij's friends and colleagues into purchasing Ash's book; the link was broken. He returned to the 'Kashmir' search and began prowling through the files.

Everything was work-related. Ash had been wary of discovering a diary, but all these research papers were its opposite, each one clinically titled, the language academic and bland. His father's career had been spent *writing*, enough to fill a dozen books. All of it about sleep. Yet nowhere did he mention dreams.

'Any luck?'

Ash shook his head, kept scrolling. 'Nope.'

'Well, ob-la-di, ob-la-da. Looks like we're going to India so you can finish it.'

'I told you, no.'

'Why not?'

'Going to Kashmir? After my dad dies? What a cliché. Picture it: me scattering the cremains from some mountain, and then honouring his memory by completing his opus. And then what? People read it and are so moved that peace descends on the Valley? Or, worse, I win a prize?'

'So what *are* you guys doing with the ashes?'

But Ash had come across a JPEG, and for a moment Matt ceased to exist.

Titled, 'Poonch, July 1965,' the file was a black and white image of four men seated on a sofa—or crammed into it, as was often the case with real estate in India. The picture took Ash aback because the guy second from right looked so familiar. An old friend? Some cousin he'd not seen since childhood? Only upon recognizing his uncle among the other men did Ash realize that this person was, in fact, his father.

Brij as a twenty-year-old. Brij with buddies. Brij *with hair*, the part like a fissure in petrified magma. Photos from this era, in the Indian way, were usually posed: people shoulder-to-shoulder as if for a police line-up, faces stoic. But this one was candid. Brij's smile was cheeky. His right arm was slung around some lean and beaming pal. His shirt bore an absurd, hysterical print, unbuttoned to release a froth of chest hair; his trousers were white and flared. He was so young!

And smiling so blithely, his own death an unseen shadow flitting beyond the frame. A version of Brij who didn't know the son he'd father, nor that one day that same son would be chasing his future self through the ether (computers! the internet!) only to find him, here, lodged among friends upon small furniture.

Ash missed this person he'd never known, this smirking hippie, this alternate Brij in bellbottoms and a sensationally patterned shirt, faraway in Kashmir. The Brij who never left India, who existed forever in bliss within the borders of this photograph, ignorant to the Troubles, to exile, to anything beyond lounging each day away in perpetuity. Who coasted through life without loss.

'Dhar?'

'Yeah.'

'What's shaking over there?'

'Nothing.'

'Honestly? Then why so quiet and weird?'

'Want to see something funny?' Ash said.

Matt came over. 'Whoa, is that a brown boy-band?'

'That's my dad.'

'Sweet Shiva's frozen schlong! Holy crud, it is. And the fella with the moustache, the one your dad's feeling up, that's his fiancé?'

'What do you mean?'

Ash had been looking so intently at his dad's face that he'd not noticed Brij caressing, with a single index finger, the forearm of the man beside him.

'No, smart guy, that's just the way Indian men are with one another. Affectionate.'

'I'll say. Look at the grin on Mister Moustache.'

'It's not like that. They'll hold hands, cuddle on park benches. It's not sexual.'

'Sure doesn't sound it.'

'Weirdly they're super homophobic too.' Ash laughed at a sudden memory. 'Listen to this. So when my dad was not much older than he was in that photograph, twenty-two or so, he came to New York for a conference. And he met up with a friend of his— maybe even that guy—who was living in the States. They went for a walk, and as they'd do back home they linked arms. But walking through Central Park or whatever people start yelling at them: "Get a room, faggots," "Go to hell, you queers," stuff like that.'

'If that was me and you, Dhar? I'd frigging murder them.'

'Keep in mind this is the seventies. But the thing is? My dad and his buddy have no idea why anyone is saying anything, because being gay—*actually* having a romantic relationship with a man—is so far beyond their realm of comprehension. As far as they're concerned, they're just two pals out for a stroll.'

'So how come you never hold my hand when we're at the bar?'

'Wait, listen. This is the best part. Eventually they realize what's going on, so they let go and keep walking without touching. And then they make it to the Village.'

'Gaytown?'

'You got it. Men everywhere are holding hands, cuddling, doing whatever they want. So they link up again, and walk around the rest of the day just like they would at home.'

'Man, the more I hear about India, the more it sounds like the place for me.'

'So you can cuddle guys?'

'I don't know. Don't you think it'd be nice?' Matt pushed a little closer. Ash was assaulted with familiar odours, the body spray not masking the weed-stink so much as candying it. 'Honestly though,' said Matt, 'they *do* make a cute couple.'

'Oh, for god's sake!'

'Dhar? Would you frigging relax and look at them?'

Ash did: at the two young Pandits smushed together at the end of the couch, at Brij's finger snaking into the crook of his friend's elbow, at their faces alight with happiness. Had he ever seen his dad so comfortable, so at ease, so at home in himself or the world? Though now Ash also realized why it had so disoriented him at first: Brij's gleeful expression was one he'd rarely seen on his father's face. That smile—that ironic, slightly smug, self-satisfied smile—Ash knew better as his own.

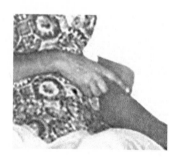

## 4

'THIS IS THE BEST,' Matt declared from the head of the table, and raised his beer and chugged it down. It was a command to do the same, so Ash and Chip obeyed.

Idly Ash turned his attention to a nearby big-screen—two shirtless men caged and wrestling, limbs entwined and cheek-to-cheek—and finished a text to Sherene, who was touring brew pubs with friends on the Plateau. *You should come downtown*, he begged. Her reply was instantaneous: *Not in a million years*.

The bar—Matt's choice—was a dingy basement with faux wood-panelled walls and framed hockey jerseys and a steady grind of corporate rock. It was a hive for a certain type of man, a man like Matt. Ash felt edgy. In these places difference was cause for suspicion. Matt, who relished any chance to play alpha, understood this, and he kept glancing around for an excuse to defend their honour. At a similar spot in London, some poor sap had once splashed beer on Ash and found himself pinned to the wall by his earlobe. 'You got a problem,' Matt had snarled, 'with my little brown friend?'

*Maybe we'll head that way*, Ash messaged Sherene. Which was doubtful. Matt was in his element. Montreal's language politics and warren of one-way streets made him anxious, but a generic sports bar offered refuge. These were the places he'd spent half his life, either as client or staff. He ordered another round with a twirl of his finger, then blew their kilted server a kiss.

On TV, one of the fighters hitched his legs over the other guy's shoulders, crossed his feet at the nape of his neck, and hauled him in.

*No you won't*, wrote Sherene.

Their pitcher arrived.

'Mare-see, Claudine,' said Matt, reading her name tag, and filled their glasses. 'The three of us together again, boys? Honestly? This means the world to me.'

'So good to see you guys,' said Chip. 'Cheers.'

As always the drinking was purposeful, and the other two fell instantly into their old dynamic: Matt holding court, Chip egging him on. Ash was meant to play the straight man, calling out Matt's lunacy with cutting asides, to which Matt would respond with physical terror—noogies and nurples and swift, backhanded blows to the groin. And Chip would laugh. Yet Ash didn't feel up to it, and the beer had a coppery, bloody taste.

While the other two bantered, Ash brooded behind his phone. The air felt static with what was left unspoken, the real reason they were together. Since Ash's childhood Brij had existed to his friends as a shadowy figure often 'away at a conference' or 'on call' or just absent and unaccounted for. Even though Matt had seen Brij for his apnea their relationship had never progressed beyond the clinical, as far as Ash knew. So with no point of entry, what could anyone say? Besides, they'd long ago established that trauma was best tiptoed around like a coiled snake, its bite numbed with booze.

*Packing it in, see you tmro*, came Sherene's reply. *Don't drink too much! XO*

Ash returned his attention to the TV. Though he knew nothing about martial arts of any stripe—and refused to trust anything that awarded merit by belt—the fight transfixed him. It was animalistic, but contained. Fierce, yet coyly intimate. And, as one man buried his face in the other's neck, their grappling struck Ash as tender.

*Sure you don't want to rescue me?* he wrote back.

Claiming to have recognized someone from his acting days, Matt went loping across the bar, arms out for a hug.

'There he goes,' said Chip. 'Making friends.'

'Or foes.' Ash checked his messages: nothing. With Matt gone, the space between Ash and Chip seemed to contract. They watched the fight together for a bit, then Chip handed Ash his Blackberry to admire some photos of his son. Ash obediently thumbed through a dozen blurry selfies.

'See the one at the Raptors' game? Got courtside and everything.'

'Cool,' said Ash, returning the phone. 'How old is he now?'

'Ten! Grade five, can you believe it?'

'Wow.'

'Puberty, man. It's happening. Pretty soon he'll be chasing girls around.'

'Right.' Ash drank. 'Otherwise though? Things are good?'

'One sec.' Chip keyed out a message and set his phone beside his glass. 'Ty's alone at the hotel so I can't stay long. I mean, he's fine, he's a big boy. I just can't get too drunk.'

Matt returned with a fistful of shots. 'Wasn't who I thought it was, but such a great dude! I told him my buddy's dad just died and he bought us a round of tequilas.'

Across the bar, some guy in a backwards visor shot Ash a thumbs-up.

'No salt, no lemon, no pussying out,' growled Matt. 'Just down the hatch.'

Ash tipped it back: the wince, the burn, the shudder.

'Horrible,' moaned Chip.

The table of francophones beside them cheered and Matt high-fived each man in turn. 'Where's Claudine? More drinks for my gar-sawns here!' Matt roared and beat his chest. 'Holy frig, boys, I feel so *alive* tonight. And my finger barely hurts or anything.'

ON TV THE FIGHT ENDED. Someone had won. Ash watched, mesmerized, as one bloodied, battered man had his hands lifted in a kind of coerced triumph. The look in his eyes, while trainers and media thronged around him, was blank and lifeless.

'Dhar!' Matt clapped him on the back. 'Get in here for a photo.'

Claudine framed the three friends with Chip's camera phone. At the last second Matt took Ash's hand and placed it on his arm. 'Just like your dad and his boyfriend.'

'Stop it.'

'I nearly forgot,' said Matt. 'Guess what our brown buddy here did earlier, Chip.'

'Please,' said Ash, 'don't.'

Chip leaned in. 'Go on.'

'We hit one of the clubs on Saint Kat-treen, I buy this guy a dons-con-tack, and—get this—oh man!—what a champ!—he tries to suck face with the stripper!'

'We didn't *suck face*.'

'What was it then? A peck on the cheek? That's even creepier.'

Chip slapped the table. 'You never been to the peelers before, Ash?'

'Are you kidding? Ash has a history of blowing it at the nudie bar,' hollered Matt. 'Literally, first time I took him? Busted a nut in his pants, stashed his dirty gitch in the back of the toilet and spent the rest of the day at school bare-balling it in his Levi's.'

Everyone howled—even the Quebecers at the neighbouring table.

Ash sunk his face into his hands. Though a part of him was relieved: playing the fool provided a function.

Matt slung an arm around him. 'Aw, I only rib you because I love you.'

'This is what love is? I'd hate to be your enemy.'

Claudine returned with another tray of shots. As she placed them on the table, Matt casually touched her forearm. 'Mare-see bow-coupe, sherry.' He slammed one back and pounded the table and jumped to his feet and announced, 'Gotta go see a man about a horse, i.e. me taking a horse-sized piss.'

Ash watched him go, shooting double-guns at strangers: *hi there, cross me and die.*

Chip checked his phone. 'I should get going. Want my tequila?'

Ash gulped Chip's shot, then his own.

'Tough guy, eh?'

Eyes watering, Ash looked away. 'I'm not sure if you saw,' he said, 'but there was an older lady in a scarf at my dad's . . . thing.'

'Okay.'

'Well, Matt fooled around with her.'

'Making memories as always!'

'What, are you impressed? She's like seventy years old!'

'This is the dude who had a threesome the night of *his* mom's funeral, keep in mind.'

Ash shook his head.

'Though who can blame him,' said Chip. 'I can't imagine my kid finding me like that.'

Ash stared. 'What do you mean?'

'In the garage?'

'What?'

Chip leaned in. 'You didn't know?'

'He found her? Matt was the one who *found* her?'

'Yeah.'

'Jesus.'

Ash looked across the bar at the bathroom door. Matt refused to wash his hands in public restrooms, convinced that passing them under the hand dryer was somehow more hygienic. Ash pictured him thumping the button, wet fingers whisking the hot air, a smirk of pity at the fools scrubbing away in the sinks, then breezing back into the bar on the stink of steamed urine. There had once been a time when his friend's follies would cheer him. Now, more than ever, they seemed pathological.

'Don't say anything,' said Chip.

'I wasn't going to! God, do you think—'

'He's coming.'

Matt loped back across the bar, bald head glistening.

'Seriously, Ash,' said Chip, his voice forlorn. 'I'm surprised you didn't know.'

Matt loomed over the table. 'You maggots talking about me?'

'As if,' said Ash. 'We've got better stuff to—'

'Just about how well you're doing,' said Chip. 'How yourself you seem.'

Matt nodded. 'I am. I really am. Dropped finger aside, I mean.' But he seemed suspicious, didn't sit down.

Again Chip offered a reprieve: 'So how's life out west? Any stories?'

'Funny you should ask,' Matt said, at last sliding into his chair. 'I told myself I'd be good once school started. Buckle down, study. Turn my life around.'

'But not until school started,' said Ash.

'Exactly. So I had a week.'

'Uh-oh,' said Chip. 'A whole week!'

*That's like four months in human years*, Ash thought, but said nothing.

Matt gestured to the neighbouring table. 'Maize-ameez,' he said, 'aycoot-mwah. Here's one I bet you've never heard before: how I really got this dropped finger.'

As his old friend commanded the crowd, Ash observed him as he might an adversary, searching for weakness. Not to strike. Just for a glimpse of the sorrow beneath that manic facade. But Matt was too good a storyteller, his voice swelling with drama and joy, and Ash quickly joined the rapt audience (Chip, the Quebecers, Claudine, a few intrigued outliers), seeing the guy as they did: a nutcase, but loveable enough in his madcap way, eyes lingering on each listener to ensure they felt connected. What a story! Ridiculous, improbable. And, to a point, possibly even true.

'So there I am,' Matt narrated, 'wrist-deep in my own arse, and the door swings open and who's standing there but my frigging landlord.'

Everyone roared. Even Ash. This should have been the kicker, a good place to stop. But Matt wouldn't concede the stage. He shifted into a 'Pakistani' accent: '"*Mister Matthew sir, please-please are you knowing your rent is due?*"'

Too performed, too needy. Also a touch too racist. Ash sensed Matt's audience withdrawing. As the story slid from fact to fiction, he was losing them.

'So I tear my fist out of my rectum'—Matt raised his hand: the evidence—'and my ring catches on my sphincter. Tears it open. Poop everywhere.' His eyes flashed from face to face to gauge how this played.

The laughter was hesitant, perfunctory. Someone coughed. Claudine looked over her shoulder. For an out, an escape.

Matt blundered on: 'Poop down my legs, poop up my arm . . . A literal poop-storm.'

Chip giggled. But he was alone.

'I'm frigging drenched in the stuff!' he cried. 'And what'd I eat the night before? Chinese food. So there's this gross sweet and sour sauce poop, and egg noodle poop, and wonton soup poop *everywhere* and this guy's just staring at me, he's probably going to evict me. And I don't know anyone in Kelowna, I've got nowhere else to go . . .'

Ash filled Matt's glass, pushed the fresh beer toward him. But it was ignored.

'And my finger!' Matt held it up again. 'Tore the ligament right through!'

Claudine was gone. Chip was texting. One of the Quebecers stood and clapped Matt on the shoulder on his way to the bathroom. 'Great story, man.'

Matt shook his head. Chugged his pint—all of it. Refilled his glass. Stared at some point just past the edge of the table. Drank. Nodded emphatically.

'Craziest part?' he said, turning intently to Ash. 'Every single word is true.'

THE REST OF NIGHT became something that Ash could later recall only as dubious flashes of sights and sound. Had he really collapsed in tears against a payphone? Did Matt have to shush him when he began lipping the Quebecers at the next table? Was it really 'Vive le Canada!' he'd been chanting? As the bar-lights went on and the stools went up, had Ash actually been carried out by Matt on one side and an eye-rolling bouncer on the other?

And then a window of clarity. Ash was standing in the snow.

'Check this out,' said Matt, tilting his head back, mouth open.

Ash did it too: flakes sizzled on his tongue. The view above turned vertiginous, astral, less a snowfall than a plunge through the cosmos. Ash closed his eyes. The world reeled. Matt caught him before he hit the ground.

Then, something else—food, maybe? Mustard and meat, the

glare of some all-night diner. The edges of this folded inward and everything ceased to exist for a while. Next thing he knew Ash was in the backseat of a taxi with his head lolling against the window and the cabbie eyeing him in the rear-view.

'Eel-ay-bun!' cried Matt. 'Nuh-vomay-pah!'

The taxi merged onto the 20, launching out of the glitter and hum of the city into a stiller sort of night. The snow here seemed thicker, more determined.

'So,' said Matt, 'Chip seemed pretty good.'

Even the thought of speaking made Ash's stomach lurch. A perilous clot of spit had collected in the back of this throat. Let it be or swallow it down? Fearing the worst, he spat into his hand and deposited the results in his pocket.

'Classy,' said Matt.

Ash closed his eyes, ducked his head between his knees.

'Easy now,' said Matt, rubbing his back: gentle, clockwise circles from shoulder blades to tailbone.

The hand lifted, seemed to remove some nausea with it. Ash straightened.

'If you're gonna hurl,' said Matt, opening his toque under Ash's chin, 'aim in here.'

'I'm fine,' said Ash, pushing it away.

They were passing the low-rise grid of St-Henri, cathedral domes blooming like tumours. A neighbourhood Brij had pronounced *Sent Ennui*.

'So where are you from?' Matt called into the front seat.

'I?' said the cabbie. (Mahmoud Abdurrahman, according to his tags.) 'From Pakistan.'

'Cool,' said Matt. 'My buddy here's Kashmirian.'

'My dad is,' clarified Ash.

'Indian side?' said the driver.

'Where your . . .' Words were hard. Ash tried again: 'Where in Pakistan?'

'From Peshawar. You know Peshawar?'

'Is that far from Kashmir?' said Matt.

'Afghanistan is closer.' The cabbie turned down the radio. 'You speak Kashmiri?'

'When I was a kid,' Ash slurred, dimly aware this was untrue. 'I forget it now.'

'Kashmir is very beautiful,' said the cabbie.

'Should we go?' said Matt, tilting forward. 'Me and my friend, here?'

'To Kashmir? Can be dangerous.' Mahmoud Abdurrahman eyed Ash in the rearview. The particularities of this danger were contentious; clearly he didn't want to say the wrong thing and compromise his tip.

'What about the pilgrimage?' said Matt.

Ash kicked him in the ankle. *Don't*, he mouthed.

'Sir?'

Matt rolled his eyes. 'What about the women, I said.'

'Yes! My wife and I went for our honeymoon and stayed on a houseboat. The floating markets, the mountains, the shikaras, the food—the people! So kind, so hospitable. She was very happy there. Wonderful place. Paradise on earth.'

'Okay,' said Ash.

'Your father is from Srinagar?'

'Yeah.'

'But he lives now in Montreal?'

Ash sensed Matt watching him. 'Montreal, yeah.'

'Do you go back with him, to visit?'

Ash shook his head. The conversation swirled around him. He felt less a participant than its hostage.

'Well, you should go. That would be a very nice trip, you and your father.'

'He's right,' said Matt, nudging Ash. 'It would be.'

That was it. Darkness engulfed the rest of the ride to the

hotel, the walk to their room, the path to sleep, and the next morning Ash awoke with his shoes on and a shadowy murk where the previous night's memories should have been. Also a raging headache, a lurching stomach, and a first pee shocking for its colour and smell: pennies.

'Morning!' Matt cried from his bed. 'Forty-five minutes until SLAW!'

Ash managed not to vomit until Matt fed him a strawberry smoothie, and the subsequent, Pepto-Bismol-coloured expulsions weakened gradually to coarse, wracked hacking. Then he showered and, throat scorched and bleary-eyed and full of self-hatred, dragged himself through the snow to Matt's truck by 10:30.

'If it's fine by you,' said Matt, lighting his one-hitter on the way out of the parking lot, 'I'll just drop you off at the restaurant and hit an IHOP or something? Don't really need to see Barbara again. We had our time.'

Ash pressed his cheek to the window. The glass was cold, clean, punishing. 'Kill me now. I feel like someone worked a hand-mixer through my brain.'

Down the 20 they went, back into the city. Traffic was solid, and Matt weaved and zagged across all three lanes: any opening was a chance to get ahead, to win.

'Pretty crazy night,' said Matt.

'Can you drive normally, please? Unless you want my guts all over your dash.'

'Don't blame me, hero. Got to a point last night where I couldn't have stopped you if I wanted.' He chuckled. 'Let's just hope that video doesn't turn up anywhere.'

'What are you talking about?' Ash sat up. 'What video?'

'You don't remember? One of those guys at the table beside us, after we went for food. Filming you on the street?'

'Filming me? Why? What was I doing?'

'Don't worry about it. I'm sure—'

'What was I *doing*?'

'Honestly, it's not a big deal. Just some frog with his cell-phone. And it was dark, there's no way to tell who you were or what you were doing.'

'But what,' said Ash, 'was I doing?'

Matt lifted his fingers from the wheel in a gesture of abdication. Replaced them to lurch around a dawdling cube van. 'Meh, you were drunk, you're going through some stuff. We've all lost it after a few too many. You think I've never acted like an arsehole?'

'I don't think that, no. But what about me?'

'Happens to the best of us, is what I'm saying. I mean, I'm no teddy bear's picnic—'

'Matt, holy shit. Just tell me what the fuck you're talking about.'

'You really don't remember?'

'Nothing. Tell me.'

He nodded, eyes on the road. 'Okay.'

INSIDE THE RESTAURANT Ash was greeted, horrifyingly enough, by six people holding copies of his novel. Barbara Bloch indicated the seat, at the head of the table, from which he could be besieged from all angles.

'He's here!' she announced.

To his dismay, the book club applauded.

Other than Barbara SLAW included Jerry, a woman in a fur hat of feral/Soviet lineage, which upon closer inspection turned out to be her hair. Across the table, the group's 'token man' seemed straight from central librarian casting: reading glasses on a chain around his neck, grey moustache, sweater vest. 'Honoured,' he whispered with a neat tuck of his chin and a slow-blink.

Beside Jerry was 'the writer of the group,' as Barbara introduced her. 'Interesting piece,' this woman offered collegially. Her copy of Ash's book appeared unread.

Second to last was a girl with a kind, open smile. She looked about twenty, hair chopped into an asymmetrical bob and stars tattooed on both wrists. Ash wondered if she might be Barbara's daughter, dragged along with familial obligations.

'Karina's at McGill,' said Barbara. 'She found us on Facebook.'

'Undergrad?' said Ash.

'Ha!' said Barbara, perched behind the poor girl with her hands on her shoulders, as if presenting her for Ash's assessment. 'She's here on a Fulbright. From Princeton.'

'Sounds impressive,' Karina said with a laugh, 'until you hear my French.'

Ash smiled. He liked her. And her copy of his novel was thoroughly dog-eared. A decent, modest human being—and a real reader! His headache and shame eased a bit.

Finally, as a sort of afterthought, Barbara indicated an elderly woman at the end of the table so faded and gauzy she seemed crafted from dust. 'Good for you, writing a book, something I'd always wanted to do,' she rasped.

'Well!' said Barbara. 'We're so pleased you could come, Ash. Especially'—her face drooped into a mask of tragedy—'considering the circumstances.'

Condolences rippled through the group.

'Thanks,' said Ash.

A waiter announcing the specials was interrupted. 'He wrote this book,' Barbara proclaimed, tapping her copy: the proof.

'You?' said the waiter, eyeing Ash, who shrugged and ordered French toast.

This merited Barbara's approval: 'They do a superb job of that here.'

Wine came. The librarian went for it with aplomb, filling his glass and tipping half its contents down his throat before anyone else had a turn with the bottle.

Barbara commanded a cheers. 'To Ash Dhar,' she said. 'Our *author.*'

The writer knocked Ash's glass especially hard. As Ash mopped the spill, he attempted to mollify her. 'So, what sort of writing do you do?'

'Mostly diptychs,' he was told cryptically. And then she withdrew.

'So,' said Barbara, wagging Ash's book in a faintly menacing way, 'who will begin?'

'I thought it was *wonderful*,' said the elderly lady.

'Thank you,' said Ash.

She shook her head in awe. 'I don't know how you writers do it—type all those words, all the way to the end. Very impressive.'

Ash held his smile.

'Who else? Jerry, you had some questions about sales?'

'Yes,' said a voice from beneath the stacked hair. 'How many copies?'

Ash felt pressure, per Karina's goodness and humility, to deflect this question. 'I'd tell you,' he joked, 'but then I'd have to kill you.'

Too much. Six sets of eyes retreated to their plates. Save Karina, who hid her grin behind her drink. One ally, at least.

Barbara rallied: 'Karina, you had some questions about what you thought to be some . . . misogyny.' This she pronounced *my*, as if the sogyny were her own.

Ash turned his smile upon Karina, hoped it seemed hospitable and self-aware: misogyny, yes, of course. They were friends. Ash had read Cixous. They could talk!

'Such a scary word, "misogyny,"' said Karina. 'Not really where I'd hoped to start.'Across the table the diptychian reached at the librarian. He handed over his reading glasses. They were married, Ash realized. A team.

Karina held Ash's eyes steadily with her own. They glittered with intelligence. Ash thought of the alleged video from the night before. Perhaps it did exist. Perhaps it had been posted. Perhaps this young woman had *seen it.*

Ash itched to pull out his phone, to message Sherene: *Help me, I'm being book clubbed!* Instead he went for his wine. Swallowing took effort.

'I mean,' she said, 'I want to understand your intentions before accusing you of anything. I believe that's only fair.'

Ash tilted his head: of course, proceed.

'I guess what I'm wondering is what you wanted the book to be about.'

'About,' said Ash.

Karina smiled. And waited. They were all waiting.

'Well, it's about a guy who—a harmless guy—'

'How so, "harmless"?'

'Oh, you know.' Ash laughed, drank more wine. He was sweating. 'I just mean not an exceptional person. Just, you know. Harmless?'

'I've read interviews where you say the character is based on you.'

'Oh?' Ash felt like a trapped rabbit, snared and struggling and only further entangling itself.

'So then, what about the love interest?' Karina opened her book. 'Here is she is—page thirty-two: "She dressed in revealing clothing, which her various fleshes swolled"—a new word to me—"and escaped." It goes on: "Her brazen sexuality was as much a liberation from social strictures as it was from her own homeliness. The gelatinous cleavage, the dimpled buttocks, the great crests of flesh that heaped themselves over her waistband, these were grotesqueries, more a travesty of male desire than a rejection of it. And still he loved her."' Karina looked up. '"Still." Is that meant to be somehow . . . generous?'

From the end of the table, the old lady's cackle sounded like a goose being throttled.

Karina continued: 'This is based on someone you loved? Or someone you once loved, maybe, who left you, so you're getting some sort of—sorry—revenge?'

'No! That's not the intention at all.'

'Hey, come on,' Karina's voice was soft, assured. She reached across the table toward him. 'I'm not accusing you. I'm just trying to understand.'

'Sounds like my-sogyny to me,' said Barbara. The diptychian snorted.

Ash looked to the exit, imagined Matt crashing through the plate-glass window with his pickup, hauling Ash to freedom, saving the day.

Karina flipped to a new page: "'He'd never understood her, never gotten a sense of how to negotiate her various moods and cycles and faintly amphibious smells.'"

'Can I see your book?' Ash croaked at Barbara.

'No,' she said, clutching it to her chest. 'I'm using it.'

All goodwill around the table had vanished. Karina read another excerpt; everyone listened with fealty and reverence. And hearing his own words—careless words, despicable words—Ash began to share SLAW's disgust. The book had long embarrassed him as a document of youth, like a school photo that captured some especially flagrant hairstyle. It was something, too, that he and Sherene never discussed; he'd always got the sense she didn't think much of it. But now he felt confronted with something essential and harder to disavow: he was a vindictive creep, a sogynist of everyone's, and his book was the proof. And there might be recent video evidence, too.

Worst of all was Katrina's benevolence. She parroted his insipid words with a compassionate smile. She seemed to believe she was doing Ash a favour, revealing this truth about himself to which he'd been oblivious. And as her oration concluded and the old lady actually nudged Ash's book away, he felt looked upon not with revulsion, or even disappointment, but mercy.

'So, again,' said Karina, 'I don't want to point any fingers. I just thought this might be a chance for you to clear the air.'

Everyone stared at him. An explanation or apology was due.

The French toast arrived, saving him momentarily. 'Wow, looks great,' Ash squawked, and filled his mouth.

'I think,' said the librarian, 'that we might need to separate the *character* in the novel from the author.'

Ash glanced up, chewing. Not an escape route he'd considered.

'Of course you take his side,' said the diptychian. 'You men always stick together.'

Shit. The guy's breadcrumb trail to salvation only indicted Ash further!

'And it's based on *himself*,' said Jerry. 'He told us so.'

'Exactly,' said Barbara. She had forced this loathsome sexist upon the group and, honour on the line, was trying to distance herself from him entirely.

Ash lifted a hand to wipe his forehead—the hand that held a fork of sopping toast; syrup dripped down his shirtfront. He searched for his napkin. Discovered it at his feet like a dead and trampled dove.

All eyes were upon him. Ash fondled his phone in his pocket.

'Maybe that's enough now,' whispered Barbara. 'The boy's father did just die.'

Everyone eased back from the table as if his grief might be contagious. Croissants were buttered, coffee was sipped. And 'the boy,' mercied upon his dad's grave, poked his French toast, which had congealed to a doughy lump on his plate.

When he looked up, Barbara was smiling at him with strained charity. 'I so enjoy our club's ability to have these frank discussions,' she said.

Ash pictured her dress hiked to her waist, Matt with his pants around his ankles. At his father's funeral. And now she had the gall to take the moral high ground. His humiliation developed edges, needling outward—but Barbara was moving in again.

'There's just one more thing I have to ask.' She placed a cold, thin hand atop his. 'Tell me, Ash: what are you working on now?'

IT HAD BEEN YEARS since Ash had visited the Montreal studios. So much orange, so much brown, so much tinted, bevelled glass. The design seemed based on a 1970s notion of what a spaceship might one day appreciate looking like, provided the future were locked in some perennial, analogue autumn of carpeted walls and LSD.

'Kind of a porno set vibe in here,' said Matt, and played some slinky slap-bass on his leg while he and Ash waited to be buzzed through security.

Ash was cleared and stickered, but, they were informed, since no guest had been pre-authorized, his friend would not be admitted inside. Matt eyed Ash from other side of the turnstiles with the look of a refugee.

Sherene was summoned. She came gliding across the lobby, dressed to the nines as always and moving with an ease and confidence that suggested an enviable serenity in the world. She hugged Ash and stood back, smiling, seemingly glad to see him. And for a moment he felt redeemed.

But then it all collapsed: 'You look terrible.'

'I told you last night to come rescue me!'

She held his eyes. 'You sure you want to do this? If it's too much right now—'

'It's fine,' said Ash. 'Though there is one problem. Can you get my buddy in?'

'You brought someone?' said Sherene. Matt, leaning on the security desk, lifted a peace sign in salutation. She turned Ash away by the elbow, spoke in a hushed voice. 'Sweetie, this isn't my building. They've already given me a hard enough time about booking studio time.'

So it fell to Ash to tell his friend he wasn't welcome. 'I'll be an hour,' he said. 'And then we can go do whatever you want.'

But something had been triggered; Matt's eyes were skittering back and forth. 'This is BS. I'm your best friend.'

Before Ash knew what was happening, Matt had launched himself halfway over the desk to grab a handful of the security guard's uniform. 'Who do you think you are?' he roared, rattling the guy by the lapels. 'My taxes pay your salary! But when I try to come in here to audition or hang out with my friend, I'm suddenly human garbage?'

'Stop it before you get Tasered or something,' Ash begged, shooting an apologetic look at Sherene. But she was on the phone for, he assumed, backup.

Grudgingly Matt relented, lowering the guy and shaking his head. He turned on Ash, a fat sausage of a finger wagging at him from the far side of the turnstiles. 'I drove across the country for you, Dhar, and what do you do? Act like I'm your chauffeur.'

'Hey, come on—'

But Matt waved him off, turned his back, and stormed out of the building, leaving Ash in a swirl of guilt, disgrace and relief. Also bewilderment: what had just happened?

He turned to Sherene, who looked as stunned as he felt.

'So,' she said, 'that's a friend of yours?'

'From childhood. Not someone I see much anymore.'

'Whoever he is, he's certainly got a thing for you.' Sherene checked her watch. 'Anyway, sweetie, let's get a move on. We've got a Behemoth to interview.'

Ash was led down a memorabilia-lined hallway to their borrowed studio. By the console was Sherene's copy of *Into the Night*, the spine bowed and cracked, a rainbow of Post-its sprouting from the pages.

'I'll need to borrow this,' he said. 'Left my copy in the car.'

'Did you at least get the script I emailed you?'

'Shoot,' said Ash. 'Sorry, I forgot that too.'

She pulled one free from a clipboard. Ash glanced over her questions. Looked up. 'Thanks for doing this. Just, with this whole week—'

She waved it away. 'Good thing, is all, that you had so long with the book.'

'Yeah, about that . . .'

'Ash!'

'I read some of it!'

'How much?'

'The first . . . part.'

'Did you get to the flood at least?'

'Flood?'

Frowning, Sherene filled him in quickly. 'Which,' she concluded, 'happens at the end of the first part.'

'Sorry, just, the thing is? I found something Brij was writing.' It was a cheap shot but Ash felt cornered. 'And I read it instead. It felt . . . like he was back with me, for a bit.'

'Your dad wrote a book? What about?'

Ash gave her the gist.

'Wow, my old man gets up the wherewithal to write me a birthday card and I fly over the moon.' Sherene shook this thought away and looked at him with a new kind of focus. She sighed, took his hands in hers. 'Oh, Ash. I'm sorry for not being much support lately. With your dad and everything. Work's no excuse. I've been a bad friend.'

'It's okay.' Ash allowed himself to be petted. 'Anyway—The Behemoth, right?'

'Okay, but let's talk about this later. Lunch when we're back in Toronto, maybe?' She released his hands and glanced again at her watch. 'We have to get a move on, but please don't worry too much about the book. I've listened to a dozen interviews with this guy and *holy* does he like to talk. Just stick to the script and sweetie? You'll be fine.'

Ash spent a few minutes pairing Sherene's prompts with page numbers, dog-earing as he went. But his thoughts kept caroming back to Matt's breakdown, to the book club disaster, to the possible ignominies of the night before: all connected. Ash rolled over to the studio's computer and searched for the alleged video—*Hotdog steam, Un con soul et son pen*, etc. Nothing. *Ash Dhar*, of course, returned no recent hits at all. He hoped it stayed that way. Not being famous was infinitely better than sudden, disgraceful infamy.

A voice materialized in his headphones: 'Okay, Ash. He's on the phone. As soon as you're done checking your email I'll put him through.'

So harsh, so business. Where was the love? Matt, Sherene— on their lives went; Ash's sorrows were his alone. And now like a penned bull The Behemoth lurked on the end of the line, a man's man who trampled the frail and left a trail of ruined bodies in his dust. Best to play the matador, sword bared for the death blow.

Ash rolled up to the microphone. 'Let's do this.'

'Here he is.'

Ash opened with an ad lib: 'I'm quite enjoying your book.' (The gerund indicating that he hadn't bothered to finish it; 'quite' to suggest *not really*.)

These nuances were ignored: 'Appreciated.'

In the booth Sherene held up the script. Ash gave her the thumbs-up and returned to it: 'Can you tell me about the main character?'

'Hardwick? He just came to me: "You need to tell my story."'

'So he isn't based on you?'

'Well, we have certain commonalities, sure. He's a guy, I'm a guy. About my age. Military background. Talks like me. Maybe even kind of looks like me. But writers should never treat their characters as proxies for some personal agenda. A writer's job is to honour the reader, and to do that one must write in service of the reader.'

On it went. Ash asked a question, The Behemoth monologued, and on they moved to the next talking point. Although Ash wasn't really listening, he sensed impatience in The Behemoth's replies: same old, same old. So he thought to shake things up bit.

'Your character kills his wife and child. In a fire.'

'He does.'

'What's that about?'

'Well, he loses it. This is a guy, keep in mind, who's experienced trauma. Real trauma. Not just I-didn't-get-the-promotion-I-want trauma. And there are no mechanisms for him to deal with that trauma. So he implodes. And his implosion is so severe that he takes down with him the only people who might have kept him afloat.'

'A woman. And a child.'

'Yes.'

'Isn't that a bit manipulative? Cruel, even?'

'What fiction isn't manipulative? The whole enterprise of the novel is simply one scheme of manipulation upon another. But I don't think it's cruel. I don't approach my characters or readers with cruelty.'

'It's not cruel to burn people alive?'

'Of course it's cruel to burn people alive.' The words were sharp, fairly spat down the line. 'In what scenario would that not be an act of cruelty? To fictionalize that sort of trauma, though, is something else. To use it—'

'To *use* the death of a woman and child?' Sherene was glaring at Ash through the glass. But they were jousting now. Ash puffed himself up and went for the kill: 'Some might suggest that sounds . . . misogynistic.'

'Sorry, what does?'

'Exploiting women for the sake of a story.'

Sherene was sawing a hand across her throat.

'Exploiting,' echoed The Behemoth, in a voice like low thunder.

Ash went on to critique the dead wife's characterization: a type, a victim, a sacrifice for the sake of the male hero's personal journey. He was on a roll. The Behemoth remained silent. Humbled, probably. 'You talk about how the writer should disavow control, but the truth is you're totally in control. And you have a responsibility—'

'Oh, boy,' sighed The Behemoth.

'A *responsibility*,' continued Ash, 'to whomever you're representing. Don't you think.'

'No.'

The air went dead around that *no*. Sherene buried her face in her hands.

'Yet here you are,' continued Ash, 'doing the *man's man* writer thing. The Hemingway pose. Fisticuffs and whiskey and killing off women and whatever else. I mean, wasn't this whole thing a little played out fifty years ago?'

Silence.

Ash flailed forward with his attack: 'And this whole ridiculous performance of masculinity, of men who fail in relation to this dumb imagined ideal of manhood. It's absurd. A man kills his woman so he's got to drink hard and fight hard and fuck hard and chop wood and build a cabin and kill a bear and gut a bear and wear the bearskin as a cloak so he can walk among the bears and kill them all, one by one—'

'Okay!' Sherene's voice severed Ash's rant like a blade. 'We're done here.'

A click. The line went dead. The On-Air light extinguished. Ash panted, breathless.

'What the hell,' said Sherene, 'was that?'

'He wrote a bullshit book!'

'Did you not read my notes? Or anything about this guy? He lost his wife and child, Ash. In a car crash. He was driving.'

'What.'

Ash stared at The Behemoth's author photo: that look in the eyes he'd mistaken for machismo struck him now as melancholy. Ash felt suffocated. And then the feeling flared into rage. He swung his legs up from under the desk and kicked the computer screen. There was a cracking sound; it buckled, the display went scrambled and wild.

Ash met Sherene's eyes through the glass. 'What?'

She stared back with a look of not shock or anger, but dismay.

A bodily, almost cellular fatigue rose up from within him then. Something profound from some place beyond sleeplessness. The computer screen, sagging, buzzed and flickered. Ash removed the cans from his ears. Closed his eyes. Bowed his head.

What had he done?

THE COBBLESTONE STREETS and stone buildings of the Old Port looked like a film set. As Matt drove them past the cathedral, what was supposed to be the most authentic part of the city struck Ash as contrived. Here the past seemed artificially pre-served, and time prevented its natural rot and decay.

Even so, he stared out the window. Immediately upon getting in the truck, Ash had noticed that the knuckles on Matt's right hand, gripping the steering wheel, were split and bloody. Whether from a wall or door or someone's face, he couldn't say. And still hadn't asked. Neither of them had yet to speak.

A ramp sloped down into the tunnel. Driving into it, with the neon lights rising up and strobing past, seemed less like locomo-tion than time travel—back to the future, thought Ash. Or at least to the here and now, such as it was.

And then they were bursting out the other end into the light again.

'Straight to the hotel?' said Matt. (*Sir*, he seemed to imply.)

Ash told him yes.

The rest of the ride continued in tense silence, heightened by

Matt's atypically careful driving: full stops and shoulder-checks and the speed limit met like a pact. By the time they reached the airport hotel, jumbo jets screaming by above, Ash realized what was going on. There was no conversation to be had. Matt had been wronged and had likely enacted some disproportionate wrong of his own. And now he was leaving.

Forgoing the parking lot, he drove up to the lobby doors.

'Not coming in?'

'Nah.' Matt stared through the windshield. 'I should get back.'

'What about your finger?'

'Not to BC. Home. To London. Be good to see some people.'

'The people you moved out west to escape, you mean.'

'They're still my friends, Ash.' Matt reached for his one-hitter from the cup-holder—and resisted. 'Feel free to take a toot for the road if you want,' he said, gesturing.

'I'm good.'

'Cool.'

The engine was running, the truck still in drive.

'Is this it, then?' said Ash. 'When do I see you next?'

'I'll be around. Always am.'

'Making memories?'

'Something like that.'

No joke followed. Ash looked out the window: in the hotel's lobby, someone wheeled past waxing the floors. He turned back and attempted a final salvo: 'Listen, if you're going to stick around Ontario for a while, you should come by the Toronto studios. Get you a tour, whatever you want. Sit in the big desk, even?'

Matt flexed his fingers on the steering wheel. The blood was scabbing darkly over his knuckles. 'Sounds awesome, bro.'

'Really sorry about earlier—'

'Honestly?' Matt's voice was a growl. 'Just shut up, for once. Okay?'

Ash went still. Every so often, the guy could still scare him.

But then Matt's demeanour changed completely: his shoulders slackened, he put the truck in park, killed the engine. And turned to face his friend. 'What I mean is, be quiet for a sec. There's something I remembered I wanted to tell you, before I go.'

Ash nodded, wary of the impending revelation. Something horrific, surely, with a preamble such as this.

'So, here it is. The last appointment I had with your dad in London, he told me this story about you when you were a kid. But he got angry telling it, like it was happening all over again.'

A little blast of air escaped Ash's nostrils, a reluctant laugh. Brij could never just tell a story. He had to relive it.

'Do you remember this? You guys went to India together. You were ten, I think. When you left Canada your dad had a big beard—it's funny, I remember afterward not recognizing him when you guys came home.'

'That trip was right around the time he and my mom split.'

'And I last heard from *my* dad. Grade five.'

'So, yeah, I would have been ten.'

Matt nodded. 'I guess it was real hot in India, too hot to have a beard. So after a few days he was just like, "Gotta shave this thing off." And I can totally picture your pops in a rage, all sweaty and swearing and hacking it off with like a steak knife or something.'

This is exactly how Ash imagined it too: the itch, the complaints, the blistering irritation that would have burst in drastic, panicked action. Yet the other person in the story, that ten-year-old version of himself—he couldn't see that person at all.

'You guys have been there like a week, visiting family, and he's shaved off his beard, and now you have to fly from one place to . . . Kashmir, maybe?'

'Doubt it. This would have been right around when things were getting really dicey. And I haven't been to Kashmir since I was tiny.'

'Well, wherever you were going, you didn't get there.' Matt

grinned. 'Because, get this. You're in line with your dad at the airport, you get to the counter and the security dude asks to see your passports. Except in your dad's picture he's got this massive beard. Buddy looks at the picture, at your dad, and goes, "Kashmiri?" And Brij goes, "Canadian." And the guy goes, "No, Dhar. *Kashmiri.*" Remember what happened next?'

Ash did not. But this story was loosening something. Not a memory. He couldn't shake the image of Brij and Matt, together, rehashing a past that had escaped him.

'This is the point where you—you little poop-disturber—pipe up and scream, "He's not my dad, he's a terrorist.'"

'No!'

'Honestly. As you can imagine the security people all go on high alert and snatch up your pops and take him off for interrogation. Full strip-and-cavity search, latex gloves and probes up the pooper and everything.'

'He told you this?'

Matt laughed. 'Nah, but you of all people should appreciate a little artistic licence.'

'What about the rest of this story? Are you sure it's true?'

'Just telling you what your dad told me, bro. Anyhow, so he has to show all these documents proving who he is, and they call the consulate and it's hours later before he sees you again, so you miss your flight, and he is royally pissed at you, but of course he has to act like he's your loving dad because the security people are still watching.'

'That's funny in itself.'

'Once you leave the airport he asks you why you would have done something so stupid. Like, were you mad at him, were you trying to get back at him? He was really honest with me in this part.'

'Just sitting there in his office?'

'Uh-huh. He talked about how he and your mom were divorcing, and he'd taken you to India to connect with that side of your family, and him too, I guess, in a way. So you selling him out felt like a real kick in the nards.'

'Where was all this when I was writing his fucking eulogy?'

'Honestly? Seemed like he was only telling me this so I'd tell you.'

'Then why didn't you!'

'I am, bro. I'm telling you now.'

Ash looked out the window: the hotel lobby was empty. Back at Matt. Whose eyebrows vaulted nearly clear off his forehead.

'Dhar, listen.' It sounded like a plea. 'What you told him? When he asked why you'd said that? You weren't mad. It wasn't revenge or you punishing him or anything. Get this: all you said was, "I wanted to make something happen."'

'I said that?'

'One hundred percent. Right away I was like, "Yeah, I feel you, Doc, he was a maniac when we were kids too! Always stirring up stuff, causing trouble." You and me, Dhar. Making memories.' Matt's expression shifted from wistful to sombre. He leaned into the space between their seats, his bald head looming like a rising moon. 'What I'm wondering, though, bro? Is what made you stop?'

# 5

WHENEVER HE'D GONE AWAY AS A KID, upon returning home Ash was always surprised by a strange and foreign smell in the house. Since this was usually after a few weeks' vacation (visiting cousins out east, off in India with his dad) in which the family home had sat empty, he'd assumed it was the olfactory result of closed windows and undisturbed space, a gradual putrefaction that set in as the air turned stagnant and stale. And as his family stirred the place back to life, the odour faded. But it was something he noticed in other people's houses too. Each one had its own smell.

'Why does your apartment smell like ketchup?' he'd asked Matt in grade six. Which it did: that sugary red aroma clogged every room.

'Take it back,' said Matt, and put Ash in a chokehold until he admitted otherwise.

It wasn't until adulthood that Ash recognized that he was simply smelling the particular scent of families. Out in the world everyone's smells were loose, melding into the generic odours of civilization, of community. But your house trapped you with yourself: your pores and breath and farts released, and the walls soaked it up. Like a sudden long hard look in the mirror, returning home offered self-revelation—until you acclimated again, and your smell simply became the air you lived in and made.

So why wasn't this the case, now, with his condo? Ash stood sniffing in the doorway, but nothing came back: not cookery nor body odour nor laundry nor garbage nor even some fecal reek lingering in the pipes. The air wasn't even sterile. Instead this was pure absence. The place smelled of nothing. Ash had worried since moving in that the building, a converted factory, was a nothing sort of place, its past reduced to aesthetic flourishes: exposed brick and plumbing and lofty ceilings from which dangled chrome light fixtures with affectations of industry.

Carved from the long open main room were a kitchenette and, up four steps, a curtained-off bedroom; clustered by the bank of windows at the far end was some staid Nordic furniture. And books, of course, were everywhere: filling the shelves, piled on the coffee table, stacked by his bedside. But that was it. Ash's previous apartments (often shared, always rented) had been adorned wall-to-wall with cheaply framed posters and photos tacked right to the wallpaper, every spare space cluttered with thrift store oddities. All of that stuff was in storage; it didn't befit the sleek angles and marble countertops of fancy downtown digs. This was adult living and it demanded commensurate decoration, not the dorm-room kitsch with which he'd long adorned his life.

He got a beer from the fridge, sat down on the couch, peeled off his socks and checked his phone: a dozen unanswered messages from Sherene.

Ash called his mom.

Right away she launched into Christmas—was he coming? Mona and Harj were coming. Ash should come! It had been years! Rick was asking specially!

He needed something else from her now. So he derailed her requests with the news.

'What do you mean,' she said, 'a *leave*?'

'A month. Maybe two.'

'They didn't specify?'

'Bereavement, they said.'

'That's a long time for bereavement, Ashy.'

The pet-name made him a little sad—for her, for himself. He switched the phone to his other ear.

'Did something else happen?'

'I likely won't take the full two months,' he said. 'But some time off might be good.'

'It will. You work so hard. Too hard, I've always said. Haven't I told you that?'

'Yeah.'

'So. What will you do?'

'Not go to India.'

'Were you thinking of going?'

'Matt has some crazy idea that we'll travel there together to scatter Brij's ashes or something similarly inane. A pilgrimage, finding ourselves. All that lost boy bullshit. Keep in mind the guy is nearly forty. Did Mona tell you that he just showed up in Quebec and stayed the whole weekend? Drove all the way from BC.'

'He drove all that way? Just to see you? What a good friend. You're so lucky to have someone like him in your life.'

Ash considered this.

'If you and Matt go to India together you should do a radio project about it. Wouldn't that be fun?'

'No, no it would not. Matt's out of his mind. He can go solo, if he wants, though I don't know what he thinks he's going to find over there. He'll probably end up in jail for defiling an idol or something.'

'So if you stay in Toronto what will you do?'

'I don't know.'

'Write?'

'Maybe.'

'Doctor Litke is always asking me, "When's your Ash going to publish another novel?"'

'So I should write a book to satisfy your colleagues.'

'You could work here, in London. There's still a desk in your old room. No one will bother you. Just remember to thank me in the acknowledgements!'

'I just got back. I haven't really thought about it.' Ash thought about it. 'Maybe.'

'Think how much quieter it will be here at home than in Toronto—to write, I mean!'

'Mother, Toronto *is* my home. I haven't lived in London for nearly twenty years.'

A pause. Then: 'You're not mad at me, are you? For missing the funeral?'

'Of course not. Don't be silly.'

'I just—Ashy, please don't think it was an easy decision not to come. In the end though I really didn't feel comfortable intruding like that. The old ex-wife from another lifetime, lurking in the back? No thanks. And obviously Rick couldn't go. So, what, drive all the way alone to Montreal? You know how my back's been lately.'

'No, it's fine.'

'Was your sister disappointed?'

'Mona?' Ash had no idea how she felt—about their mother's absence, about anything. 'You'll have to ask her,' he said. And added hurriedly, 'But I really don't think so.'

'So when will we see you? Christmas Eve? Before? How long will you stay?'

'Listen, this whole business, this leave of absence or whatever they're calling it, wasn't my choice. They seem to think I'm losing my marbles, but what do they expect when they foist these awful people on me?'

'You had a bad conversation with a writer?'

Ash pictured his mother holding the phone with two hands, listening greedily. 'Yes.'

'Was she rude to you?'

'He.'

'He. You were rude to him?'

'Yes.'

'Oh, Ashy. Why?'

'Because . . . I don't know. No good reason, I guess.'

'Who was it? Anyone I know?'

Ash told her.

'Oh, my, he's so famous! Ashy, that's very impressive.' He waited while she listed The Behemoth's various awards and accolades. 'But, sorry, dear. It didn't go well?'

Ash's phone flashed: another message from Sherene. 'Whatever,' he said.

'How are you doing, my love? This business with your father, it was so sudden, wasn't it? Did you have any time with him . . . before?'

'Not really.' Ash's voice was very quiet.

'There are things you didn't get to say.'

'Yes.'

'Oh.' He could sense his mother panicking a bit: she'd led him down this path, but she was no better at navigating emotion than he was. 'Like what?'

Ash choked back a sob. 'I don't know.'

'Is there anything I can tell you? Obviously I haven't spent much time with him in years, but I was married to the man for a decade. I'm not sure what you'd want to know . . .'

She trailed off. He cried quietly into the silence.

'We had our issues,' she continued, finally, her voice gentle. 'Long before we split. Especially when he drank. Not that he was violent, nothing like that. He would just drink and get distant. Maybe with the purpose of getting distant. But before he got there, after a few glasses of wine—no, what am I saying! Never wine back then. Beer. And scotch. Like a real Indian! At any rate, before he'd get past his limit, he'd tell such wonderful stories about Kashmir. You know how much he missed it there, don't you?'

'Yes,' said Ash. Half word, half gasp for air.

'And when we went! Just once, before you were born. I was terrified in India, Ashy—you know this. Delhi was just too much. But Srinagar was different. Maybe because your dad became so much more natural there. He certainly didn't seem even remotely comfortable anywhere else in India. And then in Kashmir he was like a kid, showing me the sights, introducing me to everyone we met with this gleam in his eyes. He seemed so happy and proud—of the place, but of me, too. So pleased to share us with each other. This was before '73, keep in mind. Things hadn't blown up yet.'

Ash wiped his eyes, blew his nose, waited for more.

'When we came back, your dad was so nostalgic, always telling stories about home. His voice would go soft, he'd get this faraway happy look in his eyes. But over the years that faded. The memories got too distant, like he was chasing after them. Meanwhile things turned so bad he couldn't even visit anymore. He'd start to tell a story but abandon it and go all grumpy and sullen. And that's when he started drinking seriously.' She paused. 'Sorry, Ash. Is this too much information?'

'No. I want to know.'

'I've just never really talked like this to you. About Brijnath.'

'That's okay. Tell me.' *Please*, he thought. Please fill this space.

'What else, then?' He pictured his mother tugging at her

earlobe, something she did when trying to loosen an idea or memory. 'Well, part of it was that Brij never loved Canada. You know
this. What he needed, I think, was someone to make a home with
here. And based on how he grew up, he had expectations of how
a wife would fit into that.'

'That's sad.'

'Because I didn't?'

This was not what Ash wanted, to guilt-trip his mother. A new
tack, then: 'Did you miss him? After you split up.'

'Of course I did! Still do. I mean, Rick's a wonderful person
and a far better partner—*for me*, I mean—in so many ways, but
your dad was such a voracious reader. In thirty-eight years of teaching English I've had few colleagues who I can talk about books
with so deeply, so passionately. You know how we met, don't you?'

'You were reading Shakespeare.'

'Studying for my comps! And he came breezing up, this funny
little brown guy in a corduroy suit, took one look at my book and
launched right into it: "If all the year were playing holidays; to
sport would be as tedious as to work."'

Ash laughed. 'God, what a nerd.'

'What about you, Ashy?'

'What about me?'

'Do you miss him. Your dad.'

Ash stared at his feet. Like Brij, each of his toes was garnished with a little shrub of whiskers. 'I miss what we missed
doing together. Though I don't think it's sunk in yet.'

'That he's gone, you mean.'

'Yeah,' said Ash. 'That he's gone.'


ASH'S BUILDING SHARED FACILITIES with a neighbouring hotel,
and he liked to head over for a swim just before the pool closed
for the night. There was rarely anyone using it so late, and he
swam lengths until his anxieties stilled and all that remained was

the simple repetition of stroking from one end to the other. This was the first step of a ritual (herbal tea, *The Book of Disquiet*, cataloguing the day's ignominies) to coax himself to sleep.

The pool had that sterile quality particular to everything in hotels. Its surface was as flat and taut as cling-wrap; the smell was ammonal. A spectral reflection shimmered up the walls. Mercifully, tonight Ash was alone. He left his towel, flip-flops, T-shirt and keys in a little pile and padded up to the edge. Dipped a toe: bathwater warm.

He eased in and drifted down, limbs hanging. Touched bottom. Bounced off like an astronaut on the moon. Hovered, floated. Had no thoughts. Let the moment extend. Gradually his lungs tightened. The tension spread through his chest to his neck, into his throat, up through his cheeks, until the follicles of his hair seemed to constrict and at last in a breathless surge he planted his feet and launched upward, bursting out of the water, swallowed air, then dove again and flogged his way toward the deep end.

He was a lousy, weird swimmer.

Brij, too, could never be described as naturally aquatic, plunging about with a unique hybrid of front crawl, breaststroke and doggie paddle, and surfacing intermittently with a blowholish sputter. Mona did an excellent imitation of their dad's swimming, rendered as frantic digging in the waves for something lost. Now Ash performed the routine without irony. It felt natural. This was just how he swam.

After a couple laps he stopped and, panting and clinging to the side, detected a sudden presence at the far end of the pool. A boy, maybe ten years old, stood there with a pink lip of belly crumpling his bellybutton and folding down over his trunks.

'Hi,' said this boy.

'Hi,' said Ash. 'Where are your parents?'

'They sent me down for a swim. To tire me out.' He seemed embarrassed. 'I get hyper sometimes at night before bed.'

'Me too,' said Ash. 'Come on in. The water's warm.'

If this sounded as creepy as Ash feared it did, the boy didn't seem to care. He rocked back and lunged into a mid-air tuck, crashing lopsided into the water. Waves sloshed the deck. He surfaced looking proud. 'That's my cannonball.'

'Nice.'

'You do one.'

'A cannonball?'

'Yeah.'

'Okay,' said Ash with a grin.

The scamper, the launch, the scrunch, the plunge. The fleeting abandon, the joy.

'Whoa,' said the boy, standing now in the shallow end. 'Amazing!'

Ash bobbed amid his own wake. 'Years of practice. You'll get there.'

The boy turned solemn. 'I live in New Zealand.'

'Lots of chances to cannonball there, I bet.'

'I guess. Except everyone at my school calls me Tubby Canuck.'

'That's mean. Is everyone mean in New Zealand?'

'I'm from here, though. Etobicoke Ontario. We moved for my dad's work. He teaches university. The one here was U of T Mississauga but the new one's called . . . I forget. We live in Christchurch. Like Jesus Christ, like church. There's a lot of churches there, holy.'

'What about your mom?' Worrying this might also seem creepy, Ash added, 'Mine's a professor too, like your dad.'

'She's a teacher, except of kids. Except she can't teach in New Zealand because of her experience.' The boy shook his head; he'd got it wrong. 'Because of her *lack* of experience. Even though she taught in Canada, they won't let her teach in New Zealand because she's never taught in New Zealand. But how can you get experience if they won't give you any? They say she has to go back to school. But she just stays home all day and reads.'

'That doesn't sound so bad.'

'She likes it better here. I do too.'

'Do your parents let you swim on your own all the time?'

The boy shrugged. 'I do lots on my own in Christchurch. I'm independent. I ride the bus, go to the movies. It's not a big deal.'

'What if there's no lifeguard?'

'They said to stay in the shallow end.'

'Gotcha.'

'Also . . . *they're fighting.*'

'Ah.'

Flopping onto his face, the boy floated as if searching for something on the bottom of the pool. Ash waited for him to right himself. And when he did, asked, 'So when are you flying home?'

'Tomorrow, but via LA so I can check out Hollywood.'

'Is that so.'

'The Hollywood sign, the Walk of Fame, the Chinese Theatre, Burbank Studios. All of it. I'm going to be a director and move there when I'm older. I've already got my own DV camera and everything. I've got Final Draft, I've got Final Cut Pro—'

'But why Hollywood? You can make movies anywhere.'

The boy laughed. 'Because that's where you have to go if you want to make it. Jeez, you don't know very much for an adult, do you?'

'I know they make more movies in India than in Hollywood.' Ash wasn't sure if this was true.

'What kind of movies?'

'Bollywood movies. Fun movies.' Ash ducked his chin, took in a mouthful of water, and spat it out in a fountain. 'Lots of singing and dancing.'

'Ew. I hate musicals.'

'These are different kinds of musicals. They're kind of crazy. Do you like moustaches? There are a lot of moustaches.'

'We lived in India too.'

'Really? You did?'

'Yeah, when I was five. I don't remember it though. My dad was on sabbatical. We had a servant who had *six* fingers. Four fingers and two thumbs.'

'That's a lot of thumbs.'

'On one hand!' The boy looked pensive. 'Though maybe I just saw that in a movie.'

'That happens to me sometimes.' Ash whip-kicked to the side of the pool and clung to the edge. 'Where in India did you live?'

'I don't know, I told you. I was five. It was dirty.'

'Sure. It's dirty.' Ash sensed the conversation dwindling. 'I'm Indian,' he announced.

This had the required effect. The boy eyed him with renewed interest. 'No, you're not. You don't look Indian. Or sound Indian.'

'Well, I am.'

'Nope. You're Canadian.'

'I'm that, too.'

'You can't be both. I live in New Zealand but I'm *only* Canadian.' Here he seemed to ready himself for something grand—and yet Ash was not prepared for what came belting out: '*Oh, Canada . . . Our home and native land . . .*'

'Don't you think they should change it to *our home* on *native land*?'

'*True patriot love*,' the boy sang, his hand on his chest, standing stalwart in the pool with the water sloshing around his gut, '*in all thy son's command.*'

What the hell, Ash thought, hauling himself up onto the deck. '*With glowing hearts*,' he sang, disbelieving himself even as the words spilled from his mouth—where were they coming from? He'd not sung the national anthem in years. Even when the boy switched to French he remained right alongside, clueless as to what the words meant: '*Car ton bras . . . sait porter l'épée . . . il sait porter la croix!*'

And they sang, and they sang, Ash with one eye on the exit should the kid's parents appear—should *anyone* appear—and find him here, belting out this ridiculous, nonsensical song, with everything he had, with all the fake, patriot love in his heart.

## DEVELOPMENT

*The first voice, which announced the subject, should never be silent while the second voice is giving the answer. It always accompanies with a counterpoint, which may or may not be intended for subsequent use.*

*1*

MATT WINKED AT THE STEWARDESS in the plane's doorway. She
performed a sultry bow, hands clasped at her chin as if to swan
dive into his heart, or groin. Tantric! Handing over his boarding
pass, his dangling pinkie brushing hers, he cursed himself for not
packing condoms in his carry-on. Though they could just go down
on each other in the bathroom, if things came to it.

But first: a first impression. (Rule #1: *Make yourself memo-
rable.*) As she confirmed his seat number, Matt went with a compliment: 'Cool nose-ring.' Then, noting her name tag (Rule #2:
*Always get their name*), he added: 'Meena.'

A smile, another bow, and Matt was directed to the rear of
the plane.

Groundwork, complete.

But squeezing down the aisle Matt realized that Meena
worked First Class. He and the rest of the low-lifes in coach were

stuck with a stewardess who was in fact a man. Snippily this guy (architect glasses, suspiciously hairless arms, *Raj*) told Matt he couldn't recline his seat until they were in the air.

'Look at the size of me!' Matt wailed. 'How can I relax if I'm folded up like a frigging paperclip?'

Raj sighed, pressed a button on the armrest, thrust Matt upright, and proceeded to his little demo with life vests and seat-belts, staring dimly over everyone's heads, and then the turbo kicked in and they were screaming down the runway and lifting skyward and the plane shuddered and howled while Matt, eyes closed, recalled those two bearded guys he'd watched so blithely clear airport security, baggage unchecked. Now he waited for the inevitable explosion, the plane seared in two and its flaming halves pinwheeling to earth. He was too young to die! Or if thirty-five wasn't too young, at least he'd not yet fully lived. He'd never had sex on an airplane, for instance. And here he was about to lose the chance because of a couple nut-jobs doing jihad . . .

Terror aside so much could go wrong. How did air travel even work? A car he understood: spark plugs fired and gas exploded (in a good way) and something—possibly the carburetor?—turned and so did the wheels and on you went to whatever kegger or beach. But planes? How did that same process, plus a pair of unflappable wings, get a hundred tons of steel to lift like a wish into the goshdang sky? What was 'fuselage'? Did it mean something was on fire? *Fuselage off the starboard ho!* he imagined Raj screaming while smoke billowed from a goose-plugged engine.

The intercom dinged and in a smug voice the pilot announced, 'We've reached our cruising altitude'—*our*, thought Matt, as if he and the other passengers were in on it!—'of thirty-two thousand feet.' Why so high? Why not glide twenty yards above the ocean the whole way to Europe? That way if things went wrong the plane could just settle on the water like a spoon laid upon a table, and everyone would ride those inflatable slides down to lifeboats, aboard which there'd be a huge, grateful orgy captained by Matt in all his glory.

Matt turned to the woman beside him, a spindly brown grandma with a forehead dot so vast it looked blown there with a cannon; beyond her at the window sat some nerd reading a book. 'Namaste,' he said, bowing.

'Namaste,' she giggled. 'You speak Hindi?'

'Nah. Not really. I did some yoga for a bit, but I threw out my back.' Matt slid his hand to his lumbar, winced.

'You hurt yourself doing yoga?'

'That's not why I quit though. Actually the teacher asked me to leave the class—'

'You were thrown out of *yoga?*'

'I guess that's weird?'

She giggled again. 'First time to India?'

'First time anywhere.'

'Oh!' She patted his arm.

Matt couldn't read this gesture. Approval? Consolation? Pity?

'In India, many people. Many, many people.'

'So I hear. This buddy of mine—'

'Very dirty.' The old woman shook her head with something like remorse. 'Indians are clean people. But India? Dirty.'

'Were you visiting someone in Canada?'

'My daughter, yes.'

Matt guessed this daughter to be about his age. 'Married?'

'Yes, to a lovely Canadian boy. Four grandchildren. I will show you some pictures.'

He was handed a phone. Obediently Matt swiped through snapshots of grinning toddlers and passed it back.

'So why are you going to India?' said the woman. 'To find a wife?'

'Why, you think I've got a shot?'

'Indian girls these days, very focused on career. What is your work?'

'I'm an actor. But currently? In school for massage therapy.'

'Chiropractor?'

'Not exactly.' He reached out and lightly squeezed the old woman's shoulder; it felt like a knuckle. And yet at his touch she loosened, even melted at bit. 'Oh, you feel tense,' said Matt. 'Turn?'

She pivoted in her seat and Matt began kneading.

'Such strong hands,' she cooed. 'So lovely.'

'Your daughter's husband never gives you a massage?' said Matt, planting seeds.

A cleared throat whipped him around. Raj loomed behind the snack cart. 'To drink?'

Raj rolled his eyes at Matt's request for a rum and coke. So Matt put him to work, downing it one gulp and demanding another, and when that was done, though Raj had rolled off down the aisle, Matt rang the bell to summon another refill. By the time this drink arrived the engines had settled into a distant drone, the grandma had nodded off, snoring gently, and the plane soared out over the Atlantic.

The booze had Matt feeling considerably better about the science of aviation—about everything, really. With the bitchy steward down in the little cabin by the toilets, Matt unfolded himself from his seat, reeled up the aisle to First Class, and poked his head through the curtains.

There she was, handing out pillows.

'*Meena,*' he whispered.

'Sir?'

'A-meena-meena-meena.'

'Sir, please return to your seat.'

A few First Class faces swivelled in his direction. Then swivelled away.

'Meena-meena *meeeeee*-na.'

'Sir?'

Matt bounced his eyebrows suggestively.

'Sir,' said Meena. 'Please go. Now.'

'Aw,' said Matt. 'You're no fun.'

Meena put her hands on her hips.

And Matt, with a droop of his chin, said, 'Fine.'

Still, he wasn't beaten yet. Maybe Meena lived in Delhi? Matt could play the hapless tourist. How might he survive alone in India's jungles and deserts, amid all those tigers and cobras and leprosied beggars wagging fleshy stumps, without a guide— was Meena interested? She was, or would be. And back at her place she'd conduct him through all the positions of the Karma or Kama Sutra on a bed draped with mosquito netting and lavish silks while Ravi Shankar twanged away in the background . . .

And here the fantasy inspired a hunched stagger to the toilet, Matt's seed flushed in a mist upon the ocean below. He imagined it impregnating some lucky cod, who'd hatch a batch of fishy little Mattlings oblivious to their human dad, wondering on occasion why they had hands for fins and chest hair. Sad bastards, thought Matt, back in his seat. Then he passed out, woke up over the Balkans, ate a meal, drank two small bottles of wine and a whiskey, and passed out again watching a Bollywood movie. When he woke next they were landing, and the calendar had progressed *two days* from when he'd left Canada.

To Matt's astonishment, he was the only one to applaud the successful touchdown.

Meena was at the door again, well-wishing passengers as they debarked.

'Hey,' tried Matt on his way past, 'do you maybe know—'

But a shove from behind by his elderly seatmate—'Go now,' she barked—sent him out the door, away from Meena and onto a wobbly metal staircase. Down he was herded to the tarmac, where Matt stood gazing helplessly up the steps (Rule #14: *Admit defeat and move on*) swarmed by jet-lagged travellers. India smelled oddly cottagey: the earthy stink of an outhouse, the smoke of a bonfire, the marine petrolea of a dockside gas bar. The sky was purple. Everyone, it seemed, was brown.

Dark-faced people streamed from the plane, their eyes hazy and haunted by a full day of air travel, and whisked Matt aboard a waiting bus. Where was his backpack? Stolen, probably. He imagined some baggage handler home in his dung-hut slicing the thing open with a scimitar. Would it be Matt's fault if, mistaking his penis pump for a water purifier, this guy were to spritz some malarial stew into the family teapot, and all two dozen of them perished in a heap like corpses in a zombie movie?

A zombie movie, that was India: the mindless thronging, the apocalyptic smudge of sky, the bus's twitchy blue lighting that rendered every face undead. And, perfect, here was a soldier—toting a machine gun! But the guy was folded into the crowd and Matt was left wondering whether a military presence should incite relief or alarm.

If called upon, of course, Matt would spearhead the resistance. Among the brown faces he counted four potential allies: a middle-aged chinless couple in safari outfits; a business-type wielding his phone like a compass; and a blonde twenty-something woman clutching a very dark guy in a Jays cap. Matt tried to meet her eyes as the bus groaned into motion, the doors hanging open—scratch that: the bus had no doors.

Off they went. The crowd was packed so tightly that each jostle and lurch shook the lot of them like a pudding. At the terminal the crowd was released and carried Matt inside—only to join another, huger crowd swarming the baggage carousels and beyond. There was no escaping people. India was like being caught in a continuous mudslide.

Wait, was that racist?

But it *was* like a mudslide! Or at least 'mudslide' was Matt's first thought. Why deny it? Honestly, thousands of brown bodies surged organically as one, muddy mass, sweeping him into their midst: mudslide was as good a comparison as any. It didn't mean that Matt didn't or couldn't love them all. Given the chance, sure, he'd take each one for a beer and friendly Q&A.

How few women there were! And apart from the odd grey-bearded Sikh and a troupe of nervous-looking kids in fatigues with machine guns slung over their shoulders, the men seemed to be more or less the same character: fortyish, thin as a rake, wax-sculpted hair-helmet, moustache, outfit from an unfortunate family photograph circa 1979. Not like Ash or his dad in any way. More like monkeys.

Gosh, there really was something monkeyish about these men, all lithe and sinewy, a look at once cunning and melancholy in their eyes. And like monkeys each one seemed on the verge of treachery or mischief. Though, honestly, Matt meant this in a cute, not racist, way. Besides, they were little, and he was big. He shouldered through them to the baggage claim and staked his territory in a linebacker's stance.

A siren flashed and the conveyor belt came to life and here was Matt's backpack, after all, leading the charge. The alpha, he thought, shoving Indians aside to scoop it up.

But he wasn't free yet. The corral to the exit was jammed end to end with bodies. A head above them all, Matt fell into step: the bovine plod of a slaughterhouse death march.

Though Ash had renounced this trip, he'd grudgingly arranged a pick-up and accommodations for Matt's arrival in Delhi. ('After that,' Ash had said, 'you're on your own.') Yet Matt's name was not among the signs wielded from the barricades. One-by-one his fellow travellers reached the end of the corral and were greeted and embraced and swept away. But Matt was left unclaimed while the crowd seethed and dispersed—and a new one gathered for the next flight.

One clear thought pierced the rabble: Matt was in India. And in India he was no one; he could die, right then and there, and not a soul would frigging care.

Something dripped on him from above. A flap of ceiling hung loose, drizzling brown juice. So this is how his life would end, poisoned by disease-ridden effluent on the other side of the planet. Matt pictured himself huddled in a corner of the airport, green-complexioned and feverish and succumbing all alone . . .

And then he was touched. On the arm. The fingers belonged to a diminutive, finely featured character, now easing Matt's backpack from his hands.

Matt yanked it away. 'Hey!'

The little guy was undeterred. 'Mister Matthew, sir,' he said, and bowed, and summoned Matt to follow him. What else to do? He went.

Outside dawn had broken. The sky was pink and toxic. Nimbly that pixyish brown creature weaved through the crowd, vanishing for a moment and reappearing, beckoning Matt, forging ahead. Like a freighter trailing an icebreaker Matt followed behind—until the car-park, when his guide broke into a sprint.

Matt caught up, gasping, at a Mitsubishi hatchback. 'What's the hurry, bro?'

'Bitu,' the pixie said softly, tapping his chest. 'Mister Sanjay driver.'

'How did you know it was me?'

'Come,' said Bitu, gesturing to—no, not the driver's seat, Matt realized; things were reversed. The passenger side.

But they weren't home-free yet. Cars edged bumper-to-bumper out of the lot on a chorus of horns, like geese bawling in lust or rage. Bitu nonchalantly guided the steering wheel through it all with his fingertips, humming a quiet tune. Oblivious? Or unmoved? Either way, his serenity about the whole affair made Matt feel almost safe.

Then they hit the highway.

Horns bleated, cars swerved without cause or reason. Bitu

came to life, a new fire in his eyes: veering around a motorcycle (whose female driver was *applying makeup from a hand-held compact*), slamming the brakes, screeching left, nudging a taxi onto the shoulder—more horns—and then drifting back into the roiling tide.

It was like bumper cars piloted by blind-drunk teens. It was the first lap of a smash-up derby before the collisions began. It was oceanic: schools of sealife plummeting along through the depths. It was a free-for-all, it was chaos, it was mayhem, it was terrifying; it was the most fully aware of what a car actually was—a killing machine—and what driving meant—a flirtation with death, with inevitable death—that Matt had ever been.

Yet Bitu was still humming. And clearly out of his mind.

Matt closed his eyes. If he was going to croak at the hands of this elfin psychopath, he'd at least prefer not to watch. But then he reconsidered: what if this might later become a memory? Matt would at least need to bear witness. Opening his eyes was like waking from a coma: here was this ludicrously teeming world again.

Beyond the highway were buildings upon buildings, and a hillock capped with shacks, and a pair of burdened camels— honestly!—trotting roadside. Scooters zipped through gaps no wider than their riders. And the traffic in the other direction was something to behold, too, arterial in the way it pulsed and surged past.

This felt not just a different place, but a different time, some new hour or epoch. Nothing here was *new*, nor had ever been new; this bus grumbling along the shoulder must have appeared on earth as it was, a rusty hull, trembling in its bolts and stuffed with passengers, their haunted brown faces gazing out the barred windows from some place beyond history, fumes billowing, dust billowing, horns shrieking. Everything in India was *right frigging now.*

'This one CNG,' said Bitu proudly.

'Sorry?'

'Bus. CNG. Clean gas.'

'Okay . . .'

'But bus, bad mens.' Bitu's tone had turned severe. 'On bus, bad mens.'

'Bad what?'

'Mens, mens. Make womens . . .' Bitu trailed off. He seemed genuinely pained.

Then Matt understood. He'd heard about the assaults—the rapes. In fact he'd even entertained fantasies of vigilantism in Delhi, dressing up in a sari and riding around with a shillelagh tucked into his girdle, waiting for a gang of leering men to slither into the seats around him. As soon as one made a move he'd pound them all into oblivion.

'Is that still happening?'

'Bad mens,' said Bitu, shaking his head. 'Bad, bad mens.'

They pulled up to a stoplight. Bitu turned off the ignition (interesting!) and pointed to bamboo scaffolding rigged around an overpass. A few shirtless, turbaned men were scattered upon it. Hammers tinked stone. 'Subway,' said Bitu. 'Open soon!'

A handmade subway? Before Matt could ask, someone appeared at his window. A hollow-eyed woman in rags and riotous orange hair, with a baby tucked under one arm. She tapped the glass and made a gesture of putting food to the kid's mouth, again and again: *tap-tap, eat-eat; tap-tap, eat-eat.*

Matt reached for his wallet. And Bitu held him back. 'Sir, no. No give.'

'No?'

'No give,' said Bitu. 'No clean.'

Before Matt could argue they were pitching again into that anarchic motorcade. Between trucks and buses and sleek sports cars and great, glistening sedans flitted three-wheelers with gold canopied tops. They reached a roundabout and while Bitu waited to merge Matt peered into one: in the back sat a man with his arm around a goat.

'There's so much to look at!'

'Yes sir,' said Bitu, swerving in front of a Jeep, setting off another chorus of horns. He seemed so collected about it all, so *cool*. And when he spoke next his voice had the polish of rehearsal: 'Welcome, Mister Matthew, to India.'

ASH'S COUSIN'S HOUSE was off the highway, past a shantytown and a pantless child and a boxy, neon-dappled caricature of a shopping centre, down a boulevard lined with palm trees, through a secured entrance, and finally onto a quiet side-street that reminded Matt of Florida, save the concrete walls topped with broken glass. The burbs, he thought. Or some Indian approximation.

A guard in a beret saluted the Jeep as it pulled through the gate of one of these houses, then hurriedly closed it behind them. Standing on the doorstep was a chubby fellow in shirtsleeves and Joseph Stalin's moustache. A slash of vermilion marked his forehead. He clasped his hands at his heart, looking joyous.

'Mister Matthew sir!' he announced, steering Matt inside by the elbow. 'Come!'

'What about my bag?'

'The boy will see to it. Come, sir, eat. Please.' He spoke with a pronounced lisp.

Matt was led into a dining room and deposited at the head of the table. Arranged artfully upon a turmeric-stained tablecloth were plates of pastries, a bowl of fruit, a bottle of juice, a jug of milk, and a box of cornflakes.

Matt's host stood at his side. 'A toast? Omelette?'

'No, really—'

'Coffee? Chai?' The man's head wobbled. Then it stopped. His expression turned troubled. 'Sir, Mister Dhar sends his regards.'

'Which Dhar is that, now?'

'Mister Dhar, the master of the house, is in Dubai. I am Sumit, his assistant. You will be very comfortable here.'

'Ash told me—'

'Some fruit,' Sumit instructed, producing a knife. 'You have tried banana?'

'Oh, yeah, I've—'

Sumit sliced a stack of creamy disks onto Matt's plate. 'Try.'

'Wow. Now *that's* a banana.'

'Yes, banana. This one, apple. Try.'

'Lay it on me, brother. Delicious.'

'Do you know chikoo?'

'What's that now?'

Sumit displayed something round and dully russet, like a shaved kiwi. 'Very sweet.'

His knife exposed flesh the colour of a spoiled peach; Matt peeled a gooey clump from the blade. The taste was sickly with afternotes of soil. 'Wow.'

'Chikoo.'

'Chick-ew,' said Matt.

Sumit looked pleased. 'And, sir, your itinerary?'

'Honestly? I hadn't really thought—'

'This p.m. we will show you all the sites: Jama Masjid, Red Fort, Qutb Minar.'

'Easy now, bro. I just got in!'

'Here in Gurgaon, many beautiful malls. New malls. *Beautiful* malls.'

'Wait, aren't we in New Delhi?'

'Just like in America!'

'Hey. Canada.'

Sumit's eyes fell to Matt's empty plate with a look of dismay. Tilting into the hallway he screamed, '*Omelette!*'

'No, hey. Honestly, I'm not that hungry.'

'Sir,' said Sumit.

The omelette arrived, scorched and oily, its papery edges drooping over a saucer. The man who brought it wore bellbottoms and a baseball cap. Another servant, thought Matt, which made four: Sumit, this chef, Bitu the driver and the guard at the gate. Which one was the 'boy?'

Sumit barked something. The cook scurried away, returned with ketchup, bowed and disappeared again.

'So, tell me, Soo-meat,' said Matt. 'Do any women work here?'

'One girl Tuesday only. For sweeping, washing.' Sumit nodded at Matt's plate. 'Eat.'

After breakfast, Sumit led Matt to his room, fragrant with Dettol. A flat-screen TV occupied most of one wall; another featured a calendar on which a flying monkey toted a mountain like a waiter presenting a massive, volcanic cake.

'Luggages,' Sumit said, opening the wardrobe, where Matt's backpack sat as if teleported in.

'Swell, bro. Mind if I take a shower?'

'Please.' Sumit gestured to the ensuite.

When Matt emerged twenty minutes later, glistening and pink and scrotally powdered, he still stood there, rocking on his heels and beaming.

Matt asked if he might be left alone to dress.

Sumit's shoulders hunched in a sad bow. 'Sir,' he lisped, backed out of the room and closed the door—though not all the way. As he dropped his towel, in the crack Matt could make out Sumit's shadow, lingering in the hallway, maybe even peeking in.

⋐⊕⊛⊕⊜

A DOG. ASH HAD FORGOTTEN that his mother and Rick had fostered one through some rescue organization, fallen in love, adopted the animal as their own. He knew this story, it had just escaped him. So when, rather than his mom or her boyfriend, a black Lab came bounding to the front door and went straight for his crotch, Ash worried for a moment that he'd walked into the wrong house, or that his mom had moved without telling him.

But other than the animal trying to molest him, the house was otherwise the same: the leather couch and recliner tilted amiably toward each other, the fireplace stacked and ready for ignition, the gentle ticking of the old clock on the mantle. And, of course, the smell: tea and Pine-Sol and wet wool and soup. The smell of home.

There'd been a time when Ash would have never thought of his mom's house as home. At eighteen, fleeing to school in Toronto, any association with London had risked tainting his plans for big city bohemianism, so he'd more or less disavowed it. A blandly pleasant, intermittently forested outpost of three-hundred-odd thousand people stranded halfway to Detroit, it had the trappings of similar-sized municipalities south of the border—local sports lore, an east-west divide, a gutted manufacturing sector, a shit-ton of malls—but none of the character or manic Yankee pride. Neither city nor small town, American nor Canadian, London was a nothing sort of place with no identity of its own: a place to escape, Ash had believed, in order to find yourself elsewhere.

Even as the surrounding farmlands were fractalled with sprawl, London never seemed to change. It felt somehow outside time, and each big box development and pre-fab suburb felt less like progress than a replication of more of the same. But as time passed, this constancy turned comforting. And Ash's mom's house embodied that familiarity: it always felt the same, regardless of some new knick-knack—or some new Rick. Even the dog, snuffling between Ash's legs with the tenacity of excavation, seemed almost archetypally domestic.

And here was Rick himself, galloping out of the kitchen in a great silver flaring of beard. 'Burt! Down!'

The dog collapsed as if shot, eyes fixed on his master in terror and reverence.

'Don't let him dominate you like that, my man.'

'Okay.' Ash misinterpreted Rick's extended arm as a request for a handshake.

'No,' said Rick. 'Ash, greetings. But first let me touch your chest.'

Ash waited.

Rick bowed his head, hand planted firmly over Ash's heart. 'Sorry about your dad.'

'Oh, that's okay—'

Rick shushed him. 'Wait until the blessing's over.' His voice turned sonorous:

'Fatherhood is a sacred bond, and to shatter that bond is to cast the son loose. But, Ash, you are not lost among men. You are no orphan. For wherever you go, we are with you, all of us. We call you brother. We are all brothers. All of us, as one. All men.'

Rick nodded. Dropped his hand. The spot on Ash's chest felt damp.

'My mom around?'

'Groceries,' said Rick, with a note of apology. 'She likes to go now when there's no one there, just the night owls. Back soon though.'

Ash was offered coffee. He'd had this man's coffee before, a sour, boggy concoction reminiscent of the juice at the bottom of trash bins. 'Bit late for that,' he said, and slid past Rick to the basement.

His old single bed was covered with a tenuously Aztec quilt, something with tribal aspirations that Rick had likely picked up at a yard sale. Ash set down his duffel. Checked his phone. No messages, no calls; maybe Sherene had given up. Nothing from

Matt, either, which seemed ungrateful. Without Ash's help he'd be begging for sanctuary at the gates of Delhi's Canadian embassy. The least the guy could do was drop a thank-you text.

From upstairs came the sound of Rick creaking across the kitchen floor to the top of the stairs. 'Hey, my man. You hungry? There's some tagine left, happy to heat it up.'

Ash declined, though he was starving. Tagine? He wanted his mom's home-cooking: meatloaf, mac and cheese. Not her boyfriend's orientalist putties.

*Boyfriend*—odd word for a man nearing seventy. Yet it was what Ash's mother called him. 'I can't abide this *partner* business,' she'd explained more than once. 'Makes us sound like cops.' Rick had retired from Western's anthropology department around the same time she'd been winding down at Brescia College, and soon after they'd started dating, and soon after that he'd moved his bongo drums into her basement, though he'd kept his townhouse as a showroom for their artisanal efforts. This Ash pictured: African masks on the walls, moccasins by the door, an odour of berbere and incense and beard.

If his mother's hippie tendencies had culminated in once marrying a man from the mystical east, after the divorce they'd been limited to occasionally hauling out her old six-string to strum along to Joni Mitchell. Yet now, eight years post-retirement and seven into Rick, she'd time-warped back to the sixties, eating organic, dressing in caftans, breezing through her days with an airy, floral joy. In her twenties she'd sold handmade pottery at folk festivals all over North America, but after starting grad school the one time she'd touched her potter's wheel was to lug it to the curb. Rick had reignited that artisanal spark, and now together they toured craft fairs hawking her bowls and the chunky leatherwork he referred to as his 'art.' And she was happy, inhabiting her nostalgia in ways that Ash's father, for one, had never managed.

Beside the bed a shelf held all the novels and plays and poetry that Ash had barely cracked in school. He spied *Don Quixote* and pulled it free. One of many classics he'd always lied about having read. Maybe he was growing tired of lying. Also the novel was fat enough to occupy him for a while. Also he'd long used the term 'quixotic' without really knowing what it meant. So he took it to bed, lay down and set it on his stomach. But didn't read. His thoughts instead caromed between memories of this room—the virginity he'd lost, swiftly and apologetically, on its floor; or long before that, waiting in bed for his mother to read him to sleep— and what it meant to be here now.

It had been years since Ash had made it home for the holidays, obliged as he was to attend various seasonal functions in Toronto. These were held for and among the darlings of the Canadian media industry, self-appointed *creatives* who performed such soaring feats of artistry as typing out celebrity gossip and building websites for banks. And while Ash attended their parties resentfully, he went seeking something—approval, or maybe just recognition, though invariably he lurked unheralded and unknown on the periphery like some brighter light's valet.

He felt that part of what set him apart, or below, were his clothes (Levi's, thrift store blazer, sneakers), so the previous year, in a panic of inadequacy, he'd visited some slick downtown haberdashery. Immediately he felt identified as an imposter when the nifty, vested salesman (*Yves*) asked him, with palpable irony, if he needed *help*. Ash emerged ninety minutes later having spent only slightly less than his mortgage. Yet, cheered on drippily by Yves, those duds (waistcoat, cufflinks, shoes pointy enough to skewer cubed meat) had suggested a metamorphosis: from boy to grownup, from layabout to gentleman. The outfit required a corresponding haircut and salves and gels, which would eventually coagulate to buttery sludge in Ash's bathroom cabinet.

But when Ash dressed at home, the transformation was not repeated. Instead the clothes looked like a costume and his sculpted hair replicated a toupee's naive hubris exactly. And the shoes! Their scabbard tips were sneers. On the streetcar ride down-town, the other passengers' stares—*what a dandy!*—mortified him even more.

The party, hosted by a vodka company, thumped and thudded away in a derelict warehouse turned lavish with ball gowns and ice sculptures and double-kissed cheeks. Ash checked his coat and lingered in the doorway. A few heads turned appraisingly in his direction, then back to their conversations. For the next few hours he drank his way through passive aggressive dismissals ('I had no idea people still listen to the *radio*. Good for you!') until last call, when the lights came on to dispatch the few forlorn, shiftless drunks who remained, and Ash staggered outside and vomited thunderously all over his shiny new shoes.

Upstairs the dog barked and the door clattered open and his mother whooped, 'How's my pooch? How's my pooch?' Silence followed. In it Ash imagined Rick whispering to his mother of her son's return, a note of apprehension in his voice, his mother's pointed questions—'How does he seem? Is he okay?'—and the two of them shaking their heads in a forlorn, pitying way.

So he climbed the stairs to head them off, and found his mom transferring groceries to the fridge and Rick dancing down the driveway leashed to Burt, off into the night.

'Ashy!' His mother came at him for a hug. 'Rick thought you might have gone to bed.'

'I slept on the train.' This was untrue; Ash couldn't sleep on trains.

'I got everything you'll need for Christmas dinner. Help me put it away.'

Ash squeezed a tub of cranberry sauce into the fridge beside a cling-wrapped bowl of something pasty and beige.

'You're okay taking charge of cooking?' she said. 'You do a bet-ter job than me these days anyway. Rick's the chef around here so I'm out of practice.'

'Always happy to cook,' said Ash, hoping he sounded amenable. He was handed a turkey the size of a gym bag. Kneeling, he wedged the bird into the fridge, where it occupied an entire shelf like a corpse awaiting autopsy.

'I'm so glad you're here,' said his mother. 'And your sister should be in tomorrow morning—the whole family together again! We've got the craft fair at the arena most of tomorrow, but Rick's really looking forward to spending some time with both of you.'

'Rick.'

'He finally read your book.'

Ash stood. 'Why'd you let him do that?'

'He's just trying to get to know you. He's a very interesting man. Well read, well travelled. Give him a chance.' Her ironic smile suggested that Ash never gave anyone, or anything, a chance. 'You're not mad, are you?'

'If you really wanted to blow the lid off all my secrets, I've got some old journals downstairs. Or I can give him my email password.'

'Ashy.'

'I wrote that book like ten years ago. It isn't *me*. When you write, you change things. You make stuff up. You're just trying not to make something bad, not expressing yourself or whatever inane thing people say. That's it. It's no way to know someone!'

'You're yelling.'

He'd also seized the edge of the kitchen table, he realized, as if he might tip the whole thing over. He let go, rubbed his sweaty hands on his jeans.

'You look tired,' said his mother.

An excuse to head downstairs. Sequestered in his basement lair Ash finally texted Sherene: *Do your parents bring out your inner Hyde too?* Waited five minutes for a reply. Ten. Twenty. Gave up and lay in the dark—for hours, was it? Though he must have

dozed off because an incoming call startled him so badly he nearly
fell out of bed.

'Bro!'

'Oh god. You realize there's a time difference, right? It's like
four in the morning!'

'Oops.'

'What do you want?'

'Merry Christmas, I love you too.'

Ash flopped back against his pillow. 'So you're there, I guess.
At my cousin's?'

'Yeah, except he's away. Sumit's here though.'

'Who the hell is Sumit?'

'I dunno, his butler or something. Dude had me on an *itinerary* today: into the city to see that big mosque in the old part,
then across the road to the Red Fort—big lineups there, but
you get the gist from the car—then out to the countryside to
see some tower, then we drove around and he yelled the names
of embassies as we went by, then back out here to Gorgon.
Dang that guy's got some sweet fruit, though. *Do you like my
chikoo?*'

'Don't do that accent. You sound like a Jamaican leprechaun.
And it's *Gurgaon.*'

'Sumit's my man, he's hilarious. I got my phone out so he
could take my picture with this broad I met at the mosque, and
he asks me how many megapixels, so I tell him four, it's old, and he
just laughs and goes, "I will be in the car." What a guy.'

'Wait, you met a *woman* at a *mosque?*'

'I've got game, what can I say.'

'At the mosque.'

'It's not really a mosque.'

'It is! It is totally a mosque! Jama Masjid? It's the biggest mosque
in India!'

'You had to take off your shoes and I was sure a leper or

whatever was going to steal them but we got out and there they were. I thought you said I was going to get ripped off?'

'So who's your new lover?'

'Oh, we didn't seal the deal. But we're going to Goa, so maybe there.'

'Wait. What? You realize that's the opposite direction from Kashmir, right?'

'That's where the party is, she says.'

'The drugs, you mean. Who is this woman?'

'Mieke. She's Dutch, from Norway or whatever.'

'Holland!'

'I know, bro. Duh. Just yanking your cord.'

'But wait. Goa? When?'

'Tomorrow, I think she said?'

'Done with Delhi already, are you? Seen enough?'

'Thing is? I don't really know when tomorrow is. Isn't it still yesterday back home?'

'Are you going to marry this woman?

'Doubtful. She's lesbian.'

'Sounds like a nationality, the way you say it.'

'Netherlands. Nether-region-lands. Heh heh. Hey, you weren't kidding about all the gay dudes here. Cuddling, snuggling, dry humping. I saw one guy with his buddy's head in his lap, combing his hair. Another two dudes walking around holding pinkies. I thought it was super homophobic here? Seems pretty homo-tastic.'

'No, no. They're not gay.'

'What?'

'They're just . . . Indian. I told you this, remember? My dad? His buddy? New York?'

'Maybe that means I've got a shot with Mieke?'

'How would it possibly mean that?'

'Just, you know. Stuff's different here.'

'I can't imagine you see her sexuality as an impediment.'
'More of a challenge.'
'You're a bad person.'
'I'm making memories!'
'I know. That's what worries me.'

# 2

MATT ARRANGED WITH MIEKE that he and Bitu would collect her
at her Connaught Place hostel and go for dinner anywhere she
wanted, price no object. She chose one of the city's five-star hotels,
of which he approved for its lack of online diarrheal testimonials;
the last thing he wanted was for his bowels to prevent a score.

Ash had provided strict instructions on what not to eat: anything raw, basically, despite however tempting a platter of sliced
pineapple might look paraded by at a stoplight. He'd also suggested avoiding street food of any type. Normally Matt wasn't
afraid of a rough gut. Through his twenties he'd lived on Taco Bell,
fifty bucks' worth at a time, eat what you can and freeze the rest as
groceries. But India was different. The stakes were higher, and
weirder, and potentially fatal.

Even if this wasn't a date, Matt prepped for one. (*Rule #8:
Doing it up = pants coming down.*) A four-hundred-dollar shirt

was all a guy needed to get a leg up, and he'd brought his go-to number. Baby blue and tastefully embroidered and tailored snug as a glove, it anchored his outfits to night clubs, to auditions, to court. Then there were his other ablutions: a scalding shower, a shave (face, throat, scalp, shoulders, perineum), a quick go with the penis pump, and a final spritz of body spray through which he nudely twirled, the mist settling into every pore.

Before heading out he eyed himself in the mirror. What he saw looked good, obviously, yet still Matt felt atypically unsure. He'd been with a lesbian before, sort of, as a third party in a threesome, though his role had been mostly observational. He'd dated a few bisexuals and even attempted a brief, gruff make-out with a coked-up Swedish guy in Whistler. The experience had been more pugilistic than sensual—like one of them was trying to win—and eventually the two men had pulled apart with a comradely, concessional pat on the back.

But he'd never turned a gay woman before, though at least four girlfriends had turned from him to one of their own. Would Mieke be down? Maybe being in India would give him a better shot, per the various laxities—hygiene, core values, etc.—enjoyed on holiday. But should he act less masculine than normal? Shaving had occasioned debate: down to the skin, or leave a little stubble? Mieke was girlish, so he figured she preferred manlier women—though how feminine a man?

Outside the door, Sumit swayed expectantly, his hands clasped behind his back: 'For this evening's meal, sir, we shall prepare veg or non-veg?'

'Whatever floats your boat, Sumit,' said Matt, edging past.

'Sir, I take my wife's food only. I bring from home.'

What was this? Sumit had a wife? And a home!

And kids, the photos displayed almost smugly on his phone. The girls were identical to their father, minus the moustache: same gap in their front teeth (Matt could fairly hear the s's whistling out), same obsequious sheen to the eyes, same pot bellies. 'I see them weekends only. Monday-Friday I stay here.' Sumit gestured to the kitchen. Did the guy sleep in the oven? 'And now, your meal?'

'Truth is, Sumit? I'm not here for supper. I've got a hot date.'

It was as though Matt had announced he was trafficking the guy's family back to Canada. The shoulders slumped, the head bowed. Sumit was taciturn in summoning Bitu, and shook his head mournfully from the front step as the Jeep reversed down the driveway. 'Be careful, Mister Matthew,' he cried.

Matt pressed a hand to the window and mouthed, *I will.*

Twilight was descending and the traffic into Delhi seemed less anarchic than restless, like a pride of lions gearing up for a nocturnal hunt. Mieke was waiting on the appointed corner wearing a sarong, her hair up in a fat bun held together with chopsticks. Sliding into the backseat she smacked Matt on the leg.

'Thanks for getting me! Is this our chauffeur?'

'My driver,' said Matt, the lift of his eyebrows indicating a whole realm of possibilities. (*Rule #5: Power wins.*) 'He'll take us anywhere we want.'

'All I want is to eat,' said Mieke, retracting to the window. 'I'm starving.'

The hotel bar was lit intergalactically with tubes of blue neon. The music gurgled and pulsed. Decaled on the walls were instructions: *RELAX, MEET, CHAT, CHILL.* And the clientele, mostly young couples in stylish western attire, obeyed. Standing in the doorway, as he often did upon entering a room, Matt was conscious of his size—and now his colour too, as a dozen brown faces turned his way.

A host in a soulpatch and Nehru jacket escorted Matt and Mieke to a table on the edge of what, presumably, would later become the dance floor.

'I've never been to a place like this in India,' said Mieke. 'So modern!'

'We can go somewhere else,' Matt offered. 'My driver—'

Mieke pointed to an imperative pasted above the bar: 'Just chill, okay?'

The menu was fusiony. They ordered a few small dishes, Mieke proceeding tentatively until Matt smacked down his credit card. 'Whatever you like. It's on me.'

She lowered the menu. 'Give us one of everything.'

'And a fork,' said Matt, holding up his hands sadly. 'Can't do chopsticks with these meathooks.'

Drinks came. Mieke began telling a story about Burma or Bhutan or Bangladesh, which Matt ignored: three people had slid into the adjacent table, and one of them was the most stunningly beautiful woman he'd ever seen. More of a girl, really, maybe nineteen, and boasting that severe brand of beauty particular to former Soviet states. Flanking her were two men in pinstriped suits, hair slicked wetly to their scalps. While she examined the menu, they peered around the room with predatory intensity.

'My god,' whispered Mieke, nudging Matt under the table. 'That girl is *gorgeous*.'

Did this make the Dutchwoman an accomplice or competitor? Matt played it cool. 'You think?'

'God,' said Mieke. 'Are you joking? Look at her.'

Given permission, Matt did, and met the girl's eye, and winked. She smiled back—a smile that went sizzling through Matt's soul and landed hotly in his lap. Was it on? It might be. But how to dispatch Mieke? And who were the girl's companions? They looked old enough to be her dads. So, what, a family vacation—father, daughter . . . uncle? Or business associates. More likely: the CEO and VP of some Russian conglomerate, here on business with their finest executive assistant along for the trip.

As Matt stared, one of the men spoke into the girl's ear. She nodded, rose, moved into the empty space in the middle of the room and began dancing.

All conversation ceased. Every face—patrons, staff, Mieke, Matt—turned to watch her. The girl knew it: she wriggled and writhed, hands twisting in gestures both eastern and serpentine, slinking down into a crouch and then shimmying back up. Her dress was sheer and short and slack; beneath it the contours of her body appeared for tantalizing glimpses only to dissolve inside the fabric.

'Sweet merciful Vishnu,' whispered Matt.

Mieke echoed him in Dutch.

Then something happened: one of the men stood, buttoned his jacket, strode across the lounge, and joined two middle-aged/middle-management types in a corner booth. His comrade, who remained at the table beside Matt and Mieke, checked his watch.

Meanwhile, the young woman kept dancing.

'Should I ask her friend to join us?' Matt whispered.

Mieke shook her head. 'Are you crazy?'

'He's all alone!'

The guy must have heard this, passed a gaze of appraisal their way. A scar curled from his eyebrow to cheekbone, like a fishhook poised to snag his eye.

A young couple had interrupted the girl's dancing to have their picture taken with her. Matt jumped up and offered to play photographer. He framed the shot just-so, taking a moment to ogle the young woman through the viewfinder: her eyes seemed to look right through him. Then the flash flashed and the couple retreated to their seats, checking the camera's display screen and beaming as though they'd met the queen.

Matt sat, winked at Mieke, and tilted his beer at Scarface. 'So,' he said, 'where are you from?'

Mieke dove at her drink.

'My friend and I come from Moscow. But her'—he gestured toward the dancing girl—'we have brought from Ukraine.'

The other Russian returned with the Indian men in tow. Scarface summoned the Ukrainian girl. She received some instructions and, with a roomful of people watching, took one of the Indians to the elevator and upstairs into the hotel.

'Oh,' said Matt.

And Mieke sighed.

Dinner came, then. A second table had to be provided to accommodate the spillover dishes. While Mieke spooned noodles onto her plate, Matt gazed at all that excess with shame and revulsion. So much food. Too much food. His appetite vanished.

Mieke ate in silence. Matt sipped his beer. At the neighbouring table, the Indian guy ordered a bottle of rum—to celebrate, Matt thought grimly. But the Russians covered their glasses with their hands.

After a while the first man returned. It was his friend's turn to go upstairs.

'Frig this,' said Matt. He pushed back from the table, rocketed to his feet and stormed the elevator. *Rule #17: Be the best man in every room.*

The button for the top floor—the penthouse suite—was illuminated. The doors closed and up they went. Matt's fellow passenger seemed cut from the same portly, moustachioed cloth as Sumit. But he lacked the charm, the twinkle. His hair was styled haphazardly, as if by rival barbers. His shoes were green.

The floors moved into the teens.

Matt's voice filled the elevator like a foghorn: 'So! What's your name?'

'Barat.' Said with a pause between syllables, as if it might be retracted midway.

'Nice to meet you, Bar-rat. I'm Richard Gere.' They did not shake hands. 'Your night's going well, I hope. Though it's about to get a lot better, am I right?'

Barat stabbed the lit button.

'Penthouse, pretty swank. You must have paid good money for

that room.' Matt moved a little closer. 'Though I guess it's not the room you paid for, so much, is it?'

Barat coughed.

They were into the twenties now.

'Nearly there,' said Matt.

They eased to a stop. The doors opened with a digital chime. Yet Barat didn't exit.

'Go on,' said Matt in a soft voice. 'She's waiting for you.'

Still didn't move, just rocked slightly on his heels.

The doors began to close. Matt pried them open. Across the hallway, on a marble dais, sat a carving of figures entwined in either combat or coitus.

And Barat bolted.

Matt laughed and followed, standing behind him while he pounded on the penthouse door.

A lock unlatched.

'All yours, hero,' said Matt.

The door opened. As Barat ducked inside, Matt, too, pushed into the room.

The girl was dressed in a robe, her hair knotted in a loose bun. She stared at Matt.

'Okay,' said Matt, moving between proprietor and client. 'This ends *now*.'

The girl took a cellphone off the nightstand.

'No, wait, who are you calling?'

She rolled her eyes, turned her back.

Matt came at her over the bed, seized the phone. 'I'm trying to help you.'

She blinked. At most she seemed mildly inconvenienced. Perhaps even bored. Not how this scene was supposed to go at all.

Meanwhile, Barat was backing out of the room.

Matt wheeled. 'Hey! Don't you go anywhere.'

For a moment everyone froze.

What came next? Matt sat on the bed with the phone in his lap, thinking how he might regain control of the storyline. Barat hovered by the mini-bar. The girl stood with crossed arms, her back pressed to the window. Where Matt sat the covers were rumpled: the bed had been made hastily, belying the recent transaction within its sheets.

The phone came to life. Matt dropped it on the floor, where it trembled and purred.

'They will come up,' said the girl simply.

'Wait,' said Matt. 'How much?'

'Pardon?'

'What are they paying you? I'll double it.'

'Double?'

Matt kicked the phone at her. 'Tell them.'

With a sigh she answered, playing absently with the tassel of the robe. Matt tried to chase meaning out of the torrent of Russian syllables that followed. But it was hard enough to think in English. The girl regarded him so casually, so mockingly.

She moved the handset away from her mouth. 'All right, enough. You get out now.'

'Wait!' Matt cried. 'We don't even have to blast. We could just talk. I'll pay you *double* just to sit here. You don't have to do this, you shouldn't—'

'No. You, leave.'

This emboldened Barat, who crossed his arms.

'Come on, please.' Matt lowered his voice to a whisper: '*I'm trying to help you.*'

The girl smirked. 'He's trying to help me,' she said into her phone in English. And laughed—such a cruel, bitter sound. 'And we say go fuck yourself.'

Matt rose with difficulty from the bed. Lugging his body from a scene of defeat always made his size feel so cumbersome. But had he been beaten? Barat was nodding—dismissive, victorious.

With one arm Matt lifted him off the floor and said, 'Looks like we're not wanted here, bro.'

Though he squirmed and kicked, effortlessly Matt carried him into the hallway. The door closed behind them. Matt set him down.

'You bloody can't do this,' Barat sputtered. 'We have paid!'

'Yeah, and that's pretty gross. She's a *kid*, bro. You're lucky I don't staple your head to that wall with your own frigging teeth.'

Barat took a step back, reaching for his pocket.

'Don't even think about calling anyone. We're going downstairs, and you're going to collect your buddy, and then you're going to head home to your wife, and you're going to cuddle her brains out and tell her how sorry you are. Understand?'

The hand retracted. A nod.

Matt went to call the elevator, but it was already rocketing from the ground floor to the top level—Russians aboard, Matt imagined, screwing silencers to their Kalashnikovs. 'What say we take the stairs?'

So down twenty-four flights they went, emerging cautiously into the lobby: clear.

'Wait here,' said Matt, depositing the guy on a couch by the front desk.

From behind a pillar, he glanced into the dining room. The Russians were gone. And so was Mieke. Matt went to the ladies room, knocked, stuck his head in, called her name. No reply. He checked his phone: nothing. He was alone.

He was in India, he'd crossed the mob, and now he was alone.

Matt had heard stories of how these Siberian maniacs enacted revenge: genitals chewed off by huskies and stuffed into their still-living owners' mouths, acid baths and eyeballs vised free like seeds squeezed from a grape. Or they'd lash their rivals spread-eagled to a bedframe and lined up horny Swedes to have a go at his butthole.

Defeated, terrified, exhausted and lost, Matt slunk out to the parking lot.

Bitu and the Jeep were nowhere in sight.

His date had stolen his ride home.

NONE OF MATT'S TEXTS to Mieke got responses. He tried explanations, excuses, apologies—nothing back, not even a ☹. And working his phone with those sausage-sized thumbs on the taxi ride to Ash's cousin's place ('Just head toward the airport,' were Matt's instructions. 'I'll figure it out.') was no easy task. Never mind finding the right words—soothing words, mending words—amid the lingering haze of jetlag and three days without weed, amid the constant, strained search for some familiar landmark, amid frenzied glances out the back window to make sure he wasn't being tailed.

They circled Gurgaon's business parks and interminable sprawl, the metre ticking upward. Here was a mall that Matt thought he recognized. But no tree-lined lane threaded past the parking lot, just a mound of dirt. And here definitely was the billboard he could see from his bedroom window—except, no, this one bore a different Bollywood star lounging shirtless on a motorcycle. Around they went, the cabbie watching Matt in the rear-view, Matt peering desperately at the passing scenery, everything both foreign and familiar, the orange wash of streetlights lending it all the uncanny shimmer of a dream.

Lost, he was lost. Deserted and sold-out—by an alleged friend and conceivable bedfellow!—on the dark side of the frigging planet. What time was it? Matt's phone said one. But was that here or home, late or early, night or day? Hopeless. He collapsed in the backseat, playing out his options: move in with his driver, use his cab to start some sort of arms smuggling syndicate into Afghanistan, go to war with the Russians, end up executed by Taliban operatives in some dusty mountain cave.

'Oh, wait,' Matt said, sitting up. 'That's the gate right there. Hang a left?'

Ninety seconds later, he was home.

From the stool outside Matt's bedroom door, Sumit sprang to his feet in a panic. Clearly (red eyes, muffed hair, drool-shoulder) he'd been sleeping. 'Sir, I sent Bitu to search for you! Where have you been?'

'Just trying to make some memories, bro.' This felt false. So: 'Honestly though?'

Sumit's head jiggled like an asymmetrically weighted ball.

'I think I'm out of here tomorrow.'

A less enthusiastic wobble. Hesitant, dubious.

'Me and Mieke are heading to Goa—'

'Sir, no.' Sumit's voice trembled. 'You have only just arrived. Please. How will you go there? It is very far. Very dangerous. Goa is very murderous for westerners.'

'I think we were thinking about taking the train?'

Sumit closed his eyes, made a tsking noise; the wobble was now doleful. 'Many robberies on this train. Very long, three-four days. Very bad food only. And cockroaches!'

'Well we could fly, then.'

'No flying from Delhi. Very expensive to fly.'

'Wait. There aren't any flights or it's just pricey?'

'You will die there. You will drown. Or be poisoned. Very dangerous!'

'Really? I thought lots of tourists—'

'You will be murdered. There are sharks.'

'Listen, I should be getting to bed.'

Sumit seized him by the elbow. 'Who is this *Mieke*.'

'You met her. At the mosque. Remember?'

'These people are often up to no good. Working for gangsters. In cahoots.'

'Whoa, what? Mieke? Cahoots? Cahoots with who?'

'You are a good person, Mister Matthew. India is full of danger. No one is to be trusted.' Sumit's hand stroked Matt's arm up to his shoulder, back down. His eyes were plaintive, imploring. 'You must trust me when I say this.'

THE PROBLEM, MATT THOUGHT, packing up the next morning, wasn't that he'd done something wrong, but that he hadn't done enough. He was a man of action. He was the hero of his own story. (*Rule #9: Be the hero of your own story.*) So what else was there to do but track Mieke down, and win her over, and the whole fabulous tale would end happily with the two of them frolicking naked on some sugar-coloured beach while dolphins danced in the surf. Cue sunset, roll credits.

First he'd have to sneak out without rousing Sumit. He found Bitu in the kitchen, drinking tea. With a finger to his lips he performed a little mime of their impending escape: steering wheel, choo-choo train, Matt sailing off into the great brown yonder. When that didn't work, he dumped Bitu's tea in the sink and hustled him out to the Jeep. As the gates were closing, Sumit appeared on the front step in his pajamas. 'Sir!' he cried, clutching the railing. 'You are actually leaving? Why? *Why?*'

'Drive,' Matt told Bitu. And didn't look back.

A block from Nizamuddin Station Bitu pulled up to the curb and gestured vaguely ahead. He seemed to be instructing Matt to continue on foot. Ditched again! Fine, Matt thought, digging his backpack out of the trunk. Forty minutes and several baffling conversations later he joined a line-up designated for *Elderly, Invalid and Foreign Travellers*. The couple ahead of him reached roughly to his waist, a pair of collapsed question marks who took turns horking into a greasy handkerchief.

The line didn't so much progress as clot and burst. Things were stagnant and then suddenly surging ahead, and everyone scrabbled forward like twigs swept downstream. More people appeared, looking neither particularly foreign nor elderly nor invalid, and wedged themselves in line, and after twenty minutes Matt found himself further from the wicket than when he began.

Another hour to reach the ticket counter. Where the agent seemed to be gloating.

'One for Goa.'

'Class?'

'First, please.'

'A/C class?'

'A.'

The agent stared.

'When does that leave?'

'Ten minutes. Nine-twenty.'

'And arrives?'

'Madgaon, half past eight.'

'Jesus. What is that, eleven hours?'

The agent roared with laughter. 'Half past eight tomorrow!'

'So nearly twenty-four hours, you're saying.'

'Sir! Tomorrow *evening*.'

'Good sweet lord.'

The agent's head wobbled.

'Fine,' said Matt, thrusting a fistful of bills under the glass. 'Just give me the most expensive ticket.'

'Most?'

'Yes!'

'Not paying now.' The guy ducked away and returned with a form. 'First fill please.'

'What's this?'

'Request form for ticket.'

'But . . . I just told you what ticket I want.'

'Fine. Must first fill form.'

Matt resisted an urge to smash the glass and rake that haughty grin through the shards. 'You have a pen?'

'No sir.'

'Then?'

'Pens you may purchase at kiosk.'

'And then? Line up again?'

Wobble. Smile.

'Are you kidding me? But that'll take another hour!' Matt checked his watch. 'And I'll miss this train! When's the next one?'

'Eleven a.m. Must hurry.' The agent looked past him. 'Next!'

Racism, thought Matt, stalking across the departures hall to the gift shop. Or some postcolonial payback. He'd seen *Gandhi*. He knew retribution was fair—what with those folks gunned down in that courtyard and the whole salt ordeal—but he was a far cry from some twirly moustachioed dandy whipping coolies with a switch. His family was Canadian as far back as it went! And Canadians were *good*. Given the chance, Matt could do good here. His whole plan to beat up rapists, e.g., and the business with the Russians. Why was India foiling him at every turn?

From a little bin in the train station gift shop he selected a pen and was charged some arbitrary, exorbitant fee by the shopkeeper. Finding it nearly dry of ink as he scratched out his travel details on the form, the ever-present muddle of jetlag and weed deprivation fogging the edges of things, Matt stood back and took stock.

He was still letting India happen to him. This wasn't his way. Nope! Life was the thing you bent over and held by the earlobes and rogered like a champ. You kicked life in the guts or clutched it fast and smooched it hard lip-wise. You made memories out of your days—or you went forgotten.

So he shouldered his way to the wicket, slapped down the form and snarled, 'There you go, bro. Now fire off my frigging ticket.'

It was printed in silence. No head wobbles, no grin. Just a dead stare from the agent and a faint scuffling among the old folks and invalids Matt had plowed through in line.

Ticket in hand, Matt check his phone: 9:30. Ninety minutes to kill. And he would frigging murder them.

First he'd eat something—anything he wanted. There were food stalls outside: one guy stuffing oversized Rice Krispies with Bits & Bites and some pesto-looking sauce, another hawking chips and bottled drinks, another stacking phosphorescent pretzelish things on newsprint. Delhi belly be damned; Matt would not be bullied by it or Ash or anyone. This trip was *his*. It was time to make some goshdang memories of his own.

But after scarfing a pair of samosas piping hot and grease-drenched from the fryer, it wasn't even ten yet. And the train station didn't offer much in the way of adventures. So he found a phone booth.

Ash answered, his voice stiff with indifference until Matt filled him in on his previous night's adventures.

'The *mob*?'

'The Russian mob, bro.'

'In Delhi? I've never heard of anything like that before. You're sure?'

'Yeah, so I'm cutting town because, frig, what if they come after me?'

'Right. What if.'

'This girl though, Dhar . . . Man. I could tell we really had something, you know?'

'Which one is this, the prostitute or the lesbian? The one you're fleeing or chasing?'

'Hey, you know these phone booths are called STDs?'

'Subscriber Trunk Dialling, genius.'

'Sexually Transmitted Dialling. You punch out numbers with your knob. Just make sure you wear a condom!'

'Stop it.'

'Hey, I ate some street food. Was that bad?'

'I thought I told you not to do that.'

'What's the worst that could happen? I can handle the scoots. I'll just hang my rump over the train tracks like everybody else. You seen this? Bunch of guys just dropping deuces right off the platform. And then they go snuggle in the park. What a country!'

'Anyway.' Ash's sigh was full of melodrama and dismissal. 'The worst thing I've ever heard of from food in India is a brain parasite. But that was from raw vegetables, likely washed in dirty water.'

'A brain what?'

'Parasite. Happened to a cousin. At first they thought she was having a stroke—migraines, slurred speech, amnesia, seizures. Took ages to figure out what was wrong. She's okay now, though not exactly back to normal. Kind of . . . touched.'

'Seizures? I've got a headache! Figured it was jetlag but—'

'You sure that isn't just THC withdrawal?'

'What if it's not? What if I start seizuring all over the place and chew my tongue off or smash my head on the curb and get run over by a camel stampede? Or the Russians find me passed out on the street and sell my organs to al-Qaeda?'

'Unlikely. Possible, but unlikely.'

'Possible? Honestly?'

'Considering all the crap you've put into your body over the years, that you might be taken down by a samosa? It's kind of beautiful, when you think about it.'

'If I get a brain parasite you are so dead when I get back.'

'If you get a brain parasite, I doubt I'll be the one worried about dying.'

'Well can you at least write this down? I need someone to tell my story if I don't make it home.'

'What am I, your secretary?'

'Whatever you want to call it, bro. You're the book guy. Not much point in making memories if there isn't some way to share them.'

———

ASH WAS RIGHT ABOUT ONE THING, at least. Who would have guessed that, with some Moscow syndicate hot on his heels, snacks would be Matt's undoing? Compared to a Mafia hit (drawn-and-quartered by elephants, for that particular South Asian flavour) the samosa had seemed so innocuous: glistening with oil, served in a little cardboard tray—and his doom Trojan-horsed along.

Before the train left Delhi, Matt, with a berth to himself, ignored the wallahs lugging steel cisterns ('Coffee!' 'Chai!' 'Tomato soup!') up the aisle. Though after they disembarked he wondered if filling his stomach might neutralize the parasite en route to his brain. So at the next station-stop he was on the lookout for grub—chips, a Kit Kat, something pre-packaged and safe. The doors clattered open; passengers bundled out and others bundled in. The brakes hissed. Silence. Matt waited for the touts to board. Instead, someone down the far end of the car began singing.

He sat up.

The voice was heartbreaking: at once jubilant and doleful, full and fragile. It was the warbling love-cry of a hurt bird, the siren song of some beach-stranded mermaid. Who was making this song—a woman, a boy, some Rajasthani castrato? The high notes threatened to crack, as if they pained the singer to the verge of collapse.

Matt felt desperate. He was too alone for something this haunting, this beautiful. He thought to run to another berth— 'Listen! Listen!' But he didn't dare move for fear of wrecking the spell. Matt tilted his head into the aisle. Shuffling up the car with weary grace was—impossible—a *man*. Khakis and flip-flops; bald spot and beard. A man! What angel was he channelling? What did the words mean? Something tragic. An elegy for the guy's family, starved to death: kids dead, woman dead—the blues, the blues.

The singer was now a half-dozen berths away. Matt dug out his wallet and readied a hundred rupees. He watched the guy approach, stocky and mincing. Yet his eyes were wide with mystery, as if possessed by some spirit calling from the ether. Now four berths away. Matt added a thousand rupee note. Not enough. So, another. Pocket change to Matt, it'd buy the singer rice for a year. It'd make him happy. It would save him. It would make a fine, fine memory for everyone involved.

A steamy hoot sounded from the head of the train. A clack from the tracks. The singer went silent. It was as if a mask had been flung off: *like that* he transformed into any nameless face thronging the streets of Delhi. And it was this man, this mortal, who ducked out the doors as they closed. The train pulled away. Off they went. Matt sat back and tried to recall the song. Only a faint sense of it remained, like the tenor, but not the details, of an interrupted dream.

A couple came up the aisle and arranged their baggage under the bunk opposite Matt. Before he could ask about the singer (*Had it really happened?*) they had organized themselves for sleep: pillows, blankets, heads tilted back, eyelids swiftly shuttered like windows for a storm. Within seconds they were snoring in chorus.

The light outside was turning richer. Evening approached. The train chugged south through farmland and villages. Matt nodded off. An hour or so later he woke to dusklight and palm trees and his berth-mates slopping curries around tin plates with their fingers. The smells were pungent; Matt's stomach grumbled and rolled. But Indian food was dangerous. The slightest nibble might hasten his demise.

'Would you like some?' said the woman, gesturing at the spread. She looked to be in her fifties—matronly, with a kind and open face. 'Please. Go ahead.'

The offerings ranged from an off-yellow goo to a lumpy brown sludge. 'Looks fantastic,' said Matt, 'but honestly I'm okay, thanks.'

His stomach cried out in protest.

The woman's husband grunted something at her in their language. He was lean and long, dressed in crisp white pyjamas, with big square glasses perched upon a beakish nose. His wife replied, gestured at Matt, seemed to be indicating his size. The husband belched and returned to his meal.

Here was the next stop: Gwalior. Matt had a fistful of money ready as the local caterers came aboard. After passing up dishes similar in odour and consistency to that of his seatmates, Matt was delighted to discover a guy selling boxed sandwiches at thirty rupees a pop. He took a huge bite—and was shocked by a vegetal crunch. He opened the sandwich to discover a green layer secreted between the cheese and bread. If the samosa didn't take him down, this surely would: cucumber.

India!

Matt held his breath, closed his eyes, tried to sense if he could feel anything wormy swimming in his guts. Should he barf? (In his boozier days a finger down the throat had been a weekly manoeuvre.) Yet the hygienic implications of kneeling at the train's shit-splattered cistern—a hole in the floor, the tracks coasting by beneath—negated the benefits of puking. And maybe the sandwich was feeding the parasite. Why upchuck the very stuff preventing death from venturing skullward?

He eyed the couple slurping at their fingers. Maybe Indians carried some sort of brain-bug anti-venom?

'So,' said Matt, 'heading to Goa?'

'Goa, no,' said the woman.

The man's eyes narrowed. 'You are going to Goa?'

'That's the plan.'

'Quite a distance! Over two thousand km.'

'Is it that far? They told me two days . . .'

'You are American,' the woman said eagerly.

'Canadian.' Matt indicated the flag stapled to his backpack, yet to be acknowledged by anyone.

'We are Indian,' she said.

'Visiting our son in Madhya Pradesh,' said her husband. 'He works in IT. Many changes coming to India, even in these backward places. What is it you do? In Canada.'

'Currently? I'm in school—'

'Ah, yes. Studying. At McGill University?'

'No. No, at a college—'

'Queen's University. Very good medical school.'

'No, it's out West. In British Columbia? Though we have to do anatomy and all that, it's sort of like med school. I'm on a break. To travel. To . . . see your country.'

This seemed to please the woman: she smiled approvingly.

'I wanted to ask,' said Matt, leaning forward, lowering his voice. 'I just ate something that might have not been washed properly. Or washed, but in *dirty water*.'

'You will have diarrhoea,' announced the man.

'No. No, that's not it.'

'You will vomit.'

'No! Though do you think I should?'

'This is what happens to you westerners—Brits, Americans.'

'Canadian.'

'Delhi Belly,' said the woman.

'Delhi Belly,' agreed her husband. And the two of them sat back, nodding like judges who'd passed a particularly satisfying verdict.

'Not Delhi Belly!' Matt's sudden surge in volume made them jump. 'Sorry. Just, I heard you can get a parasite in your brain. From veggies. Anything raw.'

'Preposterous,' said the man. 'No such thing.'

'But—'

The man waved him off and reached into his pocket. For medicine, Matt hoped, the magic antidote. Instead he produced a pack of cards. 'Gin rummy. Come, we will play.'

For the next three hours Matt played cards with the man, Doctor Joshi, and his wife, Mira. The train rocketed along as evening ceded to night, their travel halted intermittently by some palely lit backwoods station. Though they never quite stopped, just slowed alongside the platform and then eased out again into the dark.

Doctor Joshi's play was ruthless, cunning, each trick laid down with a crisp, smug flourish. Mira kept score in a little notebook. Soon, Doctor Joshi was up four hundred points. Was his wife passing him cards, or sabotaging Matt in some sly eastern way?

Though maybe the secret was in Doctor Joshi's shuffling: a fat wedge repositioned twice to the top of the deck before he'd proceed to 'distribute.' So Matt got more or less the same cards every time, and like a fool he kept chasing runs and sets, only to discover Mira withholding his missing matches when her husband displayed another winning hand. Their conversation, meanwhile, consisted of long silences interpolated with Doctor Joshi volleying questions at Matt and then ignoring his answers.

Finally, Doctor Joshi reached the appointed thousand-point mark, swept up the cards, offered Matt a limp handshake, and pocketed the deck. Out the window, amid the blackness a serrated horizon suggested mountains or trees.

'Where are we?' said Matt.

'The south,' said Doctor Joshi.

'Is that where you're from?'

'From, no,' said Mira. 'From Gujarat.'

'Is that near Kashmir?'

'Not so close,' laughed Doctor Joshi. 'How do you know Kashmir?'

'My buddy's from there. Or his dad is anyway.'

Doctor Joshi asked Ash's surname and rolled his eyes. 'All Kashmiris are "Kaul" or "Dhar." It is like your American "Smith."'

'Canadian.' Matt waited; no response. 'Have you been to Kashmir?'

'We used to go every year,' said Mira. 'Very beautiful.'

'A paradise on earth,' confirmed Doctor Joshi. Then his mood soured. 'But now these bloody Muslims have ruined it.'

'I'm pretty sure my buddy's family are Hindu,' said Matt. 'Or were.'

'*Were?* Not *were.* We are Hindus or we are not. He is a Pandit, your friend?'

'Uh. He's got his own radio show, if that's what you mean?'

But Doctor Joshi's attentions had fled. When he spoke it was through gritted teeth, peering out the window and appraising the countryside—or the whole nation—as it went slipping dimly by. 'Since times immemorial these Muslims have caused trouble. First they invaded India, fifteenth century; it was a bloodbath. They beat their women, they thieve, they wreak terror upon the globe, and yet we allow them in our government, to run a secular country. A secular country, mind, yet still we have communal violence.'

'Oh, they're not *all* bad,' said Matt, grinning. But when he looked to Mira for support she shook her head.

'Can you show one Muslim country where Hindus are extended the special rights accorded Muslims in India? Can you show one country where the seven-eighths majority craves the indulgence of the one-eighths minority? Can you show one Muslim country which has a non-Muslim as its President or Prime Minister? In Maharashtra they have elected a Muslim as Chief Minister. Can you imagine a Hindu CM of J&K State?'

'Um.'

'In last fifty years, Muslim population of India has increased from ten percent to? Fourteen! Whereas Hindu population has sunk to less than eighty-five percent. If Hindus are intolerant, why is Islam thriving? Where are the missing Hindus? *Do Hindus have human rights?*'

Doctor Joshi had transformed. His voice trembled with rage.

White froth collected at the corners of his lips. And still he hadn't looked at Matt, staring out the window into the darkness. What did he see out there?

'No one talks of the ethnic cleansing of four lakh Hindus from Kashmir,' he continued. 'Why are Pandits denied same minority rights afforded Muslims everywhere else in India? Haj pilgrims are given subsidy, yet Hindu pilgrims to Amarnath are taxed!'

'Amarnath?'

'Amarnath pilgrimage.'

'I know, I know!' Matt smacked Joshi's knee. 'Shiva's . . . ice . . . what have you.'

'What does your friend Pandit Dhar think of all this?'

'Amarnath?'

'The ethnic cleansing of Kashmir!'

'Ethnic cleansing? Definitely against it.'

At last Doctor Joshi turned from the window. He examined Matt as he might a specimen under a microscope.

'So, hey,' said Matt, 'Amarnath. Have you done the pilgrimage?'

'Every year, as I said. Not whilst the embargo, but we will return summer next.'

'Really!' Matt quizzed the Joshis on their route, how long the hike took, the ratio of women to men, what the women wore, the sleeping arrangements. 'And, sorry, last thing: the lingam. What's it like?'

'This is one of the holiest sites in all of India.'

'So I hear. But the *lingam*. Tell me about it.'

'What do you wish to know?'

'Like, what do you get out of seeing it?'

'Get?'

'Like, after. Do you feel . . . better?'

'Why else would one lakh Hindus hike for days into Himalayas? Do you think it is some silly jaunt only?'

'Not for tourists,' murmured Mira.

'No!' yelled Doctor Joshi, thrusting a finger at Matt. 'This is not Goa or Shimla or wherever else you Americans—'

'For the last frigging time: I'm *Canadian!*'

'Canadian, American, same thing.'

'No. It's not the same thing! And don't point at me. I'll toss you out the window of this train and not think a goshdang thing of it.'

Doctor Joshi's expression clouded.

'And another thing? Being Irish I know a little about religions killing one another and let's just say it takes two to tango. Or riverdance, or whatever.'

'I thought you are Canadian?'

'My mom was a quarter Irish!' Matt affected a Gaelic lilt. 'Anyway, that's not the point. That was some racist stuff you said. Take it back.'

'Pardon me?'

'Take it back. What you said about Muslims.'

'Take it . . . back?'

Matt stood. His head grazed the ceiling. 'My girlfriend's Muslim,' Matt said, his brain scrambling through his sexual history: at some point, even for an hour, this must have been true. There had once been an Egyptian—did she count?

Mira whispered to her husband. He began collecting their luggage. 'We will be leaving now,' said Doctor Joshi. 'Pardon me, sir. I don't appreciate you threatening my wife.'

'Your *wife*? This isn't about her, you dummy. You barely let her get a word in!'

But they were already slipping past, suitcases in hand.

Matt sank back onto his seat, the vinyl puffing—so much like a sigh. The train galloped along. His brain called feebly, like a child from the bottom of a well, for weed. (*For weed!*) Outside the darkness was absolute. No moon, no stars. Matt could see nothing in the window save his own reflection: the pale dome of his head and the twin black punctures of his eyes, into which poured the night.

⟨⟨❦⟩⟩

AFTER HANGING UP ON MATT, Ash thrashed around, flipped his pillow, kicked his feet free from the sheets, wrapped himself again. The hour crept from two to three, and into those dead hours before dawn. What was Matt doing in India? His presence there felt like an invasion. Ash pictured him blundering around the country in slapstick, leaving a trail of destruction: villages in flames, women in tears, men with broken ribs—from a punch, from an overeager embrace.

At just after four Ash rose and opened his computer. No emails, and the internet's infinitude felt exhausting in the wrong way. So he fired up Word. Why? He was no writer. He sat there, staring at the screen. And then an idea struck him. He took out Brij's novel and placed it beside the keyboard. He titled the document, half ironically, *The Patrimony*—his great inheritance—saved it to the desktop, and began to copy the thing, word-for-word, into his computer.

> Toward the base of the mountain the hero proceeded, with thoughts of how he might be saved, and with each thought his strides lengthened, became stronger, he moved with purpose, there was no stopping him now. He could not yet see high above his goal but knew it was there. And as he began to ascend now and the terrain rose, he grabbed a crag of rock and hauled himself up and felt the gnarled rock warmed by the sun, and felt a slight burn in his calves as they pushed off below and he scrabbled up the little ridge. And then he was atop this boulder and stood and turned and looked back to the village where he had spent the night before, that little cluster of flat-roofed huts, only a few hundred yards below, he had not come far but he had come and every step brought him closer to glory.

Ash hadn't intended all this typing to be much more than a mechanical and mindless task to numb his brain. So he was surprised to find each transcribed line glowing from the computer with something like potential. Two pages in, he stopped to get a glass of water, and when he returned the cursor seemed to blink with the eager opening and closing of a baby bird's beak, summoning more words. Ash continued until his eyelids began to sag, his head to dip. He closed the laptop and rolled into bed and lay there with the book's voice replacing his thoughts, talking him to sleep. Toward dawn he dreamt of climbing a mountain—after something or someone, he couldn't say.

AT TEN THE NEXT MORNING Ash woke to a commotion upstairs. Burt was yelping and tearing around the living room, nails clattering on the hardwood. His sister must have arrived, no doubt towing her invasive species of a husband. Grudgingly, Ash headed up and discovered his mom hugging Mona at the front door—his sister alone, her pregnancy swelling her coat. No sign of Harj.

'Hello, brother.' Fresh tears stained Mona's cheeks.

Ash stared: that nose-mining bastard had *done something*.

'Everyone's here,' said their mom, as if taking attendance, 'just as I'm heading out the door! Rick's already at the arena setting up our table . . . You two okay on your own?'

'Why?' said Ash. 'Do you think we need a babysitter?'

'Oh, quiet, you.' She swatted at him. 'I feel bad! Here you kids are, both home for Christmas, and I'm not even here to host you. There's food in the fridge if you're hungry. We'll be home sixish. Wish me luck! Bye-bye!'

'*Kids*,' Mona laughed when she was gone, and knelt on the floor with Burt. 'Kisses,' she commanded and presented her cheek. Obediently he gave her a lick. 'At least somebody loves me,' she sighed. And looked up at Ash.

'Have you eaten?' he said, wheeling into the kitchen. 'Want something?'

'Depends. Too early for a grilled cheese?'

'Cut into triangles?'

'With Patak's, please.'

'Indian style! But does Mom have—'

Mona was a step ahead: from her purse she produced a jar of lime pickle.

'You carry that around?'

'Always come prepared,' she said, and shrugged, and laughed.

Kraft Singles and Wonderbread had been embargoed so Ash had to play it fancy with sheep cheddar and sourdough. And he felt a little surge of pride, however ridiculous, that the sandwich he presented to Mona was toasted a platonic golden-brown. She opened it to spoon in some pickle and the cheese fanned in molten filaments.

His own sandwich he burned.

Mona slid her plate at him. 'Take half of mine.'

'No, I have to endure this one,' said Ash, scraping the charred toast with his knife. 'It's my punishment.'

'For what?'

He laughed. 'For everything.'

'Oh shut up and just split it with me. We'll suffer equally, it's less lonely that way.'

They traded sandwich halves and ate. Burt prowled under the table for crumbs, occasionally emerging for a snuffle between Ash's legs.

'Hey,' said Mona. 'Do you think Rick and Ma ever act out that scene from *Ghost*? You know, where he comes up behind her at the wheel and—'

Ash nearly choked. 'For god's sake!'

'No?'

'The last thing I want to think about is . . . that.'

'Your mother being intimate, you mean? *Making love?*'

'Mona!'

This was an old game, big sister mortifying little brother. He'd not seen this side of her in ages; her eyes sparkled.

'I wonder,' she whispered, 'if Rick makes a *private line* of leather-wear. You know, assless chaps and one of those masks with a zipper for a mouth? For special moments.'

'Stop it, seriously. You sound like Matt.'

'Ouch! Low blow!'

'You do. You both live for terrorizing me.'

'Except he's an actual terrorist.' She spread a little more pickle onto a final bite of bread. 'Did he end up going to India?'

'Just heard from him. Goa.'

'Raving?'

'Ranting and raving, more like.' Ash eyed their empty plates. 'Another?'

'You know me too well.' She rubbed her belly. 'Though at least now I can blame this little guy for my appetite.'

'You know the gender?' Ash laid out four slices of bread.

'No, no . . . God, I hope it's not a boy. Especially if he takes after his dad.'

An opening. Carving pats of butter into the pan, all Ash said was, 'Yeah."

'So Ma didn't tell you Harj wasn't coming?'

'No,' he said, slicing cheese. 'Though I got in pretty late last night.'

'So she probably didn't mention, either, that my idiot husband picked my second trimester to start sleeping around over there in Turkey.'

Ash turned, knife in his fist. 'That piece of shit!'

'With, get this: a Swedish nurse.'

At their wedding Ash had welcomed Harj to the family as a 'brother.' And signed his online petitions against whatever tyrannical regime, and tolerated his self-aggrandizing moral one-upmanship and disgusting habits and insipid, passive-aggressive slights, and, for Mona's sake, never, despite several flaming urges, punched him in the face.

'Swedish nurse, Swedish nurse. It could be a round.' Mona bungled the tune of 'Frère Jacques': '*Harj the jerk, Harj the jerk . . . perving on . . . a Swedish Nurse.*'

'Are you sure?'

'Ash, I found *photos*. In his email. But before you go judging me it was because there was some tax stuff with the will that needed dealing with right away, and I'd written to him and didn't hear anything for a couple days, and I know how hectic things in those camps must be but I wanted to make sure he'd got the message . . . So, anyway, I checked to see if he'd read it. And then: ta-da!'

'I'm not judging you.' Ash hoped this was enough to keep her going. His sister hadn't opened up like this to him in years.

'In her nurse's outfit, can you believe it? Swedish or not, how cliché can you get?'

'What are you going to do? Does he know that you know?'

'No. He's in the middle of a war zone and has lives to save. The last thing he needs is me telling him off.' Typical Mona, burying her pain under practicality, the affair reframed as a logistical inconvenience. 'Anyway,' she continued, 'I told him to stay there for Christmas and we'll talk after. Too ominous?'

Ash swirled the melting butter around the pan.

'If you're keeping score,' said Mona, 'within two months I blow my first big case, my dad dies, and my husband cheats on me. I wonder what's in store for the spring?'

'These things only happen in threes,' said Ash feebly.

'What's this about you losing your job?'

'I didn't *lose* it. Just . . . taking a leave. Or been asked to take a leave.' He stacked the bread and cheese and moved it to the stovetop. 'Or put on leave, I suppose.'

'Shitty.'

The sandwiches sizzled. Ash poked them around, flipped them, then split them in two with the spatula. They ate in silence and when they were done Mona cleared their plates. Ash watched his sister at the sink. A slight hunch to her shoulders struck him as wounded. But then she straightened and announced that she was heading to the gym.

So Ash descended to the basement to 'work,' i.e. troll the internet for news of himself. Matt's alleged video had yet to surface, though Ash did track down a few speculations posted to bookish forums about his leave from the radio, however that news had leaked. His favourite: *Big coke problem I heard from a reliable source*. Ash had never done cocaine in his life, and wondered who this imaginative—or imaginary—'source' might be. Under the handle BigMatt he replied, *Hookers too I heard. Huge misogynist.*

But he wasn't erased quite yet. The following night was the airdate for his botched Behemoth interview, which Sherene would have been forced to whittle shipshape. It would be good to hear himself, to confirm his existence. But that was a whole day away. Ash closed the browser, revealing his dad's novel open in Word. The hero had reached a plateau. With nothing else to do, Ash resumed his transcription.

> And below the world spread out in all its glory, the green valley, the trees, the gurgling brook, the village far below, and the hero took it all in, breathing the clean sweet air. But his goal still loomed above. So he took to climbing again. Up toward it went the hero with the song of longing in his heart, each step then the next ever closer to the end.

Always 'his goal,' 'it,' 'the end.' So vague, the answer to a question never asked. If this really were Amarnath, the story provided no sense of impending spiritual awakening or edification or what would be achieved on the mountaintop. Ash was reminded of that adage: *the journey, not the destination.* Except the journey in Brij's story seemed futile, the destination elusive. Maybe this was the point: a novel about the unachievable, the unobtainable, and what forever might lie just beyond reach.

ASH EMERGED AT DINNERTIME, joining his sister and mom and Rick for a meal of quinoa-based sludge and mixed shrubbery, then retreated again to the basement. At just before nine, pages from the end of Brij's manuscript, a knock came at the door.

Ash froze.

His sister peeked in: 'Still up?'

He slammed the laptop shut. 'Just doing some work.'

'Not watching porn.'

'No!'

'Then why the panic?' Mona chuckled. 'Anyway, I want to show you something. Once you've, you know, cleaned up your desktop or whatever.'

'Mona! I was working!'

'Whatever. It's your business. You're an adult.'

'You leave now.'

'Aw. Come on, little brother. You're going to like this.'

From behind her back she produced a VHS tape, the spine magic markered with their mother's neat, square printing: XMAS 1984.

'No way,' said Ash, following his sister into the basement den. He sat while Mona put the tape in. 'Where did you find it?'

'Remember how I talked for years about having it digitized? Never got around to it. It's been sitting in my closet the whole time.'

She joined him on the couch and hit play on the remote. As the TV crackled to life Burt came slinking downstairs and, after his attempt to mount Ash was rebuffed, curled up between them with a grunt.

The video opened with shadows and jostling before focusing on the kitchen floor. From behind the camera Brij spoke: *Is it on, Ash? I don't know if it's working.* And then a little boy's voice, shrill as a whistle: *All systems operational!*

'Such a nerd, even then,' said Mona.

Ash kicked her gently; the dog growled.

The camera swung up: Ash, six years old, standing in the hallway. Reporters' stance, shampoo bottle microphone. *This is your correspondent Ash Dhar coming to you live from Christmas. There are reports that Mona's already opening presents. Let's go find out!* And he shambled out of frame with an ease that his adult self, watching, wished were still his own.

'You little shit-disturber,' said Mona. 'Trying to get me in trouble.'

'Let me watch!'

They found Mona reading in a chair beside the fireplace, Christmas tree twinkling in the background—presents untouched. *Say hello,* said her father. *You're on film.* She turned a page, didn't look up.

'How old are you there? Eight?' said Ash. 'So serious.'

'Just trying to have some private time away from you lunatics, probably.'

Ash's kid-version summoned the camera into the kitchen. Searching that cheerful face for some echo was like stargazing, that fanciful project of forging pictures out of dots a million miles apart—and long dead.

*Mona's reading,* the kid on TV whispered. *Interrupt her and feel the wrath.*

'The wrath,' said Ash. 'Hilarious.'

'Hilarious until you felt it. You want a reminder? Maybe an Indian burn?'

'Wait, is it over?'

The image had turned garbled. Eventually things wobbled into place and the next episode began. To the blasts and bleeps of

Herbie Hancock's 'Rockit,' Ash and Mona were dancing before the Christmas tree. In a recliner sat their mother, rapt. The kids were wearing pyjamas. Outside it was night.

Ash dove into the Worm and undulated across the floor. Mona escaped her glass box to writhe on the rug like something larval and sick. Ash's attempt at a handstand was interrupted by Brij—*Get down, idiot! That's dangerous!* For their finale they linked hands: an Electric Shock rippled through Mona's body to Ash, who passed it back, flapping his arms like a flightless, convulsive bird. Back it came, back it went.

'Did we practice that?' said Ash. 'Or is this improv?'

'You don't remember? We rehearsed for ages before telling Brij to turn on the camera. I mean, we're making a *music video* here—you think we'd just go in without a routine? You even had a plan to make copies and sell them on the street.'

The number ended. Applause from their mother. Bows. Then Brij's voice intervened: 'Okay, that's enough of that.' And the video cut to black, then static.

'That's it?' said Ash.

Mona frowned. 'I'd have sworn there was a scene of us opening presents.' She fast-forwarded through blank tape. 'Do you think it got erased?'

'It's possible. Magnets, maybe?'

'That sucks.'

'Where'd Brij even get the camera?'

'Dave,' says Mona. 'You don't remember Dave?'

'Vaguely,' Ash lied.

'Oh my god.' She sat up. 'He was this hippie who did his PhD with Ma. He lived in a trailer. We went over there once, and you went inside to use the bathroom and—this is so gross and hilarious—his bedroom had a mirrored ceiling and a waterbed and a swing, and Ma found you on it screaming, "I'm a swinger like Dave!"'

'No.'

'Yes, little brother.'

'I must have got that from Brij. Can't you just hear him, all grumpy and dismissive? "That bloody swinger friend of yours."'

'God, let's hope it was dismissive.'

'What do you mean?'

Mona tucked her feet under Burt. 'What if he and Mom were into swapping too?'

'Stop.'

'Imagine?'

'No I will not fucking *imagine*. You're sick.'

'Who knows what other movies got made with that camera?' She nodded at the static on screen. 'We should keep watching and find out.'

Ash reached for the remote; his sister snatched it away. Burt groaned and slid off the couch to the floor.

Mona sat back, curled her knees to her chest. 'Didn't we look like a real family then?'

'Are we a fake family now?'

'We were just so happy. Like there's only good in the future.' She turned off the TV. 'It's sad how much can go wrong.'

Ash thought of that loose, shambly way he'd had as a kid, so full of love and light.

Mona continued: 'Part of me wants to go back and warn those kids, "Life is going to be hard. Life is going to beat the fucking shit out of you at every turn." But then another part of me thinks, isn't it better to be like that? So blissful and oblivious? That there's just *now*, and now is good, and each next moment could only be as good as this one.'

'Yeah.'

'And *now*-now, check it out.' She polished her belly as if it were a crystal ball. 'Think of all the sadness this person is going to go through. And so much of it will be my fault.'

'Oh come on,' said Ash. 'There'll be tons of good stuff too.'

'Doesn't that make it worse?'

'No way.' A chance to bolster his sister's spirits, even against his instincts. 'The happiness of those kids has to still be in us somewhere. Which . . . is a good thing to realize, hiding away in my mom's basement with my life collapsing around me.'

'Well, our dad did just die.'

Ash's throat tightened. 'He did.'

'And my shit-bag husband is humping Swedish nurses.'

'Right. And there's that.'

'And you might have lost your job.'

'Temporarily.'

'Say it.'

'But—'

'*Say it.*'

Ash gathered a breath. 'I might have lost my job.'

'Because you're an asshole.'

'Because I acted like an asshole.'

'*Are* an asshole.'

'I'm an asshole, fine. Happy?'

'And now here we are.'

'And now here we are!'

'At our mom's house.'

'At our mom's house. With Rick.'

Mona snorted. 'Oh, Rick. Rick and his leatherwork.'

'Easy now. Rick's an artist. An *artiste*, even.'

Mona buried her laughter in a pillow. 'And tomorrow's Christmas Eve.'

Ash smiled. 'Oh, wow. I nearly forgot. And then it's Christmas.'

'And that's not so bad, is it? To be home for Christmas?'

'I believe there's a song about such a thing. *You can count on me*, and so on.'

'Even if we're Hindu. I mean, tenuously.'

'Ha!'

Ash sensed his sister watching him intently from the other end of the couch, hugging her knees. There was something imploring in her eyes. He thought of them passing the shockwave up and down the line: big sister to little brother—and back. Mona's face, so focused; his own alive with joy. And yet such harmony between them.

What could Ash say or do now?

He hoped that sitting there together in the dark, with the TV off and the dog snoring gently at their feet, might be enough.

**3**

WITH NO CALLS FROM INDIA having woken him the night before, Ash lay in bed the next morning speculating on Matt's first night in Goa. He pictured the big man arriving after dark and, having failed to book a hotel, rolling shirtless down to some beachfront rave, moshing his way into the great unwashed, pounding drinks and whatever drugs came his way, obliterating his senses, seducing a potential sexual partner with the dance-floor forays of a walrus flopping about on dry land; then, later, a moonlight stroll down the beach, his voice turned soft, a pause, a hand ruffling her dread-locks, some possibly genuine profession of love—for Matt, acting was the same as being—and a skirt hitched and a fly unzipped and a wet spot left in the sand.

And then? A desperate run into town, wild-eyed and frantic, convinced he'd contracted some infection. Finding the streets clotted with Russians, Matt would abandon his hunt for an antidote to cower in the shadows. Any pale face could be a mob informant or lackey, he'd think. Or worse: an assassin.

He'd seek refuge. He'd seek, probably, Mieke—his *real* true love. He'd text her madly. Maybe call her too, his voicemails choked with fear and loathing and the searing shame of a hangover. But it was eight in the morning; she was sleeping; he'd have to find her on foot. So he'd begin a covert search of the hostels, whose signage was not just Hindi and English—but Russian too. (They'd not just infiltrated this place; they'd colonized it!)

Still he'd enter one, stealthily, the brim of his cap pulled down, through a lobby decorated in yuletide fashion (albeit, Ash imagined, with a Desi flavour: the tinsel bushy, the lights pulsing with funhouse urgency, the Christmas tree fashioned from a broomstick and palm fronds and tape) to inquire at the desk after Mieke.

Ash pictured the concierge eyeing him with suspicion. 'Surname?'

'No idea. She's from Holland though?'

'We have many Dutch visitors.'

'About yay big, short hair, brown eyes . . . No? Nothing?'

'You describe half the tourists in Goa! Dutch, French, Israeli . . . Russian.'

'Russian,' Matt would whisper, and hitch his backpack and flee to the street.

Lost in the fantasy, Ash could see it all: the city roiled. The air was damp and thick and people seethed in it like plankton through tropical seas. Matt was swept into a market. Hawkers hawked and shoppers shopped and Matt danced between carts heaped with spices and fruit and vegetables and caged clucking chickens and here was a man lopping the tops of coconuts and dogs skittered this way and that or lay coiled under great hulking trees that sprouted from the cement. Matt stopped to pay a lean, leering man to hack a half-dozen bananas from the bunch with a scythe. These he ate on the move, dropping each peel behind him to slip up potential stalkers. (Booby traps!)

Three more hostels yielded no luck either—nor vacancies, another worry: once again, he'd nowhere to sleep. The afternoon slipped into evening; the light turned smoky, the crowds thinned, Matt's belly grumbled and rolled. Another day was vanishing with nothing to account for it. No stories to tell, no memories made, no momentum heading into the night. And what day was it? He'd lost all sense of time. Maybe some other, realer version of himself was only now boarding his flight to Delhi. Or else maybe back home, in the future, he was already recounting the trip's adventures to Ash over bong-hits and beers. Matt would feel between existences. Gutted and tired and lost.

Though, would he? How could Ash guess what Matt might feel?

The fantasy dissolved.

Ash got out of bed and checked his email—nothing. Nothing on his phone either. So he opened up *The Patrimony*. Though the title struck him as inadequately singular. From that interrupted final line threaded infinite possibilities. So he renamed it *The Patrimonies*. (Was this a word? Could you earn multiple inheritances from the same dad? Or did it imply a squadron of dads, a flock? A dozen serious men in suits, say, cresting a hill with literal baggage—briefcases, of course, the carry-all of manhood.)

His neck snapped up; he'd drifted off. And continued transcribing where he'd left off.

> And closer still drew the hero to his goal, the cave and the darkness within, while the sun burned and beneath his feet the snow seemed to be turning, yes, to slush. Everything was melting. The birds sang a song of spring a happy

burble welcoming new life. It made the hero hurry. There was less time than he'd thought to reach, and so he quickened his step, through the slush, which soaked now his stockings.

Ash crossed out ~~stockings~~ and replaced it with *socks*. Re-read the paragraph: the edit seemed false. Changed it back. Read the bit again: yes, that was it. Archaic, strange. Only a few pages remained. So Ash kept typing, saving diligently as he went.

WHILE ASH AND MONA were finishing lunch (Chunky Soup she'd smuggled in her gym bag) the front door opened. 'Ho ho ho,' bellowed a bearded voice. 'Merry Christmas!'

Preceded by a coniferous scent, Rick appeared in the kitchen doorway lugging a Christmas tree. This he stood proudly on end as if presenting a fresh kill. From the backyard where Ash had banished him, Burt barked wildly.

'A tree,' said Mona.

'Things are slowing down at the fair so your mom sent me out. Such a cruel industry, poor creatures—whoops!' Rick bobbled his grip, caught the tree before it timbered into the kitchen. 'But she said it's what you all do here. So here we are!'

'If you need to get back,' said Mona, 'we'll be happy to put it up.'

'The decorations are in the garage, your mom said?'

'We're on it.'

This job, historically, was one that Mona performed solo. Ash's function was to fetch the base and ornaments and help screw in the trunk. Then he'd retire to the couch with a beer to have his decorating suggestions ignored.

'You actually going to help this time, little brother?' said Mona.

'As long as you don't boss me around,' said Ash. 'Big sis.'

Once they'd got the tree standing on its own and its branches began to droop, Mona wrapped the branches in tinsel while Ash unravelled the lights.

'Don't be so rough,' advised Mona. 'You break a bulb and the whole thing'll go out.'

'You act like I'm some sort of monster!'

'A subterranean one, these days. Nice to see you up for air.'

'Do you want me to help or not?'

'What are you doing down there in the basement, Ash?'

'Working!'

'Really. On what?'

He'd long been subjected to Mona's lawyerly equivocations of what he did for a living: admiration at his public achievements, but skepticism that reading and talking about books comprised actual *work*—at least compared to her eighty hour weeks where people's lives hung in the balance. But when, with the intention of chastening his sister, he told her, 'On Brij's book,' it felt mostly like an admission of guilt.

'Really!' Mona turned from the tree, peering at him with interest. 'So you *are* going to try to get it published?'

'No, no. Just typing it out.' From the box of ornaments, Ash removed sparkly globes and crystal snowdrops and porcelain reindeer, laying them out along the sofa. 'There's only the one paper copy, and if we lose it the whole thing's gone forever.'

'So you're not going to add anything? Like an ending?'

'Hey,' he said, digging a figurine from the bottom of the box. 'Look who it is.'

'Ganesh!'

As a twelve-year-old intent on reclaiming her Hindu roots, this was what Mona had insisted on using to top the family tree: six inches tall, lavishly painted, regal and holy and slurping something like raspberries from his elephant trunk.

'Wanna put it up?'

'I'll get the ladder,' said Mona, and headed out through the mudroom to the garage.

Left alone, Ash checked his phone: a message from Sherene that was just a line of question marks. Pocketed it again without replying. What to say? He had no words of his own for any-thing—not her, not his sister, not Brij's book. He imagined opening salvos to talk to Mona about Harj. Something about growing up with split parents—they'd managed, it hadn't been so bad . . .

Mona reappeared with the stepladder, Burt trailing at her heels. Ash presented her with the elephant god.

'Why don't you do the honours,' she said. 'Not sure I should be going up ladders with a bun in the oven.'

So with Mona and the dog looking on Ash climbed up, hooked Ganesh over a sprig of needles, and Hinduism lorded over Christmas.

THAT EVENING, as if in a '50s cola ad, Ash, Mona, their mother, Rick and Burt gathered around the tree, with the radio on in the background. The only thing missing was Santa plopping down the chimney—an image that inspired Ash to picture Matt as an old man stationed amid some Arctic food court diorama, beard grown out and frosty, hauling children onto his lap while he ogled their moms on the far side of the barricades.

At 10 p.m. promptly his mother turned up the volume on the radio. 'Quiet, everyone. Ashy's on!'

Here was the opening music: still the same, they hadn't changed that. But when it faded, instead of Ash a stranger wel-comed listeners from across the country.

'Who's that?' said Mona.

'I don't fucking know,' said Ash.

'Language,' said his mother.

The host's name was not one he recognized—not a producer

dumped before the mic, not some network personality subbing in, not even a famous moonlighting author. Sherene hadn't edited anything. Instead she'd simply replaced him with a nobody.

The impostor ran down the same intro that Ash had long ago pre-recorded about 'the year in books.' But after blasting through the major awards and the bestseller list she went rogue, switching to an unlikely topic: poetry.

'Holy shit,' said Ash. 'Sherene got a *poet?*'

'Watch your mouth,' said his mother.

'This is my show! And she put a poet on it! Do you know what these people are capable of? They're the literary Gestapo. They say things like "prosody" and "objective correlative" in mixed company. They spell "oh" without the h—but always with an exclamation mark. They *feud*. And they suffer. O! How they suffer.'

'Shush,' said his mother.

'Once a month, I get a letter—they write actual letters! on typewriters!—from one of these nut-jobs complaining that I never interview poets. Never mind that the show is *specifically* about the novel. Their persecution complex is out of this world.'

'So both persecuted and the Gestapo,' said Mona. 'Quite a combo.'

'Would you two please *shut up*,' said their mother.

Rick hauled Burt onto his lap, whispered something into his ear.

The poet was boasting about what a swell year it had been for poetry. She had a slippery voice, gooey as egg yolk. Accustomed to holding court before a feeble gathering of the elbow-patched and cat-haired, she was clearly luxuriating in having poached Ash's audience. How could Sherene have done this to him? They were meant to be friends!

'She's got a nice voice,' said Ash's mother. 'Very warm.'

'She sounds like a tool.'

'She sounds nice!'

'What's all this about *nice?* Was that my problem? I wasn't nice enough?'

'Your problem, Ashy,' said his mother, turning up the volume another click, 'is that you don't know when to shut your cake-hole and listen.'

So he listened.

The poet was introducing *Into the Night*, oozing on and on about what a 'moving' and 'powerful' book it was. How could she—a woman!—believe such things? It was all so phony and gross. At least Ash had possessed the gumption to stand up for what was right.

'Great to have you here,' said the poet.

'Always good to be back in Toronto,' said The Behemoth.

So they'd flown him in. As an apology, Ash expected. The ticket, the hotel, dinner: not cheap. This both pleased and mortified him. He thought about finally messaging Sherene, but his phone was in the kitchen. Besides, what would he say?

'Last time I saw you was at the Vancouver Festival,' said the host. 'Was that already two years ago now? God, time flies . . .'

'How are your kids?'

'University now, if you can believe it.'

'Wow.'

Cronies!

'So,' said the host, 'congratulations on the new book.'

'Congratulations on *yours*.'

And now they were flirting. Disgraceful!

'Let's talk about *Into the Night*. Such a brave book.'

'Thank you. Obviously this story took time to find the right form.'

'I want you to tell me about the characters.' Her voice was fairly melting. 'I want you to tell me about Hardwick. But first I want to talk about *you*.'

'She sounds like Oprah,' said Ash.

His mother smacked his leg. She and Rick leant toward the radio like plants guzzling sunlight. And Ash knew, then, that they'd both read that ridiculous book—and loved it. The conversation ebbed into the subdued murmurs of a therapy session, and at 10:30 the poet thanked The Behemoth and signed off for the year—as if she were responsible for the previous thirty episodes, as if it were her show!

Though perhaps now it was.

His mother turned off the radio. 'Very interesting,' she said. 'A shame, Ashy, that it wasn't you talking to him. But you have to admit it's quite a journey he's been on. So sad.'

'I do not,' snarled Ash, 'have to admit anything.'

Mona and her mother stood and, with a synchronicity that hinted at prearrangement, informed Rick that they would be taking Burt for his final walk of the night. Ash watched them head out, a kind of quiet melancholy between them that even the dog, suddenly subdued, seemed to respect. Halfway down the drive Mona slipped her arm into her mother's and set her head on her shoulder.

Then they were gone. From within all that beard Rick stared at Ash with—was it? Yes: ravenousness. 'Well, my man!' he yelled, eyes wide and wild. 'Just you and me.'

A proposition seemed imminent. It couldn't possibly be sexual, could it?

No, worse: 'You still play guitar?' Rick continued. 'You know any Bruce Cockburn? Because I've got my djembe here, be cool to jam.'

Ash stood; sorry, he had work to do. And fled at a gallop to the basement.

An email from Matt awaited him. Weird. The guy never wrote emails. Titled *MERRY XXXMASS!!!* it read like a tele-gram—or a street-corner, pantless rant:

BRO WOW HOLY SHIT CAN YOU BELIEVE I'M EMAILING YOU!!! ANYHOW JUST WANTED TO WISH YOU AND YRS HAPPY HOLIDAYS TO YOUR MOM AND EVERYONE AND KNOW THAT I'M THINKING OF YOU BRO!!! BRO HONESTLY ITS CRAZY IN INDIA!!! YOU DIDN'T TELL ME!!! THERES RUSSIANS PRETTY MUCH EVERYWHERE BUT I FOUND MIEKE BUT SHE'S NOT HERE IN ANJUNA SHE'S FURTHER UP THE COAST SO I'M TAKING A BUS IF YOU THINK THAT'S SAFE!!! WELL TOO LATE I'M TAKING IT ANYHOW HAHAHA!!! SO THAT'L BE MY CHRISTMAS THERE THO I BET YOU GUYS ARE HAVING TURKEY AND PRESENTS IN LONDON SO THINK OF ME!!! OK BRO JUST WANTED TO WISH YOU AND YRS HAPPY HOLIDAYS SO MERRY CHRISTMAS AND I HOPE THINGS ARE GOOD WITH YOU LITTLE BUDDY LOVE YR BEST PAL MATT!!!

MATT WAS FAMILIAR with makeshift Christmases. That winter he'd spent out in Whistler, while the rest of his ski team sucked hash from a bisected pop bottle he'd headed into the woods with a hacksaw and returned four hours later hauling a twenty-foot cedar like a carcass through the snow. Or years before that, when he and his mom had been invited to the Dhars': after too much mulled wine his mom had fled to the bathroom, hand to her mouth, and Matt had to crank the carols to drown out the roar of her pukes.

Christmas, generally, got Matt down. Too many expectations, too many ways to fail. His mom had tried hard for years, struggling on her crossing guard's salary to stuff his stocking (Snickers bars, Certs, Archie comics); though they never had a tree, one year she sprung for a Butterball she roasted to dust. 'At least we're together,' she'd said with a sad laugh, which had seemed to Matt a pretty meagre thing to celebrate—they were together all the time! What was the big deal about it now?

Which is to say the holidays weren't the primary thing on his mind on the three-hour bus-ride from Anjuna to the resort where Mieke was staying. Instead he imagined their reunion: him on his knees begging forgiveness, then the two of them seizing each other like something out of Bollywood and rolling around on the floor. After all, she owed him an apology, having stolen his ride and stuck him with the bill, plus cabfare home. But would she slap his face? Would he let her? Would that, maybe, be kind of hot, and lead to a release of passion and bodily fluids all over her room?

The bus was a rickety thing, clad with rust, the luggage slung up onto the roof and not tied down. For the first hour of the trip Matt kept checking the road behind them for his backpack tumbling loose and bouncing away. Driving here was less chaotic than Delhi, but still the bus weaved and pitched, and the horn was a steady pulse. The other passengers were unfazed, staring blankly ahead until their stop—though 'stop' was a generous term for the bus slowing to a crawl and whoever's luggage flung from the roof.

As with everything he experienced in India, Matt felt on the margins. (Even just one little pull on the tiniest pinner of a joint would set him straight—but where to get some?) At home Matt was the star of the show. Here he was at best an extra, expendable and unobserved. And even as he thought this, a woman in a yellow sari came lurching up the aisle and fell directly on his lap. Not to cozy up! It was like Matt wasn't a person at all—just a big old piece of white male furniture.

Frig these people, he thought, as the woman's blade-like buttocks carved into his thighs. At least with Mieke he'd have a companion, someone who knew him, someone to talk to. And maybe someone to love.

'I've got a bad knee,' Matt told his passenger.

Nothing.

'Anyhow,' he said. 'Enjoy the ride.'

And on they rode through palm trees and little seaside towns, until at last Matt recognized the name of Mieke's resort, and he shook the bony woman onto the floor and stormed from the bus into the daylight, liberating his phone from his back pocket.

*On the beach*, Mieke had texted. Matt found her amid sunbathers, sprawled on a towel. Her bikini was green. What there was of it. Mostly he saw skin, coppery and smooth. His knees went a little wobbly.

'You made it,' she said. 'Finally.'

'I did,' said Matt, and before he could apologize, or rub sunscreen on her back—a fantasy he'd enjoyed, with various climaxes—or say much of anything at all, Mieke was up, clapping him on the shoulder. 'Stay with my stuff,' she said. 'I'm going for a swim.'

Matt watched her tear down to the water and disappear into the sparkling waves. He dropped his backpack, rolled up his khakis and unbuttoned his shirt. It had been days since he'd done any grooming, so he didn't dare unleash his stubbly shoulders or back. But at least he could ventilate. His chest hair had the look of moss bathed in fresh dew.

After a while Mieke returned, swept up her towel, and stood dripping before him. 'So,' she said, 'sounds like you've been having some adventures.'

'Just making memories,' said Matt unconvincingly. 'It's what I do.'

'As you say.'

Why so casual? She'd abandoned him to the mob! A bug was eating his brain! And here was this blithe Dutchwoman, carelessly towelling off her dampest parts and acting like he'd crossed a room, not a country, to find her.

She sat. 'You want to swim?'

Matt pulled his shirt closed. 'Nah.'

But she wasn't looking at him, just staring out at the sea, which glittered in the late afternoon sunshine.

'So, India,' he began.

'Amazing place.'

'Yeah?'

'No?' She shaded her eyes, looked at him briefly, then away.

'I just . . . Do you feel—I don't know—like yourself here?'

'Like myself? Are you joking? I feel totally free here! You can be whoever you want. There's nowhere else like it.'

Matt dug his feet into the sand, felt it trickle between his toes.

'You probably just miss home,' said Mieke. 'Plus it's Christmas. But with this sunshine, the ocean, palm trees, it doesn't look like Christmas, does it?'

'I guess not.'

'In Dutch we say *slechtgehumeurd*. What is the English? Feeling out of source?'

'Sorts.'

'That's why you're out of sorts. You should join me and some friends tonight, mostly foreigners. We're getting together to have a real Christmas.'

*Friends?* Weren't friends the folks you knew your whole life— who you knew better than yourself? Did she even know their last names? (Matt didn't know Mieke's, though he wanted to.) Was a friend over here just any non-Indian?

'With a tree and all,' Mieke continued, 'as you Americans celebrate.'

'Canadian.'

'Canadian, exactly! And there's me, Dutch, and the host is from Chicago, and there's an English, an Israeli—very multi-national. We need you to complete the UN.'

It wasn't until he'd committed to joining her, and she'd texted the host to expect one more guest, that she told him they were playing Secret Santa.

'I'm supposed to buy a present,' he clarified, 'except I don't know who it's for.'

Mieke leaned in. The swell of her breast against his arm, tongue wetting her lips. In that moment, she could have convinced him to suit up in red velvet and plunge down every chimney in India. Matt scanned his brain for a pertinent *Rule*.

'Ho ho ho,' he said, pushing closer.

'That's the spirit,' said Mieke, and moved her phone between them to send another text.

PERUSING THE SEASIDE SHOPS that afternoon, Matt's gift options seemed limited to live chickens and freshly netted fish. He pictured himself showing up with a trout wrapped in newspaper, blood and scales and marine juices trailing across the marble floor of some palatial vacation home. So, no. But what then? A sari? A cellphone? A statue of Ganesh? His brain ached—the parasite muddying his thoughts, he was sure. And he was also sure, diagnostically, that even the faintest puff from a joint would sweep that fog away.

Eventually he found a stall selling toys, and in a bout of TV movie nostalgia (a nerd, a rifle, a blinding, revenge) settled on a gun. An airgun, sure, but a dead replica for the real thing. For lack of wrapping paper Matt used a couple of jute sacks bound with a shoelace. Only later, placed alongside Mieke's ribbon-adorned gift bag, tissue paper artfully frothing forth, did this seem like the craftwork of a serial killer.

An auto-rickshaw took them inland from the resort to a block of housing with the look of an hourly-rate motel. Up a set of stairs, down an external hallway, three knocks on a door with a wreath of beach grass hanging from a nail and they waited, Matt's gift concealed behind his back.

An Asian guy (Korean, Matt guessed, based on his passing resemblance to Chip) flung open the door and screamed, 'Christmas!'

Matt stood aside so the Korean and Mieke could hug.

'You must be Matthew,' he was told. 'I'm Ed.' The accent was pure Midwest, the handshake eager, festive, possibly gay. 'Oh great, you brought a present for Secret Santa!'

'Yeah, but—'

'Great!'

Ed turned back to Mieke, took her by shoulders and danced her inside the flat. Matt trailed behind like a lost puppy.

In the living room a man and a woman were stringing toilet paper around some sort of potted bush; instead of a star riding the uppermost bough was a—good Lord Ganesh!—swastika.

There was music too: 'The Little Drummer Boy.' Matt's favourite Christmas carol—although now it seemed like a dirge.

More hugs were exchanged. Matt hovered by the shoe-rack. The girl was Indian, very small and dark, and very young. The man could have been anywhere between thirty-five and sixty; his body was lean, but his face had that shell-shocked look shared by lifelong backpackers and cancer survivors. He stepped away from Mieke and eyed Matt across the room. 'And who,' he said, 'do we have here?'

The accent—Russian? Possibly. Might Matt be about to arm the very people who wanted him dead? Even if just with an air gun. Because these canny agents could poison-tip the pellets. Or replace them with specially crafted bullets—the kind that explode and shatter inside the body, liquefying everything in their wake.

Matt mumbled hello, kept his head down, immediately forgot the couple's names. Maybe he could make a quick switch and slip a fistful of rupees into the gift pile?

Ed steered him into the room by the elbow. 'Come on in, don't be shy. Put your present under the tree.'

Matt submitted. While the other offerings actually resembled gifts, his looked like the corpse of a small child bound for cremation. The Russian watched him intently.

'You'll never believe this,' said Ed, 'but I found a *turkey*.'

'I told him it was impossible,' said the Indian girl. 'There are no turkeys in India.'

The Russian laughed. 'Probably just a monkey with a beak.' Such a racist, Russian thing to say! But then he added, 'Though what do I know about Christmas.'

'I'm not Jewish,' said Mieke, 'but I've not had turkey either. It's not eaten in Holland.'

Was the Russian posing as a Jew? Could Jews also be Russian? Or hired by Russians? For the first time, ever, Matt wished he paid more attention to global affairs.

'You eat turkey in Canada?' Ed asked Matt, with a grin like an open door.

Transience, Matt was learning, let you reinvent yourself as anyone. 'Sure,' he said. 'My mom makes it every year. With dressing, cranberries.' What else? 'Caesar salad.'

'Wow,' said Ed. 'I hope the little lunch I've put together will be okay. Pressure's on!'

Matt nodded benevolently. 'I'm sure it'll be awesome, bro.'

And so it was: not just turkey but sausages, gravy, grits, sweet potatoes, carrots, creamed spinach, two kinds of stuffing, a soufflé that Matt avoided, and homemade apple pie for dessert. Matt's preferred mode of eating was to mash everything into a pulp for easy face-shovelling. This had long bewildered Ash's mother, and whenever Matt came for dinner she watched him with awe. ('Hey,' he would shrug, 'it's all gonna end up like this anyway.')

The talk around the table turned to Indian politics, the existence of which Matt hadn't considered. (A government! Just like a real country! Who knew?) The Russian/Jew seemed to hold the most virulent views, tethered as he was to a voting citizen—literally clutching her hand as he sounded off on corruption and the economy. Meanwhile Matt puréed and gulped his food-paste in silence.

Lost in his thoughts, a line popped into his head, something an acting coach had once told him: *If a gun appears in the first act, it must go off in Act Three.* (A Russian had concocted this formula! Predetermined murder was in their blood!) The clatter of silverware was slowing; the evening's second act drew to a close. Soon enough his gift would be unwrapped—and the weapon turned upon him.

Ed stopped Matt from clearing the dishes. 'We'll wash up later. Secret Santa first.'

While Ed laid the gifts out on the coffee table, Matt assumed a spot near the door, should he need to flee. The Indian girl went first. Though her eyes lingered on it for a moment, she bypassed Matt's contribution and chose Mieke's gift bag.

'You can either keep it or pass,' Ed explained.

Inside were a tasteful array of local handicrafts: a bracelet of colourful stones, a hand-embroidered purse, a letter-opener made from sandalwood, a marble elephant.

'Oh,' said the Indian girl. 'Indian things. Wow.'

'Not so fast,' said Ed. 'Any of us could steal those from you!'

'Who's next?' said Mieke.

'Me,' announced the Russian. He eyed Matt's weird parcel. 'Looks interesting!'

'Now, hey,' said Matt. 'I bet someone else's—'

'Easy,' said Ed. 'Don't give away which one's yours.'

Mieke laughed at this: one sharp burst like a rifle report.

The Russian held the box to his ear. 'Nothing ticking . . .'

'Why would there be!' Matt yelped.

'Quite a wrapping. How is one meant to . . . enter?'

Ed went to fetch scissors. From the kitchen came a jangle of knives as he rummaged through a drawer. Matt felt the killer's eyes on him. How would he do it? Walk Matt down to the beach, make him kneel in the sand, blast an expertly placed pellet through some essential cord in his brain, then push the body out to sea? What a way to go, floating dead into the Indian Ocean to be devoured by sharks—on Christmas!

'Who knew Jesus's birthday could be so fun,' said the Russian, smiling a hitman's cold and joyless smile.

A single bead of sweat trickled icily between Matt's shoulders, down to the waistband of his pants. 'It can be,' he said.

Ed returned. Expertly, as he might slice a jugular vein, the Russian cut the twine. He peeled off the outer sack and folded it neatly on the couch beside him (belying, Matt thought, his military training). It was all so excruciating. Then the second layer came off, and the box was revealed.

'What is it?' said the Indian girl.

'A gun,' said the Russian.

'A pellet gun!' screamed Matt. 'It's not real!'

'A gun?' said Mieke. 'Really? That's a strange gift.'

But the Russian was delighted. 'An air gun! I had one like this when I was a kid in Israel. Right on! Great present. I'm keeping this, thank you all very much. And I'll shoot you if you try to take it from me.'

Matt returned the high-five, suddenly recalling something Mieke had said about an Israeli being part of the group. But was this part of the executioner's ploy, lulling his victim into false security before unleashing vengeance in a volley of pellet-fire?

Matt was next. He chose a small box. His last act as a living man, perhaps.

'Ah,' said the Russian, or fake Israeli. 'That one's mine.'

'Don't say,' wailed Ed.

The package was very light. Maybe even empty.

Inside Matt expected a note: *Meet me at the water* or *Say good night . . . forever.* Or even simpler: *Prepare to perish!* Or anthrax.

Or a poison gas, an odourless wisp of the stuff seeping into his nervous system and within minutes dissolving his internal organs to stew. So he opened the box with dread.

Never could he have guessed the Christmas miracle waiting inside.

# 4

NO ONE SEEMED TO KNOW the beach's name, or if it even had one. All Matt and Mieke had been told was which bus to take from the station in Panjim and where to get off, over a little rise and through a gauntlet of roadside stalls and down into a tropical grove. 'A great place to smoke that,' promised the Israeli, and Matt lifted the guy into another off-ground hug and thanked him again, from the bottom of his heart—his Secret Santa gift secreted in his pocket.

Life was good. No, life was *great*. The gods had shone down: not only had Matt's life been spared, his dreams had come true. Or if not his literal *dreams*, certainly his fantasies. Certainly his medical necessities. What were the chances that his Secret Santa would provide weed? And now this perfect plan: head to the beach, burn the Israeli's 'doobie' with the sunlight dimming romantically and surf lapping the sand like tongues up thighs. And then, as the stars came out, Matt and Mieke would finally tilt their alleged friendship horizontal—or at right angles, whatever. However they did it in Europe!

The bus stopped beside a bank of communal toilets so fetid the air seemed to shudder. A sandy trail led through reeds to the beach. The sand squeaked as they passed a woman in traditional garb wading out of the sea, past a game of cricket played by a dozen shrieking shirtless boys, past a cart selling cold drinks and snacks, past an emaciated steer feasting on a mound of trash, around an outcropping of rocks to a little cove. And here they found solitude. The waves shushed and frothed; the palm trees were jostled by a languid breeze. Dusk was settling. There wasn't another person in sight.

'Holy crud,' said Matt. 'I'm living in a postcard.'

Mieke laid out her towel, sat.

'I can't believe that Jew gave me weed,' said Matt. 'Best Christmas present ever.'

'So you keep saying.'

He took the joint from his pocket and gave it an adoring sniff. 'Is it any good?'

'Yaniv's marijuana can be quite strong.'

'*Marijuana*,' Matt giggled. A new giddiness had come over him. 'Wanna blaze?'

'Let's swim first. You go ahead, I'll watch our things.'

'Swim?'

'Come on. You can't come to Goa and not go in the ocean.'

'What about sharks?'

'Stop being such a baby!'

Matt stared at her. Was this his chance? He pictured the two of them cavorting in the surf, their bodies slick and saline, his trunks yanked down and her bikini bottoms shifted aside . . . 'Fine,' he said. 'I'll swim if that's what you want so bad.'

Craftily he disrobed, shielding his furrier parts from Mieke's purview, angling a shoulder or kneecap this way or that. Once down to his boxers he tore roaring to the water's edge, arms out, like a jetliner cleared for take-off. And then he was in it.

The water was cooler than he expected, even bracing. He dove under, came up, breast-stroked out. He stopped, stood, the sand churning under his feet. A big wave knocked him down. Saltwater flooded his nose; he came up spluttering, called, 'I'm okay!' But on the shore, Mieke was lying back to watch the stars come out.

Matt swam further out. The water purpled in the twilight. He splashed some on his face, scrubbed the stubble on his head and dove again, wiggling along underwater like a sea lion on his way to the rutting of a lifetime.

He swam like this until he felt his lungs constricting, and even then kept on, pushing himself until he couldn't take it any longer, and then rushed gasping to the surface. And Matt was shocked to discover a boy treading water beside him.

'Hello,' said the boy—not a boy, really. Maybe twentyish.

'Namaste,' said Matt.

'You are swimming?'

'You got it.'

'And your good name?'

'My? Oh, my name! Matt. Matthew.'

'Matthew. And you are from?'

'From? Like, country?'

The boy nodded.

'Canada.'

'Canada, very nice.'

'You've been?'

Head wobble.

Matt tried to stand but was out of his depth; his feet kicked madly to stay afloat. The kid dove, rump in the air (a bloom of white y-fronts). He came up a little closer, spouted water from his mouth.

'You would like to swim with me?'

'Swim?' Matt was confused. 'Aren't we swimming now?'

But the boy extended his hand, beckoned Matt with his fingertips. 'We will swim together now. Come.'

'Careful. I had a dropped finger recently.'

'Come.'

Matt was led to shallower waters. Still holding hands, he and his new friend set down their feet and turned to face the horizon, a crease out there in the dusk.

'One . . . two . . . three,' instructed the boy, and leapt the first wave that came rolling in.

Matt stared.

'Next one!' said the boy, and began his countdown.

This time Matt jumped in time with the boy. Another wave came and they jumped again. And again. And paused, laughing.

'Here comes another one!' cried Matt.

But the boy released Matt to splash him, then they were chasing each other through the waves, laughing, and when at last the boy swam off—'Goodbye, sir! Goodbye!'—Matt waded back to shore with a grin he couldn't shake. Mieke eyed him sideways.

'Have fun out there?'

'You see that? Some weird little Indian kid just swam up and—'

'Became your boyfriend.'

Matt laughed. 'You want to swim now?'

'Is he still out there?'

The water ruffled dimly to where it met the sky. No sign of the boy. Or anyone.

'Looks like you're out of luck,' said Matt.

'Don't go anywhere,' said Mieke, and Matt watched the two lobes of her buttocks jostle in their green holster all the way to the water's edge.

⟨⟨✦⟩⟩

THOUGH IT HAD BEEN A FEW YEARS since Ash had participated, Christmas in London went like this: everyone rose early, someone put on coffee, and then they did presents. There were assigned roles, too. Mona got the fire going and their mother distributed gifts, while Ash watched for anyone invading with unsolicited Yuletide cheer.

Now he delegated Rick to lookout: 'If carollers ring the bell, you send them packing.'

'I'll do my best, my man,' Rick promised.

Ash kicked back in the recliner beside the tree. Rick and his mother took the couch. Mona lay with Burt by the fireplace, releasing him intermittently to jostle the logs.

Like old times, his mom had gone overboard, with a half-dozen parcels each for Ash and his sister. But they happily played along, tearing through the wrapping paper and tossing the trash in the fire. Ash loved presents. He opened them greedily, in a frenzy, only distantly aware of Mona's mounting haul a few feet away. 'Socks!' he announced. Also: a box of chocolates in paper sleeves, lip balm, a paring knife—and a humidifier.

'Rick thought you sounded congested,' explained his mother.

'I've needed one of these for years,' said Ash, amazed: Rick!

Together he and Mona, as they did every year, had renewed their mother's (and Rick's, by association) magazine subscriptions, and given each other books. Or, rather, he'd bought her a book, and Mona had given him a gift certificate to an online wholesaler.

'I wouldn't dream of picking something. You snob,' she said.

'Well that novel I got you is terrible,' he said, 'though probably just the kind of garbage you like.'

They high-fived.

Rick's turn. He handed Ash an envelope. Cash?

'Just a little something to help you get back to yourself,' Rick explained, beaming at his own largesse.

The card featured a person of ambiguous race and gender gazing anthropologically at the First World from beneath a straw hat.

'UNICEF,' provided Rick.

Inside was an inscription:

To my dearest Ash,
Congratulations! You're in a creative writing workshop at the library tomorrow. I hope it provides the regeneration you need.
         From one artistic spirit to another,
               Rick.

Rick had his arms out for a hug. Ash allowed himself to be clutched for a two-count.

'Figured it would be good for you,' said Rick. 'If I ever get down, all's I need's a little push in a creative direction. Luckily I've got your mom!' Who offered her cheek for a kiss.

'Right,' said Ash. 'Well, thanks.'

Meanwhile Mona had opened her gift from Rick: a box set of *Law and Order*, a show that Ash knew for a fact she loathed.

'Oh,' she said.

'Because you're a lawyer,' Rick explained.

'Great,' said Mona, and winked at her brother as she fell into Rick's embrace.

ONCE PRESENTS WERE DONE, it was time to start dinner. Ash rinsed the turkey in the sink while his mother hauled out the required groceries and supplies. The plan, as always, was to eat precisely at 5 p.m., with the rest of the evening dedicated to the unbuckling of pants and naps and, probably, Ash moaning that he'd eaten too much.

They'd just gotten going on the stuffing (bread in the food processor, everything from scratch!) when Mona appeared in the doorway in full make up, hair falling elegantly to her shoulders, and announced she was going out for coffee with an old friend.

'Ran into them at the gym,' she said casually, eyes flitting between her mother and brother. She went to wait by the front window, peeking through the curtains every few minutes and relentlessly checking her phone.

'You think *them* is a *him*?' Ash whispered to his mother.

'I think,' she replied slyly, 'that your sister deserves to be treated nicely today.'

A car pulled into the drive and Mona raced to it. Ash recognized the guy driving: an old boyfriend whose picture still graced the bulletin board in his sister's bedroom, and whom the whole family had adored.

Ash's mother wagged a spatula at him. 'Let's not get too excited.'

So she hated Harj too! Ash had never loved her so deeply.

Rick had taken Burt to the ravine, so Ash and his mom were left alone with Schoenberg's Christmas Music on the stereo for their food prep. She gutted a squash; he chopped onions and sage. The old routine. For the first time in months, Ash felt happy.

'You remember the first time we teamed up like this?' she asked.

'I was in high school. Grade ten or eleven, maybe?'

'You were sixteen, with dreams of being a chef, and wanted some on-the-job training. No, wait. That wasn't until later.' His mom covered her mouth with her hand. 'Remember, before that, how you went on that kick about being a house-husband?'

'No! What?'

'Oh, Ashy. You did! You'd decided that you were going to marry a banker and write books and raise the kids and cook and clean. Not sure where you got the domestic instinct from. Not like *I* ever set much of an example in that realm.'

'What are you talking about? You were a great mom. Are, even.'

'Oh, don't get me wrong. I'm the best. All I'm saying, Ashy, was that I was never much of a Martha Stewart around the house. An academic first and a homemaker second, maybe.' She laughed. 'Though I must have been better than Brij.'

'Oh god. Worst ever.' Ash's eyes began to water—the onions.

'I hate to speak ill . . . But around the house the man was beyond useless.'

'I once caught him vacuuming *the sink*. He'd dropped something down the drain and he had the whole vacuum up on the counter trying to suck it out.'

'I suppose it's cultural. He'd never had much occasion for housework in India.'

Ash wiped tears on his shoulder. 'Onions,' he explained.

His mom handed him a Kleenex, then took one and dabbed her eyes too. Sniffed, shook her head. Laughed again, but a little more sadly.

Ash studied her. Why the sudden nostalgia? His memories of his parents involved either one or the other—never both, never together, even when they were married. And post-divorce their relationship had consisted mostly of terse exchanges from each other's doorsteps as they traded custody of their kids. Yet here was some echo of whatever had come before that. Maybe before him.

His mother blew her nose and moved to slicing potatoes. They worked in silence for a while. Ash crammed handfuls of stuffing into the turkey. She laid out the spuds in a dish and got a cheese sauce going on the stovetop, stepped aside so he could put the bird in the oven. The music switched over to Bach's Christmas Oratorio.

'What else?' he said.

'Nothing for now. We can do the veggies in an hour or two. Do you have work to do?'

He watched her sauce the potatoes and sprinkle paprika over-top. 'Do you know anything about this novel Brij was writing?'

'Oh, god. Was he still talking about that?'

'The guy hiking up into the mountains? Amarnath?'

'Right, and the whole impotency epidemic.'

'Sorry?'

She wiped a finger around the edge of the pot, tasted the sauce, frowned, nodded. 'He finds the lingam melting, and when he comes back down he turns impotent and infects every man he sees, and they infect everyone else, so the women of Kashmir take over and bring everyone together—as far as I remember it. God, this was years ago. But he used to talk about it all the time. Really thought he was onto something.'

Ash stared. 'That's what happens?'

'Isn't it?'

'I don't know. I found a piece of it, I guess. It's just the guy, the hero, climbing up to the temple, though he never gets there. But it's about impotency? How does it end?'

'Oh, he'd never written a *beginning*, as far I knew. He just used to brag about his Great Indian Novel at parties, swaggering around after a few drinks telling everyone that it was going to be his ticket out of medicine. But then his career got in the way. Stopped even mentioning it before you kids were born. Though he did end up writing something?'

'He started to. I have no idea if he ever finished it.'

'Maybe,' said Ash's mother, 'he just ran out of time.'

—

IN THE INTERVENING HOURS, while the turkey sizzled and the house flooded with its rich odour, Ash went downstairs and scrolled through the pages he'd typed to find some clue of what was to come—not an end, another beginning.

The text ended with the hero at the mouth of the cave:

> And he gazed in upon the blackness there and squinting
> saw it, his goal, and readied himself to enter, and entered.
> And when he reappeared

End of page, end of section. And when he reappeared *everything changed*, Ash guessed, and typed, and stared at for a while. Was this right? He tried to keep going: *The hero stepped*—no, 'stepped' struck a false note. *The hero . . .* what? Ash frowned. The cursor blinked. *Went, strode, descended*—nothing felt right. So what to write?

Ash's phone buzzed. The number was Indian. He answered with a sigh. 'You just calling to say good night?'

Matt sounded panicked: 'Bro, I need to talk to you.'

'The connection's terrible. Where are you?'

'Goa, at a resort.' A crackle, words were lost. 'Something bad happened.'

'God, what did you do now?'

'Dhar, honestly? Shut up. This is serious.'

Ash closed his laptop.

'So we had Christmas with a guy I thought was Russian and was going to kill me, except he gave me weed, and then Mieke and I went—' The line sputtered. A few syllables broke through: 'Lagoon . . . swimming . . . somebody . . . frigging murder him!'

'Slow down, I can't hear you at all.'

'I'm telling you how it was!'

'I'm confused. Does this have to do with the Russians?'

'No! No, this was—' The rest was mangled.

'Hold on.' Realizing that the weak signal might be on his end, Ash took his phone out of his room and up a few steps from the basement. 'You there? What happened?'

A digital garble.

Ash continued up to the kitchen. 'Hello?'

No answer. The line was dead. Matt was gone.

'EVERYTHING LOOKS PERFECT, GUYS,' said Mona, her face aglow in the candlelight. Since returning from her coffee outing she'd been giggly and light, and the way she held her belly as she sat seemed less to leaven the burden than to honour it.

The table was laid archetypally, as if to tantalize a Dickensian urchin peering through the window. At the centre sat the turkey, glossy and golden and platonically trussed, surrounded by carrots, peas, leeks, a big bowl of stuffing excavated from the bird, scalloped potatoes, gravy, cranberry sauce, and candles burning like the signal fires of an imminent attack. Everything was the same as it had been through Ash's childhood, save the glassware: gone was the elegant crystal that their mom saved for special occasions, replaced with blue, chunky handblown stuff—the stuff of Rick.

Mona tilted a bottle of pink wine in Ash's direction. Rick, whose wife had died from cirrhosis, didn't touch alcohol, so neither now did his mother—such solidarity. With his sister also abstaining, drinking alone risked seeming wounded. Yet so did resistance. In the end Ash accepted half a glass, neighing, 'Whoa,' in what he hoped was a carefree way.

'Merry Christmas,' said Rick, lifting a can of organic root beer. 'To you all. Great to have the family together for the holiday.'

'And it's so nice, Rick,' addended Ash, 'to have you here with us.'

Mona kicked him under the table. Ash rolled his eyes, sipped the syrupy rosé.

'Last Christmas, when it was just the two of us,' said their mother, 'we did an all vegan meal. Got a turkey made out of— what was it, honey?'

'Tofu and gluten,' said Rick. 'And the sides—your mom did the spuds with soy milk and cashew cheese. Tasted exactly the same.'

'Pretty close, anyway,' she said, eyeing the bird with what seemed like relief.

Mona carved and served while the sides were passed around. Ash accepted his standard leg and two slices of breast while Rick made a great show of refusing turkey, yet painted his plate with gravy. As Ash watched everyone fill their plates, Matt's hysteria on the phone came paddling into his thoughts. He took a big drink of wine to drown it.

The conversation turned to food: reminiscences of past triumphs and failures, comparisons with the current meal, murmurings of approval that Ash dismissed with self-critique—'bird's a little dry, potatoes underdone'—which caused Mona to threaten him with the carving knife. 'Would you just shut up and appreciate a compliment for once in your stupid life? Everything is delicious.'

Since most of the food memories were from before his time, Rick kept torpedoing the discussion with embarrassingly territorial references to more recent Christmases. 'Remember the year at my brother's? That whole dishwasher ordeal?' he said with a sad, private laugh to be shared only with Ash's mother. Then he peered around the table: the man had a story to tell. Dare they pry it out of him?

Ash shifted focus: 'Do you cook much wazwan anymore, Ma? I swear you got to the point where your rista was as good as any Kashmiri's.'

'Oh, no. Indian food doesn't agree with Rick's tummy.'

'Hey!' Rick threw up his hands. 'If Ash wants to eat Indian while he's staying with us, why not? Could do that tomorrow, after your writing class.'

Ash reached for the wine. He could sense the barbed edges of a nasty kind of drunk prickling within, and was aware of his sister eyeing him warily as he refilled his glass. He sipped twice and continued: 'I remember being in India and Brij's sisters spending hours teaching you to cook. They were really like family to you, weren't they?'

Rick went to the fridge for another root beer.

'And progressive, too. I mean, making Muslim-style dishes among Hindus wasn't exactly popular back then, was it? But that was just our family, I guess. I mean, they welcomed you right away, even though you were from a totally different culture.' He tipped back his glass. 'Like you were one of the family. Right?'

His mother nodded.

Ash reached again for the wine. Mona yanked it away. He laughed. 'What are you, my mom?'

'Come on now,' said his actual mom.

A big gulp of root beer seemed to have rallied Rick, who returned with renewed purpose. 'Was that in Srinagar?' This he rhymed with tree-bagger.

'No,' said Ash, 'we couldn't go there—to *Srinagar*. Unless we wanted our heads lopped off and marched around on spikes, I mean.'

'He's being silly,' said his mother. 'It was never that bad.'

But here was an opportunity to play the pedant, whether Ash knew what he was talking about or not. 'Kashmir in the mid-eighties, Rick, would have been on the cusp of a civil war. And Hindu families like ours weren't exactly welcomed with open arms.'

'Like Northern Ireland. With the Catholics and Protestants.'

'Oh, Rick,' said Ash with a sad laugh. 'Much, much worse than that.'

But this did not have its desired, discomfiting effect. Rick leaned in. 'How so?'

'It's complicated,' said Ash. He glanced at Mona for help.

'Well,' she said, 'keep in mind that Muslim Kashmiris had it bad too.'

'Now they do, you mean,' said Ash. 'Because the economy's collapsed.'

'Sure,' said his sister. 'The state's really fallen on hard times. But then too. And here's the thing Brij never talked about. All that communal harmony? That everything was fine and dandy until militants were shipped in from Pakistan and Afghanistan—'

'To wage holy war,' said Ash.

'Jihad,' confirmed Rick.

'What I'm saying,' said Mona, 'is that Brij liked to tell us that everything in Kashmir used to be perfect. Perfect for Pandits, maybe, who lived in comfort with the Muslims under their thumbs. Those so-called Troubles were also a popular uprising, the oppressed people finally having enough of being ruled and doing something about it.'

His mother interjected: 'And no offence to your father, but the Dhars weren't exactly refugees. They were very affluent and had opportunities elsewhere in India. Or overseas.' She helped herself to more potatoes. 'Not only did your dad's family not go through any of this, it was only when they couldn't return that they really began to care.'

A posthumous takedown! And Mona was shaking her head in a doleful sort of agreement.

'There's a whole narrative here that Brij never really acknowledged,' said his sister. 'Instead we get this utopian ideal of a place—*paradise on earth*, as they say—ruined by foreigners. So there's not only class and religious issues at play, there's also xenophobia.'

'Wow,' said Rick. 'So much to learn.'

And all so repulsive, Ash thought: with the patriarch out of the picture they could at last dismantle his legacy. He snatched the wine and filled his glass, and while he chugged it eyed the three other people around the table with the disdain of impending conquest. But just as he emptied his glass, his phone rang from the counter, and instead of eviscerating them all for their heresy he scampered away to answer it—Matt, he figured, with an update on whatever 'memory' he'd manufactured for himself now.

But the screen displayed a 519 number, and not one Ash recognized. He took the phone into the living room and answered in his most cloying phone voice. A full minute into seasonal bromides he realized the woman on the other end was Sherene.

'So,' she said. 'You avoiding me?'

'Sorry, my phone's been weird,' he lied. 'What number are you calling from?'

'My parents' landline in Windsor. Home for the holidays until tomorrow, then heading to London to spend New Year's with my sister. That's the *real* London, U.K.'

'You guys do Christmas?'

'Jesus's birthday isn't just for Hindus anymore.' Sherene moved away from the phone to yell at someone—possibly her dad—in Farsi. Ash felt a little twinge of envy. She returned: 'So what's going on in fake London? Was Santa good to you?'

'Get this: my mom's boyfriend's present was a creative writing class. At the library.'

'That's great!'

'Great? Seriously? Do you know what sorts of lunatics sign up for these things? Guys with rope for belts sharing their ten-thousand-page conspiracy manifestos. Or cat ladies writing stories about their cats—from the cat's perspective. Kill me.'

'No way. This could be good for you.'

'How so.'

'Get you out of the house a bit. You haven't been out, have you? Are you washing?'

'I've washed.'

'Not daily though.'

'I've washed as needed.'

'Time to break out the rope belt!'

'Are you on your computer? I can hear you typing.'

'Just seeing if there's any room in that class.'

'Wait. Why?'

'Solidarity, sweetie. Me and you.'

'No. What are you doing? Don't do that.'

'London's on my way back to Toronto. Look, here it is: ten to four tomorrow. I could totally make it, my flight to Heathrow's not until Monday. And look, there's space.' Sherene paused. 'I'm serious. If not me, who will you make your snippy comments to?'

'Snippy? Not clever?'

'Don't flatter yourself. Maybe if I was scripting them.'

Despite himself—despite everything—Ash laughed. 'This is a fiction workshop, right? Do you even write fiction?'

'Sorry, there, Mister Joyce. I didn't realize this was for modern masters only.'

'Meh, I figured I'd just use my dad's book.'

'You didn't write that!'

'No, but I typed it.'

'Ah.'

Her judgment was palpable; it weakened him. 'What else am I supposed to do?'

'Sweetie, sorry. I'm being unfair. I think if you really are serious about trying to do something with that manuscript, it's fantasy.'

'Fantasy?'

'Fantastic, I said. Anyway, okay, I'm one click away from joining you tomorrow.'

'Wait. You're not going to sell me out again, are you?'

'Sell you out how? And what do you mean, *again*?'

'I don't want anyone knowing who I am.'

'Is there a fatwa on your head I haven't heard about? You need me to put in a good word with the Ayatollah?'

'No, you know what I mean. I'm . . . a public figure.'

'Oh. Right.'

'Sherene, fuck off.' The words stuck and thrummed like an arrow in a target. Too much. He doubled back hastily: 'I mean, I *did* write a book. And now here I am—'

'Among the hoi polloi. The unwashed masses. Your adoring public. If only they knew what a towering figure of the intelligentsia had deigned to stoop within their midst. They'd bow down at your feet and hail your genius.'

'Is this supposed to be convincing me to let you come?'

'Let? Not *let*, my friend. I'll take the class whether you *let* me or not.' Her voice softened. 'But, hey, jokes aside, if you think it would be . . . good, I'll be there. It'd be nice to see you. To hang out.'

'After you abandoned me, you mean.'

'Abandoned?' Her voice quivered. 'Really?'

Ash waited.

'Sweetie, come on. I'm sorry about how things went—'

'It's fine. I was . . . out of line. I understand that you did what you had to.'

'Ah. You heard the show.'

'I did.'

'This is why I kept trying to get in touch, I wanted to let you know.' She sounded choked. 'They made me put something together so quickly. I didn't think you'd actually listen.'

'Whatever. Don't worry about it.'

'Ash, listen. I promise I'm doing everything I can to make sure you're back with us as soon as possible.'

*Us.* So divisive. Was he now a member of some generic, discarded *them*? Ash sighed. 'You aren't coming to this class just to embarrass me, are you?'

'No. Promise. Nothing like that. I won't even act like I know you, if you want.'

'You don't have to do that.'

'We could pretend to be lovers, then.'

'Ew. Weird.'

'Agreed, inshallah.' Sherene laughed. 'Do you miss me?'

'As a dog misses its fleas.'

'Is that a yes, then? I'm about to click.'

Ash palmed his face. 'Fine.'

'So eager.'

'Fine, yes, sure. It'd be . . . good to see you. Yes.'

'Yay!' Some clicking followed, some typing. 'There we go. All signed up. Seriously, this is going to be a hoot. Me and you! Go team!'

'Our swan song.'

'Oh, don't get all maudlin.' Yet her voice turned gentle, too: 'Are we friends, Ash?'

'If thou didst ever hold me in thy heart, Sherene. For better or worse. Though I was close to absenting my felicity when I heard a fucking poet in my spot, that's for sure.'

She laughed. 'Goodnight, sweet prince. And Merry Christmas.'

'Said the Muslim to the Hindu.' And Ash laughed, too, like a volley passed back over the net.

# 5

THE POLICE STATION IN PANJIM had the look of a colonial manor, garnished with drooping palms and gabled eaves and a wrap-around porch. Two monkeys up on the roof chirruped as Matt and Mieke approached. Or, rather, as Matt trailed Mieke up the steps—supportively, he hoped. More supportive than Ash had been on the phone, anyway, shouting and judging and then—the little twerp—hanging up.

Mieke still hadn't really opened up. She was just as silent now as she'd been during the ride from the beach to the resort, huddled in the far corner of the auto-rickshaw. 'I'm fine,' she'd kept telling Matt, whether he asked or not.

Back in her room, the minute they closed the door Mieke collapsed on the bed and cried softly for a while, and Matt sat there patting her back, crying a little too. Yet when she sat up he wondered if they'd been crying for the same reasons. After showering she offered him half the bed, then crawled to the far side, turned away, knees to her chest, and slept like that until noon. Matt lay awake the whole night, turning things over in his brain: how could a Christmas romance have gone so catastrophically wrong?

Despite its grand facade, the police station's interior was in disrepair: dirty walls, chipped floors, and the dim lighting of a crypt. Not exactly a place to install much faith in justice. Matt joined Mieke at the unmanned front desk while khaki-clothed officers flitted past in all directions, responding to Matt's 'Excuse me?' with curt nods and a perfunctory, 'Sir.' Finally he caught a bony guy by the elbow. Nametag: *Fernandez.*

'Officer,' said Matt. 'We'd like to report an assault.'

The man shook free, regarded Matt with suspicion. 'You are injured?'

'Not me.' Matt nodded at Mieke. 'Her.'

'Eh?'

'On the beach.'

'Which beach?'

'I . . . don't know. There's a cove and—'

'Up north,' said Mieke.

'Eh? Then not this jurisdiction.' He headed down the hallway.

Matt followed. 'We want to file a report.'

Fernandez glanced at Matt as he might an intrusive salesperson. 'You are making the complaint, or your friend?'

'Well, her.' But Mieke hung back, gazing at her feet. 'I'm a witness.'

Leaning into one of the offices, Fernandez hollered, 'Fernandez!' And took his leave of Matt with a martial bow.

A young woman in the same beige uniform appeared. (Same nametag too: another *Fernandez.*)

Matt took her to Mieke.

This woman—Anita, she told Mieke—sat them on the station's front steps and produced a ledger, the carbon paper crinkling. 'Write please your crime.'

There was no pen. Mieke was given a stick. 'Scrape it,' she was told, and Anita Fernandez demonstrated with her fingernail how this might produce a facsimile.

Mieke passed it to Matt. 'You do it. Your English is better.'

So Matt scraped. He scraped about the bus, though neither of them knew the number, describing its route with as much detail as possible. He scraped about the toilets, the walk along the beach, the cove. He scraped about swimming, about the boy—that frigging rat. He scraped about returning to the beach and Mieke taking her turn in the water. But then came the thing he hadn't seen. He looked at Mieke. She looked at him.

Anita Fernandez checked her watch. From somewhere in the police station came the rasp of phlegm horked from lungs to lips. A distant splat.

'Why don't I just write it,' said Mieke. Matt handed her the stick.

'Does this kind of thing happen a lot around here?' he asked Anita Fernandez.

'With tourists?' she said. 'Some theft, yes,'

'No. I mean . . . *You know.*'

Anita Fernandez looked uncomfortable. 'There is crime in Goa as there is anywhere,' she sloganed, and looked away—as if from, or toward, a camera. What wronger wrongs had this woman witnessed? Maybe she'd been wronged herself. Maybe she'd been through something similar. Or some horror many times worse.

'Can't I just tell you what happened?' said Mieke.

Matt eyed the ledger. She'd written nothing. 'I could probably identify the guy,' he said. 'About yay-big. Skinny. Dark-skinned . . .'

A pair of yay-big, skinny, dark-skinned officers came out of the station. Matt had to swing his legs out of the way to let them pass.

'You must write,' Anita Fernandez told Mieke. 'We require a full report.'

But Mieke had dropped her twig. At her feet lay dozens of the things, fallen from a nearby tree or abandoned by prospective plaintiffs. For a moment Matt worried theirs might be lost forever. But this thought was interrupted with panic: he had drugs on his person. They'd never had a chance to smoke Yaniv's joint so he'd stashed it back in his pocket—where it remained, now, on the literal doorstep of the law.

'You must write,' Anita Fernandez told Mieke, and retrieved a stick from the ground. 'Once a complaint is made, a report must be filed.'

The two women locked eyes.

Matt wavered. What was he doing here, dancing among the wolves with a steak stapled to his crotch? Suicide! He stood.

Anita Fernandez squinted up at him. 'You are leaving?'

'He didn't see anything,' Mieke said flatly.

'Not a dang thing,' said Matt, in retreat down the steps. Might the joint's outline be seen incriminatingly through his shorts? He jammed his hands in his pockets. 'So it's cool then if I head?'

Mieke stared. Anita stared. Matt clutched the joint in his fist—if only he'd hooped it! Surely in India all he'd need was a glass of unfiltered water to crap it free.

From inside the station came a cracking sound. Not gunfire, Matt told himself, after a quick visual check for bullet holes in his chest. Simply a door slamming closed. Still it was enough to send him tumbling out the gate.

'Text me when you're done,' he cried, with a final glimpse over his shoulder: Mieke and Anita were heading arm in arm inside the station.

MATT FOLLOWED SIGNS (many in Russian) to the ocean, as good a place as any to get rid of drugs. Crowds clotted the seaside promenade; the air had turned humid and close. Matt felt so *big*, plodding along heavily against the foot traffic. People dodged past, eyed him with annoyance. No matter where he moved he seemed to be in the way—an obstacle, an encumbrance. Useless, without cause or effect. Matt had never felt like such a burden, so dispatched and weak.

And what was the plan? Head to the water, wade out and fling the joint in the waves? No, it'd just wash up, stained with Matt's fingerprints. Better: annihilation by fire. Though if he was going to burn the thing anyway, what a waste not to smoke it. Two birds, one stoned and happy Canuck: this way he'd destroy the evidence *and* provide himself a little kick in the metaphysical pants.

But where to light up? Any of these Goans could be a shifty narc. Smoking the joint seemed yet another prologue to humiliation—flipped to the ground, the roach put out with a fleshy sizzle on his cheek. Maybe the Israeli had given it to him knowing full well what trouble it'd bring.

And what sort of friend was Mieke, anyway? Friends didn't act like they could care less if you existed or not. Sumit had warned him about *cahoots*. The Dutchwoman could be an agent in some elaborate, cahooted ploy. The joint in his pocket—might it even be laced? Possibly. Mieke's aloof seduction, the gift exchange, the remarkable coincidence that he would get *drugs* as a present; it was all a little too perfect. And what had actually happened the night before in the cove? She'd barely told him anything.

Matt paused at an archway that fronted one of the big hotels. Yes, it all made sense: back in Delhi Mieke had suggested the restaurant knowing her Russian associates would be there, that he'd muck it up and have to flee to Goa. But what was the scheme? Organ harvest? Identity theft? Or maybe she and her cronies were running the long-game: the whole affair would end with Mieke dirty-bombing the SkyDome with Ebola.

Ah, but Matt wasn't the easy mark they'd thought! He'd

reckoned their play. The ball was in his court. Time for some action. Time to make a memory of his frigging own.

First, though, he needed to smoke this joint. And before that, to steady the ship, a drink.

Beyond the gates a turbaned guy stood watch, rifle at his hip. Eyeing the gun warily Matt asked if there were a public bar in the hotel. Yes indeed there was, sir, he was told. Though it wasn't open until 6 p.m.

Matt ignored this, circumnavigated the hotel, ended up in the workout room, asked directions from the towel boy, somehow found his way into the sub-basement, escaped via service elevator, located the 'Lounge'—empty—snuck behind the bar and poured himself a couple fingers of whiskey, neat. And retreated to a booth with his drink.

Who were his allies, who could he trust? Not the police. Anita Fernandez was clearly also in the mob's pocket. Sumit? No, the guy could barely get it together to take Matt sightseeing. There was Sumit's boss, Ash's cousin, but Matt couldn't very well intro himself as the target of an international crime syndicate. Ash had other relatives, but they were up in Kashmir, or near it, and that was *far*. And Ash—never mind Ash. He'd sold Matt out for the last time. This was Matt's moment, alone.

Matt took a sip of whiskey. Lowering the drink he noticed a bus-boy setting tables in the adjoining room. A kid, really, swimming in a starchy grey uniform. Matt sipped his beer and watched: the kid worked methodically, but with fluency and comfort, moving almost musically to the ruffle of linens and clink of glassware. There was a whiff of familiarity about him, too. Not his face, the light was too dim to make that out. More his movements, which had a certain whimsy.

Matt nearly choked on his beer. Was it? Yes. Holy frigging crud—definitely. That lean, angular body and jangly limbs were unmistakeable. That flop of black hair was easy to imagine soaking wet and tamped to the scalp. Or that little walnut of a rear end inverting and plummeting beneath the surface of the sea. Or those hands, reaching for his. Or reaching for Mieke.

Head down and singing softly to himself, the kid went into the kitchen. He had that loose, oblivious way of someone who believed himself alone. So. Advantage: Matt.

He put down his drink. Looked around. Slid out of the booth and crept to the kitchen. Peeked through the swinging doors. No sign of anyone. In he went, as stealthily as a man his size could.

The kitchen smelled of steel, and egg, and spice. A single bulb cast a splash of light by the prep stations, but mostly the room was in darkness. A rustling noise sent Matt ducking behind the sink. The kid appeared with garbage bags, one over each shoulder. From a crouch, breath held, Matt watched him head out the exit. When it closed, he scuttled after him.

The door opened into an alleyway beside the hotel. The kid was down one end slinging trash into a dumpster. No one else in sight.

On the wall beside the exit was a fire extinguisher. Matt took it down off the wall. Just to spray the kid, bewilder him. Moving outside, Matt tripped and sent a tower of plastic buckets scattering— and the jig was up.

'This is the service area, Sir,' said the kid. 'Not for guests.'

'Isn't it?' said Matt, pleased with the menacing nonchalance in his voice.

The kid didn't move. 'Supper will be served at 6 p.m.'

Matt approached, carrying the fire extinguisher in one hand. 'Sir?'

'Remember me?'

'Sir, my apologies, there are many guests at this hotel—'

'*Come, swim with me. Hold my hand.*'

The kid stared.

'What, you forgot? I thought we had something, bro.' He stopped a pace or two away. Cracked his neck. Moved the fire extinguisher to his shoulder—like a bazooka.

'Sir, you shouldn't have that. Please . . .'

Matt tried to think of some witty catchphrase, something poetic and appropriately vengeful, but none came to mind. So he aimed the nozzle. But when he went to spray the kid in the face, the trigger jammed. He tried again. Nothing.

Sensing an opening, the kid bolted. Matt reacted: the fire extinguisher swung. A sickly crunch, metal on skull. A sense of bone buckling. And the kid crumpled as if shot.

Matt straddled the fallen body.

'Nothing to say for yourself? When we were such good friends? Of course, that was before I knew who you were working for.'

The kid was face down, limbs splayed.

The lights extinguished and the alley descended into shadow. Matt looked up, expecting snipers on the rooftop. But no one was there. He set down the extinguisher and waved his arms. The motion sensor ticked and the lights came back on.

'Look at me,' he said.

Whimpering from below. The face remained hidden.

'Frig,' Matt muttered. 'Enough with the waterworks already.'

But the kid wasn't crying. He was gasping. A wet, gurgling sound.

'Jesus.'

A cough, a wheeze. Silence. Still, Matt was wary. He knew this ploy, the coward feigning defeat only to jump up and stab him with a syringe full of tranqs—or AIDS.

'Okay,' said Matt, stepping back. 'Get up.'

No response. He nudged the kid's leg: the body heaved. And was still.

'Bro?'

Nothing.

Matt squatted, gave the boy a shake. And recoiled. Panic jagged through his guts. Up close, this kid was far stockier and older than the one he'd swum with.

The lights extinguished. In the sudden darkness, the world seemed to reel.

This feeling was familiar: an instantaneous mistake followed by the careening reality of time. All it took was a fraction of a second—the window smashed, the condom forgone, the pill popped, the biker mocked, the cop mooned—and whatever misstep receded unalterably into the past. With this body heaped at his feet, Matt again sensed his life diverging closer to the clifftop—to the void, to the end.

☙✦❧

SHERENE GOT STUCK in highway traffic so Ash arrived alone, making his way through the downtown shopping centre that housed London's central library. He'd forgotten that it was Boxing Day; the place was a riot of deal-seekers thronging in and out of the stores, eyes glazed and arms loaded with the spoils of their savings.

By the library's front desk a FICTION WORKSHOP sign and arrow directed him to one of the seminar/study rooms. Through the wire-hatched window in the door, four people sat equally spaced around a conference table, as if enduring a double-date or pre-trial disclosure. Ash let himself in.

Heads turned. He nodded generally and wedged himself in the corner. To his left sat a grinning woman whose OED, thesaurus, usage dictionary and coil-bound notebook were stacked neatly on the table; to his right loomed a man in Hemingway's beard and a cableknit sweater.

Ash took out Brij's book—his transcription, freshly printed—and set it fatly on the table. The 40-point title seemed to echo through the room:

## THE PATRIMONIES

It was a statement: a real writer was in their midst. But before the group could be sufficiently cowed, in trotted a character in a tweed blazer and goatee, waving like a game show host.

'Well *hello* my literary colleagues!' His accent was, exactly, Dracula's.

'Hi Milosz,' chorused the class—save Ash.

Milosz placed his valise on the table, remained standing. 'I trust you're all well?'

'Fine as wine,' growled Hemingway. 'How were your holidays?'

'Hardly ever a holiday for me, Grant!' Here Milosz mimed either stenography or Rachmaninoff, fingers dancing in the air. 'Always working,' he whispered.

'Done your play?'

Milosz's gaze swept over his acolytes, gauging their worthiness. With a shrug, he unclasped his valise and removed a ream of papers elastic-banded together. 'The manuscript!' he cried.

Amid the subsequent applause, Ash flipped his dad's novel facedown.

Milosz chuckled. 'Only the first draft. About which we know what?'

'*The first draft is a skeleton,*' sing-songed his disciples.

'If you're feeling left out,' said Milosz, eyeing Ash. 'I'm sure by the end of the workshop you'll be sick to death of me and all my slogans.'

Ash glanced at the door. Still no sign of Sherene.

'Well! Enough about me.' Milosz entombed the skeleton and peered around the room. 'So who's here . . . Grant? How's the collection coming?'

'Edits.'

'Which . . .'

'*Are the life's blood of a book*,' recited Grant.

'*Lifeblood*.' Milosz beamed at the woman with the reference books. 'Donna?'

'Oh you know. Some pieces here and there.'

'So modest! I happen to know that a poem of Donna's, which those of you who took Poetry with Panache might remember—the one about, what was it? Butter?'

'Ice cream. "On First Tasting of Chapman's Vanilla."'

'Yes, your Keats parody. A delight.'

'Yeah, it got an honourable mention . . .'

But he had already moved on: 'Bertrand? Priscilla? How is your screenplay?'

A fortyish couple with the same paper plate of a face exchanged nervous looks.

'We've had some creative differences,' said the husband.

'Thought this'd be a good place to work them out,' said the wife.

'Ah,' said Milosz, with a trace of fear. 'And last, you cowering in the back. You are?'

'My name?' said Ash.

'Yes!'

'My name is . . . Brijnath.'

'Brijnath.' Milosz sounded skeptical. 'And you're here because?'

'Because my mom's boyfriend signed me up for this class.'

He felt everyone's eyes on him—the interloper, the impostor. Also he probably sounded like some unruly teen, dumped here for remedial discipline.

'Have you done much writing previously?'

Ash stared. Then: 'Not for a while, no.'

'And? Your area of interest is what? The novel?'

'I like novels, sure.'

'Is that it? On the table?'

Ash pulled his father's book closer. 'The start of one, yeah.'
'We'll look forward to it this afternoon. Until then . . .' Handouts
appeared from the valise and were passed briskly around the room.
'Those who've taken my courses know the drill. In the morning we
free-write. After lunch, we share WIPS.'

There was a murmur of acquiescence. Ash raised his hand.

'*Works in progress,*' whispered Donna.

The hand retracted.

'Indeed, Brijnath,' said Milosz. 'You shan't miss your chance
to regale us with your novel. But first, we *create.*'

Ash, irate, slid *The Patrimonies* into his bag. He was one of the
nation's literary gatekeepers! And a published author with a major
press, not whatever print-on-demand swindle produced Milosz's
silly scripts. One email could ruin this Balkan bloodsucker's career.
Or could have until lately, he supposed. Where the hell was Sherene?

'We shall begin with a warm-up exercise.' Milosz cracked his
knuckles, cracked his neck. 'Everyone? Please . . . Close your
eyes . . . And relax . . .'

Obediently the class descended into a vegetative trance while
Milosz murmured about clouds and light and Ash entertained
murder fantasies and their related headlines: *Transylvanian play-
wright beaten to death with valise! Drama community rejoices . . .*

The door opened and Ash nearly jumped to his feet.

Sherene met his eyes, nodded in a covert way. 'Hi,' she said,
waving to the room.

'Everyone, ignore the disruption,' cried Milosz, marshalling her
in with a frantic wave of his hand—so fragile, the spell of his teaching! 'Quickly, before you lose the moment, move straight from your
subconscious to the page. Listen well and follow my prompts.
Writing is a journey and we embark upon it, now, together!'

AT NOON EXACTLY Milosz called for lunch. There was a sense of
rebirth, maybe, as the class paraded out into the blazing lights

of the library and beyond. Sherene and Ash met up in the stacks. After a quick glance around, they hugged.

'I'm so happy to see you,' she said.

'Before I forget: my name is Brijnath,' said Ash.

'Interesting.'

'Oh, be quiet. Let's go eat.'

In the food court they ordered combos and sat. All around them shoppers were refuelling between bouts of bargaineering. Their distant conversations reminded Ash of guttering candles.

'You ever heard of this teacher?' Sherene asked. 'Or his work?'

'Never,' said Ash. 'He's really got a system, though. You'd think we were in there with Stanislavski or something.'

'Oh, hush. The students seem to like him.'

'God, and now we're going to have to sit through their awful stories.'

'You're such a grump! It could be fun. Or funny.'

'Are you kidding? You know what these people write about? Themselves. Plotless stories transcribed from plotless lives. It will be terrible. Mark me, woman!'

She stole one of his onion rings.

'And you know the lyrical hogwash these types think makes for good writing. Description to the point of assault. As if meaning might be bullied loose with words.'

'So I'm assuming, Brijnath, that you did end up bringing your dad's book?'

'As if literature were just an accumulation of similes,' he continued. 'That's an indirect comparison using *like* or *as*, in case you'd forgotten.'

'Answer me.'

Ash sighed. 'Maybe.'

'Wow,' she said, stealing another onion ring. 'Bold.'

'As if I had time to write something of my own!'

'Why not? I did.'

'What?' Ash's burger was oozing; he leaned in and slurped. 'Just like that?'

'Well, don't get too excited. It's not like it's any good.'

'What's it about?'

'You inspired me, old friend.'

'What do you mean? It's not about me, is it?' Ash's thoughts fled to himself staggering around the streets of Montreal—Matt's supposed video, if it existed.

'No, no. I was just reading about where you're from and came across something cool.'

'Where I'm from? London?'

'No, sweetie. Kashmir.'

Ash mopped his face with a napkin. 'Sorry?'

'I got a book . . . I don't know, it was meant to be some way to . . . It sounds so stupid when I say it. How long have we known each other? Eight years? And I don't know, I've just felt so far away from you these past couple months, since . . . Your dad . . . And I never met him and wanted to be a good friend, but I didn't—'

'Spit it out, for god's sakes. What are you on about?'

'—know what you needed. I thought this might be one way to understand you. Your culture. Who you are.'

'Sherene, seriously. You want to understand *who I am* you'd do better to spend the day walking around this mall. Story of my early years. Shoplifting and'—he held up his ruined burger—'eating literal garbage.'

'Anyway, you want to hear this story?'

'You memorized it?'

'I can give you the gist.'

'Sure. As long as you don't think you've unlocked some key to my soul or anything.'

'Just listen. The original is from the eighth century, but the version I found was written by this poet, Kalhana, in the eleven hundreds. A Kashmiri. Heard of him?'

Ash tipped the last few onion rings onto his tray and shrugged: *of course*; *never*.

'Except I read a modern translation, which makes mine an adaptation of an adaptation of a nine-hundred-year-old document of something that happened four hundred years before that.'

'Go on.'

'There's this poet, Matrigupta, whose king offers the best poets residencies in his palace. As such, most poetry is written to please the king. "The king is good, the king is great," that sort of thing. So this is what Matrigupta writes too, because he and his wife are poor, and palace artists get nice salaries and apartments.'

'Give me some of your fries.'

'Matrigupta's wife is a weaver. Kalhana doesn't give her a name, but in my version I call her—guess?' She placed a single french fry on his tray. 'No guesses? Fine: Sherene.'

'I should have known.'

'Sherene the Weaver sells rugs and shawls at the local market. She's happy in her work, while Matrigupta isn't exactly overjoyed to be reciting poems about how benevolent and glorious the king is. Privately, of course, he writes different poems. Odes to Sherene, mainly, because she's so beautiful and brilliant and great.'

Ash laughed. Not just at the joke. The story was exactly the sort of thing Sherene loved, with its looming moral of artistic integrity. It was a laugh of comfort, familiarity.

'So eventually Matrigupta reads a poem about how terrific the king is and it goes over really well and he's invited to the palace for a residency.' She rationed out another lone fry, but moved her ketchup away when Ash went to dip. 'Note that there are no residencies for weavers. Though, you know, there ought to be.'

'Should there be?'

'Hush. A few days later Matrigupta starts reciting poetry for the king. Pretty soon that's all he's doing so he doesn't have time to write poems for Sherene, and it deflates him a bit. But a month or two later she gets pregnant and he's energized again, enough to write a poem about their child and what their life will be like as parents. It's a great poem, maybe his best work, and he decides to read it to the king instead of his regular stuff. Except the king hates it. He's told to write an ode like he's supposed to, "or else." Matrigupta worries that he's cost his family everything. Even so, all he can think about is the baby and Sherene, so when he doesn't have a new poem ready, the palace guards escort his family out the gates. Within days Sherene gives birth, way too early. There are complications and she dies in labour and so does the baby. Matrigupta falls apart. He swears off poetry forever and takes a job as the palace lamplighter: every day at dusk he circles the palace, lighting each lamp, save the one by the king's bedroom window. One night the king has had enough. He's waiting on the balcony and catches Matrigupta going past. "Hey!" he calls. "You there! Light my lamp." Matrigupta ignores him. The king is so enraged that he doesn't even summon one of his guards. He just rushes out of his room, down the stairs, through the courtyard and out the gates, where he finds Matrigupta hiding in the shadows. Oh, I like this part—he has chapped lips.'

'Chapped lips?'

'Matrigupta, yeah. For real. That detail has survived through all the translations. I didn't even add it: for nine-hundred years Matrigupta has had chapped lips.'

'Wow. Why do you think—'

'Hold on, let me finish. "I know you," says the king. "You were one of my best poets. What happened?" Matrigupta struggles to his feet, and from somewhere finds the words to speak. He tells his entire story, from his beginnings as a poet, writing poems for his wife, to his move inside the palace, to his expulsion, to the deaths of his wife and child. He tells it all, right up to that very moment, telling the king his story.'

'So what happens?'

'Well that's as far as my version goes,' said Sherene. 'In the real story, the king gives Matrigupta a kingdom of his own, Kashmir, where Matrigupta rules for years, before turning ascetic and forgoing all worldly possessions and all that Hindu claptrap.'

'But you don't include that in your version?'

'Well here's the thing. Think about this story: the "woman behind the man" is sacrificed, sending him into an emotional spiral, from which he emerges triumphant, wife replaced with land. Those themes—inspiration, dominion, property—are such typical manifestations of male power. And yet I wrote it, Ash. I mean, I didn't make it up, but I felt inspired enough to type it out. Which is maybe worse? Anyway, when I got to the ending I sat back and was just like, "What am I doing?" Me—even me, with all my feminist thinking, fell into the trap of this lame narrative. I think it's partly because I've never written fiction before, so I defaulted to a certain type of story. So I got to thinking: how do you subvert that? Maybe there can't be an ending. Because these sorts of stories are these weirdly deterministic things. There's this teleology that justifies its parts with the sum, which is usually a man achieving success—getting the girl, or the glory, or regaining his sense of self, whatever. Even if he rejects it, like Matrigupta— which, really, only elevates that success to some transcendentally higher plane. So either there can't be an ending, or I'd like to go back and redo the whole thing, retell it in some new way. Bring Sherene back from the dead to kill everyone, maybe.'

'But why is that the alternative? Why does the feminist version have to end with the woman laying slaughter to all the men? Can't there be some middle ground?'

'Oh, sweetie, I wasn't being serious.' Sherene checked her phone. 'We should probably get going.'

'Wait, though, I don't understand. What drew you to this story in the first place? I mean, other than an essential glimpse into my Kashmiri soul.'

Sherene seemed to be searching Ash's face for the answer. Her eyes settled on his mouth. 'To be honest,' she said, 'I think it was the chapped lips. Nine hundred years of Matrigupta's chapped lips. I liked that, that human touch. That fallibility. Seems to me the only true thing in the whole story.'

MILOSZ STOOD AT THE FRONT of the classroom with his arms raised like a preacher. 'I trust we are all ready to workshop our WIPS?'

Nods and smiles and murmurs of artistic camaraderie rippled around the table. Ash nodded too: of course! Fiction—what a lark!

'Good,' continued Milosz. 'Such confidence and courage. For? What?'

'*The enemy of creation,*' intoned his minions, '*is fear and self-doubt.*'

Milosz clucked his approval. 'Who will share first?'

Grant's hand shot up and, as if he were a brave soldier selflessly flinging himself upon the grenade of Milosz's intellect, he offered, 'I suppose I can go.'

'Grant! Fine.'

'It's called "Looking Back,"' said Grant. 'It's about . . . the past.'

'One of the richest sources of creative material,' Milosz explained, 'is memory.'

Ash watched Sherene watch four adults write this down.

Grant gathered the pages in his hands. 'Here goes nothing,' he said, cleared his throat, and proceeded with the monotone of a train conductor announcing station stops.

Ash retrieved *The Patrimonies* from his bag. What harm would it be to share a few pages? A chance to honour Brij's memory, maybe, even with this cult of shopping-mall literati and their madman of a master. Ash scanned the manuscript while Grant droned on and on about 'Greg,' his fictional proxy, thinking about things and putting on pants.

At last it was over. An ovation followed. Fourteen minutes had passed.

'Wonderful,' said Milosz. 'You know the character so well.'

'Well, it's just me,' said Grant.

Milosz held up a closed fist: a directive for Grant's mouth. 'This is a fiction class, remember. This story is not about you. It's about *Greg*.'

'Yeah, but Greg is me, Milosz. I mean, everything that happens to Greg is stuff that happened to me. I worked as a notary public for twenty-two years, I sail, I have a boxer-rotty cross named Stu. I just changed my name, because . . . I figured that's what writers are supposed to do. It's not like I made anything up.'

'And yet!' said Milosz.

Everyone leaned in—even Ash.

Milosz's eyes flashed wildly around the room, his thumbs drummed the table, his forehead crinkled. He looked like a robot pushed to the brink, about to short-circuit.

'Who's next?' he said, finally.

'Wait,' said Donna, 'don't we get to comment on Grant's story?'

'Of course,' said Milosz. 'Who has a critique for Grant?'

'I thought it was also wonderful,' said Priscilla.

'Very honest,' agreed her husband, whose name Ash had forgotten.

Donna reached at Grant across the table. 'I really liked the part where you—'

'Where Greg,' warned Milosz.

'Where *Greg*, sorry,' said Donna. 'Where Greg looked in the mirror and finally saw himself for what he was. That felt really true to me.'

At last Sherene spoke: 'I wonder if, maybe, you could dig a little deeper into that?'

'Oh?' said Grant. Heads turned.

'Yeah,' she said. 'You're obviously a talented writer'—Ash struggled not to laugh—'and I love what you've done so far, I just think you might be able to really get at *what* this character sees. Like, who is he? What's really going on for him?'

'Good point,' said Milosz, claiming it as his own. 'Brijnath? You've been quiet.'

Ash looked up.

'Brijnath is held captive by his own genius. Don't worry, you'll get your chance!'

The class roared. He felt Sherene's eyes on him: *Brijnath!*

'Brijnath, please. In a workshop it's imperative that everyone contribute. You wouldn't want to read your work—this mysterious novel of yours we've heard so much about—and not have anyone respond. Could you imagine such a thing?'

'I could not,' said Ash.

'And so? What are your thoughts on—what was it? "Looking in the Mirror," Grant?'

'"Looking Back."'

'Ah, yes.' Milosz titled his head. His goatee and air of inquisition leant him the look of a conquistador. One chair over, Grant mimicked him exactly.

'I agree with Sherene,' said Ash.

'That's it?' said Milosz.

'Pretty much,' said Ash. They stared at each other. The air in the room tightened.

'Fine,' said Milosz. 'Who will provide our second reading of the day?'

Next up was a story co-written by Priscilla and Bertrand set, shockingly, amid the Cambodian death camps, followed by Donna's piece about a paralegal a little too attached to her cats. ('The bestial,' lectured Milosz, 'has fascinated artists since the cave-painters of Lascaux.') Then they were down to Sherene and Ash.

Sherene read first. Her Matrigupta story went over well, and of course tantalized their classmates with its lack of ending. Suggestions followed: slay the king then and there and dress in his robes and rule the land; or what if Matrigupta took his show on the road and became a memoirist, telling tales of his pain? Sherene listened with a patient smile and thanked everyone for their thoughts.

Every face in the room turned upon Ash.

'And now, at long last,' said Milosz, rubbing his hands like a henchman, 'our friend Brijnath will regale us with his masterpiece.' He glanced at the clock: ten to four. 'Perhaps just a quick excerpt, enough to sample its genius.'

The pages in Ash's hands felt loose and inadequate. He read the first line over to himself. Looked around the room. He was reminded of the funeral, all those people he'd never seen before, invading his family's space with their agendas and alien ideas of his dad. He couldn't share the novel, no.

'Pass,' he said.

'Pass?' said Milosz. He threw his head back, roared. 'Brijnath, please. There is no *pass*. Everyone else has shared their stories. For the workshop to function—'

'Pass,' he said again.

'Pass,' said Milosz. 'But—'

'Thanks,' said Ash, and slipped the pages into his bag, and sat there with his arms folded across his chest, staring at the clock.

'DHAR?'

Ash froze. He'd been outed; someone in the group had recognized him after all.

But, streaming out of the library, his classmates were busy singing the praises of their master ('Milosz is such an *inspiration*,' swooned Donna; 'A genius,' said Bertrand. 'An absolute genius!') and the voice came from the stacks. An Asian man emerged, tired and hunched and elusively familiar. Someone's brother or husband, a former colleague? And then Ash noticed the wheelchair, and the boy upon it.

'Chip. Shit.'

'Hey!' Ash's old friend leapt at him, arms spread. As the two men embraced Sherene hovered nearby. Ash introduced her: 'My producer. She's off to England tomorrow.'

Chip shook her hand distractedly, eyes everywhere but her face. He seemed different from how he'd been at the funeral, more ragged at the edges. Even his habitual enthusiasm felt forced and fatigued. 'So, wow, buddy! You're home?'

'At my ma's place, yeah.'

'Family Christmas, nice.' Chip turned distant. Then that manic grin came splashing down again. 'Come say hi to Ty, Dhar!'

'Say goodbye to me first,' commanded Sherene. 'Dhar.'

They hugged.

'Promise you'll write?' Ash joked.

'Promise,' she said—with such wide-eyed sincerity that Ash had to choke down the lump that rose in his throat.

He found Chip and the wheelchair docked amid the multimedia shelves.

Chip rolled his son forward. 'You remember Ash, Ty?'

This inspired wailing, which inspired in Ash first fear, then guilt. He compensated with proportionate volume. 'How you doing, Tyler?' he boomed.

'He likes to shake hands,' instructed Chip. 'A real man now.'

Ash's hand was seized in a claw-like, clammy grip. The boy's eyes were fierce. They made Ash feel a bit too acutely seen. He wrenched his hand loose, leaving Ty pinching air. And sensed Chip watching him with disappointment.

'You guys checking out books?' Ash said.

'Videos,' said Chip. He held up a copy of *The Lost Weekend*. 'This one any good?'

'Of course. A classic,' said Ash, though he'd never seen it.

'Cool. Now I need to find one for Ty. Any suggestions?'

'How old is he?'

'Ten! Can you believe it?'

A decade spent rolling that wordless life around. No. Ash could not.

'Listen, if you're in town,' said Chip, 'how about getting the gang together for beers?'

'I haven't seen any of those guys in—wow. I don't know how long.'

'Perfect, just like old times. It'll have to be at my place, is all.' Chip indicated his son. 'So how about Matt, over there in your homeland? Sounds like he's having a blast.'

'Right.'

'Sightseeing, partying.' Chip leaned in, whispered: 'Banging Russian supermodels.'

'Sorry?'

'Well, just the one . . . Did he tell you he might have a role in a Bollywood movie? I guess they're always looking for white folks. And he's an actual actor, even.'

'I'd not heard this, no.'

'Too bad that guy's not around, especially if we're getting every-one together.' Again Chip's vigour seemed to falter, and again he raged ahead: 'Maybe short notice, but do you have plans tonight?'

Ash looked around, as if searching for an excuse on the bookshelves. Of course nothing presented itself, but it was Chip's expression—a grin so eager it was almost pleading—that forced him to concede. The guy *was* an old friend, after all. "Sure, why not?' Ash said, finally, with a shrug and a dry little laugh. 'I'm free.'

CHIP'S PLACE WAS IN THE COUNTRY, past the last few town-houses at the city limits, onto rural roads, past cornfields and grain silos, and down into a valley where a new subdivision glit-tered like a space station amid the darkened farms all around.

There were gates, and then a half-dozen show homes entic-
ing prospective homeowners. But beyond them wasn't much.
A trailer with a backhoe parked out front. A lot of empty lots, a
few with frames looming skeletally over frosty dirt patches with
lawn aspirations. The streetlights cast everything with a roseate
glow. In his mother's car Ash passed Poplar Grove, White Pine
Crescent, Elm Drive, each lined with saplings turtlenecked in
burlap. Even the few finished houses seemed not to be hosting or
even anticipating life so much as forsaken by it: lightless, still.

At last he came to Maple Court, a cul-de-sac anchored by
a single, squat bungalow with a string of lights tacked over the
garage. The other lots were occupied only with sprigs of wire and
a scattering of little orange flags. Ash parked behind a minivan
(vanity plate: TY'S RIDE), climbed the ramp and rang the bell. The
door flung open while the chimes were still sounding. Had Chip
been waiting in ambush?

'Dhar! You're the first one here! Just heating up some appies!
Come on in! Make yourself at home!'

Ash was swept inside. A boozy smell wafted off Chip, and a
silvery splatter of what Ash hoped was Ty's drool trailed down
the sleeve of his hoodie. He wore plaid pyjama pants and moose
slippers with velveteen antlers. Ash felt absurdly formal, and
urban, in his slim jeans and cardigan.

He was led through the house into the kitchen. The walls
were bare; the smells were antiseptic. The place had the generic,
unpeopled feeling of a hotel, as though the living that happened
within its walls was tentative, temporary. It reminded Ash, with
a pang, of the house Brij had moved into after the divorce.

Chip deposited him at the kitchen island before a huge
spread: olives and pickles, a cheese plate and pre-sliced baguette,
chips and salsa, pepperettes, a shrimp ring. Plus whatever frozen
snacks Chip was arranging on cookie sheets for the oven.

'Just some appies,' he said. 'Beer?'

'I'm driving,' said Ash. 'So maybe just one.'

Chip handed him a king can and a frosty mug. 'Might as well make it a big one.'

Ash poured it out badly and had to dive down to slurp the foaming head as it surged over the glass. 'When'd you move in?'

'Six months ago! Probably feels a bit like we're in the sticks but it's going to be great out here once the area's built up. There's plans for a community centre, a mall, a library. London's growing, man. And it's an easy enough trip into town in the morning, just drop Ty off at seven thirty and then head back out on the 402 to work.'

'Jesus. What time do you get up?'

'Five fifteen. Ty's not much of a morning person, takes a while to get going, needs his meds and breakfast and all that.' Chip spoke rapidly and his eyes flicked in Ash's direction, yet never settled on his face. 'But we have fun, we do our thing. It's all good.'

'At five in the morning?'

'You get used to it.' Chip tipped whiskey into a plastic cup, splashed in a little soda. 'To new beginnings,' he proposed.

'Cheers,' said Ash, unclear what this was supposed to mean. They drank.

'Ty's in the den watching the game if you want to join him. Still a hoops fan?'

'Not really. Not like I used to be.'

'Me neither! Who has the time? Between Ty and work? But it's all good.' Chip grinned, shook his head, drank.

'Sorry I'm a little late,' said Ash.

'Not sure where everyone else is . . . I said seven on the Evite, right?' Chip checked his phone. 'I mean, it's tough, obviously, at this age, at this time of year—and super last minute. People have families and that.'

'You still hang out with those guys?'

'Not really, you and Matt were the first folks from high school I've seen in ages. At your dad's . . . thing.' Chip took another big slug of his drink.

'Thanks again for coming to that.'

'No sweat, it was fun.' Chip shook his head. 'Sorry, dumb thing to say. I just mean it was good to see you—and Matt. I wish I could have stayed out and really tied one on like we used to. Ty's mom was supposed to take him that weekend, but . . .'

The night out, the video: Ash pushed it away. 'You guys don't share custody?'

'Nah. Ty and I are good. We've got our routine. We do our thing.'

'Right.'

'God, where is everyone?' Chip opened the oven, poked the hors d'oeuvres around. 'Got to eat these while they're hot. Nothing worse than a cold cheese stick, right?'

'Few things.'

'Hey, did you see I got olives? Just for you, Mister Fancy-pants. The girl at Loblaw's said that kind is good.' Chip refilled his cup, drank, refilled. 'Careful though, they've still got the stones in them. I got wine too, if you want some?'

'Beer's good.' Ash ate an olive. He did not like olives.

'And?'

He spat the pit into his hand. 'Great.'

BY NINE O'CLOCK no one else had shown nor replied to Chip's messages. So they withdrew from the food, most of it untouched, to the den. Ty sat in his wheelchair a foot from the TV, blocking the screen. Ash took the couch, dodging the bows of a massive Christmas tree that towered in the corner of the room, shaggy and unlit.

'My kid *loves* hoops,' said Chip, standing beside Ty with the bottle of whiskey in one hand, cup in the other. After every sip, he refilled. 'Just like his dad.'

'Superfan Junior,' said Ash.

'God, we had a fun team in high school, huh?'

'Didn't we even make you a top with your name on it?'

Chip laughed. 'Hold on.'

He raced down the hall and reappeared wearing the jersey: bulging in rolls at the hips and tits with SUPERFAN 00 printed on the back—this had been the centrepiece of Chip's get-up at Ash's high school games, along with face paint and pom-poms. There'd been something worrisome about his enthusiasm, even then.

'Score it!' Chip hollered. 'See my kid there, Ash? Loving that and-one?'

He high-fived one of Ty's hands.

'Bedtime soon though,' said Chip. 'The grownups've got some drinking to do.'

But then he seemed almost remorseful. He set his cup aside, knelt and stroked his son's cheek with a knuckle. Ty kicked his feet. When Chip started kissing Ty, Ash looked away—out of respect, out of embarrassment.

'Yeah, Ty-Ty,' Chip murmured. 'We're buds, huh? Me and you? Best buds.'

Chip turned and stared hard at Ash. 'I love this kid,' he said. 'Greatest kid ever.'

'Totally,' said Ash.

Chip nodded. He seemed satisfied. He joined Ash on the couch and set to his drink with renewed tenacity.

Ash was coerced into a second beer, the game ended, and as the postgame banalities wrapped and the credits rolled Chip swayed to his feet. 'Say good night to our buddy, Ty.' But Ty wouldn't look at Ash, despite his father's coaxing. 'Can't win 'em all,' said Chip with a shrug, and rolled off down the hall, propping himself on the wheelchair.

The news came on. Ash got up to search for the remote. Piled by the TV were '80s NBA bloopers on VHS, that library copy of

*The Lost Weekend*, an anime box set, an unopened workout DVD, *Home Alone*. At the bottom of the stack was a disc with MATT'S SHOW-REEL written in black marker on the case. Ash slid it into the player and sat on the floor with his beer.

The disc opened with Matt's first commercial: a background role in a thirty-second spot that featured an elderly white woman praising a fast food chain in an ad-man's approximation of rap slang. At the end, as she zoomed off on a skateboard with a mouthful of fries, Matt dropped his jaw in wonder. God, thought Ash, he looked so young, slim and trim and luxuriantly coiffed, eyes nearly delirious with ambition and hope.

The next clip was from a pilot for a sci-fi show that had never been picked up. As the bespectacled spaceship doctor, Matt delivered his two lines with gravitas: 'I'm sorry, but I've got some bad news.' *Stare awkwardly as purple-skinned patient responds.* Then: 'You've contracted a virus from time travel that is reversing the growth of your cells. I'm afraid it's terminal.' *And: pause for effect. And: scene.* ('I was going to become a major character,' Matt had claimed.)

Up next was an ad campaign that featured Matt and a half-dozen other men playing loving dads. Dads cuddling babies, dads pushing swings, dads fake-shaving their toddler sons. The pitch, with an eye to selling soap, linked emotional sensitivity and skin-care. Matt's child was about kindergarten age. In the first clip they were watering sunflowers; in the next, baking muffins. In the final spot, Matt kissed his son's tiny feet.

Chip swayed into the doorway. 'I love those bits.'

'Why do you have this?'

'Same reason I've got ten copies of your book.' His voice was slush.

'Ten?'

'I'm proud of my boys, what can I say.'

The reel ended; the screen went blue.

'Here's the thing,' Ash said, 'and I don't mean this in any disrespectful way, because I know how dedicated you are to Ty—'

'He's everything to me. Everything.'

'Totally. But that campaign? How come it's just dads? There have to be other ways for men to be decent people than fatherhood. Shouldn't that be a given, anyway? And why does being a dad have to be the only way to be a caring man? What about being good to your mom? Your sisters? Your friends?'

Chip shrugged and drank.

'And Matt never really had a dad, so don't you think it must have felt weird pretending to be one? That it might have even fucked him up a bit?'

'No idea, man,' said Chip, shaking his head. 'But speaking of soap and kids, can I ask you a favour? I've maybe had a few too many. Can you help me get Ty in the tub?'

Ash froze. 'Sorry—in the bathtub?'

'There's a harness I use but it's broken. So you just gotta put him in. Come on.'

Ty was sprawled naked on his bed, gurgling happily. When he saw Chip and Ash he lifted his legs and kicked. Just above his belly button was the valve, capped with plastic, through which he took his meals. Ash took a step back.

'Okay, hero,' said Chip. 'Pick him up.'

'Just like that?'

'Unless you know another way.'

Tentatively Ash stepped to the side of the bed. Ty froze—with dread, Ash felt certain. He knew whom not to trust.

'Go on,' said Chip. 'Get in there. He won't bite.'

One arm went under Ty's neck, another under his knees. Ash anticipated a struggle, or seizure, but the boy eased into his arms, even clung to him a little. He was heavier than he looked and Ash staggered a little lifting him off the bed. Steadied himself. Awaited instructions.

'There you go,' said Chip. 'Now down the hall. The bath's already run.'

Ty began to slide, so Ash hitched him closer and firmed up his grip. The kid giggled and pressed his lips to Ash's cheek.

'That's it,' said Chip. 'You got him.'

The bathroom was steamy. Ash stopped. 'How do I get him in the tub?'

'Kneel down. Slowly. No rush.'

Ash did as he was told, terrified he might stumble and smash Ty's face through the shower door. But the boy had gone still.

'Easy,' said Chip. 'You're doing great.'

Ash was on one knee with Ty resting atop his other thigh.

'Now put him in.'

As if offering the boy in sacrifice, Ash moved Ty over the water and let go: he landed with a splash and cried out. Water slopped up over the edge of the tub.

'Shit! Sorry!'

Chip laughed. 'No way, man. Look how happy he is.'

Ty was grinning. Waves rocked him this way and that. He hummed and burbled and his body made a rubbery squelch as it skidded around the tub.

Chip patted Ash on the shoulder. 'Nicely done,' he said. 'You did great.'

And then Ty rolled onto his belly and Ash saw the cuts, healing but recent: one long one along his spine, and another shorter gash between his shoulder blades. Around them was a massive, yellowing bruise.

Ash froze. Caught himself staring. Stood hurriedly.

'Okay, that's good,' Chip said quietly, guiding Ash by the elbow out of the bathroom. And the door closed, stranding Ash in the hallway, where he listened for a moment to the soft splash of water from within before fleeing to the living room.

—

'I NEVER BOOZE LIKE THIS,' Chip said for the third time since putting Ty to bed. 'But it's the holidays, right? And how often do we get to hang out?'

The late game was on TV, the sound down. Ash watched it in silence, thinking about Ty. That body, so dependent and defenceless—and wounded. Chip still hadn't said anything about it, which felt to Ash like an admission of guilt. And Ash, as witness, was complicit. But guilt over what, and complicit in what? Negligence? Abuse? The only option was escape, best introduced casually: 'Actually, I should probably get going.'

'What are you talking about? It's not even eleven!' Now Chip drank straight from the bottle. 'And there's still all that food. You barely ate any.'

'Sorry, man. I just shouldn't be home too late, staying at my mom's . . .'

'Fine, go if you want.' A pause, a switch: 'Just sleep here. The couch folds out.'

After one quarter, the game was already a blow out; the teams retreated to their benches looking equally unenthused at the chore of the remaining thirty-six minutes.

It went to commercial and Chip killed the TV. He turned to face Ash, sudden sobriety shadowing his face. Here it was, the confession; Ash braced himself. Instead Chip gestured outside, down the path of some other story. 'Around the corner, on Poplar, like three weeks ago this guy moved in. No kids, no wife. Solo.'

Ash's phone buzzed in his pocket. 'Oh yeah?'

'Every few days he's throwing out these industrial-looking chemical containers. Ten-gallon tubs, right there on the curb. And stuff's getting delivered at weird hours and people are coming and going all the time. People in *lab coats*.'

The phone quieted.

'So I start watching them, right? Because what's the most obvious thing going on?'

'I don't know.' But the story wouldn't proceed until Ash participated. 'Meth lab?'

'Exactly.' Chip tapped his temple. 'Last thing I need is a fire or explosion or something and my kid inhaling toxic fumes. Or addicts breaking in here to steal my TV.'

'You really think they're cooking meth?'

'Check it out.' Chip held up his phone, swiping through photos of vans in the driveway, a woman in a white smock, a pair of plastic drums on the lawn. 'I had all the evidence, ready to call Crime Stoppers, and then one day that lady comes knocking. I hide Ty in the bedroom before I open the door, because what if she's here to'—he made a gun, pointed it at Ash, pulled the trigger—'take me out? But nope! Guess who she is?'

Ash shook his head: *no idea.*

'A—get this—nurse. Guy who lives in there is on dialysis. Guy my age. Our age.'

Ash's phone began ringing again.

'Anyway, she wants a neighbour to keep an eye out—like, if I don't see him for a while or if something just seems wrong.' Chip shook his head, made a clucking sound. 'Imagine? Being sick and not having anybody? No parents or kids or wife? You could collapse one day and no one would have any idea. Die there on the floor, totally alone.'

Ash checked the number: foreign. India, probably.

'What, you're taking calls now?'

'I think it's Matt.'

'Go ahead.' Chip shook his head. 'Not like I was telling you something important.'

'No, it's okay—look, he hung up.' But the caller was persistent: the phone started up again, humming insistently. 'Maybe I should see what he wants. What if he's in trouble?'

'Trouble?' Chip snorted. He drank. Shook his head. Drank some more.

Ash fingered his phone. Its ringing seemed urgent.

But Chip was standing now, reeling and shouting. 'Suddenly you're Mister Big Heart who cares about everyone? You act like my kid's got a fucking contagious disease—don't shake your head, you always have—and then you go judging *me* for how I'm raising him?'

'Whoa, Chip. That's not what's going on,' said Ash, hands up. 'Hey.'

'The moral of my story, if you'd listened? Don't think you understand anyone. What they're going through, what they're about.' Chip fell onto the couch, tilted his head back, closed his eyes. The bottle slipped from his hand; the last bit of whiskey dribbled onto the carpet. 'I'm a good dad,' Chip said quietly, nodding to himself. 'I'm a good dad.'

And Ash's phone buzzed faintly through the room.

FINALE

*In some fugues all the voices enter with either subject or answer in the final section . . . This is followed by the coda, [which] is a passage added at the end of a piece of music to bring it to a satisfactory conclusion.*

## 1

HEATHROW: A ROW OF HEATHS UNFURLING moorishly over the land, Ash thought, searching for Sherene among the travellers rushing past the airport pub. He'd claimed their intersecting flights to be coincidence, though his need for her was obvious. And like any good friend she was happy to oblige.

Ash took a sip of his beer and imagined what the surrounding countryside might have been before the airport ruined it. A series of undulating hills, windswept and misty, billowing down to the fetid metropolis of London. Two shepherds gazed down into the valley, the city domed with smog. One sucked from a pipe, the other held Bo Peep's staff, and around them flocked their wooly charges. 'Change is afoot,' said the first. 'Ay,' said the second. ''Tis true, 'tis true . . .'

And here was Sherene, cutting across the terminal. Even through a crowd she moved with breezy nonchalance, slipping this way and that with a playful half-smile. This spread into a full grin when she saw Ash. She broke into a jog, arms out.

He stood. They hugged.

'I'm glad I got to see you,' she said, sitting opposite him. And winking.

The verb tense was strange, suggesting the purpose of meeting had already been achieved. Ash passed her a menu; he'd already settled on the tandoori chicken wrap.

'Oh, I'm saving my appetite for Brick Lane,' she said, waving it away. 'Speaking of: you ready for the subcontinent?'

'Ready as I'll ever be.'

'Aren't you excited?'

Ash stared at her. 'Excited that I'm being dragged over there by my idiot friend?'

'Come on, Ash—*India*. When was the last time you went?'

'When I was twelve, maybe? All I remember is Hindi soap operas on full blast all the time. Boredom, resentment. And never feeling clean.'

'Well you're welcome to stay with us in London, hit the clubs.' She examined him. 'I'd love to see that. I bet you dance like a dad—cross-country skiing with handclaps.'

'Like my dad, then,' said Ash. And they laughed.

Their server came over. Sherene asked for a tea, then Ash waited for some racialized reaction to his order. Not even an ironic flicker, just a nod and withdrawal. He wondered if, to the outside eye, Sherene might look like his date. But why the airport rendezvous? The end of some illicit foreign affair, this final goodbye before they slunk home to their families. Or two assassins trading dossiers. Yes—less melodrama, more action.

'So, your friend Matt,' said Sherene. 'He's in jail?'

'No, the High Commission put him up in some sort of guesthouse until his trial. Not sure why the royal treatment. He did break the goddamn law.'

'He seems troubled.'

'*Troubled*? He's an idiot. Trust me. It was inevitable that something like this would happen to him, acting like the world is his personal playground. Spare him your pity.'

'Yet you're going all the way to India to help him. To support him.'

'Well I already helped him, god knows why. I paid his fucking bail.'

'Call it loyalty, maybe?'

'More like obligation.'

'Dharma,' Sherene said with a grin.

'Let's not lose our minds.'

The tea and tandoori wrap arrived, the latter garnished with a sprig of parsley masquerading as coriander.

'I'm not sure where they're firing their tandoor,' said Ash, 'but you can't argue with a colonialism sandwich.'

'McEmpire,' said Sherene, pouring hot water through the strainer into her cup. 'over 1.2 billion ruled.'

Two bites in, the wrap was disintegrating. Pink sauce splooged down Ash's arm. He wiped his elbow with a napkin. 'Oh, I nearly forgot.' He dug through his carry-on. 'I bought you a present. Merry Christmas. Or Eid, whatever. Sorry I didn't have time to wrap it.'

Sherene accepted the book: *Don Quixote*. 'Wow. Just some light reading for the holidays, huh?'

'I'm reading it too. I thought we could . . .' He trailed off, watching her fan through the novel as if it might be judged by the flap of the pages. 'Have you read it before?'

'No, never. A very nice idea, sweetie. A little book club. Thank you.' She nodded at his carry-on. 'What else have you got in there?'

He surveyed her for a moment, wiped his hands and reached down again. Out came the grey box that held the remains of his father. Its weight surprised him every time—almost frightening—and he felt the contents shift as he set it on the table between them.

'Is that . . .'

Ash nodded. Did he detect her shiver?

They were silent for a moment. With the box sitting there beside his ruined lunch, Ash felt like Brij himself were perched on the table and glaring at him in reproach.

'Some winter so far,' he said. 'November, Mona calls with the news. Then the funeral. Then that stuff at work.' He watched Sherene for some response—forgiveness, an update. None came. 'Then at Christmas I find out my sister's marriage is falling apart. I've got one friend living in a kind of suburban nightmare while another one goes and nearly kills some kid in on the other side of the goddamn world. And now here we are,' he said, nodding at the box. 'Mona figured if I'm going to India anyway why not . . .' He couldn't manage the word *scatter*—a term for birdseed or buckshot, not a person. 'You know what kills me most? I keep forgetting he's gone.'

'Oh, sweetie.'

'It's just—life goes on. Living becomes coping. But isn't coping just forgetting?'

Sherene reached around the box, touched his forearm.

'It's got to the point that I have to actively remember he's not around anymore. And the feeling that comes isn't sadness, exactly. More guilt and'—he spread his hands—'emptiness. Just this void where the grief ought to be.'

'That sounds hard.'

'Anyway, here we are,' he said again, tapping the box and laughing drily. '*Ash to Ash*. To, I don't know, some Indian drain. Not like Brij cares at this point, right?'

Sherene winced. Drank some tea. 'They say you haven't dealt with someone's death until you dream about them,' she said finally. 'Do you dream about Brij?'

'Weirdly, I've been dreaming about that book he was writing.' Ash looked around the pub. Other than a solitary character sipping a martini at the bar, he and Sherene were the only customers.

'What I want to know,' said Ash, leaning in, 'is who this *they* is who know so much. I picture an underground laboratory in the desert, guys in lab coats with clipboards, secret trials behind two-way glass. See that dude at the bar? Do you think he's one of *them*?'

'Ash, come on,' said Sherene, reaching again for his arm. She squeezed, let go. Sat back with her tea. Eyed him for a moment. 'So what else did you do in London? Ontario, I mean. Not the real one.'

'Don't you know that authenticity is a hoax? The faker the place, the realer it is.'

'What about that Asian guy you ran into at the library? Didn't he have some party?'

'Yeah, Chip. He's the one I was talking about.' Ash assumed a regretful, pained expression and paraphrased the evening, stressing its pathos with key details: the olives, the whiskey. Even that Chip had been adopted. Yet he didn't mention Tyler at all.

'Well, now at least you'll get to see Matt.'

'Not by choice.'

'Oh, come on. That guy seems so devoted to you. The Falstaff to your Hal. The Yogi to your Boo-Boo.' Sherene laughed. 'No, you're more like that squirrel . . .'

'Rocky? Sure, he was an aviator, a hero! Though wait, that would make Matt—'

'Exactly. You're his little Rocky, and he's Bullwinkle the big dumb moose.'

SOMETHING HAD SNAGGED IN ASH'S BRAIN, though he wasn't sure what—just a nagging feeling of irresolution—and on the connecting flight to Delhi he sorted through his conversation with Sherene, topic by topic. It wasn't until they were well over Europe that he identified it. The realization was like a fishhook yanked free from a tangle of reeds, the line zipping up out of the water and reeled swiftly to shore.

Chip. He'd told Sherene about that night out in the sticks, the failed party, watching his friend drink himself into oblivion, yet avoided the detail of Ty's wounds and whatever they might mean. The omission was less about a fear of outing his friend than self-preservation, as if that sanitized version might replace his memories of what really happened, and fill the worrying space of what he didn't know.

Before saying goodbye, Sherene had raved about the impressive fraternity of flying halfway around the world to help out a pal. But he'd abandoned another. Chip hadn't seen him out after Ash had hung up and explained Matt's arrest. He'd just sat there on the couch rolling the empty whiskey bottle under his foot, eyes glazed. Travelling to another continent to play the hero was easy. Chip had required something else, something beyond action: to be met and seen. Instead Ash had fled.

Ash lifted the blind and watched the wing tip blink amid the ozone. After a minute or two he closed it again. Through the darkened cabin a few TV screens glowed from seatbacks. Mostly people were asleep. The air was static and sterile; there were no smells. Ash never slept on flights. He watched movies, read (though he'd barely cracked *Don Quixote*), and monitored the live map of the plane's progress, its outsized icon blotting out entire nations below. Now this seemed too much of a cartoon. He dimmed the screen until it went black.

On the other side of all this was Matt, waiting in some consular safe house for Ash—to what? Save him? There was no plan and nothing he could do. Ash had no power in India, didn't speak the language, found its labyrinthine bureaucracies mostly disorienting and mindless. All he could offer was a feeble act of companionship. At best. His feelings weren't of vigilance, or even duty. He was mostly just tired—a fatigue so profound that it was indistinguishable from sadness.

The hours passed; the airplane hummed. Ash dipped in and

out of restless, head-snapping naps until the pilot announced their descent. Up went the window shade and there was Delhi, a sprawling orange glitter like something radioactive spilled below. One of Brij's old, waddling sisters had ended up here amid the Hindu exodus of 1989, and her concrete apartment block had been a required stop whenever the Dhars visited from Canada. Even Brij had loathed those trips, complaining about the crowds, the heat, the filth, the noise, the inescapable fury of that massive, bewildering city.

Though it wasn't just Delhi. He harboured such disdain for anywhere in India that wasn't home. The south was a particular target for scorn. Dravidians were darkly treacherous and backward; Aryan Kashmiris were superior in every way—better looking, more intelligent, more honourable. Kashmir had the tastiest food, the most exquisite handicrafts, the richest culture, the bluest lakes and most magnificent mountains. It wasn't until university, when Ash found himself on a rec league basketball team with Keralite brothers, that these certainties were revealed as pure chauvinism. 'Kashmir is fine,' said Shik, 'but to hear your people talk about it you'd think they were the chosen ones.' Shal was less delicate: 'That kind of bullshit is how the Nazis got started.'

The landing was almost delicate: the wheels nudged the runway and the plane eased down behind it carefully. As they taxied to the terminal Ash eyed the palm trees edging the tarmac: he'd forgotten that even India's north was so tropical, a civilization hacked from jungles and deserts. The airport itself was a rickety building patched with billowing tarps, though signs threatened improvements—*Coming soon*, like a Bollywood blockbuster.

The New India seemed to thrive on this sort of thing: everything was *coming*, in process, under construction, all of it projected into some misty, utopian future. A place perennially in transition. Which it might always be, Ash thought, heading to the baggage claim with one of the same wobbly carts that Brij had let him commandeer as a kid.

Ash's memories of India were sensory: mothballs and diarrhea, car-horns and horking, the custard-like squish of some Auntie's bosom as he was ensnared for another rampage of kisses. Childhood irritation due to missing March Break for interminable family time and forced lunches of yellow dhal and yellower paneer now, on his clandestine return, found more adult targets: the clutter, the inefficiency, India's dubious embrace of everything that was wrong with the West. And at Matt for dragging him here.

If Brij were to be believed, Kashmir was different. But Ash had only visited once before the place had turned inhospitable. He'd been four. All he recalled of that trip were a mountainside resort—trees and snow and a woodsy smell—and that his socks, soaked through and draped over an electric heater to dry, had been left so long that they charred to a brown crust. As consolation, someone had given him a strange, pink, milky tea brackish with salt, which Ash had struggled not to barf all over the floor.

Mona had spent lots of time in India, often on philanthropic missions. In fact she and Harj had met while eradicating the systemic poverty of Bihar's village people, one well-digging at a time. But even before that she'd maintained more of an affinity for the fatherland. Since she was older her memories of Kashmir were more vivid: houseboat stays, shikara punts around Dal Lake. She even had some basic facility in Hindi, and was close enough with certain relatives that they exchanged regular emails.

Over the baggage carousel was the requisite billboard of the Taj Mahal. When Ash was in eighth grade, upon discovering that her nephew had never seen this Wonder of the World, that Delhi aunt had guilted Brij into taking him. The car ride south had a perfunctory, grudging tone, and they'd barely entered the grounds before Brij was complaining about the touts, the monkeys, the tourists. So Ash had not, in the end, joined the queue into the world's most spectacular monument to love. 'The view's better from outside anyway,' his father had told him, already in retreat to the car.

While India was essential to how Mona understood her-self—down to the Bengali she'd married—Ash had mostly inherited his father's resentments. Brij had never really *liked* India; on their family trips he'd been tense and weird and Ash had found it hard to know him there. After their aborted Taj tour they'd headed north to another uncle's house in Jammu, the borderlands refuge for exiled Kashmiri Hindus and, in Brij's words, 'the most useless place on earth.' In the late afternoon he'd led Ash to the rooftop and gazed through the smog at a lumpy smudge on the horizon. 'The mountains where I grew up,' he'd told Ash. Then the pained tremor in his voice had stiff-ened: 'Not that you can see it for all this bloody pollution.' And then he'd spat off the roof and gone inside.

Consular Services had provided an address but no directions to the place where they'd stashed Matt, so once Ash had collected his luggage he rolled out the Departures gate with the astonished, cautious look of any newcomer. Having not alerted any family to his trip, he was faced with the prospect of cabbing into the city. But instead of a honking fleet of the bulbous yellow and black taxis of his childhood, a bunch of slick-looking men on cellphones loitered almost coquettishly outside the terminal.

Ash bee-lined for the least shifty of the lot, an elderly Sikh who nodded at the address and led him wordlessly to a waiting Maruti. And then they were off into, as Brij liked to say, 'the worst traffic in the world.' Ash, numb with exhaustion, was only distantly aware of all those autos and bikes and garlanded, tootling lorries careening around the car. That chaos was nothing he needed. So he closed his eyes, feeling like some time-travelling interloper, passing through this temporal purgatory, on his way home to whatever Now he lived in.

A BLOCK FROM THE SAFE HOUSE, or whatever it was, the Maruti stopped. Neighbourhood kids occupied the street with a cricket game. Ash had barely paid the driver when he felt a tug at his duffel. Wheeling, he expected to be faced with thieves. But two grinning boys were simply thrusting a paddle into his hands. 'Batsman, batsman!' they hollered, and Ash was dragged to a water-bottle wicket.

As a kid, Ash had played a little cricket with cousins and their friends in Jammu: a courtyard oval ringed with fruit trees, all that back-and-forthing as if the runner had forgot something at the other end. Now, in the pose of a baseball slugger, he cocked the bat over his shoulder. The young bowler, a spindly boy of ten or eleven, jogged into his windup: a bounce, a swing, and Ash hammered the ball over the rooftops.

'Six!' he cried—and his playmates cheered.

Following the path of his homer, Ash noticed a bald, pale head leaning out of an upstairs window: Matt, looking anxious. 'Third floor,' his friend whisper-yelled, glancing around the street, then retracted and shuttered the window behind him.

In the stairwell of Matt's building, Ash was reminded again of the Jammu house, also a low-rise with pale blue cement walls and paneless gaps for windows. Even the sounds seemed familiar: as he made his way up, birdsong twittered from the rooftop, while down below the cricket game resumed with calls and taunts and laughter.

On the third floor he discovered Matt—or, again, his head, poking out of a barely cracked door. 'In here,' he said in that same hushed and urgent voice.

The flat was modest: a living area with a two-seater and a TV, a small table with matching chairs, a hot plate and bar fridge.

A curtained doorway led to the bedroom. Light streamed in the window, as did the murmur of the main street. Matt and Ash stood by the door, like a realtor with a prospective client, taking it in. And then, as if remembering an obligation, Matt seized Ash in a quick hug. 'Thanks for coming.'

'Nice place.'

'Can's through my room,' said Matt, gesturing. 'Regular toilet, not one of those snake holes you've gotta squat over like a gosh-dang mongoose.'

Over the kitchen table was a calendar that, Ash noticed, expired in two days.

'The couch doesn't pull out but you're not exactly the Jolly Brown Giant. Unless you got designs on joining me in my love chamber?' Matt smiled, briefly. But then it vanished.

'Who's paying for this?'

Matt took Ash's bag and set it on the couch. 'Me. Who else?'

'But the Consulate owns it?'

'They helped set it up. All's I know? Way better than my last accommodations.'

'Jail, you mean.'

The sounds of the cricket game drifted in through the window: the chuckles, the shouts, the cries. Matt moved to the kitchenette. He looked thin, stooped. 'Want a beer?'

'Are you okay?'

'Honestly? Say la vee, as they say in Quebec. Beer or no?'

'Is it even noon yet?'

'Sack up, bro. It's almost last call back home.'

Ash sat beside his luggage; the cushions were firm as stones. 'Sure, what the hell.'

Matt popped the tops off a couple of Kingfishers. Handed Ash one and clinked it with his own. Ash drank. The beer burned his nostrils, sizzled down his throat, while the cricket game pitched into a mad jabbering littered with the slap of footfalls.

'Thanks for bailing me out,' said Matt. 'Soon's I get home I'll pay you back.'

'Sure.'

Matt leaned against the wall by the calendar. 'Frig,' he said, shaking his head.

Ash waited for an apology, some contrition.

But his friend looked up brightly. 'You want a shower or something?'

'A nap, maybe, first.'

'You got it. Feel free to take my bed, I'll be fine out here.'

From the street came a resounding smack and a roar, seemingly all the boys at once.

'Sounds like someone scored,' said Ash.

'Nah, I bet he's out.' Matt drank. 'That's probably it. They're done. Game over.'

WHEN ASH WOKE IT WAS LATE AFTERNOON, the light golden and slow. He listened for Matt in the other room. And from the stillness knew that the apartment was empty.

Again he'd dreamt of the mountain, that figure ascending, himself trailing behind. A dumb dream, so frustrating—he never got anywhere. Ash chased the climbing figure but the top never grew any closer. And the rote symbolism of this, too, depressed him further.

An amoebic splotch on the ceiling captured his attention. In it he tried to imagine something interesting and unlikely. But all he could see was a crudely decapitated head.

Rolling onto his stomach he recalled the only time he'd slept over at Matt's mom's place, in seventh grade. She and some scraggly, shirtless guy had commandeered the living room couch, so the boys were confined to Matt's room the entire night. After an hour of trying to ignore the grunts and moans through the walls, Matt, twelve years old but already pushing six feet tall, stormed into the hallway and screamed, 'If you guys are going to pork at least be frigging quiet about it!'

The front door opened. Ash listened to the jangle of keys tossed on the table, the fridge opening, the clink of beer bottles stacked inside. A fast-food odour wafted in as well, as out of place as a Mountie on horseback tramping through the room. Ash's stomach gurgled: he'd not eaten for an entire day.

Matt's face emerged between the curtains. 'Here's Matty!'

Ash clamped the pillow over his head.

'Come on, you've been napping for hours. Get up or you won't sleep tonight.'

'What are you, my dad?'

'I got us some Mickey D's. Maharaja Macs, bro. For real!'

The sandwiches were gooey and tasted weirdly of cigarettes, but Ash wolfed his down, chasing each bite with beer. Once the food was gone they took turns belching. Compared to Ash's, Matt's burps were like thunder drowning out the chirp of crickets.

'So I hear you're heading to Bollywood?'

Matt nodded, face stern and professional. 'I guess they're always looking for white guys. Who knows, if all goes well with the trial maybe I'll stay, get some work?'

'Back to acting, huh.'

Matt balled up their trash and stuffed it in the takeout bag. 'Maybe a chance to be something other than an extra.'

'To be a star?'

'Honestly? I would settle for a frigging speaking part.'

'But what about your life? Aren't you the star of that?' said Ash. 'Making memories?'

Matt ignored the insinuation of the most recent, catastrophic memory he'd made. 'I mean, for years I thought I'd be a World Cup skier. Then I did my goddamn knees.' He replaced their empty bottles with full ones. 'Then acting didn't really work out. And now, gosh. What am I? A massage therapist? Not even. Well, not yet.'

They drank in silence for a while. Malnourished and jet-lagged, Ash felt the booze zipping to his head.

'Honestly though?' Matt resumed. 'One thing about traveling? It's a lot like acting. You can be whoever you want. Everything that happened before, whoever you were—gone. You're just whatever you say you are.'

'Until you can't escape yourself.'

Matt drank, eyeing Ash from behind his bottle.

'Sorry,' said Ash.

Matt shrugged. Checked his phone again.

'You expecting a call?'

Matt stood, went over to the fridge. 'You can get wireless in this spot,' he said, lofting the handset to the ceiling. Signal achieved, he tapped out some words and handed it to Ash. 'Check it out. Flights to Kashmir are super cheap right now.'

The screen was tuned to some flight-saver page.

'That's because it's winter. No one goes there in winter. It's basically shut down.'

'Because of the snow?'

'So much snow they have to move the capital outside the state.'

'Yeah, and down here it's nearly January and like twenty-five degrees and there's palm trees and mangoes everywhere. Feels wrong. Wouldn't that be a hoot? Going somewhere with an actual winter? And rocking New Year's Eve in your pop's hometown?' Matt leaned forward. 'How much snow are we talking—enough to ski, right?'

'Are you allowed to leave Delhi?'

'I think so.' He took some papers off the top of the fridge. 'Yeah, right here: "The applicant shall not leave the territory of India without the prior permission of the Court." Kashmir's in India, right? Should be fine.'

'They call you an *applicant*? What are you applying for?'

'Honestly, we've got time. Pre-trial isn't till January 4.'

'You realize this is insane, right? That you could be going to jail? And you're talking about a ski vacation?'

Matt looked grave. 'I'm not a frigging idiot. I know what this is.'

Ash sipped his beer.

'But it would be nice to, you know, do something. With my best friend. In case I do get locked up.' Matt's smile was weak but affecting.

'And what you want to do is go to Kashmir?'

'Your home turf!'

'Canada is my home turf,' said Ash. 'Kashmir was barely my dad's anymore.'

'Still. Heritage and all that. See where your people come from.'

'I'm not sure how rocking New Year's is going to be in Srinagar. It's not like there are nightclubs or anything. I'm not even sure you're allowed to drink.'

'Who cares. We'll just, like, hang out. Talk to people. No presh.'

'I don't feel any *presh*.' Ash moved into the hot spot, did a quick search on Matt's phone. 'Well, there's heli-skiing in Gulmarg. My dad talked about that place. Apparently it's really beautiful.'

Matt pointed his beer at Ash. 'There you go.'

'God, I haven't done any serious skiing in years. Let alone from a helicopter.'

'Bro, it's like riding a bike! You just strap on and go.' Matt grinned. 'Don't you want to strap it on with me?'

But Ash wasn't listening. The grey box in his duffel tugged at his thoughts: he pictured himself tipping it from the open door of a hovering chopper, the cremains dispersing upon the snowy slopes below.

'Come on, we didn't get a chance to ski in Quebec. You made me stare across the highway at that resort the whole time.'

This Ash heard. 'I'm sorry my dad died and wrecked your vacation.'

'Come on, that's not what I meant.' Matt's eyebrows arced—his version of an apology. 'All's I mean is it'd be fun, like old times. Remember our ski trips in high school?'

'I remember you disappearing to have sex in the change room at Blue Mountain.'

Matt nodded. 'Adeline.'

'You remember her name?'

'I remember them all . . .' Matt's tone was mystic; he tilted his head to contemplate the mental rolodex of every woman he'd ever slept with.

'Anyway,' Ash said, 'we'd need to look into some other stuff before we go booking anything. Like, is it safe, for example.'

'Nothing in the news. I've been checking.'

'How much do you hear in the Canadian media about the far north? Such as that entire towns don't have running water, for example.'

'You sound like your sister. Or her husband.'

Ash shook his head. 'I don't want to even think about that asshole.'

'Frigging commie.'

'Frigging cheater, is what he is.'

'No. No way. On *Mona*?'

'Can you believe it?'

Matt stood. 'I'll murder him.' And sat. 'If I don't go to Indian jail, I mean.'

'And be a wanted man on two continents. Good idea.'

Matt's expression shifted: the forehead crinkled into worry.

'Hey,' said Ash, 'there's a good chance you're going to get off, right? The kid's fine. And surely they won't lock you up for one little joint.'

Matt palmed his own head, rubbed it briskly. 'This trip—I really need it.'

'Heli-skiing. In Kashmir.'

Matt nodded. He looked more frightened and desperate than Ash had ever seen him.

'Maybe.'

'I'm going to take that as a yes.'

'I said maybe!'

Matt motioned for his phone, a wild grin on his face.

'Oh god,' said Ash. 'I know that look. What have you done?'

Matt passed him the phone: displayed on the screen was an email confirmation from some tour company. 'Four-day package, bro. Gulmarg, just like you said. Bought it while you were sleeping. Merry belated frigging Christmas.'

**2**

AFTER SEVEN HOURS FLYING from Pearson to Heathrow, then another dozen hours to Delhi, and now back up in another plane to Srinagar, Ash was losing touch with the ground. All he knew was sky. Also Matt was very big. He spilled both into the aisle and upon Ash, crammed in the middle row. The minute they were airborne Matt thrust his seat back—fine on roomier flights, less so on this cramped little shuttle. Ash offered a sympathetic look to the discomfited woman behind him.

'Should have sprung for business class,' Matt grumbled.

'The flight's only an hour. Suck it up.'

'Suck it up? Easy for you to say. Not everybody's a munchkin.' Matt surveyed Ash from head to toe. 'I could probably fit you in the overhead bin. Better watch yourself or it'll be like that time you took a swing at me and you spent the afternoon in your locker.'

'I still hate you for that.'

'Shouldn't have tried to sucker punch me then.'

'You were being relentless! All day you kept smacking me in the balls.'

'Which reminds me: what's the capital of Thailand?'

'Don't.'

Ash cupped his crotch just in time, barely deflecting the backhand.

'*Bang-cock!*'

'We're nearly forty years old,' said Ash. 'You realize that, right?'

But Matt was on a roll. 'Do you have a sleeping bag?'

Ash failed to get his meal tray down before Matt delivered the punch line: '*Wake up!*'

The blow caught him squarely in the testicles and a sour, cloudy pain swam up from his gut. Matt giggled like a madman. The guy in the window seat edged away.

'Fun times,' said Matt.

'No,' wheezed Ash, 'they're not.'

Once the pain had subsided to a dull ache, Ash took out *Don Quixote*. But again he couldn't focus on the words. Beside him Matt writhed and grunted, stretched his legs into the aisle, wedged a pillow against the headrest, adjusted, flopped, curled sideways, leaned on Ash's shoulder. Kissed his cheek.

'Go away,' said Ash, cringing.

'But I love you.'

'No you don't. Love doesn't clock people in the balls.'

Matt sat up. 'How's the book?'

'*Don Quixote*? A masterpiece. Obviously.'

'What's it about?'

'About?'

'Is it like the Lone Ranger? He's got a buddy, right?'

'Sancho Panza.'

'Right, the sidekick. Like Tonto. Or Robin. The Luigi to his Mario. The Chewy to his Han. The Ash to his Matt.'

'Of the two of us, *I'm* Chewbacca?'

'No way. Don Quixote is all me.'

'Maybe you've forgotten who had to fly across an ocean to rescue you.'

'Like any good sidekick.'

'You haven't even read the book!'

'Well, let's hear a scene from it and we'll see.'

'A scene?'

'Story time.' Matt nuzzled into Ash's shoulder. 'Read me something, Papa.'

The seatbelt sign extinguished. A baby wailed at the rear of the cabin. Ash shook his friend away and thumbed the pages, looking for—what? He'd no idea. He didn't know the book at all. He was only biding his time until Matt gave up, lost interest, left him alone. But the look on his friend's face had turned intent, almost studious.

And then a line jumped off the page. 'Okay, here, tell me if this sounds more like you or me: "I am a fire afar off, a sword laid aside."'

'A fire and a sword? Honestly? Me! It's not even close. You're more like a puddle and a plastic spoon.'

Ash closed the book.

'Hey, come on. This is fun. Read more.'

'No.' He thought about that fire, everything he'd never done. And the sword not laid but stabbed, the blade twisting—with his own hand on the hilt. But how could he explain this to Matt?

'Bro! Read!'

Ash sighed, flipped around. 'Okay, here's a bit where Sancho is calling Don Quixote "The Knight of the Sorrowful Face."'

'I've had those.'

'Those what?'

'Nights of a Sorrowful Face.'

'What are you talking about?'

'Those nights, bro. Not that you'd know. Your life is so put together and perfect.'

'Sorry, my life is what?'

'I just mean those mornings you wake up and there's a blank second or two but then the whole night before comes crashing in until you're drowning in it. And you have to wade through it all day, up past your neck, and you can't breathe. It's suffocating you.'

Ash did not correct Matt's mistake. Nights, knights—what did it matter?

'Sorrow, yeah, that's the word.' Matt nodded, said it again: '*Sorrow*. Sorrow about not just what you've done but who you are. And it's all there on your face for everyone to see. Like those mornings before the sun comes up you're feeling around for your clothes in the dark and dressing as quiet as you can and creeping out of some woman's room whose name you can't remember and past her kid sleeping, but the kid is up watching you through the bars of its crib with big wide eyes. What are you gonna do? You can't stay. You're no good for anyone. So you just leave with those sad, sad eyes following you out the door because you effed up again.' He shook his head. 'And then you're hurt and there's nowhere to put it but on someone else. Again.'

Ash glanced at the man in the window seat. He was asleep. Or pretending to be.

But Matt seemed indifferent to eavesdroppers. 'Like that kid in Goa. That's what happened, Dhar. Another Night of the Sorrowful Face.'

'Errant nights,' said Ash.

'What's that?'

'It's what Don Quixote believes in. Kind of.'

'Errant means bad?'

'It means lots of things. But, yeah, it can also mean a kind of mistake. And *ab*errant means something even worse. Like unnatural. But disgracefully so.'

Matt shook his head sadly. 'Yup. Too many nights like that, bro. Too many sorrowful, aberrant nights.'

Ash held up the book. 'You want me to read something else?'

'Nah. That's enough.' Matt leaned back and closed his eyes. 'I'm tired. I don't want to think about anything. Leave me alone for a bit. Let me sleep.'

THE LANDSCAPE TURNED ALPINE so suddenly. Ash wondered if he'd missed the transition through foothills, some slow steady rise of the land. Because in an instant, it seemed, the dun-coloured desert below ceded to snowy peaks. A settlement appeared like confetti speckling the snow, the detritus of some long-gone parade. The suburbs of Srinagar, Ash thought. But it dispersed, leaving only landscape. Then a new valley and a new cluster of houses appeared, and vanished again, and on and on they flew with no sign of descent.

What was out there, Ash wondered; who? Were those villages teeming with militants? Like the tribal lands outside Peshawar—gun markets and sharia law, sleeper cells in mountain caves with rocket launchers propped by the door. Funds pooled, IEDs wired, martyr videos shot against an Arabic-scrawled backdrop. But this was just the stuff of movies and TV. Surely there were other, homier truths out there: two girls cheating off each other's math tests, workers with pickaxes hacking a roadway to rubble, a spindly grandmother slurping yogurt from the fingers of her daughter-in-law. Lives. People.

And he'd come here to ski.

This trip, and his own willful ignorance, reminded him of the time he'd gone to Cuba with his dad and sister. The Christmas of the millennial New Year, with the fanfare of an Oscar presenter Brij had presented his adult children with envelopes. Inside were flight itineraries and brochures for an all-inclusive resort (Windex-coloured ocean, salt-coloured sand, all-you-can-everything, all the time). 'All of us, together,' Brij announced, 'to ring in Y2K.' Ash and Mona traded looks of astonishment. Such an extravagant, unlikely gift. Not just misguided but lonesome—and too lonesome to say no to.

The resort was sequestered safely from the nearest town, yet not so removed from civilization that they could ignore the poverty at its gates. The Dhars went snorkelling, played volleyball, gorged at the buffet and dutifully pounded rum and Cokes until they passed out on their deck chairs, the grotesquery tainting the air like smoke from a funeral pyre. Mona had the hardest time of it politically, of course, until two of the more attentive male staff invited her to a party off-site on New Year's Eve. (Ash, though technically never asked, used his father as an excuse to stay behind.)

Before heading home Ash had unloaded his suitcase on these same guys: clothes and books and toiletries—even a crappy MP3 player with nothing on it but books on tape. Yet this excess of charity shamed him even further. On the flight back to Canada he vowed never again to participate in such decadence, the disgrace of hiding behind barbed wire for all-you-can-eat/drink gluttony while the locals starved just beyond the fence. Or, worse, waited on him and cleaned up his mess.

Yet here he was, heading to Kashmir on another package tour. While nuclear war threatened on either side of the border. While the military 'disappeared' suspected insurgents from homes throughout the Valley—maybe those same homes passing below. While mass graves were unearthed and bereaved mothers waited, hearts knotted with hope and despair, for a glimpse of their sons' remains. While Kashmiri refugees and exiles from Kathmandu to Newark woke homesick each morning; and every night, as they lay down once again in whatever foreign land, their souls crumpled inward a little more: the only home they'd ever known existed solely in their dreams.

Or so Ash imagined.

Beside him Matt snored and drooled, bald head lolling like a beach ball. Matt: This lunatic whom Ash had flown across the ocean to help, yet who was now dragging him to this broken, wounded place that had shattered millions of hearts, so they could climb into helicopters, unleash themselves upon mountaintops—and *ski*.

It occurred to Ash that he ought to stay in Srinagar. He imagined himself sipping kava among the Kashmiri literati in some dingy cafe. They would tell him how hopeless life was here for writers, that their poetry and searing polemics were produced only in samizdat, that they—the voice of the people!—were routinely harassed, beaten, jailed, silenced. Through his publishing connections Ash would bring their work to the masses, igniting a global phenomenon of 'Writing from the Vale' akin to the Latin American boom of the seventies. He'd be its saviour and hero; he'd endow an award in Brij's name.

Meanwhile Matt could ski his big clueless heart out, chopper up to any illicit glacial peak he wanted, and like something out of a spy movie slalom back to base camp amid the crackle of gunfire. If he weren't kidnapped and executed, after three days of powdery alpine bliss Matt could slink back to Delhi for his day in court. In a bolt of malice, Ash wished for a conviction—not some particularly cruel and unusual punishment, just a little time behind Indian bars. It might do the guy some good, set him straight, force him to admit that the world didn't revolve around his whims.

Skiing! Ash had not skied in six years, almost exactly. The last time had been at his dad's place one February, when he and Mona and Harj had all packed into Brij's Volvo and crossed the highway and spent the day on the slopes.

Brij had picked up the sport in his fifties, much to his children's astonishment. 'You expect me to sit in my bloody house and watch people having fun?' he'd railed. (Mysterious, too, was his sudden interest in 'fun.') From a series of private lessons Brij had developed the methodical style of a novice chef obeying, to the letter, a particularly thorough recipe. Skis impeccably parallel, in a strained crouch he made wide, deliberate turns with such precision that a parabolic function could plot the trails he left behind.

Mona had never been much for winter sports (or winter, or sports) and after two bored forays down the bunny hill she fled for the clubhouse. 'See you two later,' she told them at the T-bar, unclipping her rented skis. 'I'm too Indian for ice-capades.'

So Ash spent the day with Brij, riding the lift together, skiing down in tandem (Ash's technique, his dad pointed out, was more like power-skating from one edge of the hill to the other), meeting at the bottom and then heading back up. They didn't talk much. Then, near the end of the day, the chair lift stalled. After a minute or two of sitting there, feet dangling, Brij began to speak.

'I never understood what you Canadians like about this,' he said. 'Growing up in Kashmir there was no skiing. Some Europeans, certainly, would go up into the foothills and ski down, and a few would die every year because nothing was cultivated. It seemed absurd. But I suppose now Kashmir is developing some mountains for tourism.' He was soliloquizing now—gazing into the distance, into the past. 'You know,' he said, 'I did try to ski once, however. As a very young boy.'

'Oh?'

'We would hear of these idiot Danes and Germans going up into the mountains and sailing down on boards stuck to their feet. So one day we decided to try it for ourselves.'

'How old were you?'

'Eight? No, nine.'

'Cute.'

'We had some idea that boots were attached to the skis, so we nailed a pair of shoes to some boards—though of course we knew nothing of poles—and convinced our friend Sharif's father to take us in his Jeep around Dal Lake, up past the Mughal Gardens, into the hills. Then there was much snow in Srinagar. Now, with this global warming, who knows. So he dropped Sharif and me and the rest of our gang, six boys in all, at the base of a path that led to a lookout. Up we went, three of us carrying each ski. Our skis, mind, were ten feet long. Thick chinar timbers. The sort used to build houseboats.'

'Not exactly Rossignols,' said Ash.

Brij nodded and smiled. 'So we reached the lookout and set the skis down—'

'But, wait. If there was only one set of skis, who went first?'

'Ah! Precisely the problem. Though we often went sledding, the idea of going down a hill standing up was absolutely terrifying. So we argued about who would be the initiate. Sharif said not him, as his father had driven us. Another boy said not him, as his feet were too small and didn't fit the shoes.'

'What about you?'

The lift creaked, hummed, lurched forward. And stopped again. The chair swayed. A cry from somewhere—'Crisse d'osti tabarnak!'—echoed up the mountain; laughter rippled back down. Ash thought of avalanches, all that billowing annihilation triggered by a few careless words. But this was not the Alps. Just some mound in Quebec. Most of the snow wasn't even real.

'So,' said Brij, 'we were debating, and it came to my turn, and I had no excuse. They were in fact my shoes. The whole thing was my idea. I had even suggested the spot. So I agreed. Someone took my boots. I slipped my feet into the shoes. They were so cold! I remember the leather had hardened. Like wearing sheaths of ice.'

Below a pair of skiers were winding between the trees, their tracks braiding. In silence Ash and Brij watched them until they were down the hill and out of view.

'So then what?' Ash said. 'How did it go?'

Brij laughed. 'The other boys had to push me to the edge because the skis were too heavy to move. They had no edges. Just big pieces of lumber strapped to my feet.'

'Amazing you lived to tell the tale.'

'Just wait.' Brij kicked his feet a little, one then the other: the tips of his skis appeared and vanished beneath the chair. The gesture was so childlike. 'One of my friends took one of my hands, and another had the other, and one steadied me from the front, and another from behind, while Sharif coordinated. They moved me to the edge of the hill so that the tips of those boards were pointing into space.'

'I love that feeling.'

'Now, yes. Of course. If you are a skier, that moment before you release is exhilarating. But then? It was only . . . disembodying. It felt . . .' Brij looked up the mountain—or over it, beyond it, to the sky. He nodded. 'Like dying. Not even that I *would* die. I wasn't envisioning an accident. In that moment I remember thinking, "This is what dying is like." An in-between feeling. On the cusp, before the fall. And then over you'd go, leaving everyone behind, and nothing left.'

'No heaven?'

Brij snorted. 'Heaven, idiot? You believe in *heaven?*'

The lift started up with a groan, and off they were tugged to the top of the run.

'There,' said Brij.

'So did you go down?'

'What?'

'The hill.'

'When?'

'When you were a kid! What we were just talking about.'

'Oh.' Brij seemed irritated; with a dismissive wave he dispatched the story back to the past. 'I crashed. And that was the end of it.'

Now all that was left of his father was stuffed into a box at Ash's feet. Bringing it along—on a ski trip to Brij's homeland!—was a travesty. *It*, thought Ash, and cringed inwardly. Though *him* was even more absurd, and *them*, for the ashes, plural, was hardly better. There was no language for that clump of heavy dust. *Father*, Ash thought, and pictured himself cradling that grey box to his chest, tears streaming down his cheeks, before dumping the contents between the lily pads of Dal Lake.

What was he meant to do with it/him/them? Brij's will had provided no instructions. Perhaps a crop-dusting flyover, right now, would be best—his dad's powdered bones atomizing through the ozone. Ash looked past the sleeping man at the window: the mountains continued, on and on, all that snow streaked with gleaming black ridges where the rock showed through. And the sky, pale and feeble, more like a lack of sky. With a chill he realized that he was in it too: a nothing kind of place.

Ash sat back, shook the thought free from his mind.

And when it was gone, nothing replaced it.

Something had shifted. He felt weightless, untethered.

Had he fallen asleep? He couldn't remember. No dream lingered. Though it seemed as if he'd snapped out of unconsciousness, or a coma. He looked around: the cabin of an airplane. They were flying . . . somewhere. Yet he'd no recollection of boarding or any idea where they were headed. And the men on either side of him, who were they? A dark-skinned man at the window, sixtyish; a big bald white man sprawling into the aisle. He searched their faces for recognition, but none came. Strangers.

Where was this? What land passed below? Mountains—the Rockies, the Andes, some range upon the moon? He didn't know. He sensed only that he wasn't heading home. Though where or what was home? All he knew was that he had a body, which ended at the tips of his fingers and toes. A man's body. Everything else was a mystery.

He searched his thoughts for anything that preceded this moment, but it was like peering into a bare-walled room.

There was only desolation where the past ought to have been.

His mind had been emptied. There was nothing there.

Even his name. He tried to summon it and could not. Whoever's body this was, it was nameless. He had no name.

The edges of panic closed in.

He shut his eyes, took a few slow breaths.

Opened them.

The big man beside him was grinning. An expression that conveyed familiarity. But how to mirror it back? He tried an upturn of his own lips. But this felt orthodontic and forced, and the big man's smile collapsed into concern.

'Sheesh, bro. What gives? You look like you've seen a ghost.'

# 3

SO THIS WAS INDIA; they were in India. The airport was dimly lit and derelict, with black-on-yellow signage (TOILETS, DRINKING WATER, SECURITY) subtitled in Hindi and Urdu—he somehow knew the names of the scripts, but couldn't make sense of the words. And for India, or what he thought he knew of India, the airport was uncommonly quiet.

Other than the sixty-odd folks unloaded from their flight, the only people in the terminal were a few harried-looking staff and a flock of wild-eyed young men in fatigues, rifles strapped to their backs. There was so much space. But to enter those spaces alone felt perilous, so he hung close to the big man, his companion or keeper, the one who seemed to know him and yet whose face was as unfamiliar as this foreign land.

He trailed the big man to the baggage claim, reluctant to admit to having no idea who either of them was. It seemed a betrayal of their camaraderie—a failure, even. He merely listened politely when spoken to, responded with as few words as possible and followed along. Even so he kept having to squirm away from looks of scrutiny: one eyebrow scrunched, the other scuttling up the big man's broad, corrugated forehead. *Who are you?* these looks seem to ask. An excellent question.

Soldiers flanked the baggage carousel, rifles shifted to ready position, half-cocked. Fingers hovered over triggers. Beyond them, out the windows and past the tarmac, the horizon was serrated with mountains. These had the look of teeth.

'Kashmir, huh?' murmured the big man.

Kashmir, then. But why?

He sensed the big man watching him and thought for a moment to confess: fine, yes, who *am* I? and who are you? and what's going on? and what's happened to my brain? But he resisted; no need to panic when surely it all would soon return. The altitude had likely just scrambled his memory. It couldn't have been wiped clean. All he needed was a bit of time to get back on track to finding himself again.

The conveyer belt heaved into motion; a siren wailed and a red light twirled.

'*Goal!*' said the big man, pointing at the light. 'Like hockey. Get it?'

This seemed to require laughter. So, obediently, he laughed. But the big man shushed him. 'Easy there,' he whispered, indicating a nearby soldier with a sideways twitch of his eyes. 'Don't cause too much of a ruckus.'

Luggage tumbled down the chute, circled, was collected piece by piece; the crowd dwindled. A nearby billboard flipped through tourism ads: a laneway through autumnal trees, a meadow of vibrant flowers, a houseboat floating on a lotus-clogged lake. He'd no idea which bag was his. Though perhaps on sight he'd remember it. Or his friend might. He eyed the big man for some flare of recognition. But the guy had turned his attention to his phone, madly thumbing the screen.

'I'm not getting a signal,' he whispered. 'You?'

He patted his pockets, located a phone in his jacket: on the home screen was a photo of someone in headphones behind a microphone. He worried it might be himself. What breed of raging narcissist would carry around his own picture? He touched his face, tried to match the features to those in the image. But his skin felt pouchy and battered, while the guy in the photo seemed so vibrant, so alive.

'Bro?'

'Sorry. No. It says, *No service.*'

'Huh.'

Again the big man seemed to be eyeing him a little too penetratingly, so he turned back to the carousel. All that remained was an ominous package, unlabelled and bound with twine and tape. Surely this wasn't his? If he made a move for it might the big man caution him away? Or encourage him—*Yeah, go for it, that weird one's yours!*

But it was lifted free by a soldier and carted off.

The belt stopped with a shudder.

'Can we go now? All we brought's our carry-ons anyway, right?' The big man passed him a duffel and hitched his own backpack; he'd been carrying both.

'Oh. Thanks.'

'No sweat. Just figured you were waiting for the snipers to disperse. Only following your lead. All you out here, Hometown Hero.'

Was this home? Kashmir? It seemed unlikely; his thoughts came only in English. And the big man had a Canadian flag stitched onto his backpack. He suspected that he too was Canadian, though he wasn't sure how this was meant to feel; certainly the realization conjured nothing in particular. He needed a look at himself—the bathroom would have a mirror—but the big man was leading them toward the exit.

Two guards stepped into their path. The big man flung up his hands in surrender. But the intervention was harmless; they were required to sign in as foreign visitors. From behind a desk an indifferent-seeming woman provided pens and clipboards. The forms bore the heading, THE STATE OF JAMMU AND KASHMIR, and an official crest.

Kashmir. Some facts swam up from the murk: an uprising, an occupation. A dangerous place to be traveling. *Why were they here?*

'Passports,' demanded the woman behind the desk, hands out and palms up.

A passport—yes! In his bag he located a navy booklet: Canadian indeed. Inside was a name that belonged to the same face pictured on his phone; both, evidently, were his own. Still no memories tumbled free. He copied his names—first, middle and last—onto the form, five strange syllables like the lyrics to a tune he didn't know.

Most of the required information could be gleaned from a flight itinerary folded into his passport: his address was in Toronto; he was here for, apparently, *pleasure*. Many of the questions were baffling and he cribbed as best he could from the big man's answers—*Matthew*, read his companion's form. When he came to, *What is your distinguishing feature?* he checked Matthew's page: *Bigness*. So he answered: *Small*.

And then they were through.

A man in a leather jacket and massive orange beard held up a DHAR – GULMARG sign. 'Bro, check it out, our ride.'

'Luggage?' said the driver, offering to take their carry-ons.

This felt like an imposition. The duffel bag's contents were *his*; any object could be the key to unlocking the secret of himself. So he clung to it, shook his head. The driver shrugged and led them to a waiting Jeep. Matthew cried, 'Shotgun!' and dove into the passenger seat, leaving him to slide into the back cradling his duffel like an infant.

On the way out of the airport they laboured through multiple checkpoints, including one posted with a massive armoured vehicle, some hybrid of tank and elephant. Scrolls of razor wire lined high fences on either side. From behind sandbag stockades snipers trained rifles at the traffic. At the exit a spiked barrier had to be rolled aside so the Jeep could pass through.

'Serious,' said Matthew. He turned to the backseat. 'Was it this bad last time you were here, or do you remember?'

'I don't remember.'

A flash of their driver's eyes in the rearview suggested reconnaissance.

Outside the airport military police lined the road, batons clenched in their fists.

'Is this normal?' Matthew asked. 'All these soldiers everywhere?'

'BSF,' said the driver. 'Border Security Force.'

'In the city? All the time?'

'Also CPRF, and army. And police.'

Matthew shook his head. 'Yeah, but are they always everywhere like this?'

'Yes, sir. Always.' From the backseat this conversation had the detached feel of a TV on in another room.

'My buddy's from here,' said Matthew.

The driver looked in the mirror again. His eyes narrowed.

'Or his dad was anyway.'

The driver twisted a little in his seat. 'You speak Kashmiri?'

'No.'

'But, who? Your father is Kashmiri?'

'Yes.'

'He is a Pandit? He will be returning?' There was a hopeful lift in the man's voice.

'Returning?'

'Home.'

No, home was Canada. A safe answer: 'We're just here for vacation.'

'Skiing package,' said Matt.

*Skiing.* Ah.

'But you should come first to my house.' The driver's voice chimed like a bell. 'My wife, my friends, my children—we would be pleased to have you join us. It has been twenty-thirty years since we had Hindus in our home. Please. We will have tea.'

'Can't do it,' said Matthew. 'It's nearly noon and we're scheduled for a run this aft . . . I mean, we paid for a package, better use it. Right, Ash?'

*Ash*, he thought. Not the name on his passport. A short-form, a nickname: Ash. 'Right,' he said.

The Jeep drove on. High walls on either side of the road fronted palatial homes.

Pausing at a traffic light, Ash (*Ash*, he repeated to himself; *my name is Ash*) eyed two schoolgirls waiting on the corner. One whispered into the other's ear; the second girl's face lit up and her hand flew to her mouth. Everything about them was so familiar. (Was that possible? Did he know anyone here?) Perhaps they reminded him of someone—a wife, a sister, a daughter, a friend? Who were the people that he, Ash, knew?

'Anyhow, the tea party's a nice idea,' said Matthew. 'But maybe another time.'

The driver seemed to deflate. 'As you wish.'

The light turned green. Off they went. The girls were gone.

Then they were wheeling around a roundabout and the city receded behind them. The road scrawled toward a ridge of mountains looming against a dishwater sky and along it they went, with a light snow fizzing down from above and the steady whir of the wheels and the hum of the engine and the roar of the vents blasting warm air into the backseat, and Ash felt lulled and lost, fading, fading . . .

He jolted awake; Matthew was handing over his fleece. 'Use my vest as a pillow.'

Ash scrunched it into a ball under his cheek. For some indeterminable amount of time he passed in and out of sleep, dreaming of being jostled around the backseat. When he finally sat up again they were heaving up a series of rutted switchbacks through a hillside forest of dim, shaggy pine. For a moment Ash wondered if his amnesia had been a dream. But he was still unable to conjure a single memory. The furthest back his life seemed to go was that flash of sudden awareness on the plane.

They reached a plateau. Everything opened up: a little roadway led out from the trees to a great swath of white land and white sky and white fog swallowing the treetops.

'Gulmarg,' announced the driver.

The place had the look of ski villages the world around, Ash thought—and was surprised by the clarity of the images this inspired; there were things his mind had retained, then. Hotels lined a gravel slash through a wide, snowy valley and a gondola cycled up into a bank of low-slung cloud at the far end.

'Frigging *nice*,' said Matthew, drumming the dashboard with his knuckles.

They rumbled past a corral where a dozen men in shawls and woolly caps waited with meagre looking horses, eyeing the Jeep with the look of buzzards sizing up a corpse. Halfway down the strip they pulled up to an A-frame building with a paint-flaking sign—HOTEL PARADISE—and the eaves humped with snow.

'Hotel,' said the driver.

'Paradise,' said Matthew.

Other than the horsemen there weren't many people about, though the place seemed designed for tourists. As such Gulmarg had an abandoned, funereal air, with the gondola ascending into the mist offering something like celestial escape.

Ash's teeth rattled as he climbed down from the Jeep. 'Cold,' he said.

'Check out that curry powder,' said Matthew, gesturing all around.

Ash nodded, watching the Jeep rattle off down the road. Along the shoulder the snow was cratered erratically with horseshit.

'Honestly, that's what they call it here.'

'Curry powder,' said Ash. 'Okay.'

The eyebrows were mobilizing again. 'Something wrong? You don't seem yourself.'

*Myself*—who would that be? Ash was his name, he thought. But having a name and being that person were very different things. Who was Ash?

Matthew sighed. 'Let's go check in, you frigging weirdo.'

So Ash followed him inside.

The hotel seemed inspired by Swiss chalets: sloping walls of unvarnished wood, an open lobby, a fire roaring away in the hearth. The man at the desk, though, was very Indian, with a big brown forehead and a luxuriant coif swept from it with pomade.

Matthew gave Ash's last name and explained that they were on a package tour for three nights. Three nights: Ash figured that after one good sleep his memory would return. A temporary short-circuit—like a computer, he just needed rebooting.

A ledger was scanned, pages were flipped. The concierge was at a loss. Matthew looked at Ash. Ash looked at the concierge. The concierge squinted at the ledger, then at Matthew, then at Ash. Nobody said anything.

A room off the lobby labelled BAR & RESTAURANT disgorged a huge, gingery character. In an Australian accent, through a baleen of beard, he yelled, 'They're mine, mate!' and swept his arms around Ash and Matthew, claiming them both. 'The Canadians!' he announced, squeezing their shoulders. 'How you going?'

'Good,' said Ash. 'Great.'

Matthew stepped back and clapped hands with the guy in a rockers' salute. Although the Australian was as luxuriantly furred as Matthew was shorn, they were otherwise physical replicas: same size, same shape. Like a pair of minotaurs reuniting for a ceremonial greeting.

'Guessing you're David?' said Matthew.

'Dave-o, mate. Only folks call me David round here are the locals.' He shot a furtive, ironic glance across the desk.

Forgoing the concierge's offer for help, Dave-o acquired keys and steered Ash and Matthew upstairs by the backs of their necks. The room was clean and simple: two beds, a single dresser, a piny smell. No TV.

'Get settled in,' Dave-o instructed, 'quick bite in the pub, then some runs this avo?'

Ash sat on one of the beds with his duffel in his lap. 'This what?'

'Avo, mate. You want to fit in round here, better learn to speak Australian.'

'Afternoon,' decoded Matthew. 'Sounds good to us.'

'Actually—'

'Shut it, Ash.' Matthew slung a leg up on the windowsill to stretch his calves. 'We didn't come here to sit around and read books.'

'No, it's not that. I just don't know . . .'Ash caught Dave-o grinning at Matthew; in their exchange was something transactional and exclusionary. 'If I can ski,' he finished.

'Oh give it *up*.' Matthew shook his head. 'You're not exactly La Bomba but you get down okay. And we're not going up in the chopper today, anyway. Eh?'

'Nope,' said Dave-o. 'Just some quick runs, then we'll rip it up for New Year's tonight. Get the heli out tomorrow.'

'See, Ash? Quit being such a mons.'

Ash stared at his hands, palms then backs, as unknown to him as those of a stranger. 'No, that's not it,' he said, looking up. 'I don't think I can remember how.'

'To ski? Are you out of your mind? I told you, it's like riding a bike.'

'Or a lady,' said Dave-o.

Matthew's laughter filled the room.

'It's not just skiing.' Ash let the silence that followed swell with portent, wanting Dave-o and Matthew to experience the full burden of its emptiness.

And then, when he spoke, his confession sliced through it like a blade.

'YOU NEED TO STOP calling me that. Just say Matt.'

'Okay,' said Ash from his bed. Matthew—*Matt*—was at the window. The open bag on the floor held Ash's things. Picking through it had felt like invading someone else's life; even its smells were foreign. 'And me? I'm just Ash?'

'Yeah, only your dad ever used your full name.'

'What's Ash like?'

'You're Ash!' Matt's face crinkled in worry. 'You swear you're not messing with me?'

'Swear,' said Ash. 'I don't know what happened. Everything's . . . gone.'

'You don't remember *anything*?'

'I told you, nothing personal. I know what India is, I know what Kashmir is, I even know what's going on here politically. The world isn't the problem. I could tell you the starting lineup of the 1992 New York Knicks, and the first lines of a bunch of books— "If I'm out of my mind, it's all right with me" is one that keeps coming up—and sing the national anthem, but anything to do with me just isn't there anymore.'

'So, like, what you did last week. Nothing?'

'Last week, yesterday, last year—all gone. But *history*? If I wasn't there? I remember just fine. It's all the stuff I was around for that's the problem.'

'Crud. So what do we do?'

'No idea.'

'Well who better to help you get it all back than your best bud? I know you better than anyone.' Matt seemed suddenly enthused; he had a function now. 'Your favourite food is pizza. Your favourite pop is root beer. You play hockey left-handed but golf right. In grade five you broke your leg mountain biking in Medway Creek and I fireman-carried you home but your dad blamed me anyway. As if it was my fault!'

'Keep going.'

In a kind of informational mania Matt provided Ash's age, employment, birthdate, birthplace, and so on. Some of it he'd already covered—that Ash hosted a show on the radio, that he'd written a book. When the facts were exhausted Matt listed some important people in Ash's life—family, friends. But none of these names conjured faces or feelings. And when Matt finally paused for a breath Ash was still left with a vacuum where his self should have been.

'Well what about more recent stuff?' Matt said, collapsing on his own bed. 'Do you remember getting here?'

'I told you, everything starts on the plane. It was like waking up. Or like being born.' He frowned. 'That's not it either. I want to say being reincarnated—like having my consciousness flash into a new body with no sense of what was there before—but that sounds cheesy. How Hindu am I?'

'Not very. But, wait. You don't remember flying to India?' Matt seemed to say this carefully; when Ash shook his head he continued with gusto. 'Not much to remember, I guess, just two old pals heading to your homeland. Or your dad's homeland anyway.'

'My dad's from here?'

'He . . . is.' Matt's voice wavered.

'But he lives—'

'Yeah, in Quebec.'

Before Ash could pursue this line of questioning (What was his dad like? Did they get along?) there was a knock on the door. An alp of polar fleece and beard loomed at the threshold. 'How's he going?' said Dave-o, peeking into the room. 'Anything coming back?'

This was directed at Matt. Ash waited for the assessment.

'We're working on it,' said Matt. 'Piece by piece.'

'Putting Humpty together again,' sighed the Australian. 'All right, I've done some checking and it looks like this sort of thing isn't totally unheard of. Happens sometimes to travellers, no real reason for it. Mind just goes blank for a bit. Comes back eventually.' He handed a stack of paper to Matt, who passed it to Ash. 'Some info I found online.'

Ash scanned the pages. Half were about transient global amnesia; the rest, dissociative fugue. Did he trust this grizzled bushman with a diagnosis?

'Not to worry, mate!' Dave-o's buoyant pitch made Ash feel not just absent, but mentally delayed. 'You'll be right soon enough!'

'One sec?' Matt said to Ash, and gestured to Dave-o to join him in the hall.

The door closed behind them. Murmuring followed, nothing Ash could make out. He flipped through the printouts, which included testimonials by survivors and clinical notes. *The word fugue comes from the Latin word for 'flight,'* explained one website. What was he fleeing?

The door reopened; Matt was now solo. 'Dave-o's going to try to get a doctor in later this evening. So if you want we can just hang in the room until then.'

'Oh, no, come on,' said Ash. 'Aren't you here to ski?'

'Bro, no way. I want to help you remember who you are.'

'I don't think that's how it works, like something will trigger me and everything will come pouring back in. Listen: *No treatment is needed for transient global amnesia. It resolves on its own and has no confirmed after-effects.* Basically I just have to wait it out. I bet by dinnertime I'll be back to my old self.' Ash laughed. 'Whoever that might be.'

Matt brightened. 'So it'd be good to do something. As opposed to sitting around.'

'Like what?'

'Well, not to pressure you or anything, and if it doesn't work out we can come right back, but muscle memory's a different type of memory, isn't it?'

'What do you mean?'

'Me and Dave-o were talking. Maybe your body has memories stored that your brain doesn't. And something physical could kickstart things again.'

'Okay.'

'All I'm saying, honestly?' said Matt, kneeling beside Ash's bed as if in prayer. 'Is once we get out there I bet you'll remember how to ski."

IN THE HOTEL'S BAR & RESTAURANT Matt and Ash met the other members of their group, an alarmingly tattooed Norwegian couple, Jens and Tove, in identical floppy haircuts and turtlenecks and perfect, rigid posture. A handful of other guests, mostly Indians, were also having lunch, which arrived in the form of partitioned metal trays spotted with lumps of yellow and brown.

The skiers would begin with drinking.

Dave-o handed out five quart-sized Kingfishers. 'I shouldn't,' said Matt, retreating, before accepting one as if defeated by protocol. A cheers to Ash's memory went round the table, the bottles clinking with so much force that Ash's frothed up over his hand.

'So when do we hit the slopes?' said Matt.

'This guy!' said Dave-o, clapping Matt on the shoulder. 'Bloke after my own heart.'

Matt grinned: a compliment. Or at least a statement of solidarity.

'After lunch we'll do some runs up the gondola. Take the chopper up tomorrow to the peaks where the real curry powder's at.'

Matt elbowed Ash. 'See?'

Ash nodded, drank. The beer had a coppery taste, but the mechanics of drinking—lift, sip, lower, repeat—offered a comforting sense of ritual. So he drank some more.

'We were up yesterday,' said Jens. 'Great conditions. Fat snow.'

'Fat snow,' said Tove.

'These two've skied all over the world,' said Dave-o. 'Ask them if they've ever been anywhere so pristine.'

Jens and Tove sat in expressionless silence until Matt leaned in and shouted: 'Have you ever been anywhere so pristine?'

'No,' said Tove.

'No,' confirmed Jens.

'Sweet,' said Matt.

Ash was half-done his beer. A giddy sensation twirled around his temples and his body felt like a fist unclenching. He chased this new lightness to the bottom of the bottle.

'What's amazing here is that they'll take you anywhere you want,' said Dave-o. 'Nowhere's out of bounds—short of maybe Siachen.'

'What's that?' said Matt.

The Australian explained the glacier's prevalence in the conflict, the Line of Control and the current ceasefire, how invariably one side would launch shells over the border and start the whole business up again. He presented this information with a kind of beleaguered futility, as it if were a story he'd long ago tired of telling, one that sprawled with no end in sight. Or spiralled back on itself, again and again.

'But the glacier,' said Matt. 'Can we ski it?'

'For the right price?' Dave-o dropped his voice as if revealing a secret. 'I bet they'd let you waterski the Ganges.'

Ash finished his beer and eyed the others' drinks covetously.

'So how many people have died here?' asked Tove.

'Yes,' said Jens, 'how many?'

'In the Troubles?' Dave-o raked his fingers through his beard. 'Couldn't tell you. If you're really interested I can hop online tonight and get all the answers you want.'

*Online*. The word had the cheery ring of a solution: surely Ash must have an email account. And archived in it would be everything he needed to know about himself. Eagerly he pulled out his phone. Dave-o intervened. 'That won't work here, mate.'

'Too high up,' said Matt.

'No, no,' said Dave-o. 'The network's closed. To get mobile service in Kashmir you got to do a whole application.'

'No Wi-Fi even,' said Tove.

'No Wi-Fi,' echoed Jens wistfully.

'You have to use the hotel computer,' said Dave-o, 'And even then someone'll sit with you to make sure you're not ordering a drone strike on Srinagar. Though? You ask me? I think they're just curious and bored. Anyway, I can set that up later if you want.'

Ash spun his empty bottle around a ring of condensation. 'Sure.'

'*Some drink to remember*,' sang Matt, thumping Ash on the back. '*Some drink to forget*. Way to go, bro. Let's get you another.'

'It's *dance*,' said Ash.

'What?'

'"Hotel California," right? Is what you were singing?'

Matt looked baffled. Ash let it go. How could he explain what he knew?

Dave-o wagged Ash's empty at the bar. The boy there sprung to attention, held up five fingers and yelled something back. The Australian responded in twangy Kashmiri.

'Wow, you speak the language?' said Matt.

'Been here seven winters now. You pick up the essentials.' Dave-o tilted his head, squinted. 'I hope this doesn't sound poofy, Matt, but I keep thinking I've seen you before. And not skiing. Maybe on the telly?'

Matt shrugged. 'I've done some acting.'

'A soap ad, was it?'

'You got me.' For Jens' and Tove's benefit, he explained the campaign.

'God, those things used to make me cry like a girl. All those guys with their kids.' Dave-o slapped his knee. 'But where's your boy now?'

'My what?'

'Your son. That little guy you were aeroplaning and pretending to shave. Cute little bastard. Back with his mum in Canada?'

'No, no. That was just an actor. All the dads and kids—none of us were related.'

'Whoa.' Dave-o appeared to be revising his worldview. 'So you don't have kids at all?'

'None's I know of,' said Matt. He seized Ash in a headlock. 'Except this little guy!'

Ash went limp as his head was knuckled, then kissed, then released as their lunches and a round of fresh Kingfishers arrived. While the others sopped up watery dhal with chapatis, Ash tipped back his beer, eyes watering as it glugged saltily down his throat.

THE CONTAINER, TUCKED AMID the socks and underwear at the bottom of his carry-on, was about the size of a child's shoebox. The weight of it was surprising: heavy as iron. Ash struggled to think what such a thing might be—a gift? He shook and sniffed it. No clues.

'Dave-o's waiting,' called Matt from the hallway. 'Get the lead out!'

Ash left the box among his things, bundled up in the few warmer items of clothing he could find—wondering distantly why, if they'd planned a ski vacation, he hadn't packed long johns or mitts—and chased Matt down the corridor.

They were to fetch the Norwegians on their way out, but at Matt's knock Tove's face appeared, looking grave. 'We won't be skiing. Jens is feeling . . . unwell.'

So it was just the two Canadians who met Dave-o at the rental shop, a shack crammed with ski equipment and staffed by a young Kashmiri in plastic sunglasses who Dave-o introduced as Karim. Ash bought cotton pyjamas to wear under his jeans and sweat-shirt. But all the men's outerwear was in large sizes.

'They're used to outfitting Germans and Dutchmen, guys twice your size,' said Dave-o. 'Going to have to get you in a kids' kit—or women's.'

After some rummaging around, Karim presented a turquoise and pink snowsuit almost shyly, as if it were the pelt of some exotic beast he'd accidentally slaughtered.

'Wow,' said Matt. 'Too bad we're not going to a gay bar on the moon. Perfect outfit.'

Dave-o affected a lisp: 'I just *love* the zigzag piping, sailor.'

Matt took out his phone to snap photos of Karim zipping Ash into his snowsuit. The jacket was ribbed and elaborately patterned; the pants flared into bellbottoms. Matt showed Ash the pictures: amid all that Technicolor, his face looked sketched in grey-scale.

'He's like a time-traveling aerobics teacher,' said Dave-o.

'Like a soccer mom on acid,' said Matt, and between belly laughs he told Dave-o about a class ski trip when Ash had caught a pole in the rope tow and been dragged halfway up the hill before the patrol jimmied him free.

'Crikey, mate,' said Dave-o. 'Not much of a rescue team in Gulmarg. Fall from the gondola and we may have to leave you up there until the spring melt.'

Next Matt chose him a pair of boots, sparkling and silver. 'See if these fit, Cinderella.'

Karim knelt and eased Ash's feet into them. Were his arches meant to feel so pinched? He couldn't remember. 'You from around here?' Ash asked Karim.

Srinagar, he was told.

To the pair of children's skis assigned to Ash, the two big men added accessories: faux-mink stole, lime green gloves, sequined toque. Then Dave-o led them outside and, lowering his goggles like an aviator, instructed the Canadians to 'Nordic over to the lifts.' Ash did not understand until Dave-o and Matt had cross-countried fifteen yards down the road. His first step was perilous: a boot unclipped and the ski torpedoed away. He pursued it sheepishly, horsemen watching from the pasture.

'Faster on horse,' one of them suggested, jingling the reins of a wasted grey nag.

Collecting his stray ski, Ash wondered if Matt was concealing the real reason for their trip—a Dhar family reunion, say, or, if he did indeed work in radio, an investigative piece about the conflict. Surely there were stories to tell. One of these pony-wallahs, for example, might once have been a champion rider, reduced by sectarian violence to shuttling tourists from one end of Gulmarg to the other.

Shouts came from down the road. Matt and Dave-o waved their poles in semaphore. 'Move it or lose it!' called Matt. 'We'll get you a horsey ride later!'

Ash caught up at the base of the mountain. The touts were closing in and Dave-o brushed away offers of guided hikes up Mount Apharwat. 'I'm the guide here,' he said through a fierce, bearded grin.

The building that dispensed and collected the gondola was under construction, with loose wires and pipes bursting from bare concrete walls. They were the only skiers in line; the few other people were sightseers who would ride the lift to the top and, without exiting, cycle back down.

'Looks like two per car,' Matt told Ash. 'You okay to meet us up top?'

'Some solo time's likely just what you need to jog the old grey matter,' added Dave-o, clapping Ash on the shoulder.

A cable car came wheeling around the track and Dave-o and Matt piled in. As it swept them up the mountain, an aide appeared to help Ash into the next car. The doors closed and out it swung into the icy afternoon light. Halfway up the mountainside, a cluster of huts swung into view amid the trees. Militant hideouts, maybe? Ash waited for some young mujahideen to come staggering out with a rocket launcher and blow the gondola to smithereens. But the little village was swallowed by fog.

With the view blanketed below, the only thing to look at was the car ahead. Ash could just make out the back of Matt's bald head and Dave-o's gingery locks through the glass. Their car rocked slightly—with laughter, he presumed, as they mocked him. 'Could barely get his stubbies on,' Dave-o would yuck, 'can't wait to see him ride the bumps.' Matt would respond with a catalogue of Ash's lifetime of incompetence: a tumble down a gulch, his torso impaled on a stalagmite. None of it even had to be true. Whatever Matt claimed of Ash was, for now, fact.

Up he went, the lift grinding and twanging as it pulleyed him skyward. Then things levelled out and the fog scattered; a treeless plateau emerged. And here was the terminus, a squat building on stilts that absorbed the gondolas in darkness. In went Matt and Dave-o; Ash's car slowed with a groan as it reached the platform. The cables clacked. The doors heaved open. Ash readied himself to debark, sure he'd find himself alone, with Matt and Dave-o (what a name, like a Dave-flavoured breakfast cereal) off on some gnarly mogul run over the backside of the mountain.

What he discovered instead was Matt leaning on his poles and the Australian nowhere in sight.

Ash skied up. 'Where's Dave . . . o?'

'Got a call on his walkie-talkie, that Norwegian guy's really sick. Looks like they're going to have to chopper him to Srinagar.'

'So he went back down?'

'Yup, took off like a bat out of hell. Left me this though.' Matt handed Ash a flask. Indian rum, musky as cheap cologne. Still, the trickle of booze down his throat was welcome. He took another sip before Matt snatched it away.

'Easy now, that's not ours!' He pocketed the flask. 'Gotta love Australians, huh?'

'Love?'

'Yeah! They're so much like us.'

'Us?'

'Canadians.'

'We're like Dave-o?'

'Sure. Australians, Canadians—we're practically brothers.'

'You two do seem very brotherly.'

Matt eyed him quizzically. 'You jealous?'

'Of Dave-o? I may not remember much about myself, but I can guarantee that nothing about that person would ever make me jealous.'

Matt laughed. 'There you are. *That's* the old Ash.'

Encouraged, Ash peered down the slope. 'Like riding a bike, you said?'

'Gosh, bro. I hope so. Do you remember how to do this?'

'I guess we'll find out.'

'Just go slow, be careful. And I'll be right beside you, the whole way down.'

Ash pushed off tentatively. Remarkably his body took over: Matt was right, it knew what to do. He turned his edges and slid off sideways, feeling ridiculous in his garish outfit—yet almost happy. This felt familiar. He smiled a little.

'There you go!' cried Matt, waving his poles in triumph. 'Looking good.'

Ash made slow, looping tracks from one side of the hill to the other. After a few traverses he eased up on his angles, let himself gather a little speed. Matt followed, weaving expertly and patiently around him. The whoosh and whisper of their skis turned hypnotic as they descended in tandem, trees looming darkly on the periphery.

Skiing felt good. Life had become halting and tentative: a stab toward himself, a retraction. Swishing along so fluidly, the air brushing icily past, lulled him—the momentum, but also the control, even as the fog thickened and Matt became a hazy silhouette bumping in and out of view. 'You okay?' he'd call and Ash would reply, 'Yup! Fine!' Though each time these check-ins seemed more distant.

A misty wall rose up ahead. Ash slowed as he neared, searching for some way around. But the fog bled from one side of the hill to the other. So he entered with caution. It submerged him completely. Wary that a turn left or right might plunge him into the woods, Ash angled his skis inward. Down he snowplowed in what he hoped was a straight line. Everything everywhere was white.

And here came fear, the glinting edge of it.

Matt whooshed past a few feet away like something out of an energy drink commercial. 'Wild!' he hollered. 'Frigging total whiteout! See you at the bottom!'

And vanished.

Ash slowed, knees trembling. He could barely make out the tips of his skis. The air was milky and motionless. He felt like a specimen floating through some miasmic jelly, and wary, too, that at any moment something huge and horrible might rise up in his path. Or, worse, that he'd ski cartoonishly off the edge of a precipice: the suspension, the dawning horror, the screaming, flailing descent. Then the fantasy dissolved, replaced by that now-familiar, blank static.

For a moment he felt lighter, airy. He was aware only of his body: a cold breeze sparkling on his cheeks, the pillowy terrain jiggling his knees, his hands clutching poles. Poles, why poles? He dropped them; they disappeared behind him. And why this knock-kneed crouch? He moved his skis parallel. And picked up speed.

The wind came more stiffly now, articulating his body within its currents. And the more rapidly he went the stronger and surer it came. For a moment the emptiness in his mind didn't matter: he was just a form moving through space, hurtling down and faster down, icy air tearing up inside his woolly hat and whistling in his ears.

The fog tattered and broke. Out of it he plummeted. A town opened up before him. And a figure stood at the base of the hill, maybe seventy-five yards away. A big man in goggles, waving his ski poles. From this figure boomed a voice of authority: 'Whoa there, Dhar. Ease up, slow it down now.'

Why? Faster was better. The faster he went, the more alive he felt.

The big man, fifty yards away, was still yelling. Matt, Ash thought: his alleged best friend, about whom he knew nothing. Beyond Matt was a fence, and beyond that the building from which a procession of those little booths climbed swaying up the mountain.

'Are you trying to kill yourself?' cried Matt. 'Bring your tips in!'

Kill himself? Surely not. The alternative appeared to be stopping. But how? He lowered his hands to his sides but that achieved little. He crouched, which only increased his speed. He willed himself mentally slower. No result.

The skis cut fast through the snow with a gristly, raking sound. Matt was a hundred feet away, eighty, sixty. Close enough to see the terror in his eyes, and now bracing himself for impact—arms out, feet set. 'I got you, bro!' he cried.

But it felt wrong and possibly detrimental to crash into this person. So what to do?

Fall.

So he fell. Leant left and crumpled, skis detaching and pinwheeling away. His body crunched hard into the snow and knotted and pitched, over and over and over, like a bit of litter balled and flung from the window of a moving train.

And then it all stopped. Pain shot from his hip to shoulder. But pain was good: it anchored him. Lying on the frozen ground, Ash gazed up at the colourless sky. Snowflakes floated down, lighted wetly on his cheeks. Winter, he thought. Simple and clear: *Winter, winter.* The word tumbled through his brain, a sock in a clothes dryer—

A memory interrupted. Something here: wet socks, a burning smell. And this place. But before these elements could connect and concretize Matt was upon him, hollering and gesturing hugely—'Gosh, good, you're alive, are you okay, what were you doing, did you break anything, that was crazy, what were you thinking?'

'I don't know,' said Ash simply. And wondered when he might answer a question with anything but those words.

## 4

'WHAT YOU NEED,' said Matt, 'is a massage.'

It had the implication of a threat. Ash, sitting in bed with an icepack pressed to his lower back, crossed his arms. 'I don't know, I'm still pretty sore.'

'So let me fix you up. I told you, I'm pretty much licensed, don't worry. Down you get.'

'On the floor?'

'Need the leverage. Bed's too soft.' Matt was coming at him now. 'Shirt off, pants off.'

'Pants off?'

'Everything off.'

Obediently Ash stripped down to his boxers. Pulling off his shirt, he cringed: pain shot through him, seeming to originate everywhere at once.

'What are you, bashful? I've seen your junk a hundred

times. Look, I'll gear down too if it makes you more comfortable.' Matt's shirt came over his head. His chest, as broad and pale as a whitewashed wall, was speckled with stubble and razor burn.

'Is that necessary?'

'What are you, afraid of a little man-on-man action?' Matt laughed. 'Fine, I'll leave my trackpants on if you're going to be so homophobic about it.'

And then he was lowering Ash to the carpet and straddling him.

'Not too hard.'

'Don't fret. I'm a pro. Just gotta be careful with my pinkie, it's nearly totally healed.'

As Matt began working his shoulders Ash crossed his arms and laid his cheek on his wrists. His view was straight under the bed to his open duffel bag on the other side. That strange grey container poked out from amid the clothes.

Matt's hands worked rigorous circles over Ash's deltoids, down across his shoulder blades, along his spine. Pinching, kneading, furrowing. 'How's that feel?'

'Okay. A bit . . . intense, maybe.'

'That means it's working. Relax.'

Ash tried to obey, but every time Matt moved to a new region of his back he felt his entire body contracting, resisting.

'Where's it hurt the most?'

'Right where you're sitting, actually.'

'Gotcha.' Matt moved lower to bludgeon Ash's calves. 'Swedish,' he explained.

Matt's hands ventured northward, up past his knees, knuckling into the meat of Ash's thighs. Ash thought he felt a stray finger snake up the inside of his boxers, but it retreated. Up it crept again, a little more adventurously, and he tried to wriggle away. But Matt pinned him in place.

'There we go,' Matt murmured. 'Some really tight knots right here.'

He worked Ash's upper legs briskly, almost aggressively, thumbs probing inward. Ash tried to bring his knees together to close the gap. But Matt pried them open again.

'Just gotta get at your glutes.'

And his hands were now cupping his buttocks, working them like balls of dough. Ash could feel the outline of each splayed digit, the thumbs delving down into the space between his legs and then pulling up and outward, stretching him—

'Okay,' said Ash. 'That's probably good.'

But Matt kept going. He pressed his prickly chest to Ash's back. His breath came in gusts. And then he went still. For a moment Matt just lay there: a quarter-ton of man spooning Ash from above. And was that? No, Ash thought; impossible. But, wait, yes: Matt seemed, almost imperceptibly, to be grinding his hips. Ash held his breath. It stopped. Nothing for a moment. And then the humping—was there another word for it?—resumed, a little more propulsively than before.

With all his strength Ash rolled onto his side, tipping Matt onto his knees.

Matt looked baffled. 'Everything okay, bro?'

Immediately Ash felt ashamed. 'Sorry,' he said. 'Just felt a little claustrophobic.'

'Pretty standard osteopathic technique,' said Matt. 'Using my full weight on you. Working out those kinks from your fall. But if it wasn't working, that's cool.' With a shrug Matt picked up Ash's shirt and pants and handed them over.

Ash felt stupid; he'd made it weird. He dressed while Matt stayed kneeling, eyes focused on some point a few inches from his face. 'Did it help?' he asked, looking up.

Bending and twisting at the waist, Ash told him yes, it had. 'Thanks,' he added.

'No prob.'

Down the hall a door slammed. A scuffing noise of footsteps raced past their room.

'Might go try to check my email,' said Ash.

'Smart,' said Matt. 'Good way to get some info. About yourself, I mean.'

'Exactly.'

For a moment, neither of them moved or said anything.

Ash broke the stiffening silence: 'Should probably clean up a bit first.' He moved his duffel onto the bed and began stuffing it with errant clothes. But zipping it closed was a struggle; the two sides bulged around that grey box. Ash pulled it free and set it on the dresser: a gift awaiting its recipient.

'You're going to need your password,' Matt said, standing at last. He came over, pushed aside the grey box and scrawled a line of digits onto the hotel notepad. 'Same one you've used since you were fifteen,' he said, tearing off the page but not handing it over. 'PIN to your bank account, alarm to your condo. Everything.'

'Thanks.'

'No problem.' Matt folded the paper in half, concealing the number, and slipped it into Ash's hand. 'I keep telling you, bro: whatever you need, just ask.'

THE SCREECH AND STATIC of the dial-up modem played like an old, familiar song. Ash smiled at this—a blast from the past, albeit a past he could recall only peripherally.

The concierge supervised over Ash's shoulder, hands clasped behind his back in a posture of official surveillance. 'Online?'

'Yeah,' said Ash.

'Proceed.'

Matt's password worked. And here were Ash's emails in a great cascade.

'Begin here,' instructed the concierge, leaning in and tapping the most recent unread message, from someone named Sherene. The subject was 'Book Club.' Ash clicked and read, the concierge following intently over his shoulder.

> Ash—
>
> So I'm 100 pages into DQ and yeah sure it's hilarious and sort of cool too I guess, and surprisingly modern, and thanks again for the gift, you're sweet—but JESUS, Ash. Talk about bro-lit. Been imagining it as you and your meathead buddy gallivanting across India instead of Spain. I mean I hope you aren't getting in fights all over the place and defending maidens' honour and whatever else, tilting at rickshaws, but seriously it's got me thinking how many men are still like this, how many men end up chasing some ridiculous ideal that has nothing to do with who they—and you too, sweetie, don't think I'm letting you off!—actually are.

The email continued but Ash stopped reading for a moment. The message stabbed at the core of something. He felt needled. She'd called him 'sweetie'—was Sherene a lover? The absence of a girlfriend or wife in Matt's rundown had not seemed notable until now. No picture accompanied Sherene's email address. And when he tried to find an image online a warning popped up on the screen.

'No web searches,' warned the concierge. 'Blocked.'

Ash returned to the message:

> But the thing for me mainly about this book, the big disappointment, is Sancho Panza. I had this idea that this was like THE BOOK about friendship. But he's more of a lackey. I mean DQ is delusional right? Possibly insane? And Sancho just trucks along with him because of this vague promise of some island fiefdom or whatever. Not to honour his friend.

And this willing obliviousness is what gets me, Ash. Like he's willing to just play the idle witness while his pal suffers one humiliation after the next, and even encourages him sometimes too when really he should be acting with real kindness and just be like, no, this isn't real, let's go home. Anyway, speaking of, it'll be nice to get back to Canada again. London's fun for a few days but I've got another FORTNIGHT here, as my cousins keep telling me and inshallah, Ash, I already can't wait to get back to work, isn't that weird?

The rest of the email eased into some book recommendations and well-wishing for his trip and a gentle sign-off: XO. And here the possibilities of romance deflated; those weren't passionate kisses. Sherene's message pulsed with the exasperated affection that blooms in the gaps between love and sex. She and Ash were close, to a point, but there it stopped. Even so, she seemed like a friend he might actually trust.

Encouraged, Ash returned to his inbox and, to the concierge's dismay, skipped the next three unread emails to click another from Sherene. It had no subject and consisted of a single sentence:

Oh, sorry to bring up work though I did talk to management and it looks like we'll be able to get you back in the chair for the spring season, so good news there and no one seems to despise you anymore than they did already! XO

A colleague too, then. But why might Ash be despised at work? Matt had claimed that he was 'a famous radio host' and loved by 'literally dozens;' no part of that biography touched on anything particularly contemptible. Though if Matt were as good a friend as he claimed, might his casually brutish way implicate Ash? Ash pictured himself in the studio mewling at a twenty-something intern as she leaned down to adjust his microphone, smacking her rear-end as she fled the room. Maybe he and Matt were more similar than he thought, or hoped. How close were they, really?

A flash of that massage invaded his thoughts. Ash shuddered, shook it away.

Better to align himself with Sherene. Ash preferred the version of himself she mirrored. And he sensed tenderness beneath her vitriol. He liked, too, how she repeated his name; there was something warmly imploring about it that spoke of shared history: they'd been having conversations like this 'for years'—and here they were, still.

'Ten minutes left,' announced the concierge.

Ash clicked back to his inbox, scanned the list. Chose an email titled 'I am so pregnant!' from someone named Mona—his sister, he remembered, according to Matt. The message contained no text, only a photo. The dial-up struggled; the hard-drive chirped and whirred. Line by line excruciating the picture unfurled on the screen: dark hair, peaked eyebrows, almond-shaped eyes. From the framing and blurred focus Ash guessed that it was self-taken. Halfway down the nose it paused. The concierge leaned in. The cursor became an hourglass tipping back and forth. Mona's expression was unreadable—coy or sombre? He could hardly admire her pregnancy from her forehead!

Ash cancelled the download and hit refresh.

An error message appeared.

He clicked back.

Nothing; the connection was down. The photo had vanished, his inbox had vanished—all that data, lost to the ether.

'Offline,' said the concierge.

'How long before it comes back up?'

'Minutes, hours.' A shrug. 'Days.'

'Days?'

'Possibly.' The concierge's hands appeared from behind his back in, possibly, the opening gambit of a chokehold. 'So, finish?'

Ash stared at the screen: *Unable to connect.* He laughed a lone, sharp syllable somewhere between 'ha' and 'huh.' And then the concierge stooped and pulled the plug.

Dreading a return to his room, Ash headed outside and stood on the steps of the hotel shivering in the winter dusklight. From the carrel across the road a pony-wallah approached with an emaciated animal. He wore only a woollen gown, hands and head naked to the chilly air.

'Take ride. Very good price.'

'Where would we go?'

'Apharwat Peak,' he said. The solicitation had the fatigue of habit, as if in obligation to some lapsed belief. His eyes were sad.

'You know what? Sure,' said Ash. 'Let's do it.'

He was helped up onto the saddle and wrapped, with surprising tenderness, in blankets. Beneath his weight the horse's spine sagged. Yet she staggered forward, snow squeaking under her hooves, with the pony-wallah clutching her bridle and clucking softly. 'You are from?' he asked.

'Canada,' said Ash meekly, as if offering an apology.

'No. Not Canada. You are . . . Indian?'

Ash enjoyed a little surge of possibility. 'My dad's from here. From Kashmir.'

'I knew it!' His smile revealed a jumble of yellow teeth. 'You have the nose. Name?'

'Dhar.'

'Hindu?'

'My dad is,' said Ash, following Matt's script.

'I am Mumtaz,' the man said, bowing. 'Welcome home, Pandit Dhar.'

They walked for a while in silence. Ash considered his nose as a marker of identity. And Mona's, chopped off at the bridge: did they share this nose? And what kind of brother was he? A protector, a confidant? Or merely a blood relation to send compulsory updates—a single picture, snapped haphazardly, but no words.

Mumtaz clucked. The horse stopped. 'You will come to my village for tea?'

'Your village?'

'Not too far.' He indicated a path up through the woods. 'No charge.'

Ash eyed the mountain.

'Apharwat, later. It is early only. Come. Please. A Hindu. At last!'

'Oh, I don't know how Hindu I am.'

'How Hindu?' Mumtaz laughed. 'You are enough Hindu. Come. We will go.'


MUMTAZ LIVED JUST OUTSIDE TOWN in a cluster of stone and timber cottages amid the trees. His house was small and modest, the interior painted in an array of pastel shades. Ash was led to a drafty, cement-floored room blanketed with worn carpets. An electric heater glared in the corner. Mumtaz heaped some cushions together and encouraged Ash to sit.

'Now I will fetch the tea,' he said, and withdrew.

The room had no decorations, no furniture, not even an end table. Ash wondered how accustomed to any of this he might be. Maybe he had relatives who lived in similar homes? Maybe he'd spent countless afternoons in parlours just like this; maybe the situation echoed some previous experience to which, now, he was oblivious.

A boy came in with a plate of—were they?—bagels.

'Hello,' said Ash.

'Sir,' said the boy. He knelt and deposited the tray at Ash's feet.

'What's your name?'

The boy looked nervous. He took a step back, eyeing the doorway behind him. 'Pastries, sir,' he said. And vanished.

Ash tried a bagel. Dry as a crouton. Stale? Or meant to be this way?

A man appeared in the doorway, broader in the chest than Mumtaz, though with the same sad eyes and wonky teeth. He touched his forehead and sat. 'Welcome.'

'Thank you,' said Ash, through a mouthful of dough.

'You speak Kashmiri?'

Ash scanned his thoughts: not a word. 'No. Sorry.'

The man nodded; his melancholy seemed to deepen. 'You are coming from? Canada?'

'Canada, yeah.' Ash felt himself being watched intently, almost imploringly. In an effort to please his interlocutor, he finished the dusty bagel.

The man was joined by another, elderly, long and lean, in thick glasses and a stark white goatee. On his head perched a peaked woolly hat.

'Hello,' said Ash, offering him a pastry: declined.

The old man knelt, joints crackling, and wretched violently into a handkerchief, which he pocketed.

More and more men piled into the room, alone or in pairs, lining the walls. Some acknowledged Ash directly, others simply squatted and stared. Soon a dozen strangers watched him with the reticent curiosity of UFO researchers sizing up their live specimen. What was expected of him? Just to eat?

Finally a woman entered in a loose silk pantsuit and matching headscarf. (*Salwar kameez*, thought Ash, with taxonomical satisfaction.) The position she assumed, facing him directly, seemed to have been reserved for her. She was acknowledged by the older guy with a nod. Then all eyes turned back to Ash, as though viewing him anew, via the gaze of the room's sole female presence. He again felt himself on display. Or trial?

With a coy smile the woman made a comment in Kashmiri that inspired subdued laughter from the group. The elder offered his two cents in a reedy little voice, which caused the men to inhale briskly, close their eyes or shake their heads.

'Please,' the woman told Ash, indicating the plate of pastries. 'Eat.'

A function: he took another bagel.

Mumtaz reappeared with a tea set. 'Ah, everyone has come,' he said, and knelt before Ash to fill a porcelain cup from a matching pot.

'Thank you,' said Ash.

The tea was hot, salty, milky. And pink.

Not everyone got tea, only Ash and the woman, whom Mumtaz introduced as a poet; her name was not provided. 'And he'—the old man in the hat and goatee—'is Doctor Sayeed.'

A doctor! Perhaps the one scheduled to visit Ash later that evening. But Sayeed eyed Ash with suspicion, his thin hands fondling each other in his lap.

'Nice to meet you,' said Ash.

The doctor tilted his chin so that sharp little beard targeted Ash like a dagger.

'So,' mediated Mumtaz. 'First time to Kashmir?'

'I'm not sure.' Ash laughed uneasily and sipped his tea. 'I've been having some memory issues. Actually maybe the doctor—'

'Surely your father brought you as a boy, before the Troubles?'

interrupted the poet. Her accent had a crisp, British officiousness to it. 'Although it is much different now.'

'Decimated,' said Doctor Sayeed. 'The whole valley.'

'But we have a Pandit returned!' Mumtaz clapped. 'And he has seen how beautiful it remains. So he will return—every year. With his father.'

'That'd be nice,' said Ash. 'It's pretty here. The . . . mountains.'

'The mountains,' said Mumtaz with satisfaction.

'You know,' said the poet, 'your own Pandit Nehru called this paradise on earth.'

'*It is here, it is here, it is here,*' provided Mumtaz, voice swelling.

She interceded in Kashmiri, delivering a possible couplet with the sonorous cadence of verse. At its conclusion a chorus of impressed tsking rippled around the room.

'Do you know Lal Ded?' said Sayeed.

'I've heard of him,' Ash lied.

'She was in fact a woman,' said the poet. '*I was passionate, filled with longing; I searched far and wide. But the day that the Truthful One found me, I was home.*'

'Very nice,' said Ash.

The poet bowed—not to the compliment, but in reverence to the work. 'Lal Ded also wrote: *Some leave their home, some the hermitage, but the restless mind knows no rest. So watch your breath, day and night, and stay where you are.* A lesson, perhaps.'

Ash sipped his tea and wondered what the lesson might be.

'You see it is the women poets who have long been the voice of this place. And Habba Khatoon is the best of the lot,' she continued. 'Sixteenth century. She wrote of scorned lovers, of longing, of loss. Even then, the story of Kashmir.'

More tsking. Ash, in an act of daring, attempted a tsk of his own.

'*I left my home for play,*' recited the poet, wincing as if the lines assailed her from within. '*Nor yet again returned, although the day sank into the West. The name I made is hailed on lips of men—Habba Khatoon!—though veiled, I found no rest. Through crowds I found my way, from forests, then, the sages came . . . when day sank into the West.'*

Ash joined the tsking and, not to be outdone, improvised an awestruck headshake.

Doctor Sayeed came to life: 'One of the great Muslim poets.'

'But Muslim, Hindu,' said Mumtaz in protest. 'Kashmiriyat, all same people.'

The doctor spat something dismissive and turned upon Ash. 'You have come as a tourist. To stay in hotel, to ski. *Highest gondola in the world*, they say. You like it?'

'Um,' said Ash. 'Yeah, really nice.'

'*Very nice*,' said Doctor Sayeed, hands twisting in his lap. 'Very nice to visit, then leave, and fancy yourself in exile. Do you know what we who live here have been through?'

Mumtaz said something cautionary, pacifying.

'No! He must know. These Hindus think they are the only ones to suffer. Mister Dhar, I am a? Doctor. My father also. And his father before him. All doctors, all down the line. As my son too would have been a doctor.'

The air in the room had turned brittle. Ash put down his tea.

'Our house is just there, down the lane.' Doctor Sayeed indicated this with a kind of karate chop toward the window. 'One evening my son was playing in our garden. Two men came over the wall with guns and chased him inside, very frightened. This was a time, mind, when people were disappearing all over the Valley. In middle of night they would come and—*whup*, like that, snatch you from your home. Understand?'

Ash nodded.

'So I went to? Confront them. It was dark, I could see only shapes. I had no weapon, no torch even. My son was just a boy, and my wife was inside. I could hope only that they wanted drugs from my dispensary. I called. They appeared from shadows. I recognized both, young men from next village. I had treated one as a boy for colic. And now they carried guns—big guns!' He sucked in his breath sharply between pursed lips. 'But they claimed to be for my protection. "People are after you," they said. "We will stand watch."'

'Bastards,' said Mumtaz.

Yet Doctor Sayeed spoke inexpressively, eyes fixed on Ash; all that moved were his lips and his hands. The room felt heavy, as if bearing the weight of this story. 'No one at this time could be trusted. Each side was terrorizing us equally—state police, BSF, Indian army, militants. But what could I do? So then I had goons here all day, harassing my patients. Very disruptive. If I or my wife went out, they would? Follow. These two boys, so strong and important. Whole time I thought something was . . . untoward. My wife also. We had never been threatened. We were respected. I would, without question, treat militants and soldiers both. To do away with me made no sense.'

'Yet,' said Mumtaz.

'Yet.' Doctor Sayeed's fidgeting hands made a papery sound. 'After some days my wife grew fed up. She slipped from rear of house and off to market to buy fruit, something like that. This was midday, October. I saw patients all afternoon. When my son returned from school my wife had not returned from market. We waited, my son and I. This is a tiny village, one road only. Very difficult to become lost. Unless she had gone all the way to Gulmarg. Which would have been foolish, very dangerous.'

'On horse is fine,' Mumtaz assured Ash.

Ash tsked.

'I call the police, but they are? Unhelpful,' said Doctor Sayeed. 'And what is interesting, when they come so-called body-guards do not hide. They remain in open. Even they are *talking* to the police officers. One would think that militants would not be so friendly.'

'Indeed not militants,' said Mumtaz.

'No,' said Doctor Sayeed. 'They were? Spies for military police. Hoping that actual militants would visit my practice so they could snatch them up. Next day I received a message: as they had seen these guards and knew them to be police, one militant group believed I was? Colluding with army. This is why they had kidnapped my wife. They would kill her if I did not pay ten rupees crore. So with all of my savings I arranged to meet them. This is how these idiots behave. They wage war like it's a? Film. I was told to come alone, then my wife would be returned, and when paid for her release only they would leave us in peace. However, I could not think of leaving my son alone. They had already taken my wife. Why would they stop at ten crore when they could double the price? So I brought him with me.'

Ash sensed that this was the turning point—not just of the story, but his own edification. He nodded: yes, the son, of course. A fatal mistake.

Mumtaz gestured at Ash's cup. 'Please, drink. Your tea will grow cold.'

The liquid had turned tepid and a creamy film slicked its surface. Ash sipped. All he could taste was salt.

Doctor Sayeed continued: 'My son and I entered the woods with this money in a lending box. And? Figures came from trees. A bag over my head, just like that. My hands bound. I was hit in the stomach, all the breath went—*poof!*—from me. We were dragged to a lorry and thrown in back. I could not say which direction we drove. My son was weeping. I told him he was safe, that I would let nothing happen. We arrived somewhere, a house. I was taken up the stairs, away from my son, to the top floor. Still I have this bag over my head. I begged them to spare my boy. They could have any sum they wanted. I was told only that I would be dealt with in the morning. And this, "dealt with," I knew to mean? Executed. And perhaps same fate awaited my wife and child.'

The story had its own energy now; Doctor Sayeed was only its medium. But here he required a pause to gather himself. Even his hands fell still.

'So what could I do?' he said after a moment. 'I waited until night. House was very quiet. Still with sack over my head I found a window. We had climbed three-four flights of stairs—typical Kashmiri house—and if I jumped? I could die. Regardless I leapt. Upon landing I heard—*snap*. Such pain! I had fractured my tibia. Fortunately bone did not pierce skin. I crawled to the road. I could only guess which direction was Gulmarg. For hours, I crawled on roadside. A Jeep approached. I signalled—but the driver failed to see me. So I continued, another hour. Through the sack I could see the sun rising, but my hands were still bound behind my back so I could not take it off, and . . .'

Doctor Sayeed went silent. He tucked his chin to his chest.

'But you made it to town?' said Ash.

'Yes.'

'And then, were you able to get back to the hideout? With the police or whoever?'

'Yes. They knew the place.'

'And your wife and son? Were they okay?'

'My wife and son?' He looked up; his eyes were fierce. 'No, Mister Dhar, they were not okay. Upon discovering that I had fled, the militants murdered them. Shot once each'—he pointed to his temple—'right through the head as they slept.'

'I'M GOING TO GET frigging annihilated tonight,' called Matt from the bathroom.

He was in there trying on shirts while Ash lay on his bed leafing through a volume of Kashmiri poetry. The poet had given it to him as he'd been leaving Mumtaz's house. 'My English translations,' she'd explained. According to the book she did have a name, or a nom-de-plume: Zoon. Ash had hoped that the poetry might kindle the embers of some memory, something elemental and ancient. But the entries tended toward godly worship and their effect was soporific. His eyelids drooped; the book fell from his hands.

Matt emerged in a paisley-print button-down. 'What do you think of this one?'

'Yeah, good,' said Ash, glancing up.

'Honestly? Don't I look like Jimi Hendrix?'

Ash smiled.

'Bro? Hello?'

'Sorry. Still a little out of it, I guess.'

Matt traded the shirt for a white kurta with green embroidery around the neckline. 'Dave-o leant me this one.' Matt bowed. 'Namaste.'

'Looks good,' said Ash.

'You're not going to make fun of me?'

'Should I?'

'Ugh, this is the worst. I can't wait for the old you to come back. It's weird.' Matt shook his head sadly. 'You're acting so frigging *nice*.'

A long, slow breath drained from Ash's nostrils with the sound of a deflating tire. He put down the book. 'Sorry,' he said.

'The least you can do tonight is tie one on. Right? I mean, if it's so wrong to drink to forget, what's the problem if you already forget everything?'

Ash laughed.

'That's the spirit. I'll make sure you have the goshdang night of your life! I mean, we're on vacation, am I right?'

'And we go home when?'

'To Canada?' Matt moved back into the bathroom to check himself out in the mirror. 'I don't know about this top. I mean, if you were a chick and went home with me, would you assume I could put my legs behind my head and go for like eleven hours?

Don't want to set too high a bar. Probably should just go with my regular GOS—going-out shirt, sorry. A little joke we used to make.' He chuckled gloomily. 'You doing okay?'

There was something beseeching in his voice. Ash nodded. 'Yeah, fine.'

Matt pulled the kurta over his head and flung it into the room. 'Anyhoo, gonna prond-ma-doosh. Can't ring in the New Year with my junk smelling like a ski boot.'

The door closed. Ash stared at it. Doors were always closing on him, it seemed. He felt on the periphery of everything, especially himself—gazing from the edge down into the chasm where his life ought to be.

He returned to Zoon's book. But again it failed to capture him, lacking some essential quality from her recitations. And it wasn't just the cadence of her oratory that was missing. She'd watched Ash so steadily, her voice trembling with melancholy and import—more of an incantation, a summoning. And then, after, pressing the book into his hands: 'Take this home with you.' Ash felt now that she'd meant something more intrinsic and ineffable than the words within its pages—maybe that irreconcilable space between document and memory, and what therein was lost.

The doctor's kidnapping story had been intended as a different type of edification, to humble and chastise him. After Mumtaz had dropped him back at the hotel, Ash had repeated the story to Matt. Yet telling it turned the events cinematic, its lessons and emotion burdened by characters and action. Never mind that Matt's response had mostly been terror: 'Bro, you went to their *house?*' he spluttered. 'Anybody here could be al-Qaeda! I know you're a little out of your mind, but there's no need for a suicide mission.'

Ash stood, scanning the room for the printouts Dave-o had left him. Among the clothes bursting from his suitcase he spied the edge of some papers, but these proved to be something else entirely—a story. He read a few pages: a hero climbing into the mountains (of Kashmir, he assumed). Something he was writing? It seemed possible, tucked as the pages were among his things. Almost secretively, at that. And Matt had told him he'd once written a book. Perhaps this was the sequel.

He settled back on the bed, flipping to the last page, which cut off mid-sentence:

And when he reappeared

A work in progress, then. Ash tried to follow that fragment somewhere: *and then what?*

He'd still not come up with anything when the bathroom door opened and Matt appeared amid billowing steam.

'Ash, hey, smell me.' He came over, a towel clutched loosely around his lower half. 'I did that dumb thing of crapping first and not flushing while I showered, so I ended up steaming my poo. Have I got a poopy bouquet about me? Be honest.'

Ash tilted toward him. Inhaled. Recoiled. 'You smell like soap.'

'You sure?' Matt looked nervous. 'There any way this amnesia messed up your sense of smell? Aren't your nose and memory supposed to be connected?'

Ash hadn't considered this. He sniffed again. Matt's zesty odour triggered nothing.

'Listen, while I've got you—do me a solid and shave my back? There's a patch right between my shoulder blades I can never get.'

'Shave your back?'

'Honestly, we do this all the time. Normally.'

'Normally.'

'For sure. You shave my back, I shave yours. It's basically our catchphrase.' Matt dropped his towel in the bathroom doorway.

Ash was amazed by how much that pale massive ass resembled an actual moon. 'I can manage my nuts and taint myself,' said Matt, 'but I'll holler when I need you.'

This time he left the door open, revealing glimpses of his body, like a zeppelin cresting the horizon. The moment loomed when Ash would be called to duty. Could he say no? He'd already panicked once at something that, from Matt's bewilderment, had likely been a perfectly normal exchange between friends—a little helpful rubdown, nothing weird at all. Ash wanted to act like himself. So he waited there on the bed, face pointed at that unfinished story, mind blank, for Matt to announce he was ready to be groomed.

'THE CANUCKS!' cried Dave-o, leaping to his feet.

The enthusiasm seemed for Matt's benefit. While the two giants thumped each other's backs, Ash watched a disco ball scatter shards of light around the hotel bar.

'Mate,' said Dave-o to Ash, and offered him a hand to shake.

Beers appeared. Ash accepted one, slurped it greedily.

'Good old Ash, always up for a drink,' said Matt. 'Even if he doesn't remember it.'

Dave-o laughed. 'How many New Yearses do *you* remember?'

They exchanged war stories: passing out in a waterfall (Dave-o), passing out in a snowbank (Matt). Dispersed around the room were a few other guests, mostly couples, all Indian. Someone had strung up leftover Diwali tinsel and a banner proclaiming HAPPY NEWYEAR EVE sagged unconvincingly over the door. The staff wore party hats, which made their anaesthetized expressions look even more forlorn.

The music, Ash somehow knew, was Madonna: *Celebrate,* she commanded. So he drank his beer. Mid-swallow a sneeze exploded from his face like a tripped landmine, spraying its misty shrapnel down his shirt.

'Easy there, mate,' said Dave-o, passing him a serviette. 'You catch something on your pony ride?'

Ash cupped his face and sneezed again. 'Sorry.' He blew his nose. 'God, that sounded just like my dad.'

Matt shot him a suspicious look. 'You remember how he sneezes?'

A memory. Ash tried to rewind his thoughts. But whatever had emerged was gone.

'Good news, anyway,' said Matt. 'Must mean your nut's getting back on track.'

Dave-o tilted his beer in salutation. 'What did I say? Just a matter of time. Anything else coming back?'

The music changed to Michael Jackson. Ash could remember all the words: *Lovely . . . is the feeling now; fever . . . temperature's rising now.* Yet he recalled nothing of his father: not his sneeze, not his voice, not his face. He blew a little cloud of bubbles from the top of his bottle, took a drink and shrugged. 'Nope.'

'Was gonna say,' said Dave-o, 'I sound just like my old man when I sneeze too. This big *harrumph.* Can't control it. Weird, right?'

Matt snorted.

'What?' said Dave-o. 'You don't sneeze like your dad?'

'You guys are out of your minds,' said Matt, and turned away. The disco lights refracted off his scalp in blues and greens.

To retrieve his friend, Ash changed the subject to the unfinished story he'd found. 'Something about a guy climbing a mountain. Any idea what the deal is?'

Matt took a second, then nodded exuberantly. 'It's a book you were writing. Part of the reason you came here was to finish it. Research and that. There's a hike in it, right? Up to a cave? We're supposed to do that at some point.' He looked at Dave-o for corroboration. But the Australian was shaking his head in awe.

'Wow,' he said. 'I always wanted to write a book. How d'you do it?'

'I wish I knew,' said Ash. 'I don't even have writer's block. More like person's block.'

'Exactly why we're going up to the cave,' said Matt. 'Unplug the toilet of your brain.'

'And then?'

'And then you write your book and find your way back to yourself.'

Ash tried to parse Matt's logic. Failed, shook his head. Drank.

Michael Jackson faded into a bhangra number and a husband and wife (green shirt, green dress) moved onto the dance floor. Dave-o nudged Matt. 'Shall we make a move?'

The room's two lone white men sidled out under the disco ball, successfully separating the woman from her partner. Looking concerned but still dancing gamely, the cuckold watched Matt take his wife by the waist and dip her, hips grinding. Meanwhile Dave-o performed a faintly menacing judo of rhythmic air-punches and kicks. When she was vertical again the woman swatted Matt away. Playfully or not, Ash couldn't tell.

The two men high-fived and returned to their table like a pair of linebackers to the huddle. Matt fell into his chair, shirt grey with sweat at the armpits. 'Groundwork laid.'

Ash drank.

Turning to Dave-o, Matt lowered his voice. 'What's the deal with swinging and open marriages and that over here?' He made a surreptitious gesture toward the green-clad couple. 'Or even, you know, *third-party interventions.*'

'Oh mate, have I got stories for you.'

Matt slung his arm around the back of Dave-o's chair. They proceeded to one-up each other with tales of sexual deviancy and conquest. Then the talk turned to skiing: who had scaled the highest peaks, seen the fattest snow, broken the most bones. While Matt and Dave-o compared battle scars, Ash watched the woman in the green dress and her husband sit at their table staring blankly into the room. They still hadn't spoken to each other by the time Ash finished his second beer.

'Well, mate,' said Dave-o, clapping Matt on the shoulder. 'Sorry again if today was a bit of a botch with the Norwegians. Going to be a real treat seeing you out there tomorrow. Sounds like if it weren't for your knee you could have gone pro. Might have met you a lot earlier out on the circuit.'

'Yeah, definitely. Too bad my amnesiac buddy here can't tell you.'

Ash offered a weak smile of apology.

'State he's in,' said Dave-o, 'we could tell him anything we want. Not just about you—about himself. Because what does he know?'

The suggestion inspired laughter, huge and cruel and boomingly full of itself. When it faded Ash felt himself examined with a new kind of scrutiny.

'Only taking the piss, mate. Bet you wake up tomorrow morning with your brain good as new. So! Happy New Year, gents. Bottoms up.'

Another round arrived, prefaced with shots of rum. Someone cranked the sound system and the dance floor filled, husbands on one side and wives on the other; their moves seemed choreographed. Huddled knee to knee, Matt and Dave-o evaluated which women might be stolen from their husbands, while Ash drank as if beer were the elixir to restore his memory—or the poison to do him in for good.

Halfway through his third quart the night started to feel dangerous. Ash swayed in his chair and everything eddied around him, vaporous and indistinct. The two figures across the table, the music grinding away, the shadowy undulations from the dance floor, the hotel staff collecting empties—all of this melted into a slush of sights and sounds. Ash squinted, tried to focus. And a clear thought arrived: he'd no idea what year they were entering.

He motioned to Matt, leaned over and asked. But the music drowned him out.

'What?' screamed Matt.

Ash repeated himself, tapping his wrist—the wrong move.

'Still nearly an hour to go!'

Ash tried again with a full charade of actions: the banner over the door, hands lifting and exploding like fireworks. He even tried miming a calendar, the flap of pages.

Through it all Matt nodded and frowned.

Ash paused, waiting for recognition. He was drunk and adrift; knowing the year would anchor him to something. But Matt just stared blankly, shook his head, then leaned over to Dave-o and whispered in his ear. The Australian cracked up, slapping Matt's knee. Everything about Ash's tablemates consumed so much space—their bodies, their gestures, their gazes trawling the room. As they drank they seemed to expand. Ash, meanwhile, cowered in his drunkenness like something caged.

Matt patted Ash on the shoulder and with Dave-o returned to the dance floor. Ash tried to watch but his vision reeled. The music slurred and thumped. He had no thoughts. His presence in the room felt marginal and vague. Though he did have beer left. So he drank, the bottle upended and his eyes on the ceiling.

And when he set it down, empty, he realized the music had stopped.

He sensed the night turning itself inside out. Something was happening. Something was wrong.

Things clicked into focus: at the edge of the dance floor Dave-o held Matt back from someone screaming in a shrill, nasal voice—the green-shirted husband.

'Easy now,' Dave-o said. 'We're all friends here.'

But Matt was livid too. He bounced on his heels, jutted his chin, widened his eyes, roared. Something had loosened within him and threatened to unspool catastrophically into the room.

For now only Dave-o kept it at bay. Some of the other men hid behind their wives; others fled to corners. The woman in the green dress pushed her shrieking husband aside and levelled a finger at Matt.

'You've no business behaving that way here,' she told him in a steady voice.

'Who the frig do you think you are?' Matt thundered. Bulging veins corded his neck. 'Disrespecting *me*? I don't care if this is your country—'

But the woman was undeterred. 'Take him away,' she ordered Dave-o.

'Mate,' said the Australian. 'Forget it. Come on, let's go.'

In a bear hug Dave-o maneuvered Matt to the door, murmuring into his shoulder. The room was hushed; nothing moved save the disco ball, still whirling its chaos of light around the room.

'Go,' ordered the woman.

Dave-o kneed the door open, nudged Matt outside. As he left Matt told the entire party he'd see them in hell. And then he was gone—into the lobby, maybe beyond.

With Matt's beer unaccounted for, Ash took it and drank. Behind the bottle Dave-o loomed into view. 'Guy could probably use a friend right now.'

'Me?'

'Yeah. You're his best mate, aren't you?'

Ash, feeling at once assessed and challenged, struggled to his feet, steadying himself on the back of his chair.

'Whoa there! Gonna be okay?'

'Going to be okay,' said Ash. And then, to himself: 'Okay.'

He staggered across the bar and out into the lobby. The concierge eyed him warily. 'Looking for your friend?'

Ash nodded.

'Outside.'

The night was another universe. The frigid air and open space smacked him sober. Enough, maybe, to shock the past back into him? Ash stood shivering on the steps of the hotel, breath steaming from his nostrils. But nothing returned. All that existed was the gaping, hollow present.

And there was no sign of Matt anywhere.

Beyond the empty pasture the black humps of the mountains blotted the horizon. A low-slung cloud cover obscured the stars. Under it, the snow looked mauve. The only signs of life came from inside the hotel: the party had resumed—though tentatively. And that swamp of sound, drizzling feebly from the hotel only to be stifled by the icy night, accentuated the massive silence.

In the middle of the pasture was a little island of trees. Ash stared at it and felt a tug. It eased, then surged again: the view twanged some chord of recognition. Maybe even a memory. He stilled his thoughts to allow whatever it was to settle. But the sensation fled and that old desolation returned. His mind was like a half-frozen pond over which life had skimmed and sunk. Ash spat—a snaking wad that carved a divot into the snow. Turned around, stumbled inside.

At the door to the bar he paused. From within came hoots and hollers, the steady thump of bass. Though the night had been wounded, the partiers were doing their best to revive it. Maybe Matt had even returned to do a pass around the room, offering sheepish handshakes and drinks. Ash sensed he would be forgiven, had likely enjoyed a life of forgiveness, of second and third chances. Of fucking up and making do.

A new year was close. A new beginning—of what? Ash had no idea what he was leaving behind. He pictured Matt and Dave-o falling into each other's arms at the stroke of midnight. The confetti, the streamers, the kisses, the cheers. All these people bidding farewell to the last twelve months and hailing the potential of what was to come; all of them with someone else. *Should auld acquaintance be forgot*, they'd sing, *and never brought to mind . . .* Too much, too much.

Ash went to his room.

He paused at the door and listened, heard nothing inside, and opened it cautiously. Empty.

On the bed was his half-written story. Ash lay down with it and tried to read a few lines, but the text went skipping around the page. He tossed the papers aside, closed his eyes. Music pulsed from the hotel's first floor and the room careened, swirling Ash away with it. But halfway to sleep a clear thought interrupted: the music had paused again—replaced with human voices. 'Ten!' they cried. 'Nine, eight . . .' But the countdown was like a song overheard from a passing train, flashing past and fading, and Ash passed out before the finale.

AT SOME POINT IN THE NIGHT Ash was shaken awake. Something disruptive was happening to his body. Strong hands turned him face down and tugged his legs straight. Ash resisted and was held there. A voice whispered, 'Shh, shh,' until he stopped struggling. Next his jeans wriggled free from his legs, and then he was being lifted at the hips, his backside hitched. The pillow stifled him. Raising his chin to breathe, he looked over his shoulder just as the pale dome of a head, silver in the moonlight, ducked down out of view. A sugary scent of alcohol—carrots and pine—lingered in its wake. Ash faced the headboard. Felt himself clutched at the hips and parted and—was it? Yes, blown upon. Nudged. And lapped. This continued for a while, a wet tickling that darted back and forth, round and round, stabbing sometimes inward. Deliberate and medical, something to tolerate. And then it stopped and he was released and a sort of quaking began. The bed shook; the headboard rattled the wall. Ash, no longer held in place, lowered his pelvis to the mattress, pressed his face into the pillow, clutched the sheets in order not to topple to the floor. Things accelerated;

that big figure behind him juddered and seized. And then there was a gasp, a grunt, and warm jelly splashed on Ash's feet. The bed shifted. The weight was gone. 'We do that sometimes, don't worry,' said a voice from the darkness. Ash's feet were patted dry. Footsteps moved away, and then there was a swish of bedding, the creak of bedsprings. 'Goodnight, bro. Happy New Year.'

## 5

ASH WOKE TO DAWN lightening the window, a strange window. Beneath it slept a strange man in a strange bed—Matt. Ash's old friend. His bro. His best bud. They were here, in Kashmir, on a ski trip, and a new year had begun. But that was all Ash knew: previous to that his life did not exist.

And now Ash's bowels were rumbling and he had, desperately, to shit.

He rushed to the bathroom, dropping his shorts and straddling the toilet mid-stride. What followed was sputtering and noxious. Though maybe his shits were always this way, he thought, as another surge galloped from his backside.

Washing his hands Ash studied himself in the mirror. A face that was his face and yet a mask stared back. Whatever life it had led seemed to exist in the world beyond the reflection, unknowable and unseen.

Ash opened the bathroom door and caught Matt's eyes flutter open, register him and snap shut. The mound beneath the sheets heaved like a beached whale gasping its last. Ash watched him sleep or pretend to. An eerie, hazy memory sifted out of the murk of the previous evening: his body used in the dark, his feet wiped dry with a sock.

Ash spun, knelt at the toilet and puked.

Eyes watering, he propped himself on the bowl. But the sensations returned, that same feeling of abjection and disgrace. Another hitch from his guts rose to the back of his throat. He vomited again. Flushed. At the sink he splashed cold water on his face, drank from cupped palms, spat. Looked at himself again: the face that looked back, unfamiliar or not, was at least real. That other thing had the wispy edges of a dream.

And so, Ash decided, it had been a dream.

On the floor beside his bed was the story he'd written. Ash retrieved it, stood there with the pages for a moment. Matt sighed and curled away to face the wall. Slipping from the room Ash eased the door shut, obliging the illusion of Matt's sleep.

In the hotel lobby, he sat with the pages in his lap. He read at random:

In places the frost where it had been warmed by the sun had turned the ground to slush and here his feet sunk and were suckled by the mud. Now the grass and rubble gave way to bigger stones and boulders and he came to a one so huge that he had to haul himself over it with his fingers gripping gnarls in the cool wet stone while his feet scrabbled for purchase below and pebbles went skittering down. And then he had surmounted the boulder and stood atop it with the land spread out below all green and grey and gazing up the slope there it was: the cave. And what lay inside he knew would change everything. And so on and on and up and up he went.

A book *he* was writing, Ash thought, flipping to the end and that interrupted last line. His words. His voice. Yet so foreign—where was it all meant to go?

An hour later Ash had read to that unfinished end, and with no better sense of either it or himself, headed to breakfast. From the doorway he spotted Matt and Dave-o in line at the buffet, both wearing the same grim and haggard look as they shuffled from cereal station to fruit bar. He was spotted. 'Little Canuck!' cried Dave-o. 'Join us for some brekkie.'

Matt didn't look up, just loaded his plate. With tense caution the other guests gave him a wide berth. Even the clink of silverware seemed restrained, as if a knife scraping a plate risked being interpreted as a provocation. Speech happened in whispers. Matt, as stoic as nobility passing among the unwashed, seemed either oblivious to all this or to be treating it as reverence. Ash snuck past him to spoon instant coffee into a mug and douse it with hot water.

Dave-o gathered the Canadians under his arms: 'Did we all hit the turps last night, or what, boys? You were smart, Ash, to cut out when you did.'

'Feel like I got ate by a bear and shat off a cliff,' said Matt, tearing a banana free from a bunch—and keeping the bunch. 'Barely remember a thing.'

Ash eyed that bald head. The bulbous gloss of it.

Dave-o guided them to a table. 'So, gents, today. Chopper anywhere you like. Untouched powder in pretty much any direction.'

Matt forked eggs into his face, spoke through a mouthful. 'How about Pahalgam?'

'Not really much skiing over there, mate.'

'No, Amarnath, I mean. The temple. The pilgrimage. Right, Ash?'

Ash looked up from his coffee. 'Oh, I don't know about that.' He paused, realizing he'd left his manuscript in the lobby, and half-rose to go fetch it.

But Matt seized him by the arm. 'Bro, I wasn't sure how to tell you this, but we're not just here to go skiing. Or for your book.'

Ash lowered tensely into his chair. Another tempestuous stirring in his gut passed only when Matt let go.

'That grey box in your luggage. You know what it is, right? That's'—Matt gulped back a sob—'my dad.'

'Your *dad*?' said Dave-o.

Matt closed his eyes. Opened and trained them on Ash. They were watery. 'I didn't have room in my backpack so you were holding his ashes for me. And I almost didn't tell you, because honestly? It was nice to forget for a while.'

Ash nodded.

'Guy was a big traveller, real spiritual, my dad. Always dreamed of coming to India.'

'So, Amarnath,' said Dave-o.

'"Holiest site in all of Hinduism," you told me, Dhar, back in Canada after the funeral. And since you're the closest thing to a Hindu I know, obviously it's important for you to come with me. That's what you promised, anyway. That's how good a friend you are.'

Here were the tears now, streaming down Matt's cheeks.

'Well, Pahalgam's not too far from here,' said Dave-o. 'Just the other side of Srinagar. One hour max in the chopper. Easy enough to head over this avo. Can't imagine in January that we'll run into any pilgrims. July would be a different story.'

This trip made sense now, Ash thought. But still the knowledge didn't quite settle as fact, and the spectre of something murkier and unsettling lurked behind it.

'It'd mean a lot to my dad.' Matt put his hand on Ash's shoulder. 'And me, too.'

Ash smiled: a mechanical twist of the lips. 'Sure, yeah. Of course.'

'That's my boy.' Matt thumped Ash's back and returned to his breakfast. 'And who knows?' he said through a mouthful of corn-flakes. 'Maybe it'll even inspire you.'

ON THEIR WAY TO THE LANDING PAD, as Matt told Dave-o about all the times he'd choppered over and into the Rockies and Klondikes, Ash wondered if he, too, had ever been in a helicopter before. But all he could picture was movies: presidential convoys and manhunts and criminal masterminds and Marine units lowering into some tropical heart of darkness. There seemed no place for a real person, let alone himself, in any of it.

As if attuned to Ash's thoughts, Matt added that, along with heli-skiing, he'd once played a paratrooper on a Second World War mini-series. 'Gunned down before I hit the ground,' he said. 'But we still jumped from a real copter. Just not that high.'

'Well get ready to get high today,' said Dave-o with a grin. 'Twenty-thousand feet and counting.'

Sure enough, near the gondola on a shovelled-off patch of field sat an actual helicopter, its Indian pilot leaning on the tail boom in aviator shades. In his phlegmiest Schwarzenegger impression Matt screamed, 'Get to the chopper!' and broke into a stooped scuttle. With a nudge from Dave-o, Ash followed behind.

The pilot, Govinder, a middle-aged Sikh with a terrific beard and military bearing, loaded their gear and outfitted his passengers with radios and helmets; Matt and Ash were stashed in the back with the supplies while Dave-o went up front. The engine coughed and the rotor thupped and the skids lifted up from the snow and, just like that, they were wobbling skyward. Matt smacked Ash's knee. 'Here we go, bro. Off to see the wizard—the wonderful wizard of cock.'

Ash watched Gulmarg spread out below and shrink and vanish as they flew deeper into the Himalayas. It was cold amid the clouds. And oddly weightless inside the helicopter, as if the machine were dangled from above like a marionette. Ash found some blankets and bundled himself up in them and shivered. Across from him, Matt bore a sober expression of duty and service, the box of ashes cradled in his arms. Up front Dave-o chattered with the pilot, a garble of distortion in Ash's headset, while the rotor deafened him in two registers: a low grumble and a high-pitched whine.

Matt nodded at Ash as if in conspiracy. Ash nodded back. But Matt shook his head and mimed writing—forefinger and thumb pursed and scribbling the air. But Ash had never retrieved his manuscript from the lobby. For all he knew the concierge was reading it now, marking it up with edits. Maybe he'd even solve the riddle of the ending and publish it under his own name. Or, more likely, Ash thought, the cleaning staff had trashed it.

The chopper banked hard into a valley and walls of ice and rock and pines veered up on either side. Outside the view was white and blinding, the mountains like the ruins of some lost civilization. Down they went. Ash's breakfast sloshed starboard in his guts and puddled there. Then off came his helmet and he knelt before it, mouth gaping. After a minute he donned it again and looked up to Matt offering a thumbs-up.

The pilot angled them toward a vast plain of whiteness. Matt watched their descent with a strange rapaciousness. Maybe the view was moving him to transcendent thoughts. Though he seemed to be enjoying the scenery less than willing it past. There was tenacity in his eyes. He gestured to Ash to switch channels on his headset.

Ash flicked through feedback until Matt's voice filled his ears: 'Nearly there. Over.'

'Okay,' said Ash.

'Say *over*. Otherwise I don't know if you're done talking.'

'Over, then.'

'Roger. Though don't say *then* at the end, it wrecks it.' Matt pointed out the window. 'Nearly at the ice cock. Over.'

Ash looked: massive peaks crested up from the plateau. At the apex of one of them was their destination. 'Are you going to walk all the way to the top? Over.'

'*We* are, Dhar. Me and you. And my dad. Together. Over.'

'Isn't that dangerous?'

*Over*, Matt mouthed.

'Over!'

'It's what he wanted, can't let him down. Over.'

The helicopter lowered, the rotor droned. Snow gusted up from below. And Matt turned sober again, bowing and holding the ashes to his forehead. Muttering followed, perhaps a prayer. Then, as the skids nudged the ground, he kissed the box and tucked it inside his jacket.

'Time to make some memories, bro,' said Matt, zipping up. 'Over and out.'

FROM THE HELICOPTER'S OPEN DOOR Ash watched Matt strike a mountaineering pose in the snow: one leg up on a drift, ski poles planted at his sides. After a reverential moment he produced that grey box from his jacket and held it aloft, as if offering its contents to the gods—a blessing? a sacrifice? With competing feelings of embarrassment and respect, Ash ducked back inside the cabin. Dave-o was dealing cards to himself and the pilot.

'You're not coming?' said Ash.

'Nah, mate,' said Dave-o. 'Seems like a private thing for you two. We'll give you a couple hours? Snow's not too deep so the hike shouldn't take you much longer there and back, strapping young lads that you are. Then we'll boot back to Gulmarg and get in some runs before tea-time.'

'You think Matt might want to go alone?'

Dave-o began collating suits. 'Wouldn't you want your best mate along if that was your old man in the box?'

Ash peeked outside. Matt was on his knees. He pressed his forehead to the box, then the snow. 'Om,' he moaned, rump in the air. 'Om.'

'Best to hurry up, though,' said Dave-o. 'Bit of a front coming in. Nothing catastrophic but snow could make the walk back down a little dire.'

Ash filled a daypack with a thermos of tea and a tin of biscuits, smeared on some chapstick and headed out into the frosty alpine air. Matt was still in a crouch, swaying slightly, either sizing up or worshipping the mountain. His cheeks were roseate. Frost matted his eyelashes and beneath them his expression was forlorn. He looked like a missing child from the side of a milk carton, that same sad innocence ironized with doom. He stood, patted Ash on the shoulder and with the grey box gestured to the cluster of rocks at the top of the rise: the cave, the temple. The penis made of ice.

'You ready to do this, bro?' Ash was given no time to reply. 'Good. Let's go.'

Matt led the way, sinking to his knees in the snow, while Ash goose-stepped through the hollows he left behind. It was slow going, cold on the face and hot through the polyester-clad body, and soon Ash was breathless. A single cloud drifted overhead like a party balloon batted from one side of the valley to the other.

Twenty minutes later the helicopter had receded a hundred yards and several more clouds had settled above.

'We're barely getting anywhere,' Ash gasped.

'You're the one who told me how holy the temple is,' said Matt. 'You're the one who said we should bring my dad's remains here.'

'All the way to the top, though?'

'Take this for me?' Matt handed him the box and Ash felt its weight: a *man* was in there. 'If you want to turn back, that's fine. I can keep going on my own.'

'No,' said Ash, zippering the ashes into the pack and shouldering it. This plan, however inane, tethered him to some previous version of himself—a dedicated friend, someone trustworthy and certain. He would not let that surer Ash down. 'I'm coming.'

'That's the spirit,' said Matt, and he turned and resumed the climb.

A breeze picked up, whistling and loosening the snow in whorls. Up top, the cave became visible, as big as a cathedral. But Ash could make out nothing inside, no lingam or anything else. Just gaping blackness, like the unhinged jaw of a monstrous fish trolling the ocean floor for prey.

Toward it they trudged. And Ash was struck by a line from that novel he was writing, the one he'd possibly lost in the hotel: *Up our hero went amid sunlight blazing like fire off copper.* Except now the sun was vanishing, with clouds drawing in from all sides with the look of suds sucked down a drain.

'Dave-o said it might snow,' Ash called ahead.

Matt stopped, swivelled at the waist. 'Bro, we're in the mountains. And it's January. Of course it might snow.'

'No, but what about a whiteout like when we were skiing?'

The comment was dismissed with a disappointed wag of the head; Matt turned and kept going. Back down the path the helicopter had the look of a toy on the plateau. Clouds lidded the valley. The wind was really singing. And as Ash watched Matt forging ahead the first few flakes of a snowfall twirled down from above.

But Matt was relentless. He moved with predatory resolve. Watching him, Ash was struck by—was it?—a memory: Matt as a kid attacking a pinata in a blindfold; a smashed window, a hospital visit, sixteen stitches up his forearm. And then an admission that he'd been able to see the whole time.

Had this happened? Was this real? Ash called out to Matt to stop, but he was out of earshot, hiking resolutely up the slope. The snow fell steadily now in great sheets of lace.

Ash caught up at a concrete landing. A handrail protruded from the drifts.

'Stairs,' said Matt, toeing the first step. 'Snow's packed solid over them. It'll be easygoing from here.'

'Wait though,' said Ash. 'I remembered something. About you. I think?'

Matt seemed not to hear him; his face pointed up the hill as if magnetized. Snowflakes lit in his eyebrows and clung there.

'Did you hear me? I think my memory's coming back.'

'Good,' said Matt. 'Now let's move.'

The surface was glassy and slippery enough in spots to warrant a firm grip on the handrail and a careful, measured ascent from one step to the next. But even so the walking here was easier than that laborious plod through the drifts. Pursuing Matt up the path Ash replayed that pinata scene, trying to expand the memory and give it some context. But nothing preceded it; nothing came after. And where was he, himself, while Matt was careening blindly about? His viewpoint seemed so peripheral: an observer, a witness. The memory seemed more Matt's than his own.

Matt stopped to announce that they'd reached the homestretch: only another kilometre to go. How he knew this Ash wasn't sure, and the temple was still just a lightless hollow barely visible through a snowfall as dense as video static.

Ash grabbed Matt's sleeve. 'Did you ever go through a window at a birthday party, trying to hit a pinata?'

'Bro, plenty of time to chat later. Gotta keep going.'

And he was off again.

'Wait,' Ash cried. 'Seriously, did that happen or not? When we were kids?'

Without stopping Matt called over his shoulder: 'I'm trying to bury my dad here, okay? Would you shut up about parties and just frigging help me already? Sheesh.'

So Ash kept following, securing one foot then the next, clutching the railing to guide himself up. Behind them the plateau was lost in mist and swirling snow. The helicopter was no longer in view. Nor was anything more than twenty feet away.

'We should hurry,' said Matt, squinting up and down the slope.

'We should go back. I can barely see anything.'

'There's goggles in that bag. Get them out.'

Along with these Ash retrieved the thermos, which chugged steam when he opened it. The tea flowed hotly down his throat and through his chest. He offered it to Matt, who shook his head. Snow that had gathered on the upturned hood of his parka tumbled loose in a little avalanche. 'We're wasting time,' he said.

From below came two blasts on an air horn, and then two more.

'They're calling us back,' said Ash, donning the goggles. 'We should go back.'

'It's not far, maybe five hundred metres. Quit being such a pussy.'

Two more blasts from below—urgent, a little frantic.

'Hey, come on,' said Ash. 'We've got another day here. We can try again tomorrow.'

Matt shook his head; his smile was mocking, almost pitying. 'You can't even see that I'm trying to help you, can you?'

The goggles were fogging. Ash removed them, huffed breath on the lenses, scrubbed them with his sleeve: streaked, hopeless.

When he looked up Matt had his hand out. 'Just give me the ashes.'

What else to do? Ash handed him the pack with that grey box inside. Wordlessly Matt shouldered it, turned, and continued climbing into that swarm of white hissing all around. His big body became a silhouette, fading as it moved up and away—and then it vanished, swallowed by snow.

A single, long wail from the air horn echoed mournfully up the mountainside.

Then silence. Stillness, save the churning blizzard.

But the handrail was a lifeline into it, and it led to a foot-bridge under which in warmer seasons surely ran a creek. And here the fog cleared a little, providing a view, like a tunnel, all the way to the top. Matt grabbed a crag of rock and scrabbled atop an ice-encrusted boulder and stood there looking back down the path through the snow.

And what did he see?

Nothing, there was nothing to see.

So he turned once again and headed further up the mountain.

THE LAST TIME ASH SAW HIS FATHER was three months before Brij died, in the university town of Kingston. The medical school there had invited Brij to deliver the keynote at some conference and he'd emailed Ash a week beforehand: *It is halfway between Montreal and Toronto. I have a hotel. You can stay and read there. Or work. We will have supper each night also.* The email, sent from his McGill account, had been typical Doctor Dhar, brusque and factual, with the staccato cadence of a telegraph. Though Ash detected something lonely, and a little sad, about it too.

*Deal,* Ash wrote back. *But we're also going to do something fun. My treat.*

Ash took the train. Brij was waiting for him at the station in his idling Volvo. He was exasperated; Ash was sixteen minutes late.

'These bloody Pakistanis,' said his father, performing a violent three-point through a fleet of taxis. 'All hanging around jabber-jabbering.'

Ash belted up. 'The cab drivers? They're just trying to do their job.'

But Brij's fury had been unleashed. 'It's Friday, shouldn't they be at mosque?'

'Okay,' said Ash. 'Enough.'

Wheeling out of the parking lot, Brij cut off a truck. The burly driver's glare fell upon Ash: one day, he'd long been sure, he would end up taking a punch for his dad. And Brij was oblivious, shaking his fist at the next car in his way. He had no idea of the enemies he made, elbowing his way through the world.

'I got jumped here, once,' Ash told him. 'Not a place to mess around.'

His father switched lanes, failing to signal or check his blindspot. The driver of an inconvenienced station wagon laid on the horn, which Brij either ignored or was incapable of hearing.

'On Princess Street,' Ash continued. 'I was visiting Chip when he was in teachers' college. We were walking back to his place after the bar and this car full of guys pulled up and just started screaming at us. One of them had a baseball bat.'

'What had you done?'

'Done? Nothing. That's the whole point. That's what "getting jumped" means.'

'You did *nothing*?' Brij snorted. 'That seems unlikely. You're always saying things you shouldn't. You always provoke. I'm sure you made some stupid comment, something to make your friend laugh.'

'Would you listen to me? These guys came out of nowhere!'

'I don't believe it.'

'Ugh, you're impossible. This isn't even the point of the story.'

Up ahead, the right lane was closed, so Brij floored the gas, skipped the stalled traffic, and insinuated himself back in at the last minute.

'This isn't Calcutta,' said Ash. 'There are rules of the road.'

'What "rules"? I'm supposed to slink about like we're at a bloody funeral? This is why these Canadians never accomplish anything. They're such cowards, with their politeness and etiquette. They never seize the day!'

'What's Latin for "being an asshole"?'

Brij swatted at his son. 'Idiot, who's the asshole?'

Ash laughed, ducked. 'Anyway. So these meatheads pile out of the car and swarm us. Six of them. And the one guy, their *leader*, steps forward, literally rolls up his sleeves, and—get this— says, "Which one of you faggot chinks is first?"'

'Chinks?'

'Chip is Korean.'

'But you—you're not a chink.'

'No. Nor gay. Neither is Chip. I don't think?'

'They thought you were a homosexual Chinese?' Now Brij was chuckling.

'Not sure how much cultural diversity they got those days in Kingston.'

'The academics too,' said Brij. 'At this conference, when I arrived to sign in, the first thing they recommended was the best Indian restaurant in town.'

'Naturally. I mean, where else would a brown man eat?'

'As if I want to stuff my face with Bangladeshi slop.' Brij thumped the wheel. '*Oh, good-good, yes sahib, delicious butter chicken, birdie-birdie num-num.*'

'You should have dropped to the ground in the lotus position, right there, and told him you needed a moment with Vishnu.'

'Perhaps,' said Brij.

There was more to Ash's story about the attack: a moral,

maybe, or at least a kind of punchline. But his dad had derailed things. Brij had never been much for stories or jokes; he couldn't even recap a film in a coherent way. He seemed, like a child, more taken in by textures and tone: he loved James Bond, for example, but less for the twists of plot than the atmosphere, the style. His memory for films was accordingly terrible, and that night, when *Indiana Jones and the Last Crusade* came on TV in the hotel, Brij turned hostile. 'This is the one with the monkey brains. Banned in India. These racist Americans!'

'No,' said Ash. 'That was *Temple of Doom*. This is the one with Sean Connery.'

'What? This is *Indiana Jones*!'

'Yes. Part three of the trilogy.'

'There are *three* of these insipid things?' But, as the opening chase proceeded through a moving train, Brij settled back against his pillow. By the time the opening credits rolled, a begrudging delight consumed his dad's face.

'Hollywood,' he whispered, shaking his head with a half-smile. 'So stupid.'

Two commercial breaks later Ash drifted off and woke to a drool-soaked pillow and Sean Connery and Harrison Ford tied back-to-back in a burning Nazi bunker.

'You're alive,' said Brij.

'Yeah. What happened?'

'The movie happened!'

'No, how'd they get tied up like that?'

'Oh.' The two Joneses wiggled over to a fireplace in the corner of the blazing room. 'The young one. It was his fault.'

'Really. Not the old man?'

'No. The boy . . . compromised them. Like a fool.'

Ford activated a lever that rotated the fireplace through a secret door into a Nazi bunker, and back into the burning room—and the station cut to commercial.

'See?' said Brij. 'Everything is the boy's fault. He is reckless. He never listens to his father.'

'That's not how I remember this movie at all. What else did I miss?'

'Oh, you know. The father's tremendous dignity.'

'Dignity.'

'Yes!' Brij muted an ad for a grotesque, oozing sandwich. 'The son, meanwhile, is rash and foolish. He craves only adventure.'

Ash liked this game. 'Is there no chance, though, that the father goes along with his son because he actually wants to have adventures?'

'No. None. He's forced to.' Brij looked over. 'What do you have schemed for us tomorrow, idiot?'

'It's a surprise. Something fun, though, I told you.'

'Just like the boy in the film. He doesn't respect his father's traditions.'

Ash grinned. 'But do those traditions really mean anything anymore, or is he clinging to them for some other reason?'

Too much.

Brij tensed, turned up the volume. A woman was mopping her kitchen floor with a delirious, medicated sort of joy. 'Look at this imbecile,' he said.

'Brij?'

'Be quiet, it's starting. Either sleep or watch the film and shut up.'

They settled back into silence, though it was a heavy one. The movie should have been distracting enough. But Brij pointed his face at the screen with the deliberateness of self-distraction. Was Ash meant to apologize? The air felt charged with hurt.

After one more commercial break it was over: Connery and Ford and two associates—one brown, one white—rode off into the sunset to the fanfare of that iconic theme song. Fade to black. Roll credits.

'There.' Brij stabbed the remote at the TV. The screen dissolved. 'Goodnight.'

He rolled over in bed with a grunt, curled away from Ash and in minutes his snoring filled the room. And Ash, with his father lost to sleep only inches away, was abandoned to the greyish-blue light of the room, the chug of the air conditioner, its backdraft rustling the curtains.

BRIJ'S CONFERENCE WAS DONE by eleven the following morning, so after lunch Ash had him drive them down to nearby Gananoque. Once there, he revealed his plan: a three-hour kayaking tour around the Thousand Islands.

Brij was horrified. 'What is this, a bloody canoe?'

'It's a kayak. A tandem kayak. You go in that front spot, and I'll be in back.'

'Are we Eskimos?'

Ash laughed. 'You'll like it, I promise.'

Brij had never been comfortable around water. He was a mountain person. He avoided, at all costs, oceans and lakes. So even putting on the lifejacket made him uncomfortable—and he looked weird in it, the padding hunched at his shoulders like hockey equipment.

'It doesn't bloody fit.'

Ash came over, adjusted it while Brij glowered.

'I look like I'm ready for the psych ward in this stupid thing.'

'Oh be quiet. You haven't even got your skirt on yet.'

'*Skirt?*'

Once these mortifications were over and Brij was fully outfitted, and accordingly miserable, it was time to get in the boat. Ash held it steady while his dad slid in. Helped him pull down his skirt. Handed him his paddle.

'Do you even know what you're doing?'

'Relax, would you? Matt and I used to go kayaking all the time.' Brij's face contorted with worry as Ash walked the boat out into the water. 'Now, if we tip—'

'Let me fucking out.'

'Stop it. If we tip, which we won't, just pull that handle and release your skirt and swim free.'

'My god, idiot! Those are your safety measures?'

'Ready?'

No reply.

'Okay, here we go.' Ash slipped in, hitched his skirt and swung them around with a broad sweep of his paddle.

'Careful!'

'Oh would you cut it out,' Ash said with a laugh. 'We're fine. Now get your paddle in and—not like that. One side then the other, back and forth. It's not like canoeing. Look at me. See?'

From the stern Ash watched his father's back as they paddled the shallows a stone's throw from shore. After ten minutes of frenzied splashing, Brij developed a mechanical rhythm, alternating strokes with the precision of an automaton. Such a scientist, even in leisure.

'Ready for open water?'

In terror Brij gazed beyond the cove. 'There?'

'Sure. We're not just going to boot around the launch all afternoon.'

'Isn't it dangerous?'

'No. No more so than your driving, anyway.'

So they headed out, and just as they entered the channel a motorboat went zooming past and sent them teetering in its wake.

'Sister fuckers!' Brij screamed.

'Don't worry,' Ash said. 'It'll take a lot more than that to spill—'

'Idiot, you're steering us right into that tsunami!'

'You'd rather hit it side-on?'

The waves settled. Brij resumed paddling in grudging silence. Once they were coasting into the St. Lawrence Ash asked his dad to pass him a bottle of water from the carryall stashed behind his seat.

'And unbalance the ship? Are you out of your bloody mind?'

'Relax. Seriously. If anything's going to sink us it's your hysteria.'

'Idiot,' Brij muttered. 'You want water, drink from the lake.'

'River.'

'What's that on the other side, then?'

'There?' Ash squinted. The far shoreline was hazy in the late-summer light. 'America.'

Brij considered this. 'Let's go.'

'To America? Did you bring your passport?'

'Passport? Who needs a passport? We'll sneak in.'

'Couple of brown guys in a boat, smuggling themselves into the United States. Sounds like a good idea to me.'

Brij pointed his paddle at a bank of rock in the middle of the river. 'There, then.'

'Probably more reasonable. Unless it's owned by France or something.'

'We'll conquer it,' said Brij, and dug into the water with renewed vigour.

Fifteen minutes later they pulled up to an island no bigger than a tennis court. Ash slipped out, steadied the kayak, and invited his dad ashore.

'What, we're exiting? Is it safe?'

'Safe?' Ash looked around the little stony patch. 'Is there a bear here I'm not seeing?'

His father crawled out, cursing his son, the world, the hubris of marine travel. But once he was sitting on the rocky slope of the little islet, his lifejacket unzipped, sharing a bag of chips, he relaxed.

'Keep your paddle handy,' he said. 'In case we have to beat away any intruders.'

Ash spoke through a mouthful of chips: 'Hey, are you almost having fun?'

'Fun? On the water? When we're not about to drown I suppose it's tolerable.'

'Bullshit. I think I even heard you laugh.'

Brij took the chips, shaking his head. 'I was retching. Sea sickness.'

'Didn't you grow up beside a lake?'

'A lake, yes. But there the shikaras have drivers. And the houseboats are immobile.'

'What's the point of a houseboat if it doesn't go anywhere?'

'People live in them, idiot. Does your condominium often go rolling down the street?'

'Give me the chips back. You always do this, take the bag and eat them all.'

Brij handed it over distractedly. His thoughts were elsewhere. 'And both Dal and Nigeen Lake are full of lotus. Thick with them, too thick in places to swim. People use them for everything. The flowers for decoration. And before they bloom there are the seeds—delicious, very sweet, like little nuts. You wouldn't have had those, but you've eaten lotus stem, I've made it. The Chinese cook it too, don't they?'

Ash nodded. This was rare, his father sailing off on a Kashmir tangent and then doubling back to see if anyone was along for the ride.

'And the leaves—big, fat leaves—they use for all sorts of things. You see women harvesting them, huge stacks in their canoes. Beautiful canoes, hand-carved.' His eyes brightened. 'And the floating vegetable market! Early in the morning the boats collect in the corner of Dal Lake. Such delicious vegetables: radish, squash, aubergine, haak—'

'That's spinach?'

'Far better.' Brij took the chips back from Ash. 'My god! You've inhaled them!' Shaking his head Brij tipped the crumbs down his throat, then smoothed the empty bag into a neat rectangle on the rocks. 'You had all these vegetables as a boy. When I took you to Kashmir.' He paused. 'Do you remember?'

'Of course,' Ash lied.

Together they looked out over the water, fractured here and there with rocky clusters. A cottage, half-hidden by trees, lorded over the closest island, with watercraft of variable size and opulence jostling below in the river.

Theirs had a shrub. Otherwise it was barren.

'What number do you think this island is?' said Ash.

'Number?'

'If there are a thousand of them, I mean.'

'Do they all have numbers? What about names?'

'I don't know. Should we name it? Claim it for the family?'

'Dhar Island.'

'We'd need a flag.'

'Here,' said Brij. He speared the empty potato chip bag with a stick, found a crack in the stones and wedged it in. His flag crackled in the breeze. 'It is ours now.'

'The land of Dhar. Where the ladies wear no . . . salwars?'

'I remember you singing that song, you and Mona. That and *diarrhea, diarrhea.*' Brij grinned, shook his head. 'So stupid.'

'So what about Mona? How does she figure in our empire?'

'Of course she is welcome. She will be princess of the land.'

'And we're the kings?'

'Idiot, I'm the king. You're the prince.'

'So who gets this place when you're gone? Me or your eldest daughter?'

'Well,' Brij said. 'Normally she would be queen. But it would be wrong not to bequeath some of my kingdom to you, since you were along for the discovery.'

'*Along*? Do you really think you could have got here on your own?'

Brij laughed.

'Anyway,' said Ash, 'if I play my cards right someday all this will be mine?'

His dad eyed him with mock distrust. 'I should be wary of these sorts of ambitions. Indian princes have a habit of murdering their fathers. Maybe I should kill you first.'

Now it was Ash's turn to laugh. He couldn't remember ever having a conversation like this with his dad before, one of shared fantasy. As a kid, maybe, though the particulars of such a thing escaped him. His thoughts raced for something to grow the story. 'Should we build a fort here to consolidate our holdings?'

Brij stared at the mainland. The look in his eyes was distant, searching. He seemed on the verge of revelation. Ash waited. But when he spoke again his register turned professorial. 'Akbar, for example. India's greatest king, a lover of art and poetry. Twice his eldest son, an alcoholic, tried to kill him.'

'Right.'

'He had a preferred son, his second eldest. A good boy. Though the older one was meant to assume the throne, despite that he'd twice attempted patricide. And he had a great deal of support among Akbar's harem. So on his deathbed Akbar ordered that his sons' elephants should fight and the victor's would be king.'

'Who won?'

'The drunk.' Brij rose, brushing his hands on his shorts. 'Whose own son revolted. And then when *that* son became king, *his* son in turn tried to overthrow him.'

'So it goes, I guess,' said Ash, and got up too.

They stood there, side-by-side, the late afternoon light golden on their faces. The kayak made sucking sounds as the waves knocked it about the rocks. All around their little patch of land the river ruffled and sparked. Brij reached over and squeezed Ash's shoulder. And let go, and patted him twice on the head.

THE DRIVE BACK to Kingston was quiet.

At Brij's suggestion they took the scenic route along the riverside. 'You've plenty of time,' he said.

He drove with uncharacteristic leisure. There was little traffic, which helped, but even when they did encounter a car Brij didn't tailgate and go roaring past in a fit of rage, but held back patiently for them to turn off the highway. Once Ash even caught a smile playing on his lips; then Brij shook his head and a little blast of air escaped his nostrils—a private, wistful laugh. What was he remembering: the afternoon they'd just spent together, or something long before?

They didn't speak, not really. The radio was turned down to an ambient murmur. The water scrolled by, indigo flashing where little whitecaps curled up and caught the sunlight. Ash rolled down the window and let his hand ride the slipstream. For half an hour they were like this, until they reached the causeway into town and Brij spoke: 'I could just drive you home.'

'To Toronto?'

'Sure.'

'Don't you have to work tomorrow?'

'Yes, of course. I would drop you, then go back to Montreal.'

'So two hours to Toronto, then you'd turn right around and do another six?'

Over the causeway they went. On the northern side the river narrowed and wiggled up into the mainland.

'It's feasible in five,' said Brij.

'Still, seems like a lot of driving.'

'Once we're past the bridge I either take you into Kingston or we go up to the 401.' He shrugged. 'You decide. I don't mind.'

Ash watched his father. He seemed tired, resigned. Old.

They reached the mainland, banked left.

Brij looked over at Ash. 'So?'

'It's a really nice offer, but to be honest I don't love the idea of you driving back to Quebec in the middle of the night.'

His father sighed. 'Well, hurry up. If we're going west I need to take this turn.'

'I don't know.'

The exit passed. Brij shook his head. 'That's it then,' he said.

His father veered to cut off a passing minivan, laid on the horn, cursed, and they drove in a new, stiffer kind of silence up through downtown, making an enemy of every motorist they encountered, all the way to the station.

ASH FOUND HIS SEAT in the last car of the train and got out his laptop. Opened up a file that contained some notes about an author he'd invited on the show in the New Year. This writer wasn't someone Sherene was crazy about—too esoteric, too 'out there'—so she'd told Ash he could take first crack at the intro-duction. Ash struggled with this sort of thing, how to say some-thing sincere or express admiration; he found it far easier to fake middling interest. He read over the few lines he'd attempted—sycophantic, trite—and erased them. Confronted with the blank screen, the blinking cursor, he found himself replaying the after-noon with his dad.

Brij had been predictably ridiculous in the kayak. Like so many things he did, his technique had seemed mimetic, like an impression of paddling based on study but not practice. There'd been something almost cute about it. Childlike. How quickly he'd gone from disgruntled and thrashing to a calculated dip and swing, the paddle rotating like a wobbly axle. There'd been that moment, too, when Ash had swung them around to open water. How serenely they'd coasted out to their island. How nice and good it was. Reserving the boat, he'd thought that three hours would be pushing it. But in the end he and his father had only reached the cusp of something—and deserted it.

Ash looked out the window. They were moving.

The train crawled out of the station. A horn blew. The platform slid away. And now they were on open track, passing the parking lot—and here was his father, leaning on his car and watching the train. The pose was typical Brij: arms crossed, head thrown back in a kind of resentful interest—a little haughty, a little suspicious, but still watching and waiting despite himself.

Brij's eyes searched the train's windows, though he didn't seem able to make out his son. Ash pressed his face to the glass, waved. Still his dad scanned left and right. It was the late afternoon light, probably, bouncing off the train. All he would be able to see was glare and reflection. So all Ash could do was watch Brij watching the train.

And it was picking up speed now, galloping out of the station. His dad and the parking lot vanished and were replaced with the fields outside Kingston, the sky opening up and deepening at its edges toward night.

Ash sat back. It was okay. He would go to Montreal the next chance he got. He and Brij could pick up where they'd left off. They could go kayaking again—maybe they could even return to Dhar Island, if they could find it, and see if their flag still flew. Ash smiled. Yes. That would be fun. Or another trip, to some other place. They could go anywhere. They could do anything. There would always be more time.

PASHA MALLA is the author of five works of poetry and fiction, including the story collection *The Withdrawal Method* and the novel *People Park*. His work has won the Danuta Gleed Literary Award, the Trillium Book Prize, an Arthur Ellis Award and several National Magazine awards. It has also been shortlisted for the Amazon.ca Best First Novel Award and the Commonwealth Prize (Best First Book, Canada & Caribbean), and longlisted for the Scotiabank Giller Prize and the International IMPAC Dublin Literary Award. Pasha is a monthly books columnist for *The Globe and Mail*, and a regular contributor to Newyorker.com, *The Walrus* and CBC Radio. He lives in Hamilton, Ontario.

A NOTE ON THE TYPE

*Fugue States* has been set in Fairfield, a typeface originally designed by Rudolph Ruzicka for the Linotype Corporation in the 1940s. The face references modern versions of such classic text faces as Bodoni and Didot, and, like its influencial forerunners, Fairfield is at its best when used in book-length text settings.